*D*over, England 1912

They had set up lanterns so that one could see what one was doing; and, even at that early hour, even in that bitter cold, two reporters and a photographer were there to record the event—Sarah Martin's attempt to be the first woman to fly across the English Channel.

Jean-Marc was there, climbing up the back of the monoplane like a human fly, his voice reassuring in Sarah's ear for a moment, "Are you all right, mademoiselle?" She gave him a shaky thumbs-up gesture, which he imitated.

Sarah took a deep breath, banishing the dream of plummeting down, diving out of the sky, from her mind. Even in the daylight she could see the horror and feel the dropping sensation in her stomach. She had wanted this since that night in Newport—was it less than a year ago? It seemed a lifetime since Roger had suggested that she make a few more firsts in her life; and now she was standing on the edge of it—an accomplishment.

She took a deep breath, and signaled to Jean-Marc. The men let go of the airplane and she started moving—faster here than normal because of the cliffs and the altitude—bumping unevenly across the grass, gathering speed, faster and faster and then . . . she was in the air, soaring out with the headland moving smoothly under her. She was over the ocean, if she could but see it, flying true and even and correct.

When she finally let her breath out, she wasn't even aware that she'd been holding it in.

Wings

Jeannette Angell

LYNX BOOKS
New York

WINGS

ISBN: 1-55802-020-9

First Printing/July 1988

This book is published by Lynx Books, a division of Lynx Communications, Inc., 41 Madison Avenue, New York, New York, 10010. The name "Lynx" together with the logotype consisting of a stylized head of a lynx is a trademark of Lynx Communications, Inc.

Printed in the United States of America

0 9 8 7 6 5 4 3 2 1

To my mother Elizabeth,
who—like Sarah—fell out of the sky
long before her time
and changed everything, forever.
With love.

Acknowledgments

This novel would not have come into being without the help and support of the following people: Daniel Rosenbaum, who gave advice (even when I didn't want it!) and who really helped start (and made me continue) the whole project; and Ellis Smith, who outlined many of the business ideas, who saw connections long before I did, and who introduced me to the very sobering real-life interactions between the industrial state and the political world.

Other people who helped with specific questions and problems were: Edwin Angell, who scanned countless publications for aviation information; John Torosian, who kindly interrupted dinner parties to answer any number of inane questions; Matthew Centorino, an enthusiastic source of historical information on automobiles; Kim Pandolfi, who helped with filing and printing; and, hardly least although last in this particular list, my editor, Christine Kinser of Cloverdale Press, who encouraged me and gave me the sense that I was not writing into a void. Our letters have been a source of real joy for me.

Especially, though, I would thank Doug, who gave me love and time and space to write this; who simplified my life so that I could take on this project and see it through on a very tight deadline; who never tired of my living in another world and another time; whose critiques and suggestions made this into a far better book than it ever would have been without him; and who taught me to fly just as Sarah taught Eric: through his eyes, through his experiences, through his judgment. I have come to love flight because of him.

Thank you all.

Contents

Wings

Prologue

The newspapers called her the "Dresden china aviatrix."

Sarah Louise Martin knew all about newspaper stories. That was her world, after all—the world of journalism, of printing machines spinning out copy into the night, and of ideas gauged by the inch, the line, and the number of words. She had written for the newspapers for too many years not to have the sense of a story and the smell of ink indelibly embedded in her mind.

It had been her world, and it still was her world, the part of her life reserved for everyday, for working, for paying the rent, for sharing her ideas and her beliefs and herself with the people who read the articles that she wrote. It was what she had always wanted to do with her life, write out all of the words that seemed to be trapped inside her head, touch hundreds of people whose faces she would never see, whose names she would never know, and yet who seemed connected to her in ways that even she couldn't define but that were very real nevertheless.

Writing had been the whole of her world until the day she had discovered the sky, and after that nothing else had ever been large enough to envelop her life.

· 1 ·

The Dresden China
Aviatrix
1906–1912

Chapter One

*S*an Jose, California, 1906.

Not the place to be, Sarah Martin reflected, when one was young and female and bored. All of which, naturally, she happened to be.

It wouldn't all have been so difficult, she decided, if she could figure out what it was that she wanted. If she only knew that there was a goal out there, a purpose, then she could think about that and ignore the sharp edges of reality. The truth would be easier to bear if there was a dream beyond it, something to take refuge in. But she didn't have a goal, a dream, and that was the frustration of it all.

When she complained, sitting with her family in the evenings in the living room of the big old clapboard house on Western Avenue, her mother would invariably look up at Sarah over her knitting and say, mildly, "Well, dear, what is it that you want to do?"

Sarah didn't know.

She took long walks out on the beach—even though people told her that she shouldn't, it was unbecoming for a young girl to be out walking alone—and thought about the future. It looked, most days, to be uncompromisingly bleak, stretching out in Sarah's mind as a series of dreary charcoal sketches: *Sarah at Home,* she called the sketches in her mind, and flinched every time she thought about them. *Sarah Cooking for Her Husband and Children, Sarah Cleaning Her House, Sarah Sewing Her Own Clothes.* That was what all Sarah's mother's friends said about her mother: "Oh, Anna sews all her own clothes!" as though it were some extraordinary feat. It probably was, Sarah thought as she walked out on the beach, sucking on a peppermint and feeling the wind clutch at her pigtails. She certainly couldn't imagine herself doing anything of the sort.

Charcoal sketches, that was the best and the most that the future could offer her; and the greatest fear of her life was that she would get trapped inside one of them and never be able to get out.

She didn't *look* like a charcoal sort of person, Sarah thought, even though hers were probably the most critical eyes to ever examine herself. She would stand for the longest time in front of the big looking glass in her parents' bedroom and scrutinize every inch of her physique. She felt guilty doing it, of course, because the priest at church often said that vanity was a terrible thing. But even more important than that was the undefined sense of secrecy that was always present in her parents' bedroom, as though, even with them absent, she shouldn't be looking there at all.

But the mirror was irresistible, particularly to a fourteen-year-old, and Sarah was drawn to it again and again. She didn't particularly like what she saw, but there wasn't anything offensive, either: clear hazel eyes (her grandmother's, people said), an upturned nose with a sprinkling of freckles ("Well, Anna, you *do* let her stay out too much in the sunshine without her bonnet," her father would say), long legs, dark red hair that was always curling, even when she didn't want it to. No beauty queen, she decided; but neither was she someone ready for the charcoal sketches.

The problem with *that* was that she wasn't quite sure what the alternatives were.

It was 1906, and she was fourteen years old, and the century was still brand-spanking-new, as her father liked to say, and said rather a lot. Her father had a certain repertoire of phrases that he used over and over again, and sometimes Sarah heard people laughing and repeating those phrases behind his back. She had gotten used to it.

The sparkle of promise that had marked the birth of the new century, however, had failed to rub off on her. She was no one, nothing special, just plain old Sarah Martin from San Jose.

So she walked on the beach all through that damp spring and felt the mist seep through her clothes and into her skin and thought about her life. What would have helped, unquestionably, was something distinctive about her, something that would have set her apart from all the other girls who sat at the plain wooden desks at Saint Mary's School and wrote boys' names on their note books and made fun of the Sisters. As far as Sarah could tell, they were all like she was herself: ordinary, with pigtails and velvet coats for Sundays, and unremarkable lives. The only difference was that she saw all of them—even her own best friend, Julia— as living out the charcoal sketches and being happy in them.

All that did, of course, was make her more frightened.

Another thing that might have helped, she often thought, was if there had been something extraordinary about her family. If her father had been a distinguished Russian noble emigré; or if her mother had suffered from one of those strange lethargic diseases that made people speak in whispers when they mentioned her name; or even if her brother had gone to prison for something. That might have made things a little more exciting. But nothing of the sort had happened: Her parents were good, solid, respectable, and unspeakably boring; while her brother on occasion showed promise of aspiring to a career of crime, it would be much too late to do her any good.

Her father had inherited his small business—Martin's Hardware—from his father who had in turn inherited it from his father (so predictable, Sarah sighed to herself); and he worked very long, very hard hours so that it would be intact to hand over to *his* son.

His son. Sarah wrinkled her nose. Her father's son was her own brother, Peter, and if ever there was someone undeserving of having his livelihood handed to him on a silver platter, so to speak, it was Peter. A younger brother, she had long since decided, was a plague she would have wished upon no one.

"Mamma! Peter's stolen my shoes again!"

"What would I want with her old shoes, anyway?"

Sarah swiped at him, narrowly missing. "Mamma! Make him give them back!"

"Silly Sarah has to go running to her mo-ther . . ." he would sing-song.

And so it went. Peter and his gang of friends, noisy and

teasing, running about in the long twilit evenings of that summer. She heard them everywhere, shouting and making fun of her, Peter urging them on.

"Silly Sarah, tell us about that hoity-toity private school of yours."

"Oh, Sister Sarah, when do you take your vows?"

"She can't take her vows! She's kissed a boy! They don't take in girls who've kissed boys!"

She would whirl on them. "I never!" And their voices would echo on, but she had stopped listening. Kissing a boy—she had never done it, of course. She would never dream of kissing a boy. Besides, she didn't know any boys who would want to kiss her. But that would certainly change things . . .

When Sarah went to her mother to complain about Peter and his friends, the response was as predictable as everything else in her life. "Well, dear, boys will be boys."

Sarah could feel the tears hot behind her eyes. "You wouldn't let me do things like that, Mamma!"

Her mother was shocked. "Of course not, dear, but you're a young lady. There are rules for young ladies."

"And none for boys?"

She was being rude, and she knew it. Later, when her father punished her for being cheeky she quietly accepted his verdict, but inside she raged. Why did boys have so much more leeway than girls? What made them so very special?

And then her mother stepped to the doorway and called Peter's name into the twilight, and it hung there for a moment and the world paused, waiting, until he burst through the door and the night gradually absorbed the calls of his mother; and he would be quiet and contrite, and everything would be well again.

Until the next time.

He would pull her pigtails as he passed the kitchen table where she sat doing her schoolwork for the summer classes the nuns continued to teach. He would mutter something terrible under his breath which her mother would never hear and would not have believed if she had . . .

And every day Sarah wondered what she could possibly do with her life that could take her away from the tedious monotony of San José. She wanted—and there, again, was the catch: She wasn't at all sure *what* she wanted. But she did know that she wasn't willing to merely settle. She wasn't willing to simply marry and produce babies—however that unspeakable thing was done—and then, like her own mother, call their names into the twilight of the summer evenings. She wanted more, much more.

Peter, she came to realize later, was her obsession only because that was her nature: to be obsessed. And it was after that same long, damp Northern California summer when she was fourteen years old that she discovered the new obsession that was to set her free from the charcoal sketches forever.

It began, extraordinarily, at school.

School, Sarah's parents had emphasized to her, was a luxury. She was very fortunate that they were so modern in their thinking as to encourage her to receive such a fine education, they said, and she really shouldn't complain. Not every girl in San Jose could go to a private school.

That was true enough, Sarah realized. But even so she wanted more, and without telling her parents that she was overstepping the boundaries of the regular curriculum she persuaded her teachers to teach her what she wanted: science and statistics, Latin and Greek and geography. At home she discussed her penmanship with her parents while Peter smirked behind her back, and the new and exciting ideas whirled round and round in her head.

It was at school that Sarah began to write: compositions at first, assignments given her in English class, narratives to accompany her history lessons. She used her study halls to work. While the other girls bent over their sewing, or passed each other surreptitious notes, or gazed out the window and daydreamed, Sarah sat and wrote. She wrote about their lives at school and she wrote about Peter and she wrote stories of places far away from San Jose and her family and the convent, worlds that she invented and populated and dreamed.

She began to keep a notebook in which she wrote her stories and her ideas and her observations, and slowly that notebook became more important to her than anything else. At Morning Mass, when she knelt with her classmates and listened to the chanting and the prayers, and watched the

smoke from the incense spiraling up and up to the high
vaulted roof of the chapel, Sarah made up more stories in
her head. Later, stealing time between classes, she wrote
them all down.

What was happening inside her head had always seemed
more interesting to her than what went on around her,
anyway.

Eventually, of course, she was caught. Illicit activities, no
matter how innocent, do not go unnoticed for long in
convent schools. Sister Mary Christopher, tall and towering
and formidable, permanently confiscated the notebook one
afternoon when the sun slanted through the windows of the
study hall and filled the air with chalk dust. But Sarah kept
writing anyway, hiding scraps of paper under her pillow and
in her petticoats, watching people and teaching herself ways
of describing them, their beings, their accents, their clothes,
their lives.

She was fourteen years old, and she knew already that the
secrets she kept from her family and her teachers, the
knowledge and skills that she acquired and nourished in
secrecy, would one day do what none of her worries and
longings on the beach would ever do for her.

Her writing would prove—of this Sarah was sure—to be
her ticket out of San Jose, and away from the specter of the
charcoal sketches forever.

Sarah Martin graduated from Saint Mary's School when she
was seventeen years old, to the smiling approbation of her
parents and the Sisters. All were pleased and confident in
her ability to confront life, to use her years at school to the
betterment of her own future and that of the family she
would, undoubtedly, soon begin.

Three days later she walked, alone and unrehearsed, into
the editorial office of the San Jose *Chronicle.*

Louis Caldwell, editor and erstwhile writer for the *Chronicle,* was barking orders in the general direction of his
assistant, a short balding man with a worried expression on
his face, when Sarah walked into his office.

She had prepared herself for this meeting with some care.
The dark auburn hair that had proved so unmanageable
when she was fourteen still curled, but it was longer now,
down over her shoulders, tied back with a silk ribbon. Blue

silk, the same color and fabric as her dress, a deep blue that highlighted her eyes. She still had freckles faintly dusted over creamy skin and dimples set in a heart-shaped face, but the figure that had gradually filled out the silken dresses belied the childishness of those traits. Sarah Martin was beginning to be a very beautiful young woman.

The editor of the *Chronicle,* however, had little time for young women, beautiful or not. He frowned at her.

"Well? What is it that you want?"

Sarah walked up to his desk. "Mr. Louis Caldwell? My name is Sarah Martin."

He ignored the outstretched hand with the glove that matched the dress and narrowed his eyes. "Yes? And what of it?"

She withdrew her hand and dampened her lips. "I'd like to come work for you. For the *Chronicle.*"

He stared at her for a split second, and then began to laugh. It was a disagreeable laugh, and it filled the room and the musty air around them and sent the editorial assistant scurrying to his side to discover the source of the problem.

Caldwell leaned back in his chair, still laughing. "See, Hughes," he said at length. "This Miss—er—"

"Martin," supplied Sarah coldly.

"Yes, this Miss Martin has come to work for us. Just like that. No advertisements, mind you. She thinks that she knows what we need better than we do. What do you say, Hughes?"

Hughes scratched his balding head. "I'd say that we could use some help, sir."

"You would, would you?" Caldwell roared, sitting forward in his chair, suddenly, and looking at Sarah again. "Well, yes, perhaps we do. But not from her. Cleaning work was it that you wanted, Miss Martin? Take a tip from me: Go home. You'll mess up all your fine clothes if you try cleaning around a printing press."

He swiveled the chair around until his back was to Sarah, and picked up the newspaper on the desk in front of him. Hughes looked nervously at the girl, who hadn't yet moved, and cleared his throat once or twice.

Caldwell looked up, obviously irritated. "Yes, Hughes?"

The assistant gestured towards Sarah, and, with an exaggerated sigh, Caldwell swung his chair around again. "You

still here, Miss Martin?" His voice was sarcastic. "What was
it that you wanted?"

"A job," Sarah said firmly. "Writing for the *Chronicle.*"

This time he didn't laugh. He just stared at her with
narrowed eyes, and at length tapped the side of his promi-
nent nose. "I got it! I have you placed, now! Herbert
Martin's daughter, aren't you? Martin's Hardware?"

"That is my father," Sarah said levelly. "He has nothing
to do with my wanting to work for the *Chronicle.*"

"And what would he say, then, do you think, if I told him
that his daughter was in here asking me for a job?"

"I cannot speak for my father, Mr. Caldwell. What did
yours say when you began newspaper work?"

There was a light in Caldwell's eyes that hadn't been there
before, an answering glint, but he wasn't giving in. Not yet,
Sarah thought, and willed her hands to stay still, to stop
trembling. She clasped them together in front of her.

Caldwell reached behind him, and wordlessly Hughes
placed a pipe in the editor's hand. "My father, Miss Martin?
Don't rightly know. Best of my knowledge, my father never
learned to read. He was a Michigan farmer who thought that
printing presses came straight out of hell. Hasn't spoken to
me in years." He started the elaborate ritual of lighting the
pipe. "What makes you think that you can write?"

She took a deep breath. "What makes you assume that I
can't?" She hesitated a moment, surprised by her own
words. "It's the one thing that I do well, sir. I have some
samples. . . ."

"Samples." He snorted. "Only thing samples are good for
is carpeting, Miss Martin. News has to be fresh, immediate,
real." He sucked in on the pipe, and finally gestured towards
Hughes again. "Give her the lightning storm clipping."

"But Mr. Caldwell—"

"Mr. Hughes, this is an English-language newspaper. I
have given you an order in English. Is there something
wrong with your hearing?"

"No, sir, Mr. Caldwell."

The clipping was a narrow strip of paper that Hughes
handed to the editor, who looked at it briefly and then held
out to Sarah. "If you're as good as you say, young woman,
you can prove it."

"What is this?"

"Information. A story, girl, a story! What else do you want me to do, write the damned thing for you?" She looked at him, and he relented. "Go write it. Now. Bring it back by six o'clock. If it's good enough, you're on."

Her cheeks were flushed. "Thank you, Mr. Caldwell," she said, already starting to leave the room.

"No promises, Miss Martin," he cautioned. "Starvation wages. And you have to be *good.*"

She smiled. "I will be," she said, firmly. "I will be."

To everyone's surprise, she was.

Her parents were aghast. That had not, her mother wailed, been the point of sending her to school. So that she could go to work. As a journalist.

Her father shook his head, but privately he was pleased. He would provide for Peter, of course. The young man clearly had a head for business, he'd do well with the store. Nothing to worry about there. But Sarah . . . Sarah was something else altogether. There had always been something about Sarah that he didn't understand, something he couldn't define, couldn't place his finger on. A streak of rebellion, of stubbornness; something wild and mysterious within her. He knew that she would never be content to simply marry, sit at home and look pretty, though God knew she had the looks for it. No, he was relieved. If she was going to do *something,* as apparently she was bound and determined to do, then it might as well be something seemly, like writing.

After all, Jacob Robertson's daughter was studying to be a doctor, so things could be much, much worse.

Sarah was the first woman to work as a journalist for the San Jose *Chronicle.* After she turned in her first story Louis Caldwell never treated her as anything but a writer. Not a man, not a woman, but a writer. He saw the things in her that were good and unique, and he encouraged her to bring those qualities to the stories that she wrote. He taught her how to form her thoughts, how to practice her craft; it was from him that Sarah learned to put her natural tendency to be obsessive to good use.

"I don't understand this sentence."

She glanced at the copy, impatient. "It says that the house was lost in the mudslide."

"Oh? Indeed? Is that what it says? Could have fooled me. Look closer, Miss Martin. That's what you may think it says, but it's not what you've written."

And she would write and re-write under the scrutiny of his unforgiving eye, and she learned not to take shortcuts, to check, double-check, and triple-check.

"Are you sure of your sources? You can't be too safe in life, Miss Martin. Remember that. You can't ever be too safe."

"I'll remember it, Mr. Caldwell."

She worked long hours to perfect her craft, staying late at the office with the huge printing press behind her grinding out the news for the residents of San Jose to read with their morning coffee. And she went home night after night, exhausted and grimy, with newsprint on her hands and cheeks and an odd new exhilaration in her heart.

People in the street would stop her, when she went shopping, and there would be recognition in their eyes. "Aren't you Sarah Martin? I've been reading your series on the farmers; it's fine work."

"Terrific piece on the new playhouse!"

"Sarah Martin? The writer? Oh, I'm so pleased to meet you!"

Her mother finally admitted that the recognition was gratifying even to her; so perhaps having a journalist for a daughter wasn't such a bad thing after all. But Sarah was more thoughtful about her success. All these people, all these faces, all these names she would never know: She was touching them. Her words and her ideas were making a difference in their lives. When all was said and done, that was the heady stuff. And she stayed later still at the office, working and reworking her pieces, until Caldwell's assistant Hughes, who lived across the street, would notice the light on and come tottering over to send her home.

"Terrible thing, nice young girl like you, walking home alone at night."

"Nonsense, Mr. Hughes. I'll be quite all right. Go back to your wife." Did he have a wife? she wondered belatedly.

"Miss Martin, it's a terrible thing you're doing, a terrible thing indeed."

And then, the next day, she was taken to task by Mr. Caldwell.

"Miss Martin, it has come to my attention that you are working late hours."

"Sometimes." She was brewing coffee in the corner, pouring the hot water carefully through the filter, and she didn't look up.

"Miss Martin, the privilege of your attention, please."

She sighed and put down the kettle, and turned to face him. Hughes immediately scurried from the room. "Yes, Mr. Caldwell?"

"I don't want you attacked or molested because you're working late here."

"Attacked in San Jose?" Sarah couldn't help smiling. "I just did a piece on how safe it is here, Mr. Caldwell. Are you trying to prove me a liar?"

He sighed heavily. "Just don't want you proving yourself one, my dear," he said gruffly.

She hesitated, gesturing helplessly. "I need the extra time sometimes, sir. I need to make my stories perfect. I need—"

"You need, you need, you need. I suppose the reporters are running the newspaper, now." He tapped his pipe out in an ashtray. "I'm not allowing it anymore, Miss Martin."

"Mr. Caldwell!" Sarah's consternation was genuine. She did need those extra hours, pools of silence stolen at the end of the day, when the bustle and hurry was over and she could listen to the rhythm of her own words. "Please. I'll be careful. Please don't tell me I can't work late. . . ."

He raised his eyebrows. "I intend to do nothing of the sort, Miss Martin. You obviously are, once again, jumping to conclusions. Unfortunate trait in a journalist." He swiveled his chair back to face the desk. "Henceforth my nephew will escort you home. He's just home from Yale and driving his mother crazy."

Sarah smiled in delight. "Mr. Caldwell!"

He shrugged. "Nothing personal, you understand, nothing personal. Can't afford to lose one of my reporters just now, that's all." He dismissed her with a gesture. "Now get back to work, girl."

"Yes, Mr. Caldwell."

The next evening the nephew duly collected her, waiting outside the office and blowing on his fingers to keep warm. Autumn was beginning to be more than just in the air. Sarah closed up, carefully, turning down all the gas lamps and locking all the doors, gathering her cloak around her and pulling gloves over her hands. She was astonished to find him waiting outside.

"Have you been here long? You ought to have come in."

His face was ordinary, nice, telling her nothing. "Uncle Louis was very clear, Miss Martin. He didn't want you to feel—hurried—by my presence."

"I see." She kept her voice polite. "I live on Western Avenue."

"I know." He offered her his arm and, when she hesitated, added, "Uncle Louis insisted."

Sarah smiled and took it. "He's very kind," she observed. "And so are you, to walk me home. I know that my parents would be pleased."

The nephew glanced up. "It's my pleasure," he said, diffidently.

They walked for a few minutes in silence, and then at length Sarah tried again. "I'm sorry," she said. "I don't remember Mr. Caldwell telling me your name. What is it?"

A brief smile. "Benjamin Todd, at your service, Miss Martin. My mother is Uncle Louis's sister."

"I see. And you were back east—at Yale?"

"For four years. Isn't this Western Avenue?"

"Yes. It's silly, actually, making you come out in the cold for me. It's such a short distance."

"Please, Miss Martin. Think nothing of it." Some ruefulness crept into his voice. "My mother says that it's the first productive thing I've done since I got home."

Sarah smiled. "What did you study at Yale?"

"Physics, mostly. A smattering of other things, some theater, you know. But mostly physics."

"So you're a scientist."

"In a very minor way, Miss Martin. And scarcely destined for glory."

She was amused. "For what, then?"

"University teaching, I shouldn't doubt." He sounded resigned. "Isn't this your house?"

"Yes. There are worse things, you know, than teaching."

He opened the door for her. "I expect you're right."

She held out her hand, and he shook it, formally. "What is it," she asked finally, "that you want to do?"

He met her eyes for the first time, then, and she was

startled by the intensity in their depths. "Miss Martin, I haven't the foggiest idea. Good night to you."

She watched him go, with a vague sense of uneasiness. But he was waiting for her again the next evening, and they talked of the tennis matches he had enjoyed at Yale. It wasn't long before her dreams were filled with dark intense eyes and bright college sweaters. That Friday there was a note on her desk: "Dear Miss Martin, tennis on Saturday? Benjamin Todd."

She played tennis with him that Saturday, to her mother's consternation and her father's private amusement, and then the Saturday after, and the one after that. Ben Todd was a new experience for Sarah: Here was someone bright and articulate, who treated her with respect for her intelligence and appreciation of her spirit.

What Ben in his turn was thinking, she couldn't fathom; for while she stretched and sparkled with his attention, he withdrew from any personal questions, any prodding, any interest. "Sarah," he would say in exasperation, "just leave it be, won't you, please? Just leave it be!"

Three weeks after they met, he kissed her for the first time while they stood together on her father's porch. Sarah closed her eyes and put her arms around his shoulders and was amazed at the rush of warm feelings that coursed through her entire body. So this was what it was like, she thought with some surprise: dark and warm and blurred around the edges, like some of the paintings she had seen at the Museum of Art in San Francisco once as a child. An agreeable feeling, all in all, though it left her with some undefined, ill-understood longing. Like drinking salted water, she thought as she slowly went up the stairs to her bedroom, leaving Ben whistling in the street on his way home: tasty, but leaving one unsatisfied.

He was to begin teaching in the new year, he told her a month later. In San Francisco. Close enough for visits, from time to time; much too far for evening walks and Saturday tennis games. He held her close and spoke into her hair, his voice muffled.

"It's what I have to be doing, Sarah. I can't just spend my life like this, one long, aimless holiday."

"I thought you were enjoying yourself!"

He stroked her neck, slowly, sensuously, and she felt her

entire body vibrate in response. "Sarah, you know—you know that I am. You know how much I care for you."

"Yes," she whispered huskily, because it was the answer he wanted; but she didn't know, not really. He had never told her. He had never told her anything.

Ben kissed her hair and tightened his arms around her. "Sarah, you could come with me, you know."

She drew in her breath, sharply, and struggled to move so that she could look at him. "What do you mean?"

"Sarah, darling, come with me to San Francisco. We can save up some money, we'd be able to marry in no time, you'll see." He put his hand under her chin and raised her face to his. "Say you will."

There was a tightness in her chest that she didn't recognize, squeezing her painfully with tight icy fingers. "What about my work?"

He bent his head, then, and kissed her, one of the long lingering kisses that she was beginning to know so very well, the ones that sent sharp impulses running up and down her body. He kissed her and then, slowly, released her. "Darling," he said, his voice slurred. "What does it matter? We're in love, I have a good job. You wouldn't have much time, you know, with all the other things you'd have on your plate."

"What other things?" Something was suddenly, terribly wrong.

"Oh, you know, Sarah. The house. The cooking. It's a lot of responsibility. . . ."

"And what I do now isn't?"

He was looking confused. "What you're doing is great, darling. I've always said so, haven't I? Just great. But you can't do it forever. Someday you have to settle down and be a real woman, with a real household and real responsibilities."

Sarah pulled away from him then, instinctively wrapping her cloak closer around herself, isolating herself from Ben, from the terrible foreign ugly words he was saying. "I am a real woman, Ben. A real woman and a real writer. That's what I want."

His eyes were cold. "More than me, Sarah? More than a husband and love?"

"Yes," she said, and found that her hands were shaking,

that there were tears burning bright and hot right behind her eyes. "Yes," but there was new conviction in her voice. "I don't even know if I love you, but I could never love anyone enough to give up who I am. Not for you, Ben. Not for anybody."

He brushed off his hat and replaced it on his head. "You'd better be sure, Sarah. I won't give you a second chance."

"I won't need one." She met his eyes. "And I won't need an escort anymore, either. Good night, Ben."

He looked at her a minute longer, then spun on his heel and almost ran down the porch steps. He turned when he reached the street. "You'll be sorry, Sarah Martin. I'll do great things, and you won't be part of them and you'll be sorry."

Sarah shut the front door and leaned against it, closing her eyes. Perhaps, she thought. Perhaps that is true. Or perhaps . . . perhaps it will be the other way around.

And then she started to cry.

The winter came and went, and when the spring leaves appeared a man named Alberto Santos-Dumont arrived in San Jose and gave Sarah the sky. After that everything was changed, irrevocably, forever.

Chapter Two

Alberto Santos-Dumont came to San Jose in 1910 on a rush of wind and a whisper of petrol fumes. He was one of the men that the American newspapers had been writing about for some months, the men who dared to defy gravity, the men who took fragile little machines made of metal and canvas and prayers up higher even than the clouds, and sometimes even brought them down again.

He was an aviator.

Sarah had gone to the fairgrounds early, notebook in hand, to describe the show that was put on before the aviation meet. She watched the preparations of the balloonists and the glamorous girls who jumped from the balloons suspended from colorful little parachutes. Although the first American Aviation Meet, which had occurred only months before, had attracted considerable attention and excitement, Sarah poked about the two airplanes with only moderate interest. She asked Santos-Dumont, the tiny Brazilian who had piloted Europe's first successful flight, questions about them.

"When did you start flying?"

He was rubbing oil into one of the wheels, his stocky little body squatting down, beads of sweat on his forehead. "In nineteen-oh-six."

Sarah wrote that down. "Why do you do it?"

He squinted up at her, his eyes dark above his moustache. "If I told you for the money, Miss Martin, would you believe me?"

"I don't know, Mr. Santos-Dumont. How much money do you make?"

He began laughing, uproariously almost, and slowly stood up; he came only about to Sarah's chin. Reaching for a cloth to wipe the grease off his hands, still laughing, he shook his head. "No money, Miss Martin. It was a joke. Every penny goes to the sponsor of the airshow—or back into the machines. I make nothing."

Sarah was surprised. "Then why do you do it?"

He was wiping his hands vigorously. "Tell you what, Miss Martin. You watch the show. If you still want to know, after that, then come up with me. Then you'll know what to write."

She gaped at him. "Come up—you mean in the air? In the airplane?"

"Of course in the airplane, Miss Martin. God did not give *us* wings. Now, go bother those pretty little parachutists. Your readers will want to know more about them anyway, and I've got work to do."

Santos-Dumont was right. Even after all the years, and despite all the accidents—or perhaps because of them—the public still, it seemed, couldn't get enough of the daring young women who parachuted out of balloons.

Sarah dutifully walked about and described the balloons in her notebook. She wrote of the wild array of bright colors as they lay on the ground, the almost ghostly *whoosh* of the hot air blowing them into towering masses of silken patterns, the people who climbed so eagerly into the baskets below them. She watched them ascend, slow and majestic, six balloons at once, all making that same blowing noise, the people in the baskets waving. She carefully wrote down what the women—there were two of them this early morning in San Jose—wore as they stood poised on the edges of the baskets and then leapt gracefully off, their parachutes opening almost immediately above them in an imitation of the colors of the balloons. She even followed one of the parachutists back to the fancy motorcar she had driven to the fairgrounds, and interviewed her. Mr. Caldwell would be happy with that.

And then the revving of an engine sounded across the fairgrounds. Sarah turned, her hand clutching her hat on her head, only to see one of the flying machines rumbling across the fairgrounds, bumping along, faster and faster and yet not fast enough, it seemed, for flight. It was too heavy. It

could never happen. And then, just as the rising sun caught
and reflected off the painted silver wings, making the
machine seem alive, the biplane rose, almost as an act of
the pilot's will, and skimmed over the tops of the trees at the
edge of the fairground, banking and turning and coming
back, a bird with a man sitting confidently inside, waving to
the people below.

Sarah didn't write a single word on her pad.

She stood rooted to the spot, still holding her hat, looking
up and watching as the airplane flew up and up and up, only
to twist in the air and dive back down, scarcely turning
before it must surely crash to the ground, and then flying up
again.

The girl-parachutist, still sitting in the car next to Sarah,
was carefully applying powder to her face. "Silly thing,
airplanes," she said crossly, as she powdered her nose and
glanced up casually.

"I think it's incredible." Sarah said.

The girl shrugged. "You can't jump from them. They go
too fast. And they're noisy."

Sarah hadn't taken her eyes off the bright airplane above
them. "But imagine flying it," she said softly. "Imagine
being able to do all those things, in the air. By yourself. You
could be whoever you wanted to be, up there."

The girl wasn't impressed. "I'd rather go up in a balloon
any day," she said, and paused to smudge her mouth with
bright red rouge. "Besides," she added finally, "I think it's
just a passing interest, those machines. I don't think for a
minute that it will last."

But Sarah was looking at the airplane with the future
shining in her eyes, and she wasn't listening to the parachut-
ist anymore.

Santos-Dumont raised his bushy eyebrows. "So you did
come back," he said.

Sarah looked at him calmly. "Of course I did. You
promised me a ride."

He laughed, then, and clapped her on the back. "Good for
you, Miss Martin. I've made that offer many times before,
and usually the people see me up there and run home
terrified." He looked at her. "You aren't terrified, are you?"
he asked anxiously.

Sarah said, "I want to fly."

He looked at her for a long considering moment and stroked his moustache. At last he said, "So you do." He paused, as though about to say something else, and thinking better of it. "Well, then. Off we go!"

It was a biplane, a Curtiss model which looked like a boxy kite with two seats and a stick for the pilot and very little else. Sarah, gathering her bulky skirts around her and leaving her hat lying with her notebook on the ground, was helped in without further ado. Santos-Dumont had another hat for her, a small caplike device that fitted closely over her red curls and snapped under her chin. He offered her goggles, and she strapped those on, too.

And then he climbed in behind her and some men who had been standing about not doing much of anything suddenly came to life and held the wings of the plane while Santos-Dumont started the engine. The 40-horsepower engine roared to life and immediately the entire plane began shaking, hard, and Sarah's heart turned inside her. She grasped the sides of the little cockpit seat and took a deep breath.

Santos-Dumont made some gesture behind her, the men let go of the wings, and then suddenly, too suddenly, they were moving faster than she had ever moved before, the ground hard and bumpy, traveling by her so fast that the people and the motorcars became a blur as the airplane gathered speed. Her stomach lurched as the little nose pointed up, and all at once the trees were beneath them where the ground used to be. They were climbing up into the sun, into the sky, and all the people below had disappeared. They were *flying*.

Sarah's heart soared with the airplane. She laughed in delight, and Santos-Dumont catching her mood playfully made the airplane dart in and out of the low clouds over the San Jose fairgrounds. Sarah felt as she had never felt before: light and unencumbered and free; free to soar and swoop and glide. Peter and his trivial teasing, her parents, even the work that she did at the newspaper were suddenly placed in a different perspective. Here was life. Here it was, hundreds of feet up in the air, where she could breathe the cold crisp wind and watch the clouds shift their patterns knowing that she was far away from anything on land. Here was life.

"Do you like it?" Santos-Dumont shouted to her over the roar of the engine. The wind caught her reply and tore it away from them, but he understood, and he laughed aloud, a spirit recognizing its kin. The airplane dipped and turned, and the world dipped and turned with it, and Sarah knew with absolute certainty that she would never ever be able to look at anything the same way again.

And then finally—in far too short a time—they landed, bumping once before the wheels caught and settled and the trees at the edge of the fairground came looming up. Santos-Dumont, turning away from them at the last instant, finally stopped the airplane by running into a stack of hay bales, placed there, Sarah guessed, for just that purpose. They slowly made their way back to the center of the field where the crowds were already dispersing, and Santos-Dumont cut the engine. The silence sounded deafening in their ears.

Sarah sat still in the cockpit, her eyes closed, reliving every moment of the flight, the wonder of it, the excitement, the feeling of *rightness*. Was it possible that this is what she had been looking for all these years? Was this what she had been born for?

Santos-Dumont reached over and tapped her on the shoulder. "Miss Martin! Are you all right?"

She unsnapped the cap and pulled it off, and shook her hair out of it, the long curls shining like burnished copper in the day's last light. "Yes," she said breathlessly, half turning in her seat to look at him. "Oh, yes, yes."

He grinned and jumped out onto the wing, reaching to steady her as she stood and stepped out, knowing that he had begun something powerful inside of her. Sarah jumped down, retrieving her hat, her notebook, and her purse. Among the retreating crowds she heard someone murmur, "Isn't that the Martin girl, Emmeline?"

"I think so. Oh, my goodness, Margaret, whatever can she be thinking?"

"And whatever will Anna think?"

What Anna Martin thought was perfectly clear from the moment that Sarah got home.

Sarah danced in through the doorway, her happiness sparkling around her so that it was almost tangible in the air, like the water splashing off a fountain. She danced in through the doorway and danced straight into a cold unforgiving silence.

They sat in their usual group in the dark sitting room: her father in his high winged-back chair next to the fireplace; her mother on the sofa, sitting stiffly erect with her hands clasped in her lap; Peter lounging by the sideboard, a half-eaten apple in his hand and a look of delighted anticipation on his face. Sarah paused in the doorway and looked at them, and slowly the laughter and the brightness faded from her face. Life had not changed so much, after all.

Sarah's father cleared his throat. "Come in here, please, young lady. We'd like to talk to you."

She walked in slowly, unwilling to hear the words which she knew now must inevitably be spoken, frightened of making the decisions which might have to be made, knowing with all of her heart and soul that this was, without question, one of the great moments of her life. A turning point. The thought was sobering.

Peter hooked the fingers of his free hand into his suspenders. He was grinning with pleasure.

Her father began to say something once more. But suddenly, as though his wife had been holding her thoughts in for too long, as if they were under too much pressure, she spoke in a rush, "It's disgraceful. We've done so much for you. We've encouraged you in so many things, and all that you can think of is how to humiliate us publicly. I don't know what you were thinking."

Sarah sat down, carefully, on the very edge of one of her mother's velvet-covered chairs. "I don't think that I understand, Mother."

Her father began again. "I think that what your mother is trying to say is that—"

"What I am trying to say," Anna interrupted, "is that we didn't send you to fancy private schools for nothing. We didn't plan and save so that you could take it all and make a spectacle of yourself. We never thought that you could be so selfish, so thoughtless, so unkind—"

Peter took a large loud bite out of his apple.

Sarah sighed. "I still don't understand how I have disgraced you. If you are talking about this afternoon—"

"If we are talking about this afternoon! And what else would we be talking about, I ask you? This wasn't one of your usual newspaper stories, young lady. We're talking about the most unseemly behavior. . . ."

Peter snickered, and Sarah had suddenly had enough.

She stood up. "Mother, Father," she said formally. "I apologize if I have embarrassed you. I am sorry if I have done something of which you do not approve. But I love what I did this afternoon—I love flying. It's like nothing else I've ever done before." She paused. "And I need to tell you that what happened today is only the beginning."

Her mother sat as though stunned, and it was her father who said, finally, into the silence, "The beginning of what?"

Sarah took a deep breath. "Of flying, Papa. I want to learn how to fly an airplane."

Anna gasped. Peter stood up straighter, his eyes narrowing, his mouth open, his apple forgotten. Again, it was Sarah's father who responded. "And, if I may be permitted a question, how do you plan to do that, young lady?"

There was a cold hand clutching at her stomach, the cold feeling of fear, of the unknown. She willed herself to be stronger than she felt, stronger than the fear, strong enough to say the words that would define her future. She had to be strong enough to make her own future. "I'm going to New York."

Peter abruptly sat down.

Anna sat up even straighter. "You cannot be serious."

"I am, Mother." She hesitated, and then went on. "*Leslie's Weekly* is looking for writers. They pay much better than the *Chronicle*, so that I could afford flying lessons, and Mr. Caldwell says that I could do it. It's just—it's in New York. And—there's a flying school there, it's run by a flyer named Marc Allard. . . ." Her voice trailed off uncertainly.

Her father cleared his throat. "I think you'd better sit down again, young lady, and tell us more about this." But there was acceptance in his voice for the first time, and Sarah relaxed a little. Perhaps, after all, it would be all right.

"Do you have everything?" Louis Caldwell's voice was gruff. It wouldn't do to show emotion. Not when one was cultivating an image of the crusty old news editor.

"I think so." Sarah looked around the room. Hughes was

nowhere to be seen. He hated to say good-bye, or so he had told her, furtively, the week before. She snapped the lock on her valise. "It feels awfully sudden, all of this."

"When it's time to move on, you can't stand around, girl. Can't let life pass you by." He concentrated for a moment on lighting his pipe. "Are you serious about this flying idea?"

"Yes." She picked up her hat from her desk and carefully pinned it on. Burgundy velvet, with a suit to match: her father's parting gift to her. "It's why I'm going, Mr. Caldwell. So that I can write—and fly."

"Yes. Right. Well," he said, tapping his pipe on the ashtray and beginning the lighting-up procedure again. "You're a first-rate writer, I've seen to that. Want some advice?"

"Of course I do."

"Well, then. Be very careful about your writing. Don't ever leave out any of the steps, and don't ever get sloppy. Be very careful, every single time. Don't know much about flying, myself, but I have a suspicion that the same rule applies. Be very careful, every time, and don't get sloppy."

Sarah smiled. "Thank you, Mr. Caldwell. That's the best of all possible advice." She picked up her valise and held out her hand to shake his. "Good-bye, Mr. Caldwell. Thanks for letting me work here—and thanks for teaching me so much."

He was gruff again. "It was nothing, girl. Go on. You're late for your train."

She laughed. "Someday I'll fly to New York."

"Only if you're careful."

She paused at the door, nostalgia and fear clutching at her again, and looked around the small dusty room. It was a year and a half since she had first walked in and talked the editor into hiring her. Now her work had earned her a place at the prestigious *Leslie's Weekly* of New York.

She turned and walked through the doorway and into her future.

November 10, 1910

Dear Mother and Father,
    Here I am, writing right away, as I promised I would.

The trip was tedious but uneventful (and how very much of this country is flat!), and I've settled in quite nicely. I'm renting a room with kitchen privileges from a Mrs. Davenport, a very genteel widow of whom I am quite sure that you would approve, Mother. No, I'm not laughing at you. Or maybe just a little . . . !

I started work this past Monday at *Leslie's Weekly*, and it's every bit as exciting as I thought it might be. It seems that I will be given a fair amount of latitude in choosing the topics I will be writing about, which is rather a nice surprise, and already my mind is teeming with ideas.

I've started taking flying lessons, too. Please don't let that distress you—it's very safe really, and I'm quite careful. I check every bolt, every screw, every gear before I even get in the airplane, so I'll never come to any grief that way. I do wish that I could explain to you how it feels . . . perhaps I should say that I've never felt more at peace, more myself, than I do when I'm flying. Perhaps someday I will take you up as passengers, and you will understand.

I am in good health, and generally doing well, but rather strenuously hoping to make some friends here soon. Oh, I love being here, of course, but New York is very big and very strange, and sometimes a little overpowering. I will write you more about the city later, but I'm falling asleep and still need to do some reading for work.

My love to Peter, and of course to both of you.

                                                             Sarah

In the spring, Sarah went to a party at the racetrack, at Beaver Pond in Jamaica. The course was laid out around the pond and the sun shimmered off the water into her eyes. She was invited by some people she met when she was doing a story for the newspaper about actors. They had a box—or friends of theirs had a box, it wasn't very clear—and luncheon was served, and afterwards Sarah went out on the balcony to watch the fourth race.

"Do you have money on any of them?" The voice came from her elbow. Sarah turned to see a girl about her own age, dressed in extravagant blue silk. She had thick blond hair swept up in a loose topknot, turquoise-green eyes, and a smile that invited one in response.

Sarah shrugged. "I haven't really got enough money to put on horses."

"How dreary," the girl sighed, adjusting a diamond pavé bracelet on her slender wrist. "I've got forty dollars on Templar, but Freddie says that he hasn't a chance of winning. I do so adore to see them win, don't you? And have you seen Freddie, by the way?"

"I wouldn't know," Sarah said, looking back at the racecourse, squinting her eyes against the brightness of the sun. "I don't know who he is."

Her companion narrowed her eyes. "You're new here, aren't you?" she asked. "I don't remember seeing you before." She had delicate hands with long, tapered fingers and a habit of tapping her fingernails on things. Sarah had never seen fingernails of that length before, and the girl had polished them to a bright ruby red—she was tapping them now on the railing, impatient, filled with excitement, as though life were rushing by and she were holding herself in check before rushing off to be part of it all. She was extraordinarily beautiful, Sarah thought, delicate with startling eyes and alabaster skin, yet under it all, shining through was an intense gaiety.

"I've never been to the races," Sarah said, at last, suddenly aware that she had been staring. "Oh, look, they're off!"

Far below them, the horses pounded around the track, the jockeys in their bright colors urging them on, faster, faster. . . .Sarah was amazed at how quickly it was all over, the winner flashing by the post in a blur of movement which vaguely reminded her of something else, something within her own experience, and then the girl next to her was talking again.

"Oh, hell, I simply knew that he was going to lose. Silly name, that should have tipped me off right away. So tiresome, losing."

"Forty dollars is a lot to lose," Sarah said with genuine sympathy.

The blue-green eyes widened and stared at her for a second. "You *are* new around here. Who are you?"

"Sarah Martin," she said politely, wondering if rudeness went along with money and resolving to watch herself lest her new salary go to her head—or to her manners. "And you?"

The blond head tossed. "Good heavens, I'm Amanda Lewis, of course. Where on earth have you been? Come and drink champagne with me."

"But you lost," Sarah said, bewildered.

"Oh, that!" Amanda laughed. "It's only money, my dear Sarah. And I have lots and lots of it, and that's what it's for, don't you know: spending! Besides, no one really loses anything at the races. They're so amusing, don't you think?" Without waiting for a response, she casually linked her arm through Sarah's and led her back into the box. Her perfume smelled expensive, Sarah found herself thinking. The perfume was deep and rich and dark, a jungle flower scent filled with sultry promise that seemed oddly out of place on an afternoon outing. And yet—it was as though Amanda were an irrepressible child, delightful and charming, a touch out of place but endearing nonetheless. "Freddie! There you are, at last, how simply tiresome of you to go off and disappear just at the most crucial moment. Don't be dreary, my love."

Freddie was young, smartly dressed, and perspiring. "Amanda, I'm so desperately sorry. I didn't have any idea that I was leaving you to your own devices. I just wanted to go down and place one more bet, just before post time, but I was too late and . . ."

Amanda was staring at him. "Don't be absurd, Freddie," she said coldly. Then, changing moods abruptly, she laughed, and there was a shift in the tension all around her. It was really extraordinary, how she seemed to affect people. "In any case, I wasn't on my own, see who I found!"

Sarah felt embarrassed, as though she had been put on display. The people she knew had long since left, and the box was occupied by a group of strangers, young people dressed in expensive clothes who peppered their conversations with witty sayings. She felt at a loss.

Amanda was still talking. "And this is Sarah Someone, who never bets on horses."

"Wise policy," observed a blond young man sitting at the table with a cigar in his hand. He reached a languid arm for the champagne bottle before him. "Amanda, of course," he said, pouring some into a glass, and offering it to her. He looked up at Sarah. "Champagne, Miss—er—?"

"Martin," Sarah supplied. "Thanks so much, but no. I really should be—"

"What nonsense!" Amanda cried, tossing her head so that the tendrils of fine blond hair which fell from her topknot swirled in the air around her for a moment. "You can't go now, we've just begun to talk. And besides, Gerald is going to tell us a story. Aren't you, Gerald?"

The young man with the languid arm inclined his head slightly. "If you wish, Amanda."

Amanda nodded and turned to Sarah, smiling ingenuously, a deep dimple on her left cheek emphasizing her merriment. "Don't you see, I always get my way. So you must drink some champagne with us, to celebrate, and listen to Gerald's story—which is sometimes tiresome, my dear, but he's such a poppet that we all simply have to listen to him—and then perhaps we can all go down and place some money on the last race. Or Freddie will, for us."

"I'd be happy to, Amanda," Freddie said.

"Miss Martin," observed Gerald, "doesn't bet money on horses."

Sarah smiled at him. "I don't make enough money to bet. Not forty dollars, anyway."

He offered her a glass of champagne, and she took it gratefully, glad to have something to occupy herself. Amanda turned to her again, arching her eyebrows. "Do you mean to say that you work?"

"Some people do, Amanda," said Gerald, his voice dry.

"I worked once," Freddie said brightly.

Amanda frowned at him. "Freddie, you worked for a week in your father's office and he sacked you."

Sarah started to laugh. "Whatever for?"

"Sleeping," Freddie said, sheepishly. "Couldn't quite get the hang of it. Early mornings, and all that."

"Such a bore," said a girl in yellow taffeta to no one in particular.

"Freddie," said Gerald, sitting back in his chair and crossing his leg, "is a burden on society."

"On his parents' society, anyway," said the girl in yellow.

Amanda laughed. "On all of us, Mabel," she said. But

Sarah noticed that she reached over and squeezed Freddie's hand, as though to take the sting out of the words, and she saw the adoration in his face as he looked back at Amanda.

"What do *you* do, Miss Martin?" asked Gerald.

There was a moment of silence in the box, and into it Sarah said, "I write."

"Great stuff, writing," Freddie said vaguely. "I read a book once."

"And his mind hasn't recovered, yet," said the girl named Mabel, who seemed to take a particular pleasure in saying things at Freddie's expense. But everyone laughed, including Freddie, and then Gerald said, "Is that what you write, Miss Martin? Books? I don't think that I've noticed you in print—"

Amanda gave a shriek. "I have! Oh, poppet, *I* have! She writes for *Leslie's Weekly*, it's such a darling little paper, and sometimes I even read more than the fashion pages because they're so sweet about reporting the news. That's you, Sarah, isn't it?"

Sarah blushed slightly. "Yes, I—"

"I knew it! I told you, Gerald, that one of these days we would meet somebody interesting at the races, and *voilà*, I *knew* that I was right!"

Gerald poured more champagne into Amanda's glass. "You were right, of course, Amanda," he said soothingly.

Then Mabel broke in, "They're taking bets for the last race."

Freddie stood up. "I'll take your bets down, Amanda," he offered, and she turned the brilliant smile on him. "You're such a silly poppet, Freddie. Here's twenty dollars, then. Put it on Sarrazin to win."

"Sarrazin," Gerald said lazily, "is going out twenty to one."

"I like his name," Amanda said simply.

"Excellent reason to choose a horse," Gerald commented. "Miss Martin, are you leaving already?"

Sarah, who had been inching towards the door, stopped guiltily. "I'm sorry," she said. "I just noticed the time. Thank you for the champagne."

Gerald waved the bottle at her in a friendly manner, and Amanda said petulantly, "You can't leave now, Gerald hasn't told us his story yet."

"I'm sorry," said Sarah. "I must." Her flying lessons cost far too much money to waste any by being late, and she had already stayed longer than she had intended.

"They're off!" cried somebody out on the balcony, and Amanda turned, her face flushed, torn between her desire to watch the race and her desire to talk to Sarah. "Well, go then," she said crossly, and Sarah felt as though she had done something terribly wrong. She understood, suddenly, how the unfortunate Freddie felt. When Amanda smiled, the world was right. When she was cross, it was as if the sun had hidden behind a cloud. Sarah wondered what it was about Amanda that made people react like that.

Amanda, oblivious to Sarah's train of thought, was still pouting. She reached out an arm to Gerald. "Come watch the race, poppet." And Sarah, watching them walk to the rails together, felt oddly let down, jealous almost, that all these people were staying here with Amanda and she was not.

Freddie stood up slowly, and flashed a smile at Sarah. "A pleasure to meet you, Miss Martin. Feel free to come again, anytime."

"Thank you," Sarah said faintly before he, too, was gone.

She was sick that afternoon, from trying to fly after drinking champagne. It was the first time that she had been sick in an airplane, and she landed quickly, running from the plane to the hangar of the Allard International Flying School as quickly as she could so that she could throw up behind it. She was just rooting in her pocket for a handkerchief when a hand appeared in her line of vision, holding a towel.

"Reckon you'll be needing this, Miss Martin."

Sarah grasped the proffered towel gratefully, and only after she had wiped her cheeks and mouth did she look up. It was John Presley, the tall, gaunt mechanic who worked on the four aircraft owned by the school. He had never spoken more than half a dozen words to Sarah at a time.

She leaned back on her heels. "Thank you. I—you shouldn't be seeing me like this."

"It's okay." But he seemed a little embarrassed, too. "Reckon everyone gets sick up in them flying machines, sometimes."

"Have you been up, Mr. Presley?"

"Me, Miss Martin? I reckon not. Not being particularly interested in risking my neck." He glanced at her. "Reckon you won't be gettin' hurt, yourself, though. I watch you sometimes, Miss Martin. Never seen you take off without looking everything over real good."

Sarah managed a smile. "That was my parting advice from California. Be careful. I think it was good advice."

"Reckon it was, Miss Martin. Can't be too careful with them flying machines. My missus, she still says, if God wanted us to fly, He'd have seen fit to give us wings."

Sarah stood up, brushing off her skirt. "He did, Mr. Presley. In our minds. The ability to dream things, and to invent them, to make them happen. That's why flying is so great, don't you see? We have the best wings of all."

He took off his cap and scratched his head. "Reckon that's so, Miss Martin. I always says to the missus, I says, it's not our place to go questioning God's ways, now, is it? And when I sees you up there, Miss Martin, it sure is a pretty sight. The only lady flier around, I reckon."

Sarah straightened her cuffs. "I hear that Jeannine Allard is taking lessons, too."

"Miss Allard? Now that's a nice lady, Miss Martin, someone for you to be friends with. Ever since her brother opened this here school, she's been hankering to fly. Glad she's finally doing it."

Sarah was surprised. "The school's been open for over a year, Mr. Presley. Why has it taken her so long?"

"Mr. Allard's been dead against it. Kept on saying it was too dangerous for a lady to fly, and his sister more than anyone else, I reckon. But then he took you on as a pupil, Miss Martin, and that was the end of that argument, near as I can figure."

Sarah laughed. "I'm glad to see that I've been of some use here."

"Reckon you have, Miss Martin. Now Miss Allard thinks you're the grandest lady on God's green earth, I can tell you that for a fact." He suddenly seemed conscious of the fact that he had been talking to her for some time. "Reckon I'd best be going now, Miss Martin, now that I sees you're all right."

She smiled. "I'll return your towel. I truly appreciated the help."

"It's nothing, Miss Martin." He was already backing away.

Sarah hesitated. "There's just one more thing—"

He turned back. "Yes, Miss Martin?"

She dampened her lips. "Please—would you call me Sarah? I'd like so much to spend some time with you, learn about how the airplanes work, how to repair damage—"

He was shocked. "A fine lady like you won't be wanting to mess about with making repairs!"

"Oh, but I will! I do!" She started after him. "What if I fly off alone someday, someplace, and there's no one there to help me? I need to be able to do things by myself!"

He hesitated, scratching his head, obviously thinking hard. Sarah held her breath. "Well, then, Miss Sarah, that's a good point you make. Reckon I could teach you one or two things. But it would be on my own time, then. Mr. Allard wouldn't take to paying me to teach you mechanics."

She said, eagerly, "Then I'll pay you myself, Mr. Presley. The same rate as my flying lessons."

He scratched his head again. "Reckon you'd have to know my Christian name, too, Miss Sarah, if we're to be teacher and pupil, same as you and Mr. Allard."

She ran around in front of him and held out her hand. "Sarah Martin," she said.

He wiped his bony hand, carefully, on the side of his overalls and then shook hers. "John Presley," he said, with great dignity.

"Then you'll teach me, John?"

"I could do worse things with my time, Miss Sarah."

She smiled. The skies were coming closer all the time.

Three months later, in July of 1911, with some public fanfare, Sarah Martin became the first American woman to obtain her license to fly airplanes. The occasion was marked in newspapers across the country by photographs and long stories detailing every aspect of the bright silks that she chose to wear flying. The San Jose *Chronicle* ran a feature on their famous hometown girl who had made good in the big city.

Sarah sat at her desk at *Leslie's Weekly* and read letter after letter telling her that she was wonderful, that she was a role model for women everywhere, that she was shameless,

that she was the devil incarnate. She read them until her
head ached, and she didn't respond to any of them until the
card came from Jeannine Allard which read, "Congratulations, dear Sarah. I shall soon take my test as well. Shall we
fly exhibitions together?"

Sarah stared at the card for a long time, the words of
Santos-Dumont echoing in her mind, "There is no money in
flying, Miss Martin. Only for love would we do such a
thing."

She smiled to herself, and took out her pen. "Dearest
Jeannine," she wrote at length, "What a lovely idea! Can
your brother set us up with some dates?" She bit the end of
her pen for a moment, and then continued, "I think that I
can get the newspaper to sponsor us. I'll ask them this week.
It would be great publicity, after all, wouldn't it?"

She cleared her desk, slowly, carefully, and it was then
that the envelope slipped out from her blotter and onto the
floor. "Dear Sarah," she read. "I *said* that you were interesting, of course, but *none* of us thought that you would do
anything so outré as *flying*! How positively thrilling! Anyway, anyway, anyway, you *must* need a vacation, flying must
be a *terribly* tiring thing, after all, so won't you come up to
Newport for a weekend? We're having the most amusing
house party, and you would make it quite complete. Be a
poppet and say yes, and I'll have Freddie or somebody
arrange everything for you. Best wishes, Amanda Lewis."

Sarah smiled again. Why not, she mused, and picked up
her pen again. There was something very compelling about
this Amanda Lewis, and Newport would be a welcome
change from the city and the letters and the newspapers. She
added the stamp and posted both letters on her way home.

And then, finally, alone and far away from the crowds, the
cheers, and the laughter, she took one of the Allard airplanes
by herself, up where she belonged, in the darkening sky.
Skimming the clouds and feeling released, she was free,
complete. Santos-Dumont was right, she decided: This was
love.

Chapter Three

I do hope that you'll like it here, poppet. It's provincial, of course, in its own way; but my mother wanted me to go to Cornish for the summer, for God's sake. She always does, and it's absolutely the last place, don't you know. At least Newport has life and comforts." Amanda was talking from the minute Sarah opened the door of the motorcar.

The motorcar had arrived that morning at Sarah's door in New York City to drive her up to Newport for Amanda's weekend, and had provoked many wondering glances from her neighbors. Large black motorcars were not common in Sarah's quarter.

The chauffeur had been very correct, very deferential, and very silent. To each of Sarah's questions—Who would be there? What was it like at the estate? Had she brought enough clothes?—he had responded merely, "I really couldn't say, ma'am." So Sarah stopped asking questions— there was really too much noise to hear the answers anyway. Amanda's chauffeur was driving a new Napier, and it did indeed appear to be living up to its reputation as a very fast motorcar. She relaxed and watched the countryside sweep by.

There was a train line between New York and Newport, but Amanda had not heard of it, and her lengthy telegrammed response to Sarah's suggestion that she travel up to Newport by train must have raised eyebrows when it arrived, it was of such a length and verbosity. Sarah smiled. Amanda certainly appeared to have her own very strong ideas about everything.

The countryside was green and lush with summer. Crickets chirped endlessly as they rattled by; the houses they

passed had all the windows open. Here and there someone
could be seen putting clothes on a line, or pulling a bucket
up out of a well: small, homey gestures which made Sarah
ache unexpectedly for the small, intimate details of her own
home. California seemed very far away.

They had followed the coast for most of the way up, and
the ocean was different here, too. It was a cold blue-gray,
and the waves weren't as big as the ones she had known in
California. Another ocean; another world. No one had yet
attempted to fly over any ocean, she thought suddenly,
though she knew that the Frenchman, Louis Blériot, who
designed airplanes, had flown alone over the English Channel. Wouldn't it be something, Sarah reflected idly as the
road flew beneath the wheels of the motorcar, to cross the
ocean in an airplane?

And then they arrived in Newport, and the time for quiet
musing thoughts was over.

Amanda lived in a mansion on a long curving road—
called, appropriately enough, Ocean Drive—overlooking
the harbor and, beyond, the open sea. It was flanked by
other equally impressive mansions, although their owners
called them cottages. They were spaced at discreet dis-
tances, of course; one could guess at, rather than see, their
large imposing shapes behind hedges and trees. "At night,
when there are parties," Amanda had told her, "the whole
street is aglow. The lights twinkle like Christmas trees."

It was twinkling when Sarah drove up, not with candlelight but with sunshine, and she marveled at the size of the
estates. Different colors, different layouts; one looked rather
like a Greek temple. Perhaps that was the way that rich
people amused themselves, she thought. Living in a house
that looked as though it came straight out of a storybook.

Sarah's family in San José had been well-off, of course,
but strictly upper-middle class. This was her first inkling of
how the very wealthy lived, the people who summered in
Newport, the people who swam at Bailey's Beach, who
played cricket at the exclusive club out on the hill and
gambled at the casino and got drunk at the White Horse.
These were the people like Vanderbilt, Astor, and Belmont
whose family names echoed in the chambers of power;
members of New York's Four Hundred. These were the
people who made the decisions that changed the country,

the people who lived in mansions such as these—houses large enough to shelter a whole town.

"Lorraine," Amanda was saying to a uniformed maid, "please show Miss Martin to her room. She'll want to rest."

"Oh," Sarah protested, "I'm fine, really I am." But she allowed the maid to lead her into the imposing front hall, which was graced by Walter Crane tiles and Morris wallpaper. She could hear the sound of water splashing gently somewhere off to her right. She took a deep breath and followed the maid up a winding, rose-colored Numidian marble staircase that felt cold and correct under her wondering hand. They proceeded down corridor after corridor, treading on richly hued carpets from Turkey. Ancestral portraits frowned down at her as she passed until at last they reached to the room chosen for her. Inside, she saw an immense four-poster maple-and-burl-walnut bed and a sweeping view of the water. Sarah walked immediately to the window and stood looking out. The sun was sparkling on the waves, bright and almost blinding, and Sarah began to relax. She had felt out of place amid the opulence of this mansion; but now she knew that as long as she could be near the ocean, she would be all right.

Amanda had followed her in, and now spoke from directly behind her. "I *do* hope that you'll like it here, Sarah. I'll give you the tour later, if you'd like, but it's really just more of the same. There's a fountain with a cupid in it, I used to like that when I was a little girl. But it's tedious after a time, don't you know. All the rooms and all the people . . . After a while, they all look alike. They talk like my mother, you know, and they talk about things like servants and the weather and parties and dresses. Well, I like talking about dresses, too, of course, but that's hardly the point. I don't ever know whether I love it here or hate it."

Sarah turned and smiled again. "It's beautiful," she said sincerely.

"Well, it's less tiresome than other places I could mention. My mother hardly comes here anymore, though God only knows why, she's got perfectly adequate servants and plenty of friends just panting to play canasta and all those silly other games that she plays. But she simply has to summer up at her estate in New Hampshire, and it's so dreary, Sarah, you have no idea. All there is to do all day is sit about and watch the river and listen to the carriages clattering over that old covered bridge at Windsor. . . ." Her voice trailed off and she sat down on the edge of the bed.

Sarah tried to hear what was behind the words, but she didn't know Amanda well enough, didn't know how far it was safe to tread. "Tell me about your mother," she suggested.

Amanda didn't even look up. "My mother," she said distinctly, "doesn't approve of me."

Sarah raised her eyebrows. "Why ever not?" she asked, half jokingly.

Amanda shook her head. "I don't know." She stood up abruptly and walked past Sarah to the window, where she, too, stared out, but with an intensity in her vision that Sarah had lacked. "That's silly, of course," she said slowly, her voice without the laughing inflection she usually gave to her words. "I do know why. I did not grow into the daughter that she wanted me to be. I haven't gotten married and produced lots of little children, and when people talk about me they don't take me very seriously." She took a deep breath. "My mother is a very serious person."

Sarah turned away from the view and leaned back against the window casement. "I should think that there's room enough in the world for both sorts of people," she said. "It's hard to accept that. It is hard for my parents to accept that."

"Is it?" asked Amanda, without enthusiasm and without interest. "Mamma doesn't accept anything that doesn't fit in with her idea of how things should be. The truth is she wants me to be what she can no longer be: completely respectable. Well, she made her choices. She should let me make mine."

Sarah, wondering how Amanda Lewis's mother could help but be respectable, very carefully didn't look at Amanda. "What about your father?"

Amanda walked away from her, back towards the bed, and encircled one of the great carved posters of the bed with her arms. "Ah, yes, my father," she said. "Your guess, dear Sarah, is at least as good as mine. Mamma thinks that if she says no evil, I'll hear none."

Sarah followed her and sat down on the bed. "You don't know your father?" A sudden vision of the simple plain hardware store her father ran flashed into her mind. She despised him, sometimes, because he was so ordinary. What if she had never known him? Perhaps, in the long run, an ordinary father was better than none at all.

Amanda swung around on the post and settled down on the bed next to Sarah. "Not only do I not know him, I don't know who he is. No one knows, it seems. It was, oh, such a scandal, but by being ever so respectable since, and of course terribly rich since she was the only heir, she's lived it down. But she won't even tell me. Mamma is so mysterious. I'd like to think that he was someone exciting and wonderful, with a sparkle in his eye and a deep dark secret in his past." She shrugged, her voice dropping to a whisper. "He was probably the milkman."

Sarah didn't know what to say. "Doesn't that bother you?"

"Only when I think about it." There was pain behind the words, forcing them out, and then Sarah watched Amanda glide behind her public face again. "It's all right, really," she said brightly, standing and wandering over to the window again, her back to Sarah. "One just forgets it, most of the time. I only wish that Mamma wasn't quite so tiresome. She wants things to be just the way she wants them, as though we were all an orchestra and she the conductor. So tiresome. She doesn't accept things that don't fit into her scheme."

"Well, you take after her in that respect, then," said Sarah mildly, and Amanda turned from her scrutiny of the ocean to look at her. "Whatever do you mean?"

"Amanda, you're lovely, and I happen to like you quite a lot. But you have to admit that you're a bit pigheaded at times. Probably more like your mother than you like to think." This is it, Sarah thought, suddenly realizing what she had done. In this moment we either become estranged or friends forever. She bit her lip and waited.

The moment stretched out between them, and then, suddenly, Amanda began to giggle and put her arms around Sarah's shoulders. "My word," she gasped. "You do see a lot, don't you?" And in her laughter Sarah sensed a beginning.

Gerald stretched to poke the logs in the fireplace, and a shimmering shower of sparks flew around for a moment. "Nice touch," Sarah said with a smile, and Amanda flounced over and sat on the arm of Gerald's chair.

"Gerald," she pronounced, "always makes a show of

everything." She took a bite out of the apple she held and offered the rest of it to him. "Want a taste?"

"As Eve said to Adam," he replied, pleasantly. "No, thank you, dear Amanda. I'll try to resist your temptations for the time being, seductive though they may be."

She shrugged. "Suit yourself." She got up and walked over to where Sarah was sitting, curled in the corner of an overstuffed damask-covered sofa, her hands clasped around a cup of cocoa. "I'll sit here with Sarah instead. At least she doesn't make insinuations."

"She doesn't have to," Gerald said. "I don't see you offering her bites out of your golden apple."

"Here," Amanda said, extending the fruit to Sarah, who playfully bit into it. Both of them giggled.

"Mixing your mythology a bit, aren't you, old man?" a voice drawled from the doorway, and Gerald turned to look. "By Jove, Roger! I thought that you were in France."

"I was. Past tense operative, don't you know." He walked into the light, a handsome young man dressed in a heavy overcoat. Economy showed in his movements as he sat down in one of the empty armchairs. "Anyone got a cigarette? I'm dying for a smoke."

"Roger," Amanda pouted. "Aren't you even going to say hello?"

He turned brown eyes benignly upon her, his classic profile, straight nose, and strong chin highlighted by the light of the fire. "Amanda, darling, hello. Have you got a cigarette?" Then he saw Sarah, and straightened slightly in his chair. "Hello, hello, and what's this?"

"I don't know," Sarah said evenly. "What *is* this?"

He raised his eyebrows and said, without taking his eyes off Sarah, "Amanda, darling, you seem to be inviting a better class of people altogether these days. I would have come back from France sooner if I had known."

"Ignore him," Amanda advised Sarah, taking a cigarette from a packet before tossing the rest across to Roger. "Just for that, Roger, you horrid beast, I'm not introducing you."

He paused to light the cigarette, savoring the first inhale-exhale, still looking at Sarah. "You don't have to, darling. I couldn't fail to recognize Sarah Martin."

"What was that," Gerald said lazily, "about a prophet being not without honor, et cetera, et cetera?"

"Don't be too clever," Amanda said to him. "It doesn't

suit you." She leaned forward for Roger to light her cigarette. "How do you know who she is, anyway, poppet?"

"You sound miffed," he said easily. "What did you think
she was, your own private find? Sarah Martin belongs to the
annals of history, darling, no mean feat."

"Sarah Martin," Sarah said coldly, "has had about
enough of being treated as Exhibit A." She put her empty
cup down on the Persian rug and encircled her knees with
her arms. "I can't say that I can identify you as readily."

"Roger," Amanda said, "isn't famous for anything."

"Infamous, perhaps," Gerald mused. "But famous, no."

"Roger Auchincloss, at your service, Miss Martin.
They're right, of course. I fear that I, too, must admit to
belonging to the ranks of the idle rich. And do try to forgive
my rudeness. One is not in the presence of a legend every
day." He shrugged out of the overcoat, revealing a shirt and
woolen vest beneath. "Ah, cocoa! Thank you, Lorraine.
Fall's definitely in the air tonight."

"Something's in the air, anyway," Gerald muttered, and
Amanda giggled again.

"Everyone's a comedian," complained Roger. "How do
you put up with them, Miss Martin?"

"Actually, there wasn't anything to put up with until a few
moments ago," Sarah said sweetly. "In what context have
you heard of me, Mr. Auchincloss?"

He regarded her over the rim of his cup, the firelight
flickering shadows across his face. "In what context, Miss
Martin? Are there many? I should think that becoming the
first American woman to hold a pilot's license would be
fame enough."

"Should you?" she countered. "It's a mistake to limit your
vision, Mr. Auchincloss."

"Sarah," pronounced Amanda, "is also a writer, Roger.
She writes darling little stories for—"

"I don't write darling anythings," Sarah cut in. "I write
serious pieces about serious subjects. I've written articles on
infant mortality, and on conditions in the slums, and on
women's rights. But I don't suppose that Mr. Auchincloss
takes the time to think about such things." She gestured
around her. "In a place like this, it must be easy to forget
that other people live differently."

There was a long pause, during which Gerald applied
himself to the fire again and Roger lit more cigarettes for

himself and Amanda. "It seems," Roger said at length, "that we've gotten off to a rather bad start. I do apologize, Miss Martin. Believe me, I have nothing but admiration for you—as a pilot, or in any other context you'd like."

Sarah leaned back against the cushions on the sofa. She could feel her cheeks flaming. "I suppose that I get defensive, sometimes," she said slowly. "It's just, sometimes, I feel—one-dimensional. As though the only significant thing that I've ever done is getting my license. And that's not even so extraordinary anymore. Jeannine Allard and Helen Rosinski both have theirs, too, now. I need more than that in my life."

Roger leaned forward, his elbows on his knees, looking at her with intensity. "Then go for another first," he said.

Sarah laughed. "Right. Such as?"

"Write a symphony whilst in the air. It would be an improvement over what we've been hearing at the concert halls lately," Gerald suggested.

Amanda giggled. "Be the first woman to be elected President of the United States!"

Roger said, "Fly across the English Channel."

The laughter slowly died from Sarah's face, and she stared at him. "You're serious."

"Of course I'm serious." He drained his cup and set it aside. "I've talked with Louis Blériot. He's working on the overheating problem that he had when he crossed, and he hasn't licked it yet, but it seems that there's—"

"You've talked with Louis Blériot? I don't believe you."

He paused, and then smiled. "Do you want to meet him? I can arrange it."

Sarah smiled in return, suddenly, spontaneously, vividly, but she shook her head. "I never could," she said.

"Why not? You could fly an exhibition or two to finance the whole thing. If you're serious about flying—"

"Of course I'm serious about flying!"

"—then you should be in France. That's where everything is happening, Sarah. Blériot, the Voisin brothers, and Beaumont, they're making breakthroughs every week. It's the center of aviation. Any serious pilot wants to be there."

"Who is Beaumont?"

"Chap from somewhere in the Loire Valley who has a company outside Paris that's making lighter engines. Or lighter frames. Or something of the sort. Company's called Aeromécanique. Or so I hear." He paused. "You might be hearing these things, too, if you were in France. You could be writing about them, Sarah. You could be living them."

"I couldn't," she began again, automatically, but Amanda broke in.

"You," she said to Roger, pouting, "are being tiresome. Here I am, having a perfectly fun little soirée, and you have to rattle on about engines and things, which I'm sure is not the only topic on earth."

Roger shrugged. "You wanted me to be nice to your friend, Amanda. I'm just telling her that she should be in Paris, not Newport."

Amanda considered it. "Paris might be amusing, Sarah."

"I couldn't. I don't know if my newspaper would let me go, and I don't know if—"

"*I* didn't know," drawled Gerald, "if airplanes could fly. You've proved otherwise, Sarah."

"That's different," she said.

Amanda turned to her, eagerly. "It's not, Sarah! It's the same thing; it's taking risks, and I think that Paris would be divine! It would be an adventure! Oh, Sarah, do let's go!"

Sarah stared at her. "*Let's* go, Amanda?"

"Why not? Cornish is tiresome, Newport is tiresome, and as you well know, darling Sarah, New York is simply too hot for words just now. It would be lovely to be in Paris, and, besides, I have just the perfect new dress. I was trying to figure out when I could possibly wear it, and parties around here are quite impossible. Oh, Sarah, do let's go!"

Sarah smiled and shook her head. But all the while the thoughts were whirling around and around in her mind. The fire flickered, and Gerald began to talk about Irving Berlin's latest, and the conversation ebbed and flowed around her, but all that she could see was the French countryside flowing by under her wings.

"Mamma thinks we need a chaperone," Amanda said, lighting another cigarette, tucking her feet daintily beneath her as she sat curled on the one serviceable chair in Sarah's room.

Sarah was frowning, trying with little success to fit her typewriter into its case. "She's probably right," she said. "That's what my mother would say if she knew. Oops—

well, it's in, I may never get it out again, though." She straightened and wiped her hands on her apron.

"Your mother doesn't know that you're going to France?" Amanda stared at her through the smoke, a slow smile beginning to twitch at the corners of her mouth. "Sarah, darling, how *outré*. I wouldn't have thought it of you."

Sarah shrugged. "I'll send them all postcards and flash your name around a little. Even in San Jose, they've heard of the Lewis's. Maybe if I don't say anything, they'll think you're proper and elderly. Besides, if I don't ask, they can't say no. May I have a cigarette?"

Amanda giggled and tossed her the packet. "Darling, I don't ever intend to be elderly. Or proper, for that matter. How positively dreary!"

"Hmm." Sarah lit the cigarette and exhaled rapidly, sitting down on the edge of her bed. "That's it, then. I'm all packed, such as it is." She stared for a moment at the glowing ember on the tip of her cigarette. "It's hard to believe that we're actually going," she said slowly.

Amanda smiled in delight. "We are," she assured her. "We are."

September 3, 1911

Dearest Mamma,

It's all nonsense, don't you know, all that rot about Paris in the springtime. It's Paris in the fall that's best, with that crisp feeling in the air, and everyone around so full of energy. Even Sarah seems to have caught it—she's been doing *splendidly*, she's flown two exhibitions already (and I *must* say, Mamma, that I just must hold my breath when she's up there in the sky; it's hard to believe that people can *do* that kind of thing). We met that Frenchman she's been babbling about, the one that flew across the English Channel, Monsieur Blériot. I must say that I wasn't impressed; he wasn't handsome at all and had the most *horrible* garlic breath. Sarah didn't seem to mind.

I've been amusing myself, of course. Thank goodness that you insisted on my taking all those *dreary* French lessons, Mamma, they're paying off quite splendidly now, and Sarah is impressively fluent herself, though I understand that she went to good schools, which of course explains it all.

I went to the races at Auteuil (and saw Lindsey there, of all people, do you know that they've given him a peerage, whatever will the English think of next?), and to a new opera by that fellow Ravel which just this month opened here, it's called "L'Heure Espagnole," but I must admit that I'd had far too much champagne and rather snoozed through most of it. And soon we are going to the Ballet Russe which is all the rage here.

I've been seeing some rather *charming* men, Mamma, but you'll be pleased to know that I haven't had a single affair yet. I shall try to remedy that, of course, it's just one of those things that one does, although I know of course that you hate for me to talk about it. So I shan't.

I don't know when we're coming back. Sarah's newspaper is letting her write stories from here that she types up *diligently* in the dead of night and then sends off to New York. I'm sure I don't know *what* she is finding to write about, but that's her concern, isn't it? She wants to set out this weekend for some God-forsaken place out in the *country* to meet this Beaumont fellow that everyone's talking about. There will probably be *mud*, but I've said that I'll go with her, not having anything else on the program just now. She's beginning to talk seriously about flying across the English Channel, and seems to think that he can help her do it. I'm sure I don't know *why* Roger had to put a bee in her bonnet about *that*.

All for now, dearest Mamma.

Loving regards,
Amanda

"Damn it," Sarah muttered, not for the first time, as she pulled the wheezing Peugeot over to the side of the road. "Damn it. I'm sure we're lost."

Amanda opened her door, looked at the muddy edge, and thought better of it. "I thought that you said you knew how to drive a motorcar," she said crossly.

"It's not the motorcar that's the problem, it's the map," Sarah said, anxiously scanning the landscape around them. "We missed the turn, and I don't know how. I was looking at every single side road we've passed."

"If Mr. Beaumont wanted people coming to see him, he

should have marked the way better," Amanda complained, taking off her rather cumbersome hat to fan herself. "I'm hot, Sarah."

"So is the car," Sarah said somberly. "And I don't think that Mr. Beaumont wants people coming to see him, particularly."

"Good. Then let's go back," said Amanda promptly, settling into her seat.

Sarah glared at her, and then at the map. "I think that we should have taken that last road off to the right," she said finally.

"I thought that he had a company," said Amanda. "And I thought that September was supposed to be cooler than this."

"He does. It is. We could go back and take that right," Sarah said, pointing at the map. "I think that will get us there. I don't know what else to try." She went around to the front of the car and unfolded the bonnet. "It's not too hot," she said, looking at the motor. "I think that we can keep going."

Amanda sighed and examined her fingernails, and Sarah wearily scraped the mud off her boots, before getting back in. They bumped and wheezed along the side road until the trees thinned out and the road all but disappeared. They found themselves in a field, with tall grasses and an odor of cows all around them.

Amanda opened her mouth to speak, but seeing Sarah's glare, closed it again.

"Don't say it," Sarah cautioned her. "Just don't say it."

The road was little more than a dirt path through the field, but as they mounted a small rise an airplane hangar appeared before them, with one or two airplanes tied down near it, and a motorcar sitting in the shade of one of the few trees about. Sarah looked at the scene and her heart moved inside her. Yes, she thought. This was her world.

Amanda had fastidiously applied a handkerchief to her nose at the first hint of cow manure in the air, and now she gestured with it towards the hangar. "This? We came here for *this*?"

"Yes. Whatever did you expect, Amanda?"

"Oh, God, I knew that this would be tiresome. We're in the middle of nowhere, and it smells. Let's do get on with it, Sarah, and get back to the city. We might still make it in time for supper, if this awful machine holds together that long."

Sarah smiled and engaged the gears. The Peugeot coughed and wheezed its way to the side of the hangar. She parked it in the shade, and with an eagerness that even she didn't completely understand, got out of the car and started walking towards the entrance. "Come on, then, Amanda," she called impatiently. "It's bound to be cooler inside."

"I knew it. I knew it! Sarah, wait for me, there's mud!"

Sarah was looking over her shoulder, laughing at Amanda behind her, not knowing the impression she might make as she opened the side door to the hangar, her dark red hair shining in the sunlight, her cheeks flushed, her laughter infectious.

There were two airplanes inside the hangar, and large pieces of others strewn all over the floor, as well as a motorcar with missing pieces. Sitting in the midst of the rubble, grimy and sweaty, were two men, both of them drinking beer.

Sarah paused, the laughter still in her face, looking uncertainly from one to the other, and then Amanda came up behind her, hopping to stay out of the mud, and talking rapidly. "This is terrible, Sarah, how I ever let you talk me into this is certainly beyond my understanding, and we could have gone to Vincennes this afternoon, think of it, only you—"

Neither of the men had moved, but Amanda had caught sight of them and stopped talking, the flow of words ceasing as abruptly as it had begun. Into the short silence which followed Sarah said tentatively, "Monsieur Beaumont?"

The men exchanged glances, and slowly one of them rose to his feet. He wasn't particularly tall, and he wasn't particularly handsome, either, with grease on his hands and a streak of it across his face. But Sarah saw more than that as she looked at him. She saw the strong muscles on the arms, and she saw the strength, too, in the dark eyes; she saw the worry in them, and the pain, and the love.

And then the moment broke and washed over them, like a wave of salt spray from the ocean, and he spoke. "I am Eric Beaumont." He stretched out his hand to shake hers, and then thought better of it, hastily withdrawing it to wipe it on the ancient coveralls he wore. Behind him, there was a movement as his companion smothered a laugh.

Sarah smiled, still looking at the dark eyes. "I am so happy to meet you," she said softly, and offered her hand to him. "My name is Sarah Martin."

Eric looked doubtfully at her hand, and then at his own, and finally completed the handshake. Behind her, Amanda started to talk again.

"Well, thank God that's done. Now the two of you please say what you have to say and we can get on with this." She came over and stood next to Sarah, looking around her with distaste. "I hadn't imagined it so—dirty," she said faintly.

The other man rose slowly to his feet and observed to her, "It is not always this way, mademoiselle. Sometimes it is worse. My friend Eric, here, he has never minded." Sarah and Eric were still standing immobile, staring at each other, and he shrugged. "Introductions appear incomplete," he noted to Amanda. "My name is Philippe."

She didn't offer her hand. "This is silly," she stated. "I can't for the life of me see that airplanes are worth all this fuss." She then looked at Philippe, a long assessing gaze, taking in the tall muscular form, the tanned skin, the jet black hair and dark moustache, the intellectual brow, and she relented. "I am Amanda Lewis," she said distinctly. "From America."

"Ah, America!" He dusted off one of the few chairs, pulled it closer, and gallantly offered it to her. "Please, mademoiselle, be seated. You must be very tired, coming here all the way from America."

She opened her mouth, and realizing that he was mocking her, closed it again. "Thank you," she said instead, sitting down primly and crossing her ankles.

Sarah finally found that she could speak. "I—I'm Sarah Martin," she said again.

Eric nodded. "The American pilot," he said. "I know."

She cleared her throat. "I've heard of you, too," she said shyly, clasping her hands in front of her like a schoolgirl reciting a poem. "I wanted to meet you because I was told that you are building innovative aircraft. I understand that you've solved the weight problem, and—" She broke off, looking at his face, the slightly raised eyebrows, and she found herself returning his smile. "I know it sounds silly," she admitted. "But I suppose that I just wanted to meet you."

"Well." He paused, and then gestured around him. "Welcome, Sarah Martin, to Aeroméchanique."

"Aeroméchanique, Incorporated," Philippe reminded him. "You always seem to forget that part."

"This," Amanda gasped, "is it? The whole company?"

"There is also an office, in Angers," Philippe assured her. "You would like that. It's very clean."

Amanda stared at him, suspiciously, and didn't say anything, but Sarah laughed. "Amanda likes things to look impressive," she said.

"I think," Philippe said, "that Amanda likes things. She has that air. Am I correct?"

"I like comfort," Amanda said daintily. "Speaking of which, I don't suppose that the famous Aeroméchanique company would run so far as to be able to offer one a drink?"

"But of course!" Philippe responded immediately, a wicked smile lighting up his handsome face. "We have beer, and it's cold."

Eric made an awkward gesture. "Ladies wouldn't want to drink beer, Philippe—" he began, sounding embarrassed, but Sarah put a hand on his arm. "I will," she said softly.

"Sarah!" Amanda sounded concerned. "Beer!"

Sarah shrugged, still looking at Eric. "Why not, Amanda? You wanted adventure."

Philippe filled two glasses with beer, handing one to Sarah, and then went over and crouched beside Amanda's chair. He gave her the glass, then touched his own bottle against it, the clinking sound thoroughly in place in that hangar. "In that case," he said with a smile, "to adventure!"

"What made you want to begin doing this?" Sarah asked.

She was seated on the grass next to Eric, on the hill overlooking the hangar; and she had another bottle of the beer in her hands. Philippe had relented and offered to run Amanda into town for supper. They had left together, promising to bring back a picnic. "Something that will do, Sarah, don't worry, leave it to me. If I can't pronounce it, I shan't allow him to buy it."

While they were gone Eric had shown Sarah his airplanes and explained his production ideas to her, and she had looked at the drawings he made. As the sun dipped slowly down until the hangar was in shadow, they walked outside, still talking about the airplanes, the designs, talking about everything but the feelings that were slowly growing between them.

"The company, you mean?" He gestured down towards the hangar with his beer bottle. "Philippe talked me into it. He'd watched me working for so long that he thought I ought to make something out of it all."

"You always wanted to work on airplanes, then?"

He laughed. "Oh, God, no. Motorcars. Airplanes. Boats. Anything with an engine. Motorcars mostly, though, especially in the really early days, out on the estate."

"The estate?" Sarah raised her eyebrows. There was nothing in Eric's demeanor or appearance to indicate that he had any money at all.

"Philippe's estate, that was. The Chateau de Montclair, just outside of Angers." He glanced at her. "Philippe is the Count de Montclair."

"I see. Well, that will appeal to Amanda, anyway," Sarah stated frankly. "She's got more money than she knows how to spend, and she rather takes it for granted that everyone else does, too." She paused. "I don't."

"That makes us even, then," Eric said cheerfully. "I grew up on the de Montclair estate, too, but on the other side. My father is the farrier."

Sarah smiled. "And you're friends with the count? Isn't that odd?"

"So is a lady drinking beer," he replied, gesturing towards the bottle in her hands. Sarah laughed in response. "Rebels, all of us," she said.

Eric leaned back on an elbow and stuck a blade of grass in his mouth. "It's not such a bad thing to be," he observed. "Got me where I am now, anyway. Philippe's really done all this, you know. He listened to me talking and went out and ordered books for me, so that I could learn what I was talking about, and when I needed money to start the company he put it up." He shook his head. "He's been a great friend to me."

"I expect," Sarah said softly, "that you've been one to him, too."

He looked at her sharply, and then shrugged. "I couldn't say."

"If he wasn't interested in all this," she said, "wouldn't he be at home now, instead of out here?"

He grinned, vividly. "I expect so. Marie-Louise hates the company." He caught her look then. "Marie-Louise is the Countess," he explained. "Philippe's wife. An arranged marriage, decided before either of them was born. She tries to make the best of it, even pretends sometimes that she's in love with him. But she's a bad actress."

"So why does she want him around?"

He shrugged. "She's expecting their first child, and thinks it's only proper that the father should be in the vicinity, instead of being out drinking with the farrier's son." He smiled and took a swallow of beer. "The only thing that Marie-Louise hates more than Aeroméchanique is me."

Sarah drew her knees up under her chin. "Philippe obviously doesn't share her feelings."

"Philippe hates the marriage. He's civil enough to her, especially in public. But he's been with more girls since he got married than he was before." He looked at her. "Am I shocking you?"

"Are you trying to?"

"Just want you to know what your friend may be getting into."

"On that score," Sarah said firmly, "Amanda can more than take care of herself. One might even say that Philippe has met his match." She looked out over the hangar into the distance, where the evening mists were settling in. "What about you?" she asked carefully.

"What about me?" he repeated. "In what context?"

Sarah tipped her head to look at him. It wasn't that his face was so handsome; it was open as if free of terrible thoughts or fears—and full only of dreams. "Are you married?"

He looked at her for a long moment, then started laughing. "Me? Me, married?" At length he shook his head, still chuckling. "My dear Sarah, the idea has never even crossed my mind." He looked out at the hangar. "I suppose, though, come to think of it, that I'm all but married to Aeroméchanique. And I never cheat on her."

"Is that a warning?"

Eric was silent for a moment, and then, pensively, he took her left hand in his and looked at it for a long time, finally releasing it and looking straight at her. "No," he said softly. "It's a promise."

Chapter Four

*S*arah and Amanda went back to the city that night, to the small *hôtel-complet* in Paris where they had been staying. The next day Sarah flew an exhibition.

It was a good day for flying, with the sun poking in and out of clouds and the winds alive but not overpowering. Sarah smiled to herself even as she got dressed. A good day for flying.

Amanda sat on the edge of the bed and complained.

"Sarah, darling, that's the silliest outfit. Why can't you wear something more feminine out there? There are people watching, you know."

Sarah scrutinized herself in the long, stained mirror. She had taken to wearing a special outfit when flying: the same burgundy silks she favored in her dresses and hats, but in more of a pantaloon style. Amanda obviously didn't approve. "It looks fine to me," Sarah said. "Besides, I'd rather be safe than pretty."

Amanda tipped her head to one side for a better look. "I don't think that you can help being pretty," she said. "But trousers, Sarah! On a girl!"

Sarah shrugged. "It's cold up there, Amanda," she said reasonably. "And I have to climb over things to get in the seat and get out of it. It's not as easy to run as a motorcar, you know. There's no wheel, there's a stick, and it's right between your legs."

"How awful!" Amanda squeaked. "Oh, Sarah, how dreadful. Well," and she got up from the bed and started rummaging in the wardrobe, "if you *must* wear those ghastly things, then at least let me help you look a little more presentable. Here," and she straightened and turned to face

Sarah, a large piece of cloth in one hand and a smaller one in the other. "*Violà*. You must wear these!"

Sarah eyed the fabric bundles suspiciously.

"What are they?"

"Well, a scarf. A scarf is practical, isn't it?" she demanded. "God knows you must be practical. Anyway, anyway, anyway, this ought to keep you warm, and it looks stylish."

It was a long, straight, white silk scarf, and Sarah tied it around her neck obediently, the long edges trailing down. She looked at Amanda, who was clapping her hands.

"Bravo, Sarah, poppet, that's just it. Now, you see, as the breeze blows, the scarf will look quite lovely, fluttering out there behind you. Oh, do wear it, Sarah!"

"What's the other thing?" Sarah asked.

"This? Oh, just a cape, don't you know. I bought it last week on sheer impulse, you see, and it isn't even my color, except that the man in the shop over on the rue de Rheims was so darling, and quite talked me into it. . . . It's your color, Sarah, darling, and silk as you like . . ."

"I can't wear that in the air, Amanda. It would get tangled up. I need to have my hands free."

"I don't see why you need to interrupt a perfectly harmless conversation, Sarah," Amanda pouted. "I wasn't going to suggest that you wear it *up there,* not at all. But wouldn't it be rather lovely to wear as you walk out to the airplane. You know how everyone is watching you go out, and you know very well, even though you pretend that you don't, that it's still extraordinary for a girl to be an aviator, and a bit of color on the airfield would be just smashing. And I could walk out with you, and then right before you climb in, I could take the cape and walk back, and off you'd go!"

Sarah was amused. "Amanda, don't tell me you're getting interested in getting closer to an airplane!"

"Well, darling, of course not. I'm just trying to be of some help to you." Then she caught Sarah's eye, hesitated for a fraction of a second, and relented. "Well, besides, Philippe did say that he might be at the exhibition today . . ."

Sarah laughed. "All right, Amanda. I'll wear the scarf, and the cape. And we'd better get going, now, before you empty out the rest of your wardrobe on the spot!"

And Sarah had time, in the long, new Mercedes-Benz that had been hired to take her out to the airfield—the motorcar firm was sponsoring the event—to wonder fleetingly if, indeed, Philippe de Montclair would be there today, and, if so, whether the farrier's son would have come along for the ride.

In the event, Amanda's plan worked wonders.

It was true that Sarah was still something of an exhibition herself. French women had been flying for some time— though, of course, not many of them—but American flyers were rare in Europe and American women all but unheard-of. Sarah, young and pretty, dressed in bright silks instead of the heavy woolens most pilots favored, was accustomed to the attention she always received.

Louis Blériot was there, and he tipped his hat politely to Sarah when he saw her, but did not come over to speak. He was talking at the moment, she noticed, to an overweight man with spectacles who kept peering at his watch as though sorely pressed for time. Sarah watched them for a minute in amusement, hoping that Monsieur Blériot would be able to free himself and come over to talk with her—she was flying, as it happened, a Blériot monoplane at this exhibition— but, realizing that the conversation was showing no signs of abating, she sighed and turned away.

And, in turning, she bumped into Eric Beaumont.

He looked different in the early-morning light, and cleaned up. His features were strong and regular. His thick dark brown hair was combed, though the cowlick rebelliously still stood. There was no grease, no sweat, just a young man wearing trousers, an open-necked shirt, and a checkered knit vest. Nothing extraordinary. There was nothing to make Sarah's heart lurch suddenly the way that it did. Nothing to set her cheeks on fire, but she could feel their flames.

"Sarah. I hope I'm not intruding—"

"Please. No. I'm glad you're here." She smiled, helpless, aware at the same time of the crowd around them and of the inexplicable urges growing inside her. She took a deep breath. "There's a fine exhibit in the hangar. Did you see the new Blériot engine?"

"No." He paused, as though searching for words. "I

didn't come for Aeroméchanique, you know. I came to see you."

Her heart was still unsettled inside her. "I'm glad," she said again, aware of how little she was saying, and how much she really wanted to say, and how extraordinary the whole situation was, but he was smiling at her. "I have to go and check the airplane," she said at length. "Would you like to come with me?"

"Yes," he said at once, and offered her his arm.

They walked over to where the three exhibition airplanes were tied down, a Voisin and two Blériots, all of them monoplanes, their wings gleaming from the hours of polish they had received before the exhibition. The couple talked about the weather and the prospects for flight, simple everyday ordinary things, while all the time Sarah's hand felt strange and wonderful and warm against Eric's arm.

Eric strolled around the different aircraft, looking first at the wires holding the wings, and then at the pitch of the canvas covering them, ascertaining the angles, stooping to get a good view of the Voisin undercarriage. Sarah turned away from him and began to examine her Blériot with much more attention, and at length he drifted back to where she was and sat on one of the ubiquitous hay bales, watching her in silence.

As she always did, Sarah started at the front and worked her way back methodically. Amanda had watched her do this once and had left, complaining within the first two minutes, "But, Sarah, darling, you're boring me to tears!"

Sarah had blocked Amanda's voice out of her mind, as now she blocked out the close presence of Eric Beaumont. There were priorities. Louis Caldwell's voice in the back of her head, reminding her: "Be careful. Be careful." The Allards at their flying school had been astonished at how long it took Sarah to get off the ground, at the amount of time she spent checking every bolt and every wire before she even climbed into the seat. The Allards, even Jeannine, made sure that they had gas and oil and left the rest to the mechanics and to God. But it was not the mechanic whose life was going up on those fragile wings of wood, metal, and canvas, and even God had not saved the people who had crashed to their deaths on fine days such as this one because something had gone wrong with their planes.

Nothing, Sarah was determined, would ever go wrong with her airplane.

So now Eric sat and watched her as she checked it all, making sure that everything was in place, that everything was functioning correctly. "Be careful. Be careful." At the front of the airplane she ran her fingers around the edges of the propellers to see that there were no nicks or pieces missing; she checked the engine, too, looking at the spark plugs to see that everything was in order. The engine was bolted to the airplane with a heavy steel frame, and she reached up and shook it with all of her might, making certain that it wasn't going to shake loose during takeoff or in flight. She had seen engines fall out of airplanes mid-flight before.

There was gasoline and oil, filled up to the tops of their respective tanks; Sarah dipped her finger in to make sure. Walking back, she scrutinized the wires running over the place where her own seat perched so precariously. It would take only one wire snapping to change the entire stress factor on the airplane.

The other wires were the crucial ones: the cables connecting the ailerons and the elevators to the stick that she would be using to control the airplane. She grasped the ailerons and pulled them, watching the stick make corresponding movements. And then there were hands next to hers as Eric moved the elevators and the stick moved again. She glanced up at him, flushing slightly, and he smiled. "Just helping," he said softly, and she smiled in return.

She completed her safety checks: There were no holes in the fragile canvas wings; the flaps were all right. The airplane was all right. There would be no accident today, Sarah thought. Or, if there were, it would involve her heart and not her airplane.

She straightened after a thorough check, ready at last. "I suppose," she said slowly, reaching for a cloth and wiping the grease from her hands on it, "that you think I'm terribly unladylike."

He handed her the cloth and wiped his own hands when she was finished. "*Au contraire*, Sarah," he said, softly. "I think that you're terribly spectacular."

Amanda was waiting for them outside the hangars. "I thought I saw you," she said to Eric. "You've been keeping her far too long. They've called her name twice already. Oh, do come on, Sarah, I've got your things ready for you."

Sarah cast an apologetic glance at Eric, who shrugged and smiled, making her heart twist again, and then she allowed Amanda to lead her off. The preflight shadows belonged to Sarah. She could hardly begrudge Amanda her time in the light.

Amanda draped the new cape over Sarah's shoulders, and it fell down over her bloomers and her boots and hid them from view. Holding Sarah's helmet and goggles firmly in her own hands—"If you think that you're putting on that awful contraption one moment before you have to, then you're quite mistaken"—Amanda draped the long white silk scarf around her friend's neck and walked out to the Blériot airplane with her. The crowd, as usual, was unpredictable. Today they were cheering wildly, yet Sarah knew that acclamation could easily be replaced by jeers for no apparent reason. Beachey, Curtiss's test pilot and one of the American exhibition pilots who flew with Sarah occasionally, once remarked, "They boo because they don't understand; and once they understand, they boo because they don't want to believe it." To which Sarah had cheerfully responded, "As long as they pay to see me fly, Lincoln, I don't care if they throw rotten tomatoes!"

Amanda walked out with her, and stood, as promised, shielding Sarah from the crowd as she removed the long cape from Sarah's shoulders, holding it for her as she took hold of the wires and lifted herself up into the precarious seat from which she would control the Blériot.

The wind was picking up already. Sarah reached for the helmet, which she put on her head and snapped the strap under her chin; she readied the goggles. Then, to please Amanda, she draped the scarf artistically around her neck and over her shoulder, and was awarded a brilliant smile for her efforts. Amanda turned then, and ran back from the airplane into a group of spectators where one could distinguish, if one looked very carefully, the tall, elegant, figure of Philippe de Montclair.

Sarah nodded to the two workmen standing by the propeller. They began turning it for her, and the world around her was obliterated by the roar of the engine starting up—the Blériot engine. Sarah wondered, fleetingly, when

she would first fly a plane manufactured by Aeroméchanique, but those were dangerous thoughts to harbor
when one's mind had to be on the task at hand. It was
dangerous to think of Eric's dark eyes and easy smile when
she was risking her life for the amazement of a few hundred
people below her; dangerous to dwell on his strength, his
cleverness, his apparent gentleness when the airplane required every bit of attention that she could muster. Accustomed to flying a biplane, the monoplane, favored by the
Europeans, was still a new challenge to Sarah. It was more
difficult to control, but could achieve greater heights and
speeds. Sarah took a deep breath, her eyes closed, clearing
her mind of every voice but that of Louis Caldwell: "Be
careful. Be careful."

She exhaled, slowly, lowered the goggles to cover her eyes,
and placed her feet gently, tentatively, on the rudder controls below her. Gently, always gently: Feel the airplane, and
you'll know when something is going to go wrong, before it
goes wrong.

They were still holding the wings for her to hold the
aircraft in place. This was another innovation, she knew,
that Eric was working on: equipping airplanes with brakes,
so that they could stand perfectly still and even stop by
themselves, instead of running into hay bales. And it would
be a great luxury not to need so many people around one
when one was starting up.

Looking up, she scanned the horizon: empty, of course,
but one never knew. Marc Allard had told her a story once
of taking off without looking and flying into a flock of
Canadian geese on their journey south. A terrible waste: The
airplane was destroyed. Not to mention, Sarah had thought
drily, a few dozen geese. She pushed the throttle down with
her right hand, a little, not much, enough to start moving to
get into position. The field was flat all around her—it had
been cleared expressly for exhibitions such as this one—but
she wanted to take off into the wind, and she wanted a point
on the horizon to aim for.

There it was: the church tower, St. Marie des Fougères,
and almost exactly into the wind. Sarah took another deep
breath, slowly counting to twelve—her own ritual; every
aviator, she was told, had one—and then she eased the
throttle all the way down and fixed her gaze on the church

tower ahead, her point of reference, her straight line to the
heavens. Faster and faster, the Blériot began picking up
speed and bumping along, harder and harder, until the
bumps became leaps and the trees at the edge of the field
were approaching. A voice inside of Sarah said, *Now.*
Listening to it, she pulled back on the stick, gently, gently.
The wheels bumped again and then were off the ground
altogether and she was in the air, skimming over the tops of
the trees which appeared only as a dizzying blur of greens
and browns and yellows. She eased up for a moment to
allow the engine power to keep up with the height, and then
moved again and soared higher still, up, up, up. . . .

The roar around her was almost deafening, and she was
grateful for the flaps of her flight helmet which covered and
helped protect her ears. The noise of the engine was bad
enough; but she was sitting just below the slipstream, too,
and the rush of the wind going by at such a high speed was
loud, as well as a higher pitch, like banshees shrieking on All
Hallows' Eve. And still she climbed, the sun sparkling bright
on the wings and tail, and the deep blue of the sky beckoning
her onwards, further up, into horizons that most people
never even dreamed of. . . .

The people brought her back to reality. They always did:
the people who had paid their money to come and watch her
fly, even though some of them were there in the hopes that
she would crash, or that there would be some accident to tell
their mates about at the factory the next day, smacking their
lips with ghoulish delight over every detail. That happened,
too, more often than any of the fliers liked to think about.
Sarah thought about it all the time; it was why she was so
careful. Lincoln Beachey, whose daredevil flying stunts had
resulted in numerous crashes, had laughed at her one day.
"Oh you," he said. "You'll die by your fire of old age!"

"I'll die," Sarah told him grimly, "when I'm good and
ready."

She turned now, using her feet on a bar pivoted in the
center to steer the airplane into a graceful arc over the
fairgrounds, until the people clustered below looked like
tiny insignificant insects, and she laughed aloud—at them,
at herself, at the absurdity of life. One could only fully
appreciate how small one's troubles were when one had
risen to heights such as these, when one had been part of the

sky and looked down upon the earth. Then, finally, one began to understand.

Perhaps even war would look ridiculous once everyone had flown in an airplane and looked down at the earth from the clouds, Sarah speculated. No one could ever argue again, or hate again, or ever be petty. The problem with that, of course, was that once one got back down one tended to forget.

She did a half-roll as she roared over the gasping crowds, and then banked the plane to turn back, her feet on the rudders moving smoothly, gently, knowingly. "Like a lover, an airplane is, and that's the way you've got to fly her," Marc Allard had said, and Jeannine had giggled behind his back. But he wasn't so very far wrong.

She swooped down low on her second pass, just a hundred feet above the heads of the crowd, and she laughed again. The first day she had flown alone she had come upon a herd of cows grazing peacefully in a field, contented with their lot, and Sarah had not been able to resist the temptation. She had gone in over them lower and lower, until the animals below panicked and scattered right and left, running hard with the fear of the great black noise-machine buzzing them from the sky. Sarah had laughed then, aware of holding the world at her fingertips, in the controls of her airplane. It was a heady sensation.

The people scattered below her. She knew that they would be hissing and booing when she landed, for no one really likes to be frightened half out of one's wits; but that was all right. They had come to see a spectacle; she would give them a spectacle.

Circling again, she began to get more height, winding her way up into the air until she could hear the engine straining with the weight of the craft and her weight and the weight of gravity; up and up, and then, when she felt the machine could not withstand more pressure, she pushed the lever forward, pointed the nose down, and let the airplane go into a dive. The ground rushed to meet her. She waited until the very last instant before pulling out, fast and graceful, and leaving the crowd below breathless with the roar of her engine in their ears and the smell of her petrol fumes wafting over them like a breeze.

Sarah had been right: No one was pleased, except the Mercedes people, who knew that everyone would be talking

about the American girl-aviator and how very daring she
had been.

"Sarah, have you any idea what you were doing?"
Amanda cried as she rushed up to her. "I thought that you
were going to crash, which would have been so very dreary,
after all. . . ."

Sarah took off her helmet and shook out her hair, the dark
auburn curls catching the sunlight, and she looked past
Amanda to where Eric was standing. "Did you think I
would crash?" she raised her voice.

"Of course not," he said easily, walking toward her. "You
know what you are doing."

She looked at him, reveled in his calm acceptance of her
competence, and her heart warmed. Philippe joined them,
bottle of champagne in hand. "Just thought we'd have a bit
to celebrate."

Amanda eagerly turned to him, taking the glasses from his
hand and distributing them. "Philippe, darling, do tell
Sarah what a pest she would be if she crashed. She really
ought to be more careful."

Philippe looked at Sarah in a friendly manner before
negotiating the champagne cork, which he popped sound-
lessly into his hand. "There we are—Eric, old man, bring
your glass round—here you are, Amanda, my dear. . . ." He
poured with the effortless grace of centuries of genteel
breeding, and Amanda giggled in delight as she breathed the
bubbles. "I should think that Sarah doesn't need us telling
her how to fly. She's doing a splendid job as it is." He raised
his glass slightly. "To Sarah Martin and her marvelous
airplanes!"

Sarah raised her glass, but she was looking at Eric. "To
Aeromécanique," she responded, "and its marvelous airplanes!"

"To us all!" Amanda cried out gaily, and the champagne
bubbles mixed with their laughter and sparkled in the bright
sunshine.

Much later, they all went into the city to eat a belated supper
at Maxim's: *paté de foie gras*, *truite aux amandes*, and crisp
green broccoli hedging the filet mignons; the mushrooms
were dark and sweet in the sauce, the steak tender and
filling. They drank more champagne, much more champagne, and Amanda was giggling at everything, wearing a

new Poiret dress of deep crimson silk with a daring décolletage and a narrow hobble skirt exposing her ankles. Philippe sat with his arm around her, resting easily on a velvet chair, a cigarette in his hand.

Sarah found herself smiling idiotically at them all. Sarah had never dared dream that she might one day be drinking champagne and flying an airplane and eating supper at Maxim's in Paris: Maxim's, the toast of the city, with its polished brass fittings over its fine mahogany wainscoting, with its beautiful women and men—those who were the pride of the opera and the ballet—laughing at each other over glasses of champagne or brandy . . . Maxim's, with its correct, deferential waiters . . . Maxim's, with its chandeliers and its soft sustained music and the people sitting about listening for the tidbits that would provide the next day's gossip. This was Maxim's, and here she was, Sarah Martin, suddenly and mysteriously a part of it all. Amanda had been born to this sort of place, but Sarah couldn't stop marveling at the incongruity of her presence here, under one of the new Mucha stained glass windows.

And there was Eric: Eric smiling at her over the dinner, Eric's arm brushing against hers, almost accidentally, his knee moving every so often under the table with its elegant white linen cloth so as to touch hers, fleetingly, quickly gone again before she was even sure that it had ever been there. Eric listened attentively to her as she told stories about her childhood in San Jose, about the majestic California redwood trees and the brilliant, bright California surf. Smiling and lighting her cigarette for her, Eric talked easily in his turn about the horses with which he had grown up at the de Montclair estate, about the crisp autumn mornings when the air was clear and frosty, and one could hear his father's anvil echoing throughout the entire valley.

Eric's descriptions made Sarah feel as if she had almost been there: She could see it all. She could smell the wood smoke and the pine forest, hear the high-pitched whinnying from the stables, and she plainly saw the young boy sitting on the fence, watching his father hammer out shoes for the de Montclair horses.

She drank in his words as deeply as he had hers, so that it was a long time before they realized they were alone at the table, that Philippe and Amanda had gone, that the waiters were discreetly turning down lights and tidying tables around them.

They walked through the streets towards the *hôtel-complet* where Sarah and Amanda were staying, walking slowly, still talking, immersed in their words, leading each other through the mazes and labyrinths of their pasts. Eric had put his arm around Sarah, and their steps blended together, and she leaned her head against his shoulder when the time seemed right for it.

There was dampness in the air, and a mist over the streets gathered around the gas lamps, creating haloes and diffusing the light so that it was soft and unobtrusive. The fountains at the Place de la Concorde splashed water from mermaids and fishes alike, and Sarah turned her face to catch some of the spray, laughing as she had laughed that afternoon up in the Blériot, laughing with the sheer delight of sensations, feelings, pleasures.

"Here," said Eric, pulling her away. "You'll catch a nasty cold. Don't do that."

She turned to him with a joyous smile still on her lips, but her eyes became serious as they looked into his. For he was asking questions, silently. Without knowing how or why, their hands came up and clasped each other, and then he pulled her closer to him, her breasts against his chest, his heartbeat strong and regular so close to hers, his breath warm and close; and then they were kissing. Sarah closed her eyes and leaned into him and into the feeling, the warmth of his embrace engulfing her like warm water flowing all around them.

Eric's mouth was gentle and strong, asking more questions than she could even imagine answers for, and yet seemingly finding the answers in her own embrace. Her arms tightened around him, and he pulled her closer still, and then the kiss ended and he was whispering something against her hair. She couldn't understand the words, but it didn't matter. All that was certain in that night of blurred images was the reality of Eric's presence, the feelings that were too great and too strong to be confined by mere words, the night and the love.

Suddenly, looming tall and dark out of the mists, a carriage clattered by, the horse's hooves drumming an irregular staccato rhythm into the cobblestones. A whiff of leather and tobacco and chestnuts followed in its wake. Sarah laughed again, and Eric laughed with her, his arm still around her. Without speaking they began walking again. When they did talk, after a while, it was of ordinary things, of the next day's work at Aeroméchanique and of the new spanner that Eric had ordered from Germany, and of the fuss everyone in the crowd that afternoon had made over Sarah's outfit, most particularly the scarf.

They stood outside the hotel for a few moments in silence, holding hands, neither of them willing to begin to articulate what was happening between them. And then Sarah leaned forward and kissed his cheek.

"Good night," he said softly.

"I need to do some work tomorrow," she said, worry moving into her voice. "I have a story to finish for the newspaper. But I could finish by late afternoon—"

"You know where to find me," he said. "I'll be there."

"Well, if you wanted to go out, or something, I'd quite understand—"

"There's nothing on earth I'd rather do than wait for you."

The nakedness of the statement, the simplicity and the utter sincerity with which it was spoken, took her aback for a moment. Strangely enough, it had more effect on her than would have speeches filled with promises of undying love. She didn't know quite what to say. She looked at him for another moment, then turned and slipped into the hotel. As she closed the door behind her, she was quite positive that she could hear him whistling as he walked away down the street.

She was not entirely surprised to find that Amanda had not yet slept in her bed. Nor, thought Sarah as she silently undressed, was she likely to at all.

"I think he's married, Sarah. Isn't that ghastly."

Sarah bent over the pad she was writing on and tried to ignore Amanda's voice. They were sitting side by side on one of the balustrades which hedge the Seine, against which artists and booksellers propped their wares, and which in this case afforded an unencumbered view of the cathedral of Notre Dame, which Sarah was attempting to describe for her article on Americans in Paris.

Amanda, for her part, was tossing crumbs from her pastry to the pigeons that were eagerly flocking around the two women. "Sarah? What do you think?"

Sarah sighed and half turned from Amanda so that she could examine the twin spires of the cathedral. "I do wish that Lawrence didn't spend so much time here. I wouldn't have to describe it, then," she said. "Words aren't enough. They simply aren't adequate for something this majestic."

"Sarah Martin," Amanda said accusingly, "I don't think that you've listened to a single word I've said."

"Of course I have. You think that Philippe's married."

"What do you think?"

"What difference would it make, if it was true?"

Amanda considered this question. "I'm not sure," she said slowly. "I don't know as I like the competition."

"That's never bothered you before."

"How would you know?" She threw down another crumb.

"Your reputation, my dear, precedes you. What Amanda Lewis wants, Amanda Lewis gets." Sarah paused, biting the end of her pen, and then turned to look at Amanda. "Judging from your absence last night, you apparently did your reputation proud."

"Oh, Sarah, darling, don't tell me that I've shocked you! How simply delicious!"

"Why," asked Sarah in exasperation, "is everyone convinced that they're shocking me? I must have quite the air of an ingenue."

"Darling, it's just that you're so wonderfully wholesome." Amanda flung down the remainder of her pastry, and a flock of pigeons immediately congregated at her feet. "But we weren't talking about you, were we?"

"I daresay not," Sarah muttered. "All right. Philippe. Do you want to marry him, Amanda?"

"Good heavens, Sarah, you do ask the most extraordinary things, don't you? Whatever makes you think that?"

"Well," said Sarah reasonably, "if you wanted to marry him, then it would matter a great deal whether or not he's married at the moment. To someone else, that is. Tell me, would you say that a spire pierces the sky?"

"That's too graphic for me by half," Amanda shuddered. "But I'm still interested in whether—"

"Oh, Amanda, get off your high horse." Sarah had no

desire to placate Amanda today. "You've slept with Philippe, and now you're feeling guilty, and you want to justify that guilt. It's all right to feel that way, just don't invent imaginary reasons. Accept that some of your mother's values, no matter how passé they may seem, are remaining with you. That's all right."

"And what if he's married?" Amanda's voice was subdued.

"If he's married, you're still going to have an affair with him, aren't you? Does it really make a difference? You may as well simply enjoy yourself, dear heart, and leave the moralizing for people who are better equipped for it."

Amanda looked at her suspiciously. "Did I detect an insult in all of that?"

"Never," Sarah assured her blandly. "Let's go have lunch."

Amanda slid obediently off the wall and brushed the remaining crumbs from her skirt. "At least I thought to bring proper clothes," she said.

"And that," Sarah said gaily, her spirits lifting as she thought of the afternoon and evening ahead, "makes all the difference."

That evening Sarah drove out to Aéromechanique alone; Philippe had business with his lawyers in Paris and was meeting Amanda there for dinner "and dancing the tango, Sarah. Isn't that marvelous?"

"What business?"

"How do I know? It's the law firm of Beneteau and Giroux, over on the rue des Lices. Old family lawyers, I gather. Very dusty and boring, I should think. I said I'd meet him later."

"Then you really don't mind being left to your own devices?"

"Sarah, darling, I can take care of myself. Besides, I shan't have to." She giggled slightly, and Sarah thought that she could detect just the faintest undercurrent of nervousness in that laugh. "You were right, of course. It doesn't matter at all. An affair, after all, is just an affair, isn't it?"

But as Sarah drove through the gathering dusk, she was asking herself the same question, and finding that her answer was quite different.

Chapter Five

We have an order! Can you believe it? Five airplanes before the year is out—five airplanes! The Italians want to use them for spying on the Turks. Sarah! I say, Sarah! Isn't that wonderful?"

Sarah looked up from the letter she was writing to her parents. She was sitting in the office of Aeroméchanique in Angers, two elegantly furnished rooms with lithographs of earlier flight attempts on the walls, and a plush red velvet chair behind the mahogany table used by Eric and Philippe when conducting business. Eric had been sitting in the chair opening the day's mail, and to fill the hours Sarah had decided to undertake her own correspondence and write her long-overdue letter home.

She was in love with Eric.

She had known him for exactly one week.

Now she looked up and smiled in amusement. "Do I gather that you are characterizing the order, and not the war, as wonderful?"

He grinned. "That you do, my dear, that you do." He sat back down excitedly, and, pulling the letterhead stationery across the table, began to write out a response. At that moment Philippe de Montclair walked into the room.

"Greetings, one and all. Dear Sarah, allow me to kiss your hand. What a fine day it is!"

"It gets better," Eric said, lifting the letter from the Italians in the air and waving it at him. "Wait until you read this!"

Sarah was studying Philippe. "What are you doing in Angers?" she asked, frowning slightly. "I thought that you were going to the theater with Amanda tonight. Has something happened, Philippe?"

Something in the tone of her voice made Eric look up, and his eyes widened in comprehension as he looked at his friend. "Marie-Louise," he said, with complete certainty. ' 'It's Marie-Louise, isn't it?"

Philippe kept smiling. "It is indeed," he said. "*Mes amis*, you can be the first to congratulate me. You are looking at a father!"

Sarah put away her letter and, standing, gave him a hug and a kiss on the cheek. "Congratulations, Philippe," she said warmly. "Is it a boy or a girl?"

"A boy," he said, his eyes shining, looking at Eric. "I've named him Pierre Eric Antoine."

Eric didn't say anything, just nodded and smiled, as though there was some communication going on between the two men that only they could understand. It was Sarah who at length pointed out that they ought to be drinking champagne. "Come on then, Philippe. You can't tell me that this isn't more cause for celebration than my little exhibition last week! Surely it's an occasion befitting the honor of at least one bottle!"

Philippe nodded, half-sitting, half-leaning on the arm of the comfortable chintz-covered chair nearest the office door, patting his pockets as he searched for cigarettes. "Indeed it is, but I haven't got the time for it. Sorry, but I promised Marie-Louise that I'd spend some time with her and the baby at the estate today, and I want to catch the six o'clock train back to Paris tonight."

"Amanda?" guessed Eric.

"Amanda, indeed," Philippe said calmly, lighting the cigarette.

"Does she know?" Sarah asked.

There was a moment of silence in the room, as though she had tossed a stone into a quiet pond and was watching the ripples widen all about them. Eric looked down and began to rearrange the papers on the desk; Philippe sighed and inhaled on his cigarette and finally turned to Sarah.

"No. She doesn't," he said heavily. "I know that she guesses about Marie-Louise, but I haven't come out and told her, and she hasn't come out and asked, and she certainly doesn't know about the baby." He took a deep breath. "Are you going to tell her?"

"Me?" Sarah raised her eyebrows. "No. Of course not. That's your business, Philippe. It's between you and your conscience and Amanda. It's true that she thinks you're married; she said so to me the other day. But it's not my place to get involved one way or the other."

"It puts Sarah," Eric's voice carried strongly from behind the desk, though his eyes still focused down at his papers, "in a damned awkward position."

"What do you want me to do?" Philippe asked, spreading his hands in a characteristically Gallic gesture. "Tell my mistress that I'm married, and a father? Tell my wife that I have a young American lover in Paris? Divorce Marie-Louise, who is the most suitable wife for me in all of France, and cause a rift in my family that will go on for generations, and then find that Amanda wouldn't marry me? What do you want me to do?"

Eric shook his head in frustration, but it was Sarah who said, "He's right, Eric. She wouldn't marry him. She thinks he's darling and fun and a whole lot of other adjectives that I could only guess at. But her life isn't here, her life is in America." She walked over to where Eric sat and touched the back of his hand, lightly, with the tip of her little finger. "She doesn't need his money and she wouldn't think much of his title or his estate." Sarah took a deep breath. "Let it be, Eric. Amanda's an adult. She can take care of herself. She'll go back to America someday and life will go on for Philippe and his family. It's not worth the bother."

"I don't like seeing you in the middle of all of this," he said stubbornly. "I don't like seeing you put in this position."

Sarah shrugged. "In what position?" she asked lightly. "It's nothing, Eric." He was still looking down at the desk. She came around and sat on the arm of the chair and looked at him, making him meet her eyes. "It's all right," she repeated, her voice soft. "It has nothing to do with us. They have nothing to do with us."

He looked at her for a long moment, and then nodded, as though affirming a decision. "You're right," he said. "Philippe, old man," he said, raising his voice to his friend, "off you go then. Take care of your baby."

"We'll see you in Paris," Sarah said to Philippe, still looking at Eric, waiting for him to respond to her.

As she waited, his fingers tightened around her hand and the warmth flowed between them again, and she smiled.

They took the night train back to Paris.

"Separate berths, sir?" the conductor had asked Eric, and he responded, "Of course," while at the same time Sarah said, "No, that won't be necessary."

The conductor cleared his throat discreetly, and Eric turned to look at Sarah. "Are you sure?" he asked her, softly, and she squeezed his hand tightly in hers, and finally he turned back to the conductor. "One berth will do, thank you very much," he said, and the tickets were issued.

She giggled when they got into the compartment. It was so small and smelled slightly musty, and they kept bumping into each other. It was one of those old railway carriages left over from days of Victorian splendor, with a gilt-edged mirror, plush flocked-velvet seats, and framed pictures of faraway places so exotic that surely this railway had never seen the likes of them. But it was welcoming to Sarah, even though it was too narrow, and the gas lamp flickered. The seats were worn, and the mirror flecked with rust; but she couldn't have imagined a more wonderful place to be, because Eric was there.

They had eaten a belated supper already, at a Breton crêperie near the railway station: delicious cheese and mushrooms and ham peeking out from the fine layers of crêpes, some of the apple cider for which Brittany was famous—benign going down, but so potent later. Sarah sat with her elbows on the checkered tablecloth and the cup of cider in her hands, and asked questions about the Italian contract, but Eric seemed to have lost interest in talking about it. "It's just production," he concluded, taking his last bite and wiping his mouth with the rough linen napkin. "Anyone can do it. I'll have to organize someone else to do it. I don't want to deal with production, I want to deal with *ideas*."

"So," Sarah said reasonably, eyeing him over the rim of her cup, "think of the ideas. Get other people to do your production. I hear that Henry Ford is doing that now, in America, with motorcars. They call it an assembly line, and every worker has one specific job to do, and does it perfectly

well, over and over again. It's faster than having one person
do everything, I understand. They're producing a lot of
motorcars that way."

"These aren't motorcars, these are airplanes."

"So what?" She put the cup down and reached across the
table for his hands. "Why can't the same principle apply?
You're right. You've got no business turning Aeroméchanique into a factory, Eric. You're too talented for
that. You have ideas to work out. You have dreams to
create."

"You have to help me."

He said it so abruptly that she wasn't sure that she had
understood him correctly. "Whatever do you mean? I don't
know anything about designing airplanes."

"You know how to fly them." He stroked her hands,
looking down at them, then raising his eyes to meet hers.
"You know what you need, up there, more than anyone at
Aeroméchanique ever will. You can tell me. You can test my
designs and tell me what's wrong with them and how I can
change them, how I can improve them." There was a light in
his eyes she hadn't seen before and she watched him,
entranced. "We can do it, Sarah, you and I together. I can
learn things from you. You can make the designs real, and
better than anybody else's."

She had caught his eagerness. "I've wanted to make
suggestions, sometimes. . . . Something lighter would be
good, something that could solve the weight-distribution
problem, and an engine with more power. . . ." Her eyes
were sparkling, and he nodded.

"That's it. . . . I know we can work together, Sarah. I
know it!"

Carried away on a wave of optimism and delight, they
drank too much of the hard Breton cider, each sharing the
other's eagerness and recognizing that the other's needs and
expertise were mutually complementary. . . . It was an excitement beyond anything physical, Sarah realized, this
excitement of mind to mind, heart to heart. The sense of
working together towards a common purpose. It was more
inebriating than the drink. And soon, too soon, it was time
for the train and Paris.

Eric turned down the gas flame almost immediately after

they had settled in, his awkwardness communicating itself to her in waves that were almost tangible in the confined space. The flickering flame plunged the carriage into shadows and, suddenly, at the same time, brought them closer to each other in the darkness. He moved slightly, closer to her. His lips on her cheek were light, hesitant. "Are you all right?"

"Yes." She turned her head, just a bit, and felt his breath on her mouth, and then he was kissing her, slowly, lightly, as though fearful. She reached her arms up around him and drew him down over her, and the kiss became more insistent, more demanding, his breath and hers quickening together. She could feel her heart hammering in her chest.

He pulled back from her, his fingers moving under her jacket, sliding it off her shoulders, gently, slowly. Sarah bit her lip and waited. He kissed her shoulders, and then began to unbutton the front of her blouse. She didn't know what to do, didn't know how to respond. There was excitement and warmth moving in her and around her, a maelstrom of feelings, all happy and frightened and confused. Entwining her fingers in his hair, she let her hands follow his movements. He had opened her shirt, and bent his head to kiss the lace beneath, the camisole which still hid her breasts.

She began to feel as though all of the oxygen had left her, and it was at that moment that the train began to move, slowly at first, the whistle shrill and piercing in the still night air, then gathering more speed as it flung itself clear of the Angers railway station. The wheels rumbled beneath them, finding their rhythm, and the pattern of their clatter beat down on the tracks. Eric's arms were around her now, and he had taken off his own shirt, and then her camisole, and her bare breasts were against his hard chest, and it felt so good, so strong.

Later, when she thought about that night, Sarah realized that from the first she felt as though she belonged with Eric, that being with him was like being with another part of her own self, that their bodies and their minds and their hearts meshed so thoroughly and so perfectly that there was no sense that they had ever been apart, or that they would be apart ever again. They were caught in a sort of timelessness, as though their love had started at the beginning of the ages,

long before either of them had been born, as if it would
outlive both of them to the ends of time.

Eric's hands came up to her chest and cupped her breasts,
gentle, timid almost, his thumbs rubbing softly over her
nipples. She felt the same excitement at his touch, the rush
of warmth all over her body, but concentrated and then
diffused and then concentrated again, in widening circles of
feelings, of pleasure. She moaned with the sensations, and
he bent his head and licked one of her nipples, and then the
other, and she clasped him tighter to her, the pleasure
mounting and changing and enveloping her until it seemed
that she could feel no more.

"Sarah. Sarah." His voice in the darkness was whispered,
his face dim, his whole body a shadow moving over her. He
had taken more of her clothes from her body: her skirt, her
petticoat, the silk stockings and garters and panties that she
wore; and he was easing her back, slowly, until she was lying
down completely in the berth. And, all the while, he kept
kissing her, caressing her, his breath warm on her neck, on
her arms, on her face, on her breasts. "Sarah. Sarah, my
love."

She clung to him, pressing herself up against him. It was
no longer a matter of not knowing what to do, but of
listening to the voice within her, the voice which knew when
to lift her airplane off the ground, the voice which knew
what she wanted, what she needed, long before she was able
to recognize it herself. She listened to it, and moved with
him, feeling his hardness against her softness, feeling the
changes taking place, first in his body, and then in hers.

When at last he entered her, Sarah cried out, in pain and
pleasure and need, and then all thought was obliterated
completely in the feelings, in the rhythm of their life
together, of their love, of his movements and her gasps and
their words, and everything spiraling up until it seemed
impossible that it could go any higher. The whole world
seemed to hold its breath for that one split second in time.

And then the spiral turned and lights were flashing
brightly against her closed eyelids, great bursts of sparkling
colors more vivid than the sun, and Eric was moaning and
moving and burying his face deeper into her neck, and at
length they both stopped moving and lay perfectly still, their

hearts pounding together, their breath coming in gasps. The greatest peace Sarah had ever felt descended upon them. All was well. All was well.

Eric moved his head slightly and whispered into the darkness, "I love you, Sarah."

She smiled and tightened her arms around him. Softly she answered, "I love you, Eric."

The train clattered on into the night in its own rhythm of need and necessity.

"It's a silly idea, Sarah. I don't know what has gotten into you." Amanda was turning the pages of *Leslie's Weekly* with irritation. It had just arrived from New York with one of Sarah's stories in it, but Amanda had not yet even focused on a page. "I can't see why you'd want to do anything like that."

"Anything like what?" As though on cue, Philippe came to the door of the hangar and paused, looking out at the two women sitting under a tree on the grassy hill. He pulled a cigarette from the packet in his pocket and lit it. "What is it that you want to do, Sarah?"

"It's silly," Amanda pouted.

"I want to fly across the English Channel," Sarah said.

Philippe raised his eyebrows and drew in deeply on the cigarette. "Indeed? And what inspired this fit of daring?"

"It's just a stupid notion that she picked up from the most awful man in Newport," Amanda said crossly. "I think that he said it as a dare. I'm sure he wasn't serious."

"I'm sure he was," Sarah said calmly. "Besides, Amanda, Roger isn't awful, and you never said so until this moment. What is it that you're afraid of?"

"There's nothing for me to be afraid of, Sarah, darling. You're the one who ought to be afraid, if you ask me."

Philippe pushed himself off the doorjamb and went over to sit next to Amanda. "Here," he said, lighting a cigarette for her. "It sounds like an ambitious idea, Sarah. How do you plan to do it?"

She looked at him sharply, not trusting the tone of his voice. But then she saw that he was genuinely interested and she relaxed. "Louis Blériot already did it," she said. "I've been talking to him. It wasn't so very difficult, just cold and miserable. I can deal with that. He wouldn't have had any problems at all if it hadn't been for his engine overheating."

Philippe drew on the cigarette again. "But I thought he made it across."

"Oh, he did. Almost didn't, but he managed. He just got lucky and flew through a rainstorm, and that cooled down his engine enough to make it the rest of the way."

"He probably looked terrible after flying through a rainstorm," Amanda commented.

Philippe reached over and took Amanda's hand in his. "What about your engine?" he asked Sarah. "Won't it overheat?"

"My engine?" She was smiling. "Hardly my engine, Philippe. More like yours."

"Don't be silly—" Amanda started saying again, but Philippe leaned over and kissed her and in the pause that followed he said, "I see. Aeromécanique's making the engine for you."

"That's right." She drew her knees up under her chin. "Not just the engine, either. The whole airplane. Eric's working on the design right now."

"Even as we speak?" Philippe inquired. "Well, well. That might mean quite a bit of nice publicity for the company, flying the first girl to solo across the English Channel."

"Trust you," Sarah said sourly, "to look at the business end of it."

"Aeromécanique is a business," Philippe replied, his voice reasonable. "I don't care how smitten the boy genius in there gets with a girl pilot, a business is still a business."

"It sounds tiresome," Amanda said.

"'Boy genius'?" Sarah said, at the same time, with an amused smile.

"I think we're ready," Eric said, appearing in the hangar doorway, wiping his hands on a cloth. "I've got Jean-Marc and Henri standing by, so we might as well make a go at it. God, it's hot for October."

Sarah jumped to her feet, smoothing out the wrinkles from the long green skirt she was wearing. "You mean it's all ready? Now? Oh, let me try it, Eric, do!"

"Don't be daft," he said, with obvious affection. "It's just the first modification, and besides, I'd rather have you watching it down here. Henri said he'd take it up." And, as no one moved, he gestured impatiently. "Come on, you'll miss the show."

They all trooped obediently around to the front of the

hangar, the side which faced out to the field. Amanda caused
her usual stir, exclaiming and turning back to grab her
outrageously wide-brimmed hat, and scolding Sarah about
leaving hers in the motorcar. Philippe was laughing. He
picked Amanda up around the waist, spinning her around in
the air before setting her down again and lacing her fingers
through his. "Stop worrying about how you look," he
laughed. "You look wonderful."

Eric had disappeared back inside and presently they could
hear the creaking and groaning of the big doors as they
opened. Sarah crossed her arms across her chest and looked
critical; Amanda and Philippe, with their arms around each
other, watched as a gaping hole appeared in the front of the
hangar. The airplane appeared first, being pushed and
pulled and maneuvered out by Eric and the two
Aeroméchanique employees, Jean-Marc Baptiste and Henri
Lefevre. The men were sweaty and dirty and looked tired,
but Eric had a light in his eyes. Sarah nodded with satisfaction. The first modification, perhaps, but they were on the
right track. She could tell already.

She ran over to help them then, leaving Philippe and
Amanda to their own devices. The breeze tugged fitfully at
her skirt as she moved away from the cover of the trees out
into the field. In the sunlight, her hair shone like burnished
copper, and she could feel Eric's eyes on her, feel the
undercurrent of love and affection and delight.

After they tied down the wings with strong ropes that were
attached to heavy pegs pounded into the ground, Henri put
on his goggles and helmet and climbed carefully into the
small seat suspended behind the motor. Eric and Jean-
Marc spun the propellers. The engine roared into life, scattering dust and pebbles and tufts of grass all around,
making Amanda squeal and hold tightly to her hat. Sarah
stood her ground, looking over the airplane, seeking flaws
with her eyes. Up on the side of the airplane, beneath the
pilot's seat, was scrawled the inscription, *Mademoiselle
Sarah*.

She looked up and met Eric's eyes across the plane and
smiled at him. He held up his hand for a moment, the
thumb turned up in hope and optimism, and she duplicated
the gesture, her laughter silent in the loud thunder of the
engine. When Henri nodded, Eric gestured to Jean-Marc

and they cut the ropes that had been holding the airplane in place. It began to move, bumping irregularly on the dirt runway the men had carved out of the field. Sarah narrowed her eyes to watch it go: It gathered speed, made the first tentative lift, then lurched as it regained the runway and strained to get off again. Solemnly, she watched as it lifted off, barely before the end of the field, and Amanda was jumping up and down with excitement, still holding her hat, and Philippe was already starting to cheer. Eric, too, was watching, gripping his wrench so tightly that his knuckles showed white. Then there was an even louder roar and the little airplane plummeted into the treetops at the other end of the field.

"*Merde*," Eric cried out, throwing down his wrench with force into the dirt, and they all began to run as fast as they could—even Amanda. The field seemed endless and when they reached the trees at the edge Eric was shouting, "Henri! Henri, old man, are you all right?"

There was a moment of horrible tense silence, during which Sarah crossed her fingers, almost waiting for the great roar of air that always preceded airplane fires. Then, almost comically because of their relief, the answer came from over their heads. "Here I am."

"Henri?" The tension was still in Eric's voice. "Say something! Are you all right?"

"I'm fine," he grumbled. "Just get me out of here." They had managed to cut their way through the bushes toward Henri's voice when Sarah looked up and saw both the *Mademoiselle Sarah* and Henri clinging to the branches above them. It was already clear that between the two of them, Henri was in far better shape.

"I told you, Sarah," Amanda said breathlessly, clinging to Philippe. "I told you. This whole idea is silly. He can't even get out of the field, and you want to cross the Channel in it?"

"It does need a few changes," Sarah conceded. "But it was just the first model, remember."

Eric was looking disgusted. "Can you take care of him?" he asked Jean-Marc. Receiving a nod in reply, he gestured back towards the hangar. "Time for a beer."

Philippe moved closer to his friend. "Never mind, old fellow. You'll get it right next time."

Amanda, still palpitating, straightened her dress and her

hat, and walked with an effort at composure by Philippe's side. "As long as the next attempt is not today," she said. "I shall die of hunger very very soon if no one does anything about it."

Sarah could sense Eric's discouragement, and she reached over in a now-familiar gesture, touching the back of his hand with her little finger. "It's all right," she said softly. "You just need more power."

Eric ran a hand through his hair. He wasn't really listening to any of them. Already, his mind was racing ahead, running projections, making allowances, correcting miscalculations. He absently put an arm around Sarah's shoulders and walked back in silence, while the conversation flowed around him like a stream parting around a boulder. Knowing that Eric was working already, and determined to protect him, Sarah talked and laughed with the others. She wanted desperately, immensely, to fly across the English Channel, but she was finding, to her surprise, that she just as desperately wanted to do it in one of Eric's airplanes. It would be something they would have together; it would last forever, apart from the fleeting moments of life, and no one could ever take it from them.

Already she knew that it was going to happen. And, knowing that, she didn't understand the voice inside of her that urged, *Hurry*. There's all the time in the world, she told herself, and still the voice said, *Hurry*.

In the fading daylight, as Eric picked up the wrench he had thrown down in disgust and Amanda giggled with Philippe about some trivial thing, Sarah didn't move to reassure Eric that all was well, or to tell him that it didn't matter. She listened to her voice and she stayed silent. And waited.

Later, after dinner had been duly consumed and appreciated in the city, Eric excused himself to go back out to the airfield.

"But it's dark!" Amanda protested. "No, Eric, it's simply too dreary for words. Stay with us, and play instead." Her cheeks were bright from the champagne and she was showing off yet another new dress, rose-gold silk cut low in the bodice. This, unquestionably, was Amanda's world.

"I've got plenty of lamps," he said. "No, I'm sorry, Amanda, I have to go. It's going to bother me all night, otherwise. I wouldn't be very good company."

"Well, if you must, but you're really tiresome. Life is too short to be spending it being too serious, don't you know."

Philippe refilled her glass. "Then let's not get too serious." He was drinking more than usual, Sarah had noticed. Perhaps he was choosing this moment to celebrate the birth of his son, or trying to get his courage up to tell Amanda about it. Who knew?

Amanda giggled. "I'll try," she said, as solemnly as she could, "not to get serious at all." She burst into laughter at that, and Philippe was laughing, too, as they drank out of each other's glasses, spilling champagne all over the place.

Eric turned to Sarah. "I'm sorry. You understand, don't you? I hope that I'm not ruining your evening."

"Of course not," she said calmly. "I'm coming out with you."

"Don't be ridiculous. I'm going to work all night. You'd be exhausted and bored to tears."

"How little you know me, Monsieur Beaumont," she said evenly. "Two things are of great interest to me just now—airplanes, and you. How could I possibly pass up an opportunity to spend a night alone in the country with both?"

He grinned, a mischievous glint in his eyes. "Well," he conceded, "it might be nice to have someone around. Just to hand me the odd screwdriver, of course."

"Of course," Sarah agreed, straight-faced. "Shall we go?"

"I expect they'll never notice," he said, gesturing towards Amanda and Philippe, who had their arms around each other and were lost, apparently to the world at large, in a very passionate embrace.

Sarah smiled. "I think," she said, in a careful stage whisper, "that this is our exit cue." He reached for her hand and they slipped away from the table, feeling silly and exhilarated at the same time.

Amanda and Philippe appeared not to have noticed.

An announcement appeared in the newspaper the following day: "Born, to Philippe, Count de Montclair, and Marie-

Louise, Countess de Montclair, of the Chateau de Montclair, Loire Valley, a son, Pierre Eric Antoine de Montclaire, to be christened at the Cathédrale of Angers. . . ."

Sarah saw the paper before Amanda did. She had just arrived back in the city after spending the night in the closest approximation to a hayloft that she would probably ever see, out at the Aeroméchanique hangar. Eric had protested that he did, truly, need to work all night, but he had been easily persuaded to rest from his labors from time to time, and their lovemaking was, if anything, more exquisite than it had been in the train. "Do you ever think we'll be in a normal bed?" Sarah had whispered into the darkness, and his reply was at hand. "With you, it doesn't matter. Anywhere is heaven."

Amanda had spent the night out, presumably with Philippe. The room they rented at the pension was empty, with the newspaper sitting politely just outside the door. Sarah bathed, and took it down with her to the dining room where she perused it over coffee and croissants.

Once she had seen the announcement, it seemed to leap out at her, to scream its message in glaring headlines. She hastily stuffed the paper away behind one of the overpowering potted plants that Madame who ran the pension kept in the vestibule. Sarah realized that she was doing the very thing she had cautioned Philippe against: protecting Amanda, shielding her from the truth. And yet . . .

And yet. One day, a day that was quickly approaching, she and Amanda would have to go to le Havre and board a ship which would take them back to America, and Amanda's memories of France might as well be pleasant. Sarah pushed the thought from her mind: Leaving was unthinkable. Leaving Eric was unthinkable.

Perhaps, if she thought about something else, it would never happen.

Chapter Six

Philippe frowned and turned a few more pages in the newspaper. "I saw it here before," he muttered. "Somewhere . . . Yes, here it is. New age of politics, they're saying."

Eric didn't look up from the drawing he was working on. "Probably so," he agreed.

"Probably so?" Philippe roared with good humor. "That doesn't sound like you. Are you even listening to what I'm saying? Politics are important, *mon ami*."

"Politics are important to rich people," Eric said, mildly. "No one else has the time or energy for them."

"I don't think that's entirely true," Sarah objected. She was sitting with the men in the living room of the house that the four of them had decided to rent together, a lovely house in the Paris suburb of Boulogne-Billiancourt, on the rue de Verdun. It belonged to an antique dealer who was more interested in running off after treasure troves all over the world than in maintaining his residence. He had been happy to sign over a lease to the Count de Montclair who wanted, he explained, a more comfortable pied-à-terre in Paris which would enable him to follow the fortunes of his fledgling company, Aeroméchanique, if indeed it could still be called fledgling. Aeroméchanique was now building and selling more airplanes than any other French company. The Italian-Turkish conflict had been very good to them, as airplanes were used first for scouting and surveillance, and then as a means to drop bombs on the enemy. Sarah had been horrified when she heard: Her own vision of flying was one of peace, and it was painful to hear of the light manmade birds that she so loved being used as a means of war. But on this point, Eric sided with Philippe. "It's good business," he said to Sarah. "We don't make the decisions, but we make money from the decisions. That's good business. Nothing more. Good for the industry. Good for Aeroméchanique."

Eric had taken the Ford assembly line idea into the world of aviation. His hangar still stood alone in a field: That was where he liked to work, where the ideas came to him, where he kept his prototypes and his lucky wrench. But in the six months that had passed since Sarah had first suggested the manufacturing concept to him, Eric had built a factory as well, outside of Angers, which turned out the small planes and engines required by the Italians. And, in this new year of 1912, the English had started buying from Aeroméchanique, too. They had established something they were calling the Royal Flying Corps, and were designating an entire branch of the service to airplanes.

Sarah didn't like it, but she didn't voice her objections. It was Eric's company, his and Philippe's. It was their company, their decision, their business, she told herself. She resolutely tried to ignore the things about it that she couldn't support, and focus on the ideas being developed. In fact, she was much more absorbed in the airplane that Eric was still perfecting, the one that would carry her across the English Channel. He promised: In the spring, she would do it.

Now the four of them sat together in the rented house on a sweet, sleepy Saturday afternoon in March, Eric working on his designs and Philippe reading the newspaper. From the next room came the sound of a piano as Amanda practiced at her most recent undertaking.

Sarah looked up from the scarf she was knitting—the one domestic skill she seemed to have acquired, she often thought ruefully, and so much for the old charcoal sketches of *Sarah At Home!*—and objected further to Eric's remark about the rich and their interest in politics. "Rich people have more leisure to participate in politics, I should think. But oughtn't everyone be interested? It guides so much of what we do."

"Industry guides what we do." Eric corrected. "The politicians are the ones who tell the people the decisions that have been made, but it's industry that makes the decisions."

She looked at him sharply. "What makes you say that? If that were so, every country would be just as capitalistic as America, wouldn't it?"

"They're all heading in that direction," Eric said cheerfully, still without looking up from his drawings.

"I don't know," Philippe said slowly. "It's not all capitalism. It's a matter of taking care of one's family, taking care of one's people. That's where money is useful, and that's where industry is useful. You're right, political life is a figurehead for something going on beneath the surface. But what's going on beneath the surface is family."

"Spoken like a true son to the mansion born," Eric said, but he said it without bitterness, merely stating a fact. "You wouldn't say that if you didn't have a title, Philippe. The rest of us take such niceties a little less seriously."

In the next room, Amanda hit a series of bad notes, and Philippe winced. "I don't think that she's ever going to master that thing," he said, shaking out the newspaper.

Sarah looked down at her knitting. "What you're both saying is that politics doesn't really matter. Either it's fronting for noblesse oblige, or it's fronting for some sort of industrial revolution, but either way it doesn't stand on its own. I'm not sure that I believe that."

Eric stood up, stretching, and shook his head with a yawn. He walked over to where Sarah was sitting and leaned over the back of the sofa, gently kissing her cheek. "Believe it or not, love, it's the way of the world," he said. "Has Annie given any thought to dinner tonight? I'm famished."

"We gave her the night off," Sarah replied absently. "If what you say is true, then why do we bother to participate in elections?"

"You gave Annie the night off? Rash move, that," Eric said. "Have we any reservations, Philippe?"

"No reservations," Philippe said, folding the newspaper and tossing it aside. "Amanda and Sarah have volunteered their services in the kitchen tonight. And Sarah, dear, the point of politics is that that is how it is done. We might be able to see through the process, but we do still try to observe the proprieties of life."

"You're cooking?" Eric asked Sarah. "That's great. I'm delighted, but puzzled. I thought you said that you weren't about to spend your life in a kitchen, toiling over meals?"

She laughed. "One night a month is hardly toiling, darling. And, besides, Amanda's just bought a new apron— God only knows why—and is keen to try it out. So there you are. Roast turkey and cranberry sauce, potatoes and corn . . . We just thought you gentlemen ought to sample some *cuisine américaine* for a change!"

"As long as it goes well with beer, Eric will be pleased," Philippe said with a smile, and they all laughed, Eric hugging Sarah even more tightly from behind the sofa.

Sarah disengaged herself from him and, still laughing, walked through the passageway that led to the back of the house, rolling up her shirtsleeves as she went. It was true, she reflected, that she had been spoiled over the past few months. Not long before Christmas, Philippe had announced his plans to rent the house, "for all of us, Sarah, so don't be difficult."

"Me?" she said, feigning innocence. "Difficult? I don't think that I am the one to cause difficulties. But are you sure that you can afford it? I can contribute something, of course, but—"

"I told you she would be difficult," Philippe had said to Eric.

Eric had shrugged. "She's like that," he said, and she could see the teasing light in his eyes. "She'd much rather type out her stories on a chair by her bedside at that pension than have a whole room for a study. I think that that psychiatrist fellow in Austria has some word for that kind of behavior."

"I knew that you were reading the wrong kind of books," Philippe had muttered, and Sarah had laughed, and agreed to go and see the house.

It had turned out to be a place from a fairy tale, hidden from the street by tall iron gates and flanked at the entrance by grim stone lions. It was filled with the treasures of the antique dealer's travels: a lead soldier collection, narrating the battle of Waterloo; ancient oil lamps from Greece; a carved fish from China; medieval manuscripts carefully framed and displayed. The rooms were filled with Victorian clutter. The tall windows were covered at night with heavy velvet draperies, and the beds all had ornate carvings on their headboards and posters. And on the third floor was a large room filled with books and tables and an immense oak desk, where from that day forth Sarah was to write all of her work for *Leslie's Weekly*. Her attic, they all called it, and even Amanda had known better than to declare it tiresome.

Now Sarah rinsed her hands and began chopping up the garlic for supper. Amanda, she remembered, had taken to the house right off. If for Sarah it represented a place to work and to converse and to live, for Amanda it was, a love nest. Here, she had declared, she and Philippe could be shielded from the eyes of the world; here they could be themselves.

Sarah had never told Amanda about Marie-Louise, Philippe's wife, but Amanda was bright and knew without asking a second time. Having decided that it wasn't of enough importance to press the issue—or, perhaps, sensing that pressing the issue would have lost her Philippe—she had chosen to ignore it, while at the same time savoring her role as wicked mistress. Philippe spent nights, sometimes, at his estate, and Amanda was perfectly aware that he was not alone there; she raged and cried when he left and played the coquette for the whole time that he was gone.

"Does it hurt?" Sarah frankly asked once, coming upon Amanda in the living room with reddened eyes.

"Of course not, darling, don't be dreary."

Then, in the next moment, the tears came again and Sarah held Amanda tightly in her arms as Amanda cried and cried. "I hate it. I hate it. I think of her kissing him and holding him and making love with him, and it's sheer bloody hell, you have no idea, Sarah. You're so lucky to have Eric really love you."

Sarah privately thought that Philippe did indeed love Amanda, just as much as Amanda loved Philippe. Each had other commitments as well, and the sensual hedonism to which they abandoned themselves when they were together was part and parcel of the kind of life they had decided to share.

Now Sarah pushed the garlic aside and started peeling the potatoes. This part of the meal preparation, she knew, Amanda would characterize as "tiresome." Amanda was much better with the spectacular flambés, the delicate

seasonings, the glazes and the desserts. Sarah's lot was the
mundane. But, somehow, playing house here never felt like
the charcoal sketches. Because of her work, her flying, her
participation in the excitement of Aeroméchanique; or
possibly because she had never known that someone like
Eric existed. . . . Life with him in no way resembled a
charcoal sketch, no matter what she was doing.

They had talked about going back to America for Christmas, she and Amanda, but by then they had just moved into
the house and were still reveling in the novelty of it all. They
had both loved the space and the sense of it being theirs, not
as individuals or even couples but as the group of four that
they inexplicably had become. And America was so far
away. Amanda had written a letter to her mother, and that
was that, as far as she was concerned. Sarah had fretted and
worried and finally bought a painting up at the Place du
Tertre in Montmartre, where all the artists were, and mailed
it to her family with an accompanying card.

Christmas had brought delights she had never known
before. Philippe spent it, as was correct, at his estate outside
of Angers, but Eric had worked very hard to make Amanda
feel welcome and cared for nevertheless. He escorted the
two women to Midnight Mass on Christmas Eve, then
brought them back to the house on the rue de Verdun for
oysters and champagne and roasted chestnuts and truffles
and a magnificent traditional Christmas log cake. At the end
of the evening they had sat about the fire, each wearing
heavy silk robes and slippers, and opened their presents.

Sarah had sat by the fireplace, with her hair loosened and
falling down her back in loose curls, and she had watched
Eric laughing and joking with Amanda over some trivial
thing. Love for him had welled inside of her until she felt
breathless, wondering how any one human being could hold
so many feelings in her body. Eric, sensing her gaze on him,
had looked up to meet her eyes, and the bond between them
filled the space. Amanda had chattered on, oblivious to
anything else happening in the room, and Sarah and Eric
had sat looking at each other, contented in their sense of
peace and security together.

Sarah's parents, surprisingly, had sent a gift along with
their disapproval of her prolonged stay abroad: a long white

silk scarf. "All the aviators are wearing them now, my dear, and apparently you were the first to do it, so I suppose that one could say that you have started a trend. Do bear in mind, however, that there are other things to do with one's life. . . ."

Sarah turned her attention to the potatoes. Christmas had been lovely, including Eric's gift to her of a ruby brooch, surrounded by dainty gold filigree. The winter seemed to have fled quickly. Sarah couldn't fly in the winter—no one could; engines iced over too quickly and invited death—so she spent January and February writing and helping Eric with his designs, and learning to knit in the long gray twilight afternoons. And now March had come, cold and wet and dreary, with endless rain and blustery winds, punctuated only by the piano lessons that Amanda had insisted on taking of late.

"Why?" Eric had asked, puzzled by the sudden appearance of reams of music in the dining room. "Why on earth, Amanda?"

"It's something to do," she had said, evasively, leafing through the first few sonatas on the stack in front of her. "Winter is so tiresome, Eric, darling. One just must find something with which to occupy oneself."

"Piano?" he had asked, doubtfully; and later Sarah had knocked on the door to the bedroom which Amanda shared with Philippe. "Have you got a moment?"

Amanda was sitting at the dressing table, carefully applying makeup. Sarah sat down, uninvited, on the edge of the great double bed. "Why are you studying piano, Amanda?"

She had shrugged and had continued to mix some blue powder in the vial in front of her. "No reason."

Sarah had said at last, "Philippe's wife plays piano."

Amanda gasped, and the precious blue powder fell from her fingers. She whirled to face Sarah. "How can you say that? How can you be so—cruel?"

Sarah sat in silence for a few minutes, and in those minutes Amanda began to cry again. And they had sat like that for some time, Sarah's caring and reassurance palpable in the air, along with Amanda's pain and fear and vulnerability.

At last, Sarah had stood up, and offered Amanda her clean

handkerchief. "You know," she had said softly, "Philippe loves you for what you are. You can't go around imitating her. You have to do what is best for you, and be who is best for you."

Amanda had said, tearfully, like a child, "Sometimes I hate her. Sometimes I want to find a voodoo doll and put pins into it, and hurt her." She took a long shuddering breath, racked with sobs. "But it wouldn't do any good. Philippe married her because it was the proper thing to do. And he needs her as much as he needs me, and I'll never be anybody's idea of proper." The words were tumbling out in a rush. "There are two people inside of Philippe, Sarah, and I see them both so clearly. There's the respectable Count de Montclair, who marries somebody suitable to live in his chateau and bear his children. And then there's the wild one inside him, the Philippe I know, who would rather be out drinking and playing, who dares to do things, who cares about Eric and Aeroméchanique and me. . . ."

Sarah reached out and took Amanda's small hand, awkwardly, feeling useless. She had never touched people very much—except for Eric, and that was different—and she didn't know how to comfort Amanda, what to do or say. "He does care for you, Amanda, I can see that."

Amanda blew her nose resolutely. "I expect," she said in a very small voice, "that she's as jealous of me as I am of her. The difference is that she's got him to keep. I've only got him on loan." She hiccuped on the last word.

Sarah sat pensively for a moment. "Are you thinking about going home?" she asked, a sense of dread gathering in her stomach.

Amanda shrugged. "Not yet. Not as long as I have as much of him as I do. I truly love him, Sarah." She paused, and then asked, "You aren't going to tell anyone about this conversation, are you? It might be—tiresome."

Sarah smiled and shook her head, and never after that did she question Amanda's piano lessons. Even when Eric asked her again about them, she merely shrugged and said, "She just likes new things. It's a phase, it will pass."

The piano had stopped, now, from the other room, and Amanda appeared in the kitchen door. "You've started without me, Sarah, how dreary for you. Have you got the recipes out?"

Sarah, her hands wet, wiped a loose curl from her face with her forearm. "No. They're still in the cupboard."

"Well," Amanda said, "do let's get on with it, then!"

Philippe and Amanda could sleep past noon, and did so with some frequency, compensating for their late nights. Sometimes Eric and Sarah could hear them in the bedroom, giggling and moaning and moving around, but then silence would prevail again until one or even two o'clock. Sarah generally woke between seven and eight—newspaper hours —but Eric was always up first, propped up on one elbow, watching her.

"What are you doing?"

"Watching you sleep. You're gorgeous when you're asleep. Like a little girl."

And she would smile sleepily and open her arms to him, and he would nestle his head in her neck or between her breasts, and feelings of warmth and pleasure would flow between them. On the rare occasion that Sarah awoke first, she would lie still, afraid to wake him, and would study the childlike vulnerability, the gentleness, the sweetness in him. Sometimes, love welled up inside of her, and she wondered at the magnitude of the treasure with which she had been entrusted.

And then came the morning, late in March, when Eric didn't wait for her to open her eyes. He came rushing into the bedroom they shared with a breakfast tray and a huge smile, and eagerly wafted coffee under her nose until she surfaced from sleep—and another strange dream of falling; she had been troubled by strange dreams lately. He hardly waited until she was fully awake to start talking.

"You've got to come out to the hangar today. You've got to."

"Hmmm . . . are these croissants fresh? They're still warm."

"I just got them, down at the *boulangerie* . . . you're not listening, Sarah. I'm ready."

She opened her eyes a little more and peered at him. "You're—ready?" she asked faintly, the cobwebs of her dreams still trailing around her, like gossamer. "For what?"

"For you to see it, silly. The new prototype." Eric sat on the edge of the bed and smoothed her hair off her forehead.

"Poor Sarah. I'm sorry to do this to you, but it's ready, now, and you really should come see it."

She looked at him, and at the smooth contours of the bed next to her, and she said, with growing certainty, "You've been out at the hangar all night again, haven't you?"

"That I have, love, and just wait till you see what I've done. It's ready, Sarah. Your airplane's ready."

She sat up straighter, almost spilling the coffee. "My airplane—you mean for crossing the Channel? It's *all* ready?"

He nodded, eagerly. "I know that it's seemed forever, Sarah, what with all the trials and errors, but I've really got it, now. It's perfect, Sarah." He took a deep breath. "If this works, if this is what we want, then you can fly any time next month. All you'll have to do is find a sponsor for the trip."

"I already have." She pushed the bedclothes off of her, and sat up, swinging her legs over the side of the bed, reaching for her robe. "*Leslie's Weekly* has said it will do it. They'll pay you for the airplane and the boat over to England and all the publicity expenses. I got the letter from Jack in January, confirming it, don't you remember? Oh, Eric, do let's go see it!"

She dressed in haste, while he left a note for Philippe and Amanda, and they hurried out to the airfield as quickly as her aging Peugeot would take them, Eric spinning the starter and Sarah driving. The hangar looked as it always had, serene and shining in the empty field. Already at this early hour there were people bustling about. Eric's people. Aeromécanique people.

Sarah sat in the motorcar, huddled in the heavy flying jacket she had had made especially for herself in anticipation of cold spring flying conditions. She watched as they pulled the new *Mademoiselle Sarah* out of the hangar. It was beautiful. Even at that distance, she could tell that it was beautiful.

"You'll think it splendid whatever it looks like!" Eric had teased her. "It'll be splendid just because it's for you."

She had smiled gravely in return. "I never had one built especially for me."

The new engine design that Eric had been toiling over for so long was sleek and compact and lighter, perching closer to the rudimentary cockpit than the Blériot design she was used to flying. The wings were slightly tilted at an angle she, not Eric, had been the first to suggest. There were two seats suspended on wires; one for Sarah and one for any equipment she might need. It was hard to pinpoint precisely how this one was different from other monoplanes: Perhaps it was a bit sleeker. Or perhaps it was different because she knew that Eric had found a more efficient way of cooling the engine so that she, unlike Blériot, would not be dependent upon a fortuitous rain cloud to keep her from overheating. Or perhaps it was different just because it was hers, he had built it, and she loved him.

She watched for a moment as they moved the airplane out from the hangar and into position, pegging it down in readiness for a takeoff into the early morning sunlight. Watching the preparations, she had an idea. She leaped out of the car, slamming the door, and ran down the hill towards the group of men who were stamping their feet in the chill and passing around cigarettes.

"Eric! Eric, where are you?"

The group parted at her arrival, everyone respectfully keeping their eyes down, and Eric looked up from the weather map he was reviewing with Henri, who had become the official Aeroméchanique test pilot. "Sarah! What do you think? Isn't she beautiful?"

"She's perfect! Oh, Eric, let's fly her!"

"We're getting ready. Henri here is—"

"No," she interrupted excitedly. "I mean us, you and me. There's a passenger seat, Eric. Let's go up together. Oh, please, love?"

He paused for a long moment and then looked at Henri, who shrugged. Sarah reached across and touched the back of his hand with her little finger. "Please, Eric?"

He grinned then, suddenly and spontaneously. "Hell, yes!" he said, her excitement catching him, and she jumped and clapped her hands in delight. She ran back into the hangar to change into her flying pantaloons and slip back into the warm jacket, and to borrow Henri's helmet and goggles, and find some for Eric, as well.

She checked the airplane as she had checked every airplane she had ever flown, ignoring the barely concealed smiles of the men all around her who had just gone over the very same checklist themselves. Sarah didn't care: It was her life, hers and Eric's, and this would not be the moment that she fell out of the sky and . . . She stopped herself for a moment, then, recognizing the dream of falling she had been having. What nonsense! She would never have problems. She was too careful, too thorough, too deeply ingrained with Louis Caldwell's sense of caution. It was just a dream. She finished her routine in silence, every bolt, every wire, and then stepped back, but the clouded sense of foreboding remained. Every pilot had dreams like that. Every pilot had to have dreams like that. It wasn't her voice, it wasn't the same at all. It was just a dream.

They got into the Aeroméchanique prototype together. It had been months since Sarah had been able to fly, and the moment was perfect, with sharp bright morning sunlight filling the air and the moist dew still on the grass all around the field. The sky and the clouds seemed to beckon to them. Eric had never flown, had never been up in one of the machines he had engendered.

Sarah's hands and feet slid into their accustomed positions, and Eric settled in in front of her. She gave the thumbs-up signal that Eric so loved to the mechanics below, and then someone was spinning the propeller and the engine roared into life. The airplane began to vibrate and shake beneath them.

Sarah signaled for the wings to be released, and slowly the airplane moved out of the shadow of the hangar. Laughing, she reached forward to tap Eric's helmet—no use trying to talk to him, with the roar of the engine all around them, but he reached up his hand and held hers tightly for a brief moment. Sarah chose her takeoff point and turned the nose towards it, and soon they were bumping along, gathering speed. Closer and closer, the trees were coming up, fast, and then the voice said, *Fly*, and Sarah forced the little nose up. They were off the ground, skimming across the trees, banking around to the right so that, in the distance, they could see the outline of Paris.

She swooped around, and reached her hand forward into the slipstream to touch Eric again; his hand came up and patted hers, and she thought that she felt him laughing with her. Then she brought the nose up and climbed again, higher and higher, until they were skimming the first few wisps of cloud. It was mist in their eyes, cold and damp, and Sarah turned the airplane once more and coasted down, plummeting like a bird from a great height, circling the field and letting Eric see his world from a new perspective altogether.

She played with the airplane then, dipping the wings this way and that, and all the time the fair French countryside flowed beneath them. The sun warmed their wings and cast their shadow over the fields and woods they flew over, and Eric kept pointing to this thing and that: a herd of cows grazing placidly by a brook; a village, with the clock in the tower far beneath them chiming the hour; a man plowing a field behind a plodding workhorse. Sarah laughed again, and went into a half-roll, to test the balance, and then they were flying low, daringly low, skimming the trees and the lake and the fields. All too soon they were back circling around the Aeroméchanique field, and Sarah was deciding which of the three dirt runways to use.

She landed into the wind, as Marc Allard had taught her, pulling up and bumping and waiting for her wheels to take hold and stay. The whine of the engine rose as she asked it to slow down, for it was turning in tighter and tighter circles to slow them. Finally aiming for the hay bales at the edge of the field, and cutting the engine, they stopped with a great grinding sound, letting their weight and the friction on the hay stop them altogether.

There was a moment of incredible silence, and then a shout went up by the hangar and the men were all running towards them. Sarah took off her helmet and goggles and scarf, and shook out her long auburn curls, and Eric half stood, turning around in his seat, reaching out to her, and then hugging her fiercely, with an intensity that she didn't recognize. He pulled his helmet off, too, and kissed her roughly on the mouth, again and again.

They were surrounded by cheering Aeroméchanique employees. It worked; that was all that mattered to them. The slow months of cold and darkness and gestation had borne fruit.

Eric jumped down and helped Sarah down from her seat. While the others extricated the airplane from the hay bales and prepared to tow it back to the hangar, Eric and Sarah walked across the field together, their arms still around each other.

"I can't believe it. I can't believe it," he was saying over and over again, and she laughed in delight and understanding. "It's the most incredible experience, Sarah. It's tremendous. It defies language. It's—"

"—flying," she finished for him, and he hugged her again.

He threw back his head and shouted to the skies. "Oh, God, Sarah. I've never felt like that before."

"Nothing feels like it," she agreed. "Nothing on earth."

"It has nothing to do with the earth. Sarah, darling, we've got to get you up over the Channel. I understand now! I understand what you've been talking about all this time. And all that I was interested in was my engines and my designs! I understand, sweetheart."

She smiled and entwined her fingers with his. "Next month?"

"Next month, the Channel!"

The voice inside her was speaking again, and once more she thought in that moment of sunshine and delight and euphoria that she could just hear it say, *Hurry.*

Chapter Seven

I don't understand," Amanda pouted, "how Aero-méchanique can make all those perfectly darling little airplanes to go off to war, and still take forever to make an airplane to carry you seventeen miles, Sarah, darling." Sarah smiled. "Because this one is going to be perfect, Amanda."

And it was.

Amanda, surprising everyone, volunteered to go to England with Sarah. "Well, after all, I've been seeing you off all these months, haven't I? And England is supposed to be heaven in the springtime."

"The springtime," observed Philippe laconically, "is the only season when England is of any use whatsoever." But he allowed Amanda to talk him into going, too, with a graceful lift of his shoulders and a generous smile. "Darling Amanda, you know that I can't say no to you."

"That's nonsense," she responded promptly. "You've said no plenty of times, when that's what you've wanted to do."

"Ah, but never when I wanted to say yes," he said, with a glimmer in his eye, and Amanda shook her head.

"You're incorrigible," she said, and he nodded in agreement.

Sarah half smiled and raised her eyebrows and looked at Eric. "A vaudeville team," she said, and he smiled and shook his head.

"They'd have to work up to vaudeville, I'm afraid. Sounds like you have company, anyway, and I'm counting on Philippe to look after the airplane."

"What about me?" asked Sarah.

"What about Jean-Marc?" asked Philippe, in unison with her.

Eric smiled again. "See! With all of you feeling so protective, she'll be fine."

They booked passage from Le Havre to Southampton for the first of April, allowing plenty of time to get the Aeroméchanique monoplane to Dover and the cliffs before the estimated departure date of April 15. Five of Aeroméchanique's people would be with them, with Eric and others waiting for the landing in Calais. Sarah packed her burgundy flying silks with some trepidation and a great deal of eagerness: It was finally happening. Finally, after all these months of planning and waiting, it was happening.

She had the dream again the night before leaving the rue de Verdun: billowing clouds and clear blue water and a clearer blue sky, and then plummeting, diving down out of the sky. She cried out, and woke up, sitting straight up in bed with sweat drenching her body and the sheets. Eric stirred and murmured in his sleep beside her, and she took long, steadying breaths of air, determined not to wake him and to spare him the horror of her nocturnal imaginings. The images receded and the familiar shapes took their place: her dressing table, the fireplace that had warmed them all winter, and the long French windows leading out to the terrace where she and Amanda planned to keep potted plants that summer. And, when her breathing was perfectly even, and her heart was no longer hammering in her chest, and she could summon other pleasanter images, she lay back down and closed her eyes.

But after that the nightmare was never very far away from her, and even in daylight she could see the horror and feel the dropping sensation in her stomach, merely by closing her eyes.

Eric took the train with them to the coast. It was a strange entourage: the aristocratic count and his society lady-friend; the young inventor, with the spectacles that he was beginning to use more frequently in his pocket; the American writer and aviator, in her famous burgundy silks; the airplane mechanics, wearing tidy suits instead of coveralls and looking distinctly ill at ease in them; and the airplane itself, the *Mademoiselle Sarah*, taken apart for the long

journey—its pieces watched over with the vigilance of a
young mother by the Aeroméchanique people.

There were reporters on hand to see them off. The flight
was being financed by Sarah's newspaper and an English
one, as well, the *Daily Mirror*. Philippe answered their
questions with politeness and civility and the odd amusing
remark; Amanda chattered gaily to them about one thing
and the other and ended up creating hopeless confusion;
Sarah smiled for their photographers—after Amanda had
adjusted her hat and skirt and parasol—and spoke to them
with the frankness of a colleague.

Eric, for his part, avoided them all altogether.

"Miss Martin! Are you sure that a woman can fly across
the Channel?"

Her eyes widened. "Of course I'm sure. Why on earth
would I be attempting to do it otherwise?"

"Miss Martin, will you be going back to the United States
after this?"

A quick glance at Eric. "No, not right away. There are
many things that I am still occupied with in France."

"Miss Martin, tell our male readers: Are there any
marriage prospects in the offing?"

"Carl, is that you? I thought so. What kind of personal
questions is the *Chronicle* asking these days?"

At length they were allowed to change from train to boat,
the steamer waiting at the port for its usual run across the
Channel, the big smokestacks billowing black fumes into the
sky. Amanda and Philippe had boarded almost immediately, gaily, talking to each other about some other ocean cruise
that they would take someday. Sarah, filled with a sense of
foreboding, stood on the dock and looked at Eric.

"I hate to leave you."

"I'll see you in no time, in Calais."

"Eric—" She stopped. She wanted so badly, in that
moment, to tell him about the dream and about her fears
because of it; to speak the words and share the heaviness of
the vision. But she couldn't, she knew that she couldn't. For
giving voice to the images would make them more real,
more concrete, more alive. It was her job to ignore them and
to get on with other things. She knew instinctively, also, that
should Eric begin to share her fear he would force her to

cancel the flight. And it was too late for that. She had gone too far down this particular road.

"Yes, love?"

She put her arms around him. "Nothing. Nothing. Just that—I love you. With all of my heart I love you, Eric."

He bent his head to kiss her. "I love you, Sarah, darling. Please be terribly, terribly careful. I'll be waiting for you in Calais."

She responded to the kiss in her turn, tightening her arms around him and pressing her body up against his, kissing him deeply, searchingly, seeking for the reassurance that only he could give. Finally they parted, both of them breathing with some irregularity. "I love you," he said again, still holding fast to her hands.

"I love you," she repeated, and then the great powerful ship's whistle was sounding, and Amanda's voice drifted down to them, "Sarah, do get a move on, we're going to leave without you!"

"Go," he said, still without releasing her hands, and she leaned forward and kissed the tip of his nose, kissed his cheek, and pulled away. "I love you," she said again, backing up towards the gangway to the ship. "I love you."

He began to wave. "It'll be great, Sarah. You'll be great. I'll see you in a few days. I love you."

She turned, and walked briskly up the gangway, ignoring the barrage of questions from reporters waiting there. At the top, she turned to look at him. He hadn't moved, and stood as though rooted to the spot, still looking after her with those dark eyes which were filled with questions . . . and which held all of her answers. He raised a hand, then, silently and impulsively she blew him a kiss, just as Amanda might have done. His face lighted up with a smile, and then they were both waving, and the whistle was bellowing, and Amanda and Philippe had taken Sarah's arms and were leading her away from the passageway.

The three of them stood by the rail, with the wind and the salt spray in their faces. Sarah stood vigil until le Havre, and indeed France, were just a speck on the horizon. Philippe and Amanda had long since gone below, to savor the warm comforts of parlor and piano and billiards, but Sarah stood and watched the coastline disappear into the mists and wondered at the tears which had come so quickly to her eyes.

After spending so much time in Paris, the sound of English being spoken was foreign to her ears, especially British English: clipped and brittle, without any of the flowing feeling for conversation which she had become accustomed to. Everyone around her seemed to be in a hurry, rushing off first to one place and then another, the staccato sound of their voices echoing in the train terminal where the Aeroméchanique entourage took the railway for Dover.

April 12, 1912

Dearest Mamma,

Well, here we are in Dover, which is a *quaint* little city, and *so* English, Mamma, you have no idea. Sarah's been here ever since we arrived. It took them all simply *forever* to put her little airplane back together, and she's been flying it off the cliffs, just for practice, although I daresay that she calls it *fun*.

Of course, we couldn't stay here *all this time*, Mamma, because once one has said that Dover is quaint, one has already summed up all of its qualities, so Philippe and I took the train to London right away, which was a *marvelously* good decision as it turned out, because everybody who is *anybody* seemed to be in London. Even *Roger* was there, Mamma, which was very comforting indeed, as one really *ought* to keep up with what's going on at home.

It was *thrilling* to show Philippe off, don't you know, my handsome French count, and Lucinda Evans-Montreat and Bessie Wallace were there and I could *swear* that they were jealous. Anyway, anyway, anyway, anyway, I expect that it will be all over Newport by the time I get back, which is simply *delicious*. No, I *don't* know when I'm going back, Mamma, and *please* don't be tiresome and keep asking. Philippe is keeping me amused for the moment quite nicely, and he's truly the most *marvelous* lover I've ever had, and I'm in simply no rush. And Sarah is getting along quite nicely with Eric, though he is rather *below* her, which I've tried to bring to her attention ever so *gently*, but she's quite smitten, so there you are.

We're going back to Dover the day after tomorrow. She's supposed to take off on the fifteenth, and it just wouldn't *do* not to be there, what with the reporters and publicity and all. And then back to London for a few days before we return to Paris. We saw that lovely Sarah Bernhardt in a film here yesterday, by the way, it's called *Queen Elizabeth*, and she was admirable. I know how you *despise* films, Mamma, but everything modern isn't necessarily *bad*, and you'd do yourself a world of good to go out sometimes and *experience* things.

All for now.

Loving regards,
Amanda

It was Sarah who decided to call it off.

She had the ultimate decision to make, of course, and the morning of the fifteenth had turned cold and windy. Too windy. She stood in the predawn chill with Eric's great overcoat enveloping her and scrutinized the cliffs. At last she shook her head and walked back to the shelter of the lean-to they had erected in lieu of a hangar.

"Well, Mademoiselle?" That was Jean-Marc, who had also been anxiously scanning the surroundings. The small brushlike trees that grew on the cliffs were bent almost double with the wind. "What do you think?"

Sarah shook her head. "It's no use," she said, and fought back the tears that welled in her throat, the sense of failure. "It's blowing too hard. I'd turn over before I left the cliffs. It's a crosswind." She looked miserable, sitting huddled in the greatcoat, her cheeks pinched with the cold. "Can anyone get word to Eric?"

He nodded. "Don't worry, Mademoiselle. He said himself that you may not be able to do it for several days. There is no dishonor here." He poured a cup of chocolate from the small gas stove he had lit in the lean-to. "Here. Drink this, and you will feel better, and then we will go back and you can talk with your friends. Me, I will wire Monsieur Beaumont in Calais not to expect you today."

She accepted the hot chocolate gratefully, warming her

hands and her face from it before she even took a sip. "This is perfect, Jean-Marc. Thank you."

He gestured. "It is nothing, Mademoiselle. We, too, want your flight to be a success."

"It will be." She put down the cup and stood up, gathering the coat around her, and impulsively leaned down to kiss his cheek. "We will all see to that, won't we?"

As she left, she felt rather than saw his surprised smile following her.

The next morning, Sarah woke well before dawn, at three-thirty. It was useless waking Amanda at that early hour, she knew. Amanda and Philippe had whiled away the evening in the lounge of the resort hotel where they were all staying, with some betting-games and music and a great deal to drink. She was surprised, therefore, when she had dressed and gone downstairs with Eric's greatcoat slung over her arm, to see Philippe waiting for her.

"What are you doing here?" Sarah asked, a slow smile lighting her face.

"What took you so long? Everyone else has gone out already. I thought I'd have to come and wake you." He reached over and kissed her cheek. "If you're going to be flying across the Channel, such a long distance, then the least that I can do is to drive you up to the cliffs."

"I'm touched, Philippe," she said. "That's very nice of you."

He shrugged. "It's nothing. I had someone start up the motorcar, so—if you're quite ready . . ."

She moistened her lips. "I am, Philippe. Thank you." He was not the person in whom she could confide her dreams, she knew. He would not understand the sense of dread she had harbored lately, the feeling of imminent disaster, or the voice inside her that urged her to hurry for reasons beyond her comprehension. Philippe was part of Aeroméchanique, and as such, he was committed to her flight. Best to stay confident, in control of herself, on top of the situation. And. let her voice take care of itself.

They had set up lanterns so that one could see what one was doing, and, even at that early hour, even in that bitter cold, there were two reporters and a photographer taking advantage of Jean-Marc's lean-to and his hot chocolate.

Sarah excused herself from Philippe and walked over to
them to talk for a few minutes. She was a reporter herself,
and she knew how important this interview might be to
them. She talked for a few minutes about the aborted flight
and about her chances for success this time, and she smiled
for the camera and told them about the Aeroméchanique
monoplane in which she would be making the flight.

"Are you afraid of crashing, Miss Martin?"

"Of course not," she said, her voice even. "I'm too careful
to crash. Besides, I'm like a cat. I don't like to get my feet
wet."

They all smiled, and wrote that down. After urging them
to help themselves to more chocolate, she left them to their
own devices.

Philippe was waiting for her beside the airplane. "Come
on, before you die of the cold," he said. She nodded and
began her ritual, Jean-Marc helping her. There was a screw
loose in the tail. He corrected it while she watched critically.
Every moving part, every wire was subjected to her scrutiny,
and finally she allowed Philippe to help her into her seat.
Gone was the greatcoat, its limited range of motion too
inhibiting. She was back in her bright silk flying clothes,
with only heavy socks under her boots and in place of her
silk scarf a warm woolen one, and gloves to attest to the
cold. Philippe climbed up on the plane, behind her, and
passed her an added gift—a hot water bottle. She smiled at
him in sudden gratitude. "Philippe! How wonderful!"

"It was Amanda's idea," he said. "She absolutely insisted." He reached forward and kissed her cheek. "Good
luck, Sarah. We'll see you in Paris."

Philippe climbed down and moved off, nodding to the
others. The sky was turning gray, and the mists had settled
in again, penetrating even the most heavy clothing. Jean-
Marc was there, climbing up the back of the monoplane like
a human fly, his voice reassuring in her ear for a moment,
"Are you all right, Mademoiselle?" She gave him a shaky
thumbs-up gesture, which he imitated; and then all the
Aeroméchanique crew was around her, holding the aircraft
in place, ready for the blast when she started the engine.
Jean-Marc slid down, and spun the propeller, and the engine
caught and rumbled and then began its high-pitched, shrill
song. As it caught and held, he backed off and others

were straining against the engine and the wind to hold the airplane in place.

Sarah took a deep breath, banishing the dream and its horror from her mind, and steadied herself. She had wanted this since that night in Newport—was it less than a year ago? It seemed a lifetime since Roger had suggested that she make a few more firsts in her life, and now she was standing on the edge of it—an accomplishment.

She took a deep breath, and signaled to Jean-Marc. The men let go of the airplane and she started moving—faster here than normal because of the cliffs and the altitude, bumping unevenly across the grass, gathering speed, faster and faster and then . . . she was in the air, soaring out with the headland moving smoothly under her. She was over the ocean, if she could but see it, flying true and even and correct.

When she finally let her breath out, she wasn't even aware that she had been holding it in.

It was cold—colder than she had thought it would be. The early hour and the ocean air combined in a terrible viselike grip of frigid wind, and she spared a thought for Amanda, and her hot water bottle. Fancy that . . . Amanda, who made such a show of not caring, who hid her acts of kindness beneath a cloak of chatter and silliness. Amanda, who was the closest friend Sarah had ever had.

There was a great deal of fog, even once she had cleared the English coast, and Sarah frowned. She could steer her course with a compass heading, naturally. It was the only way to fly over such a distance—she had worked out the route already, laboriously, and knew exactly what to do— nevertheless it was frightening to fly in a fog bank. Better, she decided, to get a little altitude and try to break through the cover into the sunlight.

She went up a hundred feet, keeping her eye on the compass that Eric had so neatly installed on the small instrument panel in front of her. He had even put the gasoline gauge and the oil pressure gauge on that same panel, which was an innovation, and one that came not a minute too soon. But there was no breaking through the fog. She sighed, and kept on course. The flight wouldn't last forever. She could manage until she got to France. Of course she could manage.

But instead of reveling in the pleasure of flying, she was all too aware that the cold mist was getting to her. It had soaked her silks, and the hot water bottle was useless against the pervasive damp of the fog bank. Sarah bit her lip. She didn't want to go much higher, the air thinned out and was difficult to breathe, but . . . she brought the nose up, ever so slightly, and then again, even farther, more abruptly in a final attempt to get out of the fog.

It was at that moment that it happened. She had miscalculated the angle of her ascent, she must have, because the engine misfired—the beautiful little 50 horsepower Gnome-Aeroméchanique engine of which Eric was so justly proud —and all the muscles in her stomach knotted at once. It had to be, it could only be the gasoline flooding. . . . She leveled out the airplane, realizing with a sick feeling that the dream was right. She was going to go down. The only thing that would save her was to go down as level as she could manage, so that she could land flat on the water—Marc Allard had called it pancaking—and hope for rescue.

It had happened to others who had attempted this crossing, but she had no idea how long the Aeroméchanique airplane could remain afloat. Of course, the reason the Channel crossing was such a daring feat was the water beneath her and no rescue vehicle in the vicinity. No safety net. Little hope of survival existed if she crashed; only an unmarked grave in the Channel. No friendly farmers or curious onlookers would help her out of a tree or a well; just the gray, cold ocean which would cover her tracks as it covered all tracks. And no one would ever know what had really happened.

The engine coughed again, interrupting her thoughts, and Sarah winced. As long as it hadn't actually died, she thought . . . But even that thought was an admission of failure. She was too far off the French coast; there was no way in a thousand years that she could glide in, not here, not now. She was deluding herself. She was living out the worst of all her nightmares, trapped inside the feelings of panic, of fear, and of terror. She would never see Eric again, never hold him in her arms or make love with him. . . . She, who had been the most careful of all aviators, would die because she had been too cold and had wanted too much to get warm again.

She was so wrapped up in her own terrorized thoughts that it took her a full minute to realize that the engine was running smoothly again, that it had burned out all the gasoline in its system. Everything was all right. When she did realize, the relief was almost overwhelming, and with it a sudden desire to be ill. She brought the airplane down a few hundred feet more and steadied it out, adjusting her compass heading, and stretched her fingers. Too close, Sarah Martin, she told herself silently, that was too close for comfort.

In that moment of relief and thanksgiving, she broke clear of the fog bank and emerged into the sunshine.

She was flying over cloud cover, the white puffy wisps extending below her as far as the eye could see, a veritable ocean of clouds, deceptively bright and friendly. It was as though one had only to step out in order to walk on them. Sarah reached up with one hand and wiped her goggles. The sunshine was so sudden it hurt her eyes, a bright morning sun rising almost directly in front of her; she reveled in its warmth, closing her eyes for a moment against it. What was that reading from the Bible of which her mother was so fond? "Raise up thine eyes to the heavens, and look at the earth down below . . ." And here she was, trapped between the two, a creature of neither. This was flying.

The clouds below her continued for some miles, stretching out towards the coastline which she knew would be visible before long; and then, gradually, they started thinning out, long trailing wisps allowing glimpses of the ocean below. Sarah had thought that the ocean would be blue, but it was green, a deep, dark green, dancing in flames of fire where the sun sparkled off it.

She eased the monoplane down another hundred feet in altitude, and the clouds darted away from her, parting to the left and the right, no longer terrible harbingers of a nightmare fate, but friendly Channel markers to indicate the way to her. In a few minutes, she knew, she would be over France. Instinctively, more than from deep faith, she sketched the sign of the cross over herself.

"Be careful. Be careful." For one terrible moment she had not listened to Louis Caldwell's words of warning, and that moment had nearly cost her her life.

* * *

She was slightly off course, in the end, but compared with what might have happened, that wasn't so very bad, after all.

They had chosen an exhibition field near Calais for the landing, but by the time Sarah saw land she was more than ready to touch down, rather than hunt out the field. The wind had picked up on this side and was gusting fitfully, and although the Gnome-Aeroméchanique engine hadn't actually overheated, it might be getting close. Sarah, looking at the long expanse of beaches ahead of her, decided to land then and there.

She lined up her sights and took one exploratory run; then she came in a second time and set down. She had never landed on sand before and the feeling was altogether different. There was no hard bouncing, just a long sliding, clutching forward motion, and then she slid to a halt, her airplane half buried in a long furrow of sand.

Sarah cut the engine immediately, removed her gloves and helmet and goggles, and experimentally began to get out of her seat. Hopping down on the sand, she tripped slightly on her cold feet. She found that she was still trembling.

Unbelievably, the sun was shining strong and almost hot on this side.

She was aware in a moment that she was not alone, and looked around her. A small child—impossible to tell whether male or female—stood not a hundred yards from her, clutching a bucket in its grimy hands, and gaping. Behind the child, a few people hastily were assembling, all of them wearing greasy coveralls, even the women. Sarah smiled uncertainly and then looked out beyond them to a pier and docked boats. A fishing village, obviously, and one that had probably not heard that an American girl was going to attempt to fly the English Channel that morning.

Sarah well knew how terrible she looked: disheveled, with the fear probably still part of her, and an unfriendly aura. She put a hand to her head and could feel her hair, correctly combed that morning, falling out of its pins. There was a long rip in the burgundy silk jacket she wore under the heavier flying jacket, and her silken pantaloons were probably, as always, seen as very daring. She took a deep breath. This might not be easy.

They gathered around her, more and more of them, fisherfolk with broad accents in their voices and the smell of the sea all about them. To Sarah, feeling rescued through no prowess of her own from death itself, they were angels. They were curious and friendly, and soon she smiled and laughed with them, and let the children crawl all over the airplane. She understood she was to wait patiently until the mayor had gotten dressed in his full regalia to come down and greet her. It wasn't every day, evidently, that someone dropped from the sky on this particular stretch of beach.

The mayor—Sarah never did catch his name—was most polite. What an incredible feat Mademoiselle had performed! How very brave she was! There would be drinks to be had, he assured her, if only she would trouble herself to venture up the headland to their village. Ah, it was modest, but they would offer her what they had. Ah, the momentary delay? (Here he reddened slightly, adjusting his cummerbund with some embarrassment.) Well, young Yves had been dispatched posthaste to the next village, for there, Mademoiselle, was to be found one of those modern contraptions that printed images of people on paper. Ah, yes, a camera, indeed. It would be a sad thing for the village if such an event were to go unrecorded.

The camera duly appeared, and Sarah agreed, laughing, to allow herself to be hoisted to the shoulders of the crowd and so borne off to the village on the headland. She saw the picture, later, as it appeared in the newspaper *France-Soir*, and studied for a long time the laughing faces.

Drinking the glass of fine strong wine that they had offered her, she was standing by the horse-drawn carriage that they had arranged for transportation to Calais. (Ah, a motor car? Such fine contraptions, mademoiselle, but alas no one in this particular village had the means. Nor in the next village, either.) When the roar of an engine rattled through the narrow cobblestone streets, everyone around her looked up at the sky, at once associating the sound with that they had heard earlier, but Sarah recognized it for what it was and turned away from them all, waiting for the Peugeot to come rattling and wheezing around the corner.

When it did, and she saw Eric sitting at the wheel, she thought that surely her heart would break.

He stopped the motorcar a few yards off, and she held out her glass without looking at it—someone, mercifully, took it from her—and then he was climbing out of the vehicle and she was running towards him, her arms outstretched. He said something, she couldn't catch it, and she cried his name, and then they were together, his arms around her, swinging her up off the ground and round and round him in dizzying circles, and kissing her all the while. He put her down eventually, and they stood there, still holding each other, still kissing. She couldn't touch him enough, he was real, he was here; she was alive, they were together.

"Twenty-five minutes," she managed to gasp. He had asked her to time the flight. But in that moment of joy and relief nothing seemed less important. The small group of villagers, led no doubt by His Eminence the Mayor, broke into a round of applause. Beyond the headland, the waves curled onto the shore, where the Aeroméchanique mono-plane, the *Mademoiselle Sarah,* rested at last.

The couple ate a belated breakfast on the road back to Paris, at a tiny restaurant in a small village where omelettes seemed the only fare available. Sarah ordered eagerly, the congratulatory wine having gone to her head, but Eric, who had eaten earlier, played with his food.

"How was the flight? How did it run? What needs to be changed?" His questions had first been eager, rushed, the words tumbling over each other in their effort to get out; and Sarah had answered all of them calmly, accurately, gravely. There had been no problems. The engine worked to perfection.

Of her own mistake, and its possible consequences, she stayed silent. There was a time and a place for everything, and this was neither, as far as she was concerned.

Now he sat and drank strong coffee and watched her eat her omelette. "The press will be all over you before you know it," he observed. "They've been haunting the Angers offices, and a few intrepid souls, God bless them, have even found their way out to the hangar."

"But not the rue de Verdun?"

"Not the rue de Verdun." Eric smiled. "You may rest easy, my lady. We will not be disturbed."

He had something on his mind, of that she was sure, but it was not until they reached Boulogne-Billiancourt that he was ready to talk about it. They went in through the side entrance, so as not to attract attention, and Sarah paused at the door. "It's good to be home," she said, softly.

He had the keys, and was jangling them about. "Actually, I wanted to talk with you about that." He sat down on the doorstep and, curious, she sat down next to him. "What is it, Eric?"

"Home. That sort of thing." He cleared his throat. "I'm not doing this very well, am I? And all the time that we were apart I was practicing so that I would get it just right."

"Get what just right?"

"My proposal." He turned to face her and took her hands in his. "Sarah Martin, will you marry me?"

It was as though the world tumbled before her eyes, and she was, once again, breathless. But there was no doubt— only peace and calm and serenity. "Yes, Monsieur Beaumont. I would be honored to marry you."

He raised his eyebrows and then smiled in delight, pulling her to him. "Oh, God, I was hoping you would say that! Oh, God, that's great! Oh, happy day! I love you, Sarah!"

"I love you, too, darling." She paused, and smiled mischievously. "If you'd get on with unlocking the door, we could go in, and I could show you how much. . . ."

He unlocked the door, and they went in, and she made good her promise. The reporters waiting at the Aeroméchanique offices to talk with the young American flyer, the "Dresden China aviatrix," waited in vain.

Chapter Eight

Amanda tried to write to her mother about the wedding, but for once even she was at a loss for words. What words could ever sum up all the feelings touched by it: the longing and the sense of completion; the love and the joy and the eagerness; the closeness and the caring?

And, behind it all, for her, was the edge of jealousy which even she couldn't understand or admit. Amanda was the wise one who stood back from events and observed—usually in cynical terms—so surely there was no reason for her to be jealous? After all, she had cautioned Sarah about making too great a commitment and trusting too much in her own feelings. All that Sarah had said in response was, "We know what we're doing."

Amanda had done what she could to warn Sarah about this whole thing. And yet the happiness in the air was palpable.

If there was ever anything true, it was that, indeed, Eric and Sarah knew what they were doing.

Sarah Louise Martin and Eric Antoine Beaumont were married on May 14, 1912, in a small and ancient parish church in Boulogne-Billiancourt, two blocks from the house on the rue de Verdun, with only Philippe de Montclair and Amanda Elizabeth Lewis in attendance.

The priest was old and muttered a great deal; and the organist became ill with a head cold only hours before the ceremony, so they had no music. But none of that made a difference to either Sarah or Eric. It did, of course, to Amanda, who complained about it, loudly and frequently.

"Well, if you must go through with this, Sarah, darling, then let's do it right. All we need is some *time*, why are you so impatient?"

Sarah, who had decreed from the beginning no formal ceremony, no flowers, no bridesmaids, no reception, stopped for a moment and listened to Amanda. Why didn't she want a large elaborate society wedding? There was no reason not to, and the newspapers would have been eating out of her hand if she had. The girl pilot who was the first to fly across the English Channel marries the man who made her airplane. The headlines were clear, and even her own newspaper, *Leslie's Weekly*, would have been delighted with her—perhaps even to the point of agreeing to making her assignment in France permanent. It made all the sense in the world. Why was she in such a hurry?

Amanda drew her own conclusions. "You didn't tell me," she said, accusingly, to Sarah. "I thought that I was your best friend."

"You are," Sarah responded, bewildered. "What was there to tell? He asked me to marry him, and I said yes."

"Well," Amanda said, fastidiously pulling on and off a pair of new gloves she had bought in England, "you're so insistent on a tiny, little, silly wedding, and you won't wait to do it right. . . . You know all the newspapers will be saying that you're getting married now because you have to."

"I do have to," Sarah responded. "I love Eric and I can't wait any longer to marry him."

"That, dear Sarah, is not what I meant, and not what they'll be saying. Don't try to be so naive, it doesn't suit you." Amanda tossed the gloves aside. "Why didn't you tell me that you're pregnant?" she asked, directly.

"I'm pregnant?" Sarah said, in astonishment. "Of course I'm not pregnant!"

"Then, poppet, what's all the rush about? Why don't you wait?"

But there was something even more compelling than a pregnancy involved, and it was something that Sarah didn't talk to anyone about. The Channel exploit had not completely silenced the voice inside of her. Nor had it changed what the voice had to say.

As though her days were in some way numbered, the voice

still took stock of the situation, and then, in its most insistent tones, urged Sarah, *Hurry*.

Philippe popped the cork on the champagne as soon as they were out of the church. "To my friends," he declared, holding his glass aloft, "Eric and Sarah Beaumont!"

"To Eric and Sarah!" Amanda echoed, and Sarah wondered for a fleeting moment, what Amanda was feeling in this moment. But then Eric was kissing her again, and she lost all thought of Amanda, all thought of the dry little priest, all thought of anything but Eric: the man who was her husband.

The sun sparkled and shone all around them, and the champagne bubbled and fizzed, and it felt as though the four of them—Eric and Sarah, Philippe and Amanda—could go on forever. As though a photograph had been taken, Sarah thought suddenly. And that was the way it would stay. Perhaps, one day, Amanda and Philippe would marry, as well. . . .

But that was nonsense. Philippe was spoken for, a solid respectable member of the nobility, with a wife and child already, and Amanda wasn't anybody's idea of a perfect countess. The four of them had what they had, their time at the rue de Verdun. One day that, too, would end, and they would go their separate ways.

Except for Eric. Sarah stole a glance at her husband, laughing at something Amanda had just said, tipping his head back to savor the champagne trickling down and tickling his throat. Except for Eric: That was something that would never end. They had spoken vows this morning, in the musty decaying odor of this old church. They had promised that nothing but death would ever separate them. Philippe and Amanda would have to work out what they wanted and how they could live that out. For Sarah and Eric, the choice had already been made, the path was clear.

They went back to the house on the rue de Verdun that evening and ate a wonderful wedding supper—the stuff, Sarah thought, of which dreams are made. More champagne bubbled and hissed at them as they sat on the big four-poster bed in their bedroom, and they sampled stuffed mushrooms, the puffs of crabmeat spilling over into the

cheese, and the fragrance of it wafting all around them.
Artichokes then, tender and sweet, delighted them as they
dipped the leaves in the butter sauce and offered them to
each other. Wine, a robust burgundy bottled at Philippe's
estate ("The least that I can do, *mon ami!*"), complemented
a perfect tournedos, prepared by Annie ("You're married?
Oh, Monsieur, Madame, congratulations!"). Cheese and
bread were followed by an immense chocolate torte, and
more champagne.

"Eric."

"Yes?" He was busily stacking empty plates on the
bedside table.

"I believe that I'm drunk."

"Ah!" He turned to her then, a smile in his voice. "All the
better for my devious plans."

"What devious plans are those?"

"To take advantage of you, Madame."

Sarah giggled. "You know that you don't have to get me
drunk to do that."

"Don't I? Hmmm . . ." He began running his fingers
through her hair. "Waste of good champagne, then."

She propped herself up on one elbow. "Monsieur Beaumont, will you love me forever?"

He reached over and caressed her cheek. "Longer than
that, Madame Beaumont."

She purred with contentment and rolled onto her back.
"It's hard to believe that this is all real."

"Well," he said, reaching out and turning off the lamp,
and lighting candles instead. "Let's show each other just
how real it can be."

He was darker in the candlelight, she thought; darker and
more mysterious. But when his hands touched her and he
moved closer to her, the same sweet familiarity came back,
the sure knowledge of each other—not just physically, but
as whole, complete beings. It was as though the knowledge
came all in one block, moving in through all of the senses
simultaneously. Eric. Her husband.

He undressed her slowly, slipping her fine lace nightdress
first from one shoulder, then the other, as though exploring
her for the first time, but with none of the awkwardness and
hesitation of the first time. Her nightdress tumbled to the
floor, and his pajamas after it as Sarah took the initiative,

unbuttoning his pajama top, pulling the trousers down over his hips and legs. She could feel the muscles rippling in his arms, and she abandoned herself to the emotions that washed over her, her head back, the long auburn curls falling down her back, her eyes closed. So much desire . . . They would be together, like this, forever. Every night of her life, from now until eternity, she could feel those same strong muscles, move her fingers delicately down his backbone and feel it stiffen under her touch, sense his breath on her neck and breasts.

She tightened her arms around him at the thought, and he kissed her forehead, and her eyelids, one at a time, gently. "Eric," she whispered, and then he was kissing her mouth, silencing her words, asking her mouth to open to his, asking her life to open to his, deeper and deeper and the intensity building between them until one could feel it, vibrating, in the air around them.

She moved under him, pressing herself up against his body in the shadows, and the sheets slithered to the floor. He was touching her breasts now as he continued to kiss her, rubbing the nipples gently, his lips moving down her neck and still kissing her there, the fingers still teasing her, pinching the nipples, leading her on, pausing, and leading her farther still. He licked one of her nipples, and she thought that she would surely go crazy with desire.

He slid his hand down over her belly, and her skin rippled under the touch. She clung to him, pulling him up closer to her and kissing his neck in her turn, light kisses, as soft and delicate as a butterfly's wings dancing across his skin. Her fingers stroked through his hair and she kissed his cheeks and his mouth, and then rolled over so that she was lying on top of him, still kissing him, moving her hips slowly and rhythmically against his.

She pulled herself up and off him then, sitting back, her legs straddling him, and she caressed his chest in her turn, moving her fingers lightly and seductively over him: his chest, his arms, his waist, pausing for a second as they encountered the beginnings of his pubic hair and then moving down, farther, to tease and touch and caress the penis below.

Eric groaned and tried to reach her, to pull her on top of him again, but she continued her slow stroking, pausing only to bend down and take the tip of his penis in her mouth. He moaned again, it sounded like her name, but she was moving and didn't stop to listen to him, didn't stop to talk, it all felt too good and the feelings were spiraling up and up and up. . . .

And then the urgency was too great; she couldn't wait any longer. It was too intense, the throbbing insistent feelings inside, and she climbed up over him again and reached down between their bodies and found him hard and ready. Quickly she slid him into her. She couldn't wait any longer, she wanted him so badly, she loved him so much. And he was inside her and they were moving together, his hands reaching up to cup her breasts as she moved over him, the candlelight casting long shadows against the velvet draperies covering the windows, keeping the night out and the world at bay.

Sarah tipped her head back and closed her eyes. Feelings flowed over her, like the waters of a stream where she used to go swimming when she was a little girl, in California. They flowed and soothed and excited her, and it was as though her love for Eric couldn't be contained in any one place or time. The moments stretched on with the feelings mounting higher and higher, getting better with every stroke, every movement, every moan that escaped her lips. When it seemed that there could be no resolution, no ending to the suspended time of movement and feeling, Eric reached down and gripped her bottom, tightly, and thrust even harder into her and moaned, again and again, and the feeling sparked inside her and all around. The world seemed to be eclipsed in a gigantic flash of lightning.

She collapsed onto his chest and listened for a few minutes to the thudding of his heart, only inches from her ear, and measured his irregular breathing against her own. She was at peace. This, then, was love.

She wasn't aware of falling asleep on top of him, only of her thoughts becoming disjointed and more diffused, and of the light gradually fading. She didn't feel him easing out from under her to blow out the candles, and gently, tenderly cover her and himself with the duvet. All was silence—and peace; Sarah slept.

The day after the ceremony found Eric back out at the Aeroméchanique hangar, where after a few minutes of good-natured teasing he was able to return to his most recent designs. Philippe had gone to Angers to spend a few days with Marie-Louise and the baby. Amanda, unexpectedly, had announced that she had met some amusing people in London and decided to spend a week with them at a country estate in Cornwall.

Sarah was at loose ends. She had written to her family and to *Leslie's Weekly*, telling them about her marriage to the co-owner of Aeroméchanique, and was waiting with some trepidation to hear what each would say about it. In the meantime, she wasn't scheduled to fly an exhibition for another month.

Jeannine Allard had written from New York, wondering what on earth Sarah was up to "besides, of course, that marvelous trick you pulled on us all, flying across the Channel," and promising a full schedule of exhibition flights "if you can only tear yourself away from France and come *here* for a while!"

Sarah wrote to her, too, explaining about the wedding. Almost as a postscript, she added, "I shouldn't think that much has changed as far as the flying is concerned. Eric is eager for me to be test pilot for his designs, but there's plenty of time in between, of course, and I don't see why I couldn't come over for one or two exhibitions, if you could schedule them close enough together."

Jeannine's answer came back immediately, with delighted congratulations on the wedding and three dates, all of them in September. "Two in New York and one in Boston, Sarah, so you see how well I've arranged everything! The Boston airshow is first, and guess what? I'm flying it, too, so it should be quite an affair. A reunion, Sarah! I can't wait for you to tell me all about your husband's designs, and Marc is quite eager to hear about that new one that you flew over the Channel, as well. Maybe we'll order some from you for the school!"

Eric brightened when he heard that, and declared himself willing to go to America with Sarah, both to be with her and also to close any business deals that might offer themselves. "Philippe's better at the business end of things, but it's not his wife that's flying." But that was September, and, in the meantime, summer had just begun.

The papers were flooding the newsstands with news of the marriage. It was, as one columnist told Sarah, "too, too perfect for words, dear, don't you know." The "Wedding of the Decade," as the more popular editions in Europe liked to put it, was seen as a match between the two darlings of the aviation world.

Eric was removed from it all. He divided his time between the hangar, where the Aeromécanique people kept any curious onlookers at a safe distance from him, and the house on the rue de Verdun, which for some reason had still not been discovered by any reporter. But Sarah was in the thick of it all, trying to do some work of her own for *Leslie's Weekly* and arrange passage to New York. And she was keeping up with Amanda who, since her return from England, was more demanding than before.

"Sarah, don't be so tiresome. If the reporters want to write about you, then let them, but don't just rattle on about it like this." Amanda's voice didn't conceal her irritation, and she looked away from Sarah as she sipped her grenadine.

Sarah frowned, first at Amanda, and then at the steady stream of people going by the café on the Champs-Elysées where they sat. Carriages competed with motorcars on the main thoroughfare, and people strolled by the cafés, waiting to see and be seen. The meeting place was Amanda's choice, not Sarah's, and Sarah still wasn't sure what was on Amanda's mind. "I don't want them to write about me," she said stubbornly, petulantly.

"Why ever not? You always used to like it, poppet, don't say that you didn't. I've seen you talking to them in the most awful weather, so there you are."

"It's not the same," Sarah said. "I don't mind stories about things that I do, like flying. I want people to know about flying, Amanda. That's important. But I don't want my personal life screaming at me from every corner newsstand."

"Why do you want people to know about flying?"

"Because it's so—wonderful." The word sounded flat, and Sarah hesitated. How could she possibly conjure up for Amanda the thrill of flying, of skimming over trees and fields, of soaring up where only the birds dared to go, of losing oneself in the clouds and coming back down again among the mortals? How could she tell her friend of the speed and utter timelessness that coexisted when flying? Words were never adequate to sum it all up. Sarah took a deep breath and started on another thought. "Because maybe they'll understand about taking risks. Maybe if they see me doing things that I want to do, they'll realize that they can, too. They'll understand that one really can reach for a dream, and attain it."

Amanda finished her cocktail and put it down on the table. "Well," she said, adjusting her lace collar. "Isn't it the same with your marriage? Some people dream about going off to a foreign land and marrying a handsome mysterious stranger, and that's exactly what you've done. That's a kind of dream, too."

Sarah was too preoccupied to notice the plaintive tone behind Amanda's words. "It's not the same at all," she said, causing Amanda to lose patience. "For God's sake, Sarah, what else do you want from me? This was all such fun at the beginning, even with the mud, though that was awful enough, but it's not fun anymore." Amanda's voice broke and she turned away from Sarah. A moment later she resumed speaking, her voice artificially high. "You've gotten all serious and it's quite frankly becoming a dreary situation, and even Philippe isn't as amusing as he used to be. He's forever dashing off to that estate of his and that wife of his and, Sarah, that's the most tiresome thing of all." She paused in her tirade, and took a deep breath. "When you go to Boston in September, I'm going with you."

"What?" Sarah was astonished, as much by this last information as by the entire monologue. "You're coming to watch me fly? What ever for?"

"No, Sarah, I'm *not* going to watch you fly. That's even getting a little tedious, if you don't mind me saying so. I've had enough of all this for a while." She flashed Sarah a quick glance and began tapping her nails on the marble tabletop. "I've been seeing Roger in England."

"Roger Auchincloss? What is he doing there?"

"Oh, well, he was in London for some sort of reception— the details are just too too tiresome, Sarah, so don't bother me with them. That was when you were over there in April to make your little Channel excursion. And he's been staying with some terribly amusing people in Cornwall, which is a dreadful little place, but they have the most interesting estate there and friends with taste, which is something that has been decidedly missing here of late."

Sarah didn't say anything, but toyed with her drink and

tried to understand what was happening. Obviously
Amanda was hurt, but being Amanda couldn't say that she
was, so she went and did something outrageous to cover her
feelings. Sarah wasn't sure what it was all about, and she
didn't feel that it was the best time to ask Amanda about it,
either. "Go on," she said at length.

"Sarah, do wake up, won't you? I'm saying that since then
I've been seeing Roger. I'm having an affair with him. We've
been sleeping together."

"I understand perfectly, Amanda," Sarah said calmly. So
that was it: Philippe kept leaving Amanda for Marie-Louise,
and Amanda had had enough of waiting for him. So she had
begun an affair with someone else, so that Philippe would be
jealous of her as well. And, underlying it all, was the
undercurrent of envy that Sarah had something that
Amanda, in her vulnerable moments, desperately wanted as
well: marriage to the man she loved.

Impossible to tell all of that to Amanda. She probably
didn't understand it herself, and would be unable to face it if
confronted. Sarah gave a mental shrug. Amanda would have
to work out her own life. "I thought," Sarah said carefully,
"that Roger was the most awful man. It seems to me that
you once characterized him that way."

"Well, Sarah, that just goes to show how silly you can be,
and how you misunderstand things. Roger is a perfect
darling, and far more attentive than Philippe has been of
late, I might add." Amanda stood up, adjusting the small
cloche hat perched atop her upswept hair. "You can keep
your marital bliss, Sarah, and your mysterious handsome
Frenchman. I'm going home."

Eric didn't leave with them, after all. It had been a glorious
summer, with Sarah flying in meets, even winning a prestigious award at Rheims, and Eric accompanying her. Long
nights at the house on the rue de Verdun compensated for
the busy days, but the various armistices had failed in the
Balkans and the war there was requiring more firepower,
more ammunition, and better airplanes. To take even the
two months off from his work that Sarah would need in
America was too much. Blériot, as always, was breathing
down Eric's neck, using similar assembly techniques and
turning out more and more airplanes.

Eric was determined that Aeroméchanique would remain the sole supplier of airplanes for the Balkan war. Any side could buy from him, as long as they paid him in cold hard currency so that he could finance still more prototypes. As he explained to Sarah, "I don't play politics. That's a rich man's game. I make airplanes."

"Those airplanes," she countered angrily, "are being used to drop bombs on people. How can you condone that, Eric?"

"I'm not condoning anything. I don't make these decisions, the politicians make the decisions. I just want to have the means to build better planes, to make better designs, to learn more about all this." He gestured around him. "This has nothing to do with dropping bombs on people."

"This has everything to do with dropping bombs on people!" Sarah exclaimed. "You're supplying the airplanes that they're using to kill people. To kill children! And as long as the war goes on they're going to keep killing people with your airplanes!"

"Of course they are. Do you think that I can change that? If I didn't sell to them, they'd still need airplanes, and they'd still use airplanes as a means of dropping bombs on people. The only difference would be that they would be buying the airplanes from Blériot or Curtiss, instead of from Aeroméchanique. And someone else would be making the money and the reputation." He came closer to her. "Relax, Sarah, honey. And leave politics to the politicians."

She stiffened in protest against him. But she was going to be leaving soon and she didn't want to leave the shards of an argument cutting into them while she was gone. She decided, instead, to try another tack. "Have you made any progress?" she asked. "You'll have to solve the inherent stability problem before long, won't you, if they're going to start parachuting out of your airplanes?"

"So you heard about that." He grinned. "First successful jump last month, and more since." He turned back to his design table. "Look. I'm almost there. All that I need is . . ."

And as he talked on, Sarah listened to him with a mixture of fondness and irritation and sadness, thinking not about the war or the inherent stability problem, but of two long months in America without him.

In early September they took the night train to le Havre. Philippe had taken Amanda out to the Brittany countryside and was going to drive her up through Normandy in his new Mercedes-Benz roadster to catch the ship: a last attempt, perhaps, to urge her to stay. According to Eric, it was halfhearted at best. Philippe, delighting in his new status as father, was in truth spending more and more time out at the estate. But what Amanda interpreted as passion for his wife was in fact amazement and love for his son. The end result was the same, however. Eric and Sarah, holding each other in silence, the thoughts and feelings flowing between them without the need for words, were both calm and a little sad.

And then, once again, a ship was bellowing its horn into the fog and mists of le Havre, and Sarah was clinging to Eric, the tears fresh on her face but the resolve to go still in her heart. "I'll write to you every day."

"You had better." He kissed her. "I'll think of nothing but you."

"Me, and Aeroméchanique!" But she was teasing, and he responded with equal affection, "Just don't get your head too lost up there in the clouds, love."

"I won't. I'll wire you from Boston. We should be there by next Tuesday."

"I'll be waiting."

The ocean voyage was long, and Sarah spent the days pacing impatiently up and down the decks. It hadn't seemed so long before. . . . And that last crossing seemed to have taken place in a different lifetime, not merely a year ago. It was before Eric, before the Channel crossing, when she had planned just a short stay to do a few French exhibitions. . . . And here she was, going back to America as a visitor, knowing that her heart and her life now belonged in France.

Roger Auchincloss had boarded at Southampton, and he occupied all of Amanda's hours. The two of them were always dancing and playing shuffleboard and drinking late into the night. They slept late in the long languid mornings on shipboard, having a belated breakfast delivered to their stateroom.

Sarah walked the decks and tried to read Chesterton's latest Father Brown novel and wrote long impassioned letters to Eric. Her skin darkened in the sun, to Amanda's disgust; Roger lifted an amused eyebrow. "Is this what French citizenship does to people?"

And then, at long last, they docked in Boston and Marc

and Jeannine Allard were there to meet her. Jeannine was jumping up and down in excitement, but Marc was still as calm and quiet as ever, a perfect foil to his sister's exuberance.

Sarah turned to Amanda, feeling awkward in this moment of leavetaking. "I hope to see you sometime," she said, not knowing quite how to bridge the recent estrangement between them.

Amanda shrugged. "Perhaps. I'm going to Newport, don't you know, and I might be in New York before Christmas. We'll see."

It was an empty good-bye, and there were tears in Sarah's eyes as she turned back to Marc and Jeannine and the Ford roadster they had hired for their stay in Boston. "We're at the Ritz, Sarah, and don't say that it's too expensive. The sponsors are paying."

"The sponsors? Good heavens. And God bless them." Sarah laughed. "Marc, can we stop at the telegraph office on the way over? I want to wire my husband."

Jeannine laughed in delight. "Only new brides say 'my husband' quite so possessively!"

"You're absolutely right," Sarah said, poker-faced. "And I plan to stay as possessive as a young bride for the rest of my life!"

The sponsor was represented by a Stanley Williams. Large and sweaty, a native of the Midwest, he had a nervous manner and was constantly wiping his forehead with a handkerchief.

He was, however, delighted to meet Sarah. "Miss Martin! Or is it? I'm sorry, I can't remember your married name."

"Beaumont," Sarah said politely. "I still use my maiden name for exhibitions, though, so you needn't worry."

"Quite so, quite so." He mopped his brow again. "Such an honor to have you here, then, Miss Martin. The first woman across the Channel. What a feat! What an endeavor!"

Jeannine said, "This is quite a feat as well, Mr. Williams." She winked at Sarah. "Quite a ladies' show, from what I'm hearing."

"Ah, well, yes," he said, uncomfortably. "Ladies in the air. Draws a crowd. Makes the whole fuss worthwhile." He consulted his watch. "Have you read the program yet, Miss Martin?"

Sarah shrugged. "I've glanced at it. A Blériot two-seater monoplane, is that what you have for me?"

"Yes, yes, quite. Not from your husband's company, of course, but that day will come, I'm sure, Miss Martin. You're flying alone, naturally, especially the big course, with Miss Allard and Miss Rosinski."

Sarah smiled at Jeannine. "I see what you mean by a ladies' event. Three of us in the air at once, Mr. Williams?"

"Yes, yes, well, it seemed the thing to do." He wiped the sweat off his forehead again. "And then, later on, Miss Martin, if I could inconvenience you, you might take me up for a ride—just around the lighthouse out there, for the photographers and all that. Good publicity, you see."

"I see." Sarah smiled. "I understand perfectly about these things, Mr. Williams, you needn't worry. I'll be happy to take you up."

Jeannine pulled her away then. "We've got to see to our airplanes, Mr. Williams," she said. As soon as they were out of earshot she started giggling. "Better you than me, Sarah; how much do you suppose he weighs?"

"God only knows," Sarah said somberly. "I hope that I can get it off the ground with him in it!"

Jeannine nodded. "You might need an extra engine. Best get Eric working on that one!"

Sarah laughed. "Shh. He'll hear you. And Eric's got more than enough on his plate as it is. He told me once that he was married to Aeroméchanique, and I'll tell you, Jeannine, there's more truth in that than meets the eye!"

The day was superb for flying, the sun peeking in and out of clouds, little wind—and none of it across the runways at Squantum Field, where they were holding the meet. Sarah went up twice, including the famous "Ladies' Event," where she and Jeannine and Helen Rosinski flew in tight formation. It was tricky: They had never practiced together, but it went off without a hitch. Here she was, once again, in her element. Here she could forget about the struggles with Amanda, about Eric's increasing preoccupation with building airplanes for warfare, about all the problems that seemed to harass her on the ground. Here she was alive, and free.

Finally, the day was over and the band was playing; the reporters and photographers all gathered about to watch Stanley Williams make his little flight around the lighthouse with the most famous of all American women pilots. He got in slowly, still mopping his brow, his face abnormally pale. "Are you all right, Mr. Williams?" Sarah asked anxiously, fearing that he might be sick when he went up, but he shook his head. "Just a little tired, Miss Martin. Don't worry. I know that I'll be fine in a few minutes."

Sarah paused before getting into the airplane, giving the photographers a brilliant smile and a good view of her fancy flying silks and long white scarf. Then she, too, was in, strapping on her helmet and giving the signal to start the engine.

The propeller caught and held and the engine roared into life for the third time that day. Sarah felt for the rudder control and slid her fingers slowly along the throttle, getting ready. She taxied into position with the lighthouse lined up directly in front of her—damn Louis Blériot for not being as thoughtful as Eric and putting an instrument panel in front of her. All she could see was Mr. Williams's head—and then they were off, the throttle open and wind catching her thoughts and blowing them around, blowing them away. The ground was racing by, and she lifted off, soaring up into the sky, free, free. . . .

They circled the lighthouse twice. Unable to gauge her passenger's reactions, Sarah looked down thoughtfully on the crowds below. Silly people, she mused, fated to live out their lives signaling to ships to come in, when they could be up here. Up here, where nothing mattered and everything counted.

She banked slightly and headed back towards the field, towards the photographers and the reporters and the questions, and, eventually, the ride back to the hotel with champagne awaiting her, and a lovely long bubble bath and a long letter to Eric. Heading back, and everything was perfect.

And then suddenly, everything wasn't perfect, everything was terribly, inexplicably wrong. The man in front of her was moving, his vast bulk off balance. Had she banked too tightly? She had thought that she was being careful. Frozen with the horror, she saw him falling, as though in slow

motion, falling out of the airplane, his weight moving it
forward and down. The tail began to flip up, and the voice
inside her was screaming, and then he was out, falling, and
the Blériot continued to tip.

This was the dream. This was the sensation of falling,
falling on a crisp clear day with the sky solid and blue, and
the water below. This was the nightmare that had haunted
her for months. As the slow-motion horror went on and
on, thoughts raced through her head: Eric, Eric, my love,
I'm sorry. I said I'd never leave. . . . And then the Blériot had tipped over and Sarah was falling, like a wounded
bird from the sky. There was a great explosion, lights
flashing in her head, and then, at last, everything went
black.

Boston Globe, September 17, 1912

A terrible tragedy marred the festivities at the Boston
Air Show today when Miss Sarah Martin, America's
first woman pilot, and Mr. Stanley Williams plunged to
their deaths in the mud flats of Boston Harbor when
Miss Martin's Blériot aircraft tipped over.

Miss Martin negotiated the much-publicized trip to
Boston light and was heading back when the tail of the
airplane flashed upwards and the entire craft seemed,
momentarily, to stand on end before first Mr. Williams
and then Miss Martin fell to their deaths. The recovered bodies were terribly mangled; the airplane righted
itself and was virtually undamaged.

Twenty years of age, Miss Martin, it will be remembered, recently married Mr. Eric Beaumont, co-owner
of Aeroméchanique Inc., of Angers, France. It was in
an Aeroméchanique airplane that Miss Martin became
the first woman to fly across the English Channel.

She is survived by her husband, and by her parents,
Mr. and Mrs. Herbert Martin of San Jose, California,
and by her brother, Mr. Peter Martin, also of San Jose.

Mr. Williams is survived by a son, Mr. Clarence
Williams, and a daughter, Mrs. Nathalie Ackerman,
both of Kansas City, Missouri.

Sarah was buried back in her hometown, at her father's
insistence, and the townspeople made much of her funeral,

since she was the first woman to die flying. Somebody picked up her favorite silk scarf and sent it off to the offices of Aeroméchanique in France, in the hopes that it might comfort her husband.

A marching band played funeral dirges, and everybody wept openly; people in the shops on Main Street shook their heads and tut-tutted about the whole thing, flying and all.

And then life settled back as it had before in San Jose, with mothers dropping their children's names into the quiet pools of twilight and the ripples spreading throughout all the neighborhoods.

No one had thought to wire Paris, where the newspapers did not reach the young genius behind Aeroméchanique until it was too late to do anything but cry.

· 2 ·

Twilight Days
1912–1918

Chapter Nine

Newport, November 1912.

"So do tell us all about France, darling! We're all just dying to know!"

Amanda Lewis turned from the punchbowl at the long, linen-covered table at her mother's estate in Newport and faced the questioner, a young woman with her hair bobbed in the current rage and dressed in the newest fashion, a dress daringly revealing her ankles. Amanda frowned. "What is there to say, Lucinda? It was divine, of course."

"Amanda always finds everything divine," complained Freddie. "Do give us the real gossip, Amanda, won't you?"

"Like who is sleeping with whom," added another woman, moving smoothly into the radius of conversation.

Lucinda raised her chin in the air. "Must you always be so crass, Katherine?"

"Usually," Katherine responded calmly. "It's the only honest way to be, isn't it? After all, it's what we're all thinking, so we might as well say it."

"Speaking of sleeping around," Freddie said brightly, "where's Roger these days?"

Somebody gasped at that, and then there was a moment of silence, and everyone in the room averted their eyes. Amanda sipped her punch. "Roger has gotten tiresome," she said. "I can't think what I saw in him, though he was frightfully sympathetic and even amusing in England. People change, and I think that it's very tedious of them."

"Why?" asked Lucinda. "Imagine you saying that, of all people! You've changed."

Amanda frowned again. "How?"

Lucinda looked at the other two for support and, seeing that she was getting none, shrugged. "Well, if you really must know, though I do think that there are things best left unsaid, I think that you've gotten a little tiresome yourself, Amanda, darling."

"Now, Lucinda—" Freddie began.

She turned to him in exasperation. "Freddie, don't be an ass. Amanda is perfectly capable of taking care of herself."

"How have I changed?" Amanda interrupted.

"Well, darling, there was precisely that thing with Roger. A perfectly darling man; I wouldn't mind a fling with him myself. And here you are, tired of him already. And last week I hear that Clara introduced you to her cousin, who is absolutely thrilling and working in the movies, don't you know, and you hardly pursued him at all. That isn't like you, Amanda. You're usually better than that at giving us things to talk about."

"Hear, hear!" said Freddie.

Amanda slowly put down her glass. "I am very sorry," she said formally, "to have stopped being a source of entertainment for you. I expect that you'll be able to find someone else to talk about. Excuse me."

She left them then, walking quickly through the French doors which led out to the terrace on the ocean side of the mansion, tears stinging her eyes. It was cold outside—well, after all, it was early November, what did one expect?—and she hugged her arms around her body and went over and leaned up against the stone wall at the end of the terrace, looking out over the gray ocean with eyes that didn't see it at all.

Nothing was the same. They were right, in their own way. Change was tiresome. Everything was awful. Why did anyone have to change, anyway? Why couldn't the world just stay simple and predictable? That kept things safe.

When had it all started to change? When Sarah flew over the Channel and they spent so much time in England? Or later, when Sarah and Eric got married and things started falling apart between her and Philippe? It was as though her friend's wedding emphasized that things could never be that way for her and Philippe. And then, Sarah's death . . .

Amanda turned her back resolutely on the ocean and leaned against the wall again, facing the house. The one time she hadn't gone to Sarah's flying exhibition. Not that there was anything that she could have done, of course—or was there? Was there some mysterious way in which she could have helped Sarah, and didn't because she was too busy with her own pleasures?

Amanda had been in bed with Roger Auchincloss the afternoon that Sarah was killed.

And now there was no way to say that she was sorry, no way to heal the anger that had come up between the two friends, nothing but feelings of guilt and loss. Sarah had been Amanda's only genuine friend. All the others, she thought, were like those silly women in there. Great fun at parties, but . . . Sarah had been more. Sarah had truly cared. And now she was gone. And Amanda was alone.

Her first thought, back in September when she heard the news of the accident, had been to leave immediately for France. Eric and Philippe would be lost in grief, and they would need her. But the more she considered going, the more she remembered of the house on the rue de Verdun filled with Sarah's laughter, of the Aeromécanique hangar where she had met Philippe. She knew instinctively that she wasn't that strong, that the sorrow and the pain there would be too much for her.

Still, she sometimes wondered if she wasn't more alone, more unhappy here, in Newport, than she would have been had she gone back to Paris. Alone in the midst of these charming, silly, witty, tedious people. It was too late to think about that now, of course. The moment had come and gone, and in the end she hadn't even responded to the long letter that Philippe had written her when he first had news of Sarah's death. She went on with her parties and her teas, her afternoons of sailing and croquet, her gossip and her flirtations, and all the while she felt separate from her friends, as though she were merely watching herself go through the motions. It was a feeling of not quite being in one's own skin—and decidedly unsettling.

No one here understood. They were so shallow in their personal lives, for all that they were the great families of the East Coast. They all had been amazed at how long she had stayed in Paris—how long she had stayed, in point of fact, with one man—and they welcomed her back with lavish dinners and decadent amusements, and a real sense of "life goes on." Amanda had resented that, and had withdrawn to some extent, even staying for a fortnight with her mother up on the estate in New Hampshire. There she had listened to the older woman tell her what a fool she had been to fall in love.

"Fall in love?" Amanda had repeated, in amazement. "It's obvious that you really don't understand, Mamma dearest, and I do wish that you would listen."

"I do," her mother had said tartly. "I listen to a lot from you, Amanda, and I must confess that I do not always like what I hear. If you must have affairs, have affairs then. I have no doubt but that you'll settle down in time and marry someone respectable, and I do have some names to suggest to you when that time comes. But in the meantime, for heaven's sake, don't fall in love. It almost always leads one into making rash decisions."

"Well, Mamma," Amanda had said, standing up and pulling on her gloves. "I'm going out riding, and I do hope that you'll get this silly notion out of your head. I am most decidedly not in love with Philippe de Montclair—or with anybody else, for that matter." She didn't stop to ask herself why her mother had phrased her warning in just that way—that love leads one into making rash decisions. She didn't have either the time or the interest to pursue that line of thought. But much later, when the question was no longer purely academic, she considered it. Her parents had never married; she had never known her father. Was it possible that her own birth was the "rash decision" that her own mother had made when she was in love? And to compensate for her rash decision, her mother had pursued an eminently respectable, staid—and loveless—life ever since.

But those musings were for another time. Now, as she walked out to her mother's stables and waited for Arthur, the stableman—with whom she had had a delicious interlude one summer when she was sixteen—to saddle a horse for her to ride, she found herself looking rather desperately for other things to think about. She didn't want to consider whether her mother might be right. She didn't have to face anything that she didn't want to face. Later, riding down on the banks of the Connecticut River which flowed by her mother's property lines, she found herself wondering what it would have been like, if only . . .

Eric sat still, gazing out over the rain-drenched field, outside the Aeroméchanique hangar. It was over a month since the news of Sarah's death had reached him. It felt like a year.

There had been no sense in traveling to America. There was no one there to comfort him. He did not know her parents—although her mother had written him an extremely kind and generous letter, expressing her sorrow for him and inviting him to San Jose whenever he wished to come—and he didn't feel like coping with anything new. His English, though passable, was shaky, and America was, in too many ways, a very frightening place. Better to stay here among his memories of her, here in this hangar where they had first met.

Amazing, he thought with a part of his mind that was a little detached, amazing that the human body can hold so much grief and not explode with it. Curious, too, that people who talked about grief really didn't know what they were talking about. Philippe had insisted on a memorial service for Sarah in Paris, and hundreds of people had attended, hundreds of well-meaning people—some who had known her and others who had read about her in the newspapers. Not one of them had understood what it was like to lose her. "You'll get over it, with time," they all said, patting him knowingly on the shoulder.

But it wasn't the intense pain that was the problem. Eric welcomed the pain, it funneled his energies. What he couldn't cope with was the dull ache of her absence, which permeated everything that he did. Her absence spread over everything—made life impossible.

He thought about dying. After the service, he went back to the hangar outside of Paris and he thought about how he could die. There were a thousand ways to do it. He could take one of the airplanes up, himself, and crash it. He could buy a gun—one must be able to buy a gun someplace—and shoot himself. He could . . . And the more he thought about how he could do it, the more he knew that he wouldn't. He wasn't at all sure whether there was any kind of life after this one—he was more sure that there was not—but he couldn't take the chance. He couldn't think of facing Sarah again, someday, somewhere, and telling her that he had been a coward.

The pain racked his whole being. He sat on the ground, with his knees drawn up in front of him, his body hurting with the force of his sobs, and the realization of her absence

washed over him, fresh and agonizing, again and again. He
could close his eyes and see her smile or hear her laughter,
and immediately on the heels of the memory came the
knowledge that he would never again hear her, or see her, or
touch her.

She was gone.

Eric took to going to the city, and spending entire evenings
in bars, drinking until he couldn't focus on anything and the
pain dulled. He wasn't always sure what he did in the bars,
but he knew that the alcohol made him feel better.

Philippe found him one night, drunk and tired and feeling
sick, and sat down at the table opposite Eric and looked at
him with concern.

"Are you going to spend the rest of the night here?"

Eric focused blearily on him. "Probably."

Philippe looked around him in disgust. "Are you going to
spend the rest of your life here?"

Eric considered the question, and then belched. "Probably," he said again.

Philippe shrugged. "I'm not enjoying watching you destroy yourself like this."

"Then go away. Or, better yet, join me. Antoinette! A beer
for my friend, here!"

"I miss her, too, Eric," Philippe said in a low voice. "But
you have to pull yourself together. She would want you to."

"Sure she would. Thanks, Antoinette. Here's your beer,
mon ami. To what shall we drink?"

"How about to Aeroméchanique? You seem to have
forgotten that lately."

"Ah," Eric said thickly. "*Au contraire.* I have thought of
little else. A terrible business, a terrible business."

"What do you mean?" Philippe stared at him over the rim
of his beer mug.

"Aeroméchanique makes airplanes. And airplanes kill
people. So the best way to save the world is to stop making
airplanes." Eric looked pleased at that exercise in logic, and
downed the rest of his own drink. "Antoinette!"

"That's stupid, Eric. Airplanes don't kill people. What
happened to Sarah was an accident." He leaned forward
across the table. "You can prevent that kind of accident,
mon ami. You can save people. You've got to work on the

design. You've got to solve the inherent stability problem."
He leaned back. "If she had been in a more stable airplane,
it wouldn't have mattered that her passenger fell out."

"She shouldn't have been in an airplane in the first place,"
Eric said doggedly. "If God wanted man to fly, He would
have given us wings."

"Isn't it a little late to start discussing theology?"

"Hardly." Eric leaned forward and lowered his voice.
"She never liked what we were doing, Philippe. She never
liked it."

"Liked what?" Philippe was feeling baffled.

"This whole business of making airplanes. For the war.
She said that if everybody went up in the air and looked
down, then there would be no more wars, because everyone
would understand."

"Understand what?"

"That it's not worth it. That nothing's ever really worth
fighting about." He drew in a deep breath, and when it came
out it caught on a sob. "Oh, God, Philippe, we fought about
so many stupid things. I argued with her about this and that,
this and that, and all the while I didn't know that I was going
to lose her. I wish I could take all those arguments back.
She's right, you know. Nothing is really worth fighting
about."

Philippe concentrated on his glass, rolling it around and
around on the table. What did one say to someone at a time
like this? The pain was there for him, too: the pain of
Amanda's departure, of Sarah's death. They were alone
again, just he and Eric, the way it had all started. But while
then it had felt good, now it felt empty, bereft, lonely. He
glanced up at Eric. How could he help him? What could he
do?

"Do you remember," Philippe said at length, "how we
used to go out drinking, like this, in the old days? From bar
to bar, all night, until they closed, and we were drunker than
roosters?"

There was an answering gleam in Eric's eyes. "Do I ever,"
he said, slowly. "Do you remember picking that fight that
time, in the little place over by Deauville, with that big
stevedore?"

Philippe grinned and took a swallow of beer. "I thought
for sure that I would die that night," he said.

"So did I. Always standing up for principles, *mon ami,* that was you. Didn't matter how dangerous the bar or the section of town, you were always standing up for principles." He was silent for a moment. "The world doesn't always run on principles."

"No. So it's up to us. To respect those principles."

"Now you're sounding like Sarah."

"She had some good ideas."

Eric turned glazed eyes on his friend. "They didn't help her much. She's dead."

Philippe finished his beer and set the glass down on the table. "Not if you choose to keep her alive," he said, seriously. "She always wanted to help you, and it seems to me that she still is. She wouldn't have died if the airplane hadn't tipped, right?"

"I don't want to talk about it."

"And the airplane wouldn't have tipped if it wasn't depending on her weight and her passenger's weight to keep it stable. It's the same old problem, *mon ami.* Isn't it time you got around to solving it?"

"I don't want to talk about it."

Philippe stood up and, reaching for his raincoat, slung it over one shoulder. "That's up to you. You can stay here for the rest of your life if you want. You know that. Aéromécanique can support you. But it's not what Sarah would have wanted, and I can't see her being any too proud of you for it."

Eric looked up at him for a long moment, his eyes bloodshot and unfocused, and then he shook his head. "Leave me alone," he said, his voice rising. "Just goddamn leave me alone!"

Philippe shrugged, tossed some money on the table, and turned away. At the door, he hesitated and looked back. It was a working-class bar, filled with men in blue coveralls, factory workers and laborers, their voices raucous and loud, their noses reddened by too much wine. And in the center of it all sat Eric Beaumont, who could move between two worlds so very easily, who because of his genius could be assimilated into any stratum of society, whose pain was now leading him to seek out the class of his youth. Able to live in two worlds but comfortable in neither. Sarah had been very good for him.

Philippe turned and went out the door, letting in a gust of wind and rain to a chorus of complaints behind him. He wasn't listening; he was trying to listen to another voice, a voice inside him that sounded exactly like Sarah, that would tell him what to do.

Christmas arrived, cold and with snow, which was unusual in Paris.

The shops filled with toys and lights. Christmas trees decorated with candles and wreaths were being placed on doors. Carriage rides through the Bois de Boulogne were temporarily replaced by sleighs, and people were friendly.

For Eric, it was almost too much to bear.

He thought of last Christmas, with Sarah and Amanda laughing at each other over their oysters, and Amanda proposing impossible toasts with her glass of champagne held high. He saw Amanda cranking up the new gramophone they had bought, and Sarah smiling at him in the firelight, and he remembered too well going to bed with her afterwards, her voice in the darkness so close to him whispering, "Happy Christmas, my love," and her skin sweet-smelling and her arms around him. . . .

He had to cover his ears to block out her voice, to block out the pain.

Philippe worried about him, and invited him to Angers for the holidays. "Come on, *mon ami*, it won't be so bad," he said, but Eric shook his head. "You go. I'd ruin Marie-Louise's Christmas."

"Don't be ridiculous." But Philippe's voice was a shade too hearty, and Eric looked at him with a tired smile. "I'll be all right, you'll see. I'll just go and get something to drink before the bars close, and then I'll make a fire and sit by it for a while."

Philippe was concerned, but Eric was right: The last thing in the world that Marie-Louise needed was to see him. She had never liked Philippe's friendship with Eric. Noticing reports of Sarah's death in the newspaper, she had said casually, over breakfast one morning when Philippe was down at the estate, "Wasn't that the girl who was living with the farrier's son?"

"She was married to him," Philippe said briefly.

"How nice. And was he faithful to his wife?"

"I wouldn't know. Why is that our concern?"

"Oh, I just wondered," said Marie-Louise, almost gaily. "If the lower classes are good for nothing else, then they might at least be faithful. Which is more than one can say for the nobility."

"What are you trying to say, Marie-Louise?" Philippe asked tiredly. "I'm not in a mood to play games with you this morning."

"Nothing, darling," she said lightly. "Do go see Pierre in the nursery before you go, won't you?"

"I'm not going to Paris again for a while," he said, frowning as he stirred his coffee. "Eric's not doing any work, and any Aeroméchanique business that comes up I can handle out of the Angers office."

Marie-Louise raised her eyebrows. "My, my! So we are to be blessed with your presence! Maybe that girl-aviator going back to America wasn't such a bad thing, if it could interest you in your family once again."

Philippe had had enough and stood up. "Marie-Louise," he said heavily, "at this moment I'm not extraordinarily proud of how my family is behaving. If you will excuse me?"

No, bringing Eric to the estate for Christmas would not have been a good idea. Marie-Louise would have made Eric feel self-conscious, and undoubtedly would have hurt his feelings with her sharp tongue. Better to let him work it out, alone, himself. That was the only way.

But, damn it, it had been three months since Sarah's death. Three months, and Eric was still drinking himself stupid every night. Three months, and although Aeroméchanique's production was sensational, there had been no new ideas, no new designs, nothing.

Three months. There had to be a way out.

Philippe found it, almost accidentally, in January.

Leslie's Weekly continued to arrive on the doorstep of the rue de Verdun with some regularity. Eric couldn't bring himself to either read it or cancel the subscription. He used the newspaper, mostly, in the fireplace, and would sit for hours morosely watching it burn.

It was Philippe who picked it up and read it whenever he happened to be in Paris, read it with interest and detachment, the same as any other newspaper. The second week in

January *Leslie's Weekly* ran a story about Stanley Williams. Philippe's interest sharpened. He read of the comforts of life in the Midwest of the United States; he read of the family man, who worked with Boy Scouts on his free Saturdays; he read of the small company the man owned, and the nephew he encouraged to fly airplanes. He had always been fascinated with airplanes, had Mr. Stanley Williams.

Williams's company had fallen on hard times, it seemed. The Williams Tool and Die Co., Inc., had been recently bought as a subsidiary of a larger company. Still, it seemed that even the buyout was not enough to save them. There was not enough interest by the parent company, apparently, to keep Williams Tool and Die as a viable enterprise. Bankruptcy was imminent when Mr. Williams himself was so unfortunately killed in Boston.

His children had had no interest in the company. His son was in banking; his daughter was married with a family of her own. Mr. Williams had been a widower for nearly a decade.

Philippe frowned. It was a profile piece, no more. Surely that was all that had been meant by the newspaper? And yet . . . and yet. It posed disturbing questions. Mr. Williams's company was bankrupt. Mr. Williams's wife was dead, his children self-sufficient. How did one start over again in middle age in a small midwestern town when one was seen as a civic leader in one's former occupation?

No one had understood why Sarah's plane tipped. No one at the time, no one since, had offered any plausible explanations. The Blériot monoplane was steady enough to resist a rogue wind or air current.

No one had understood. But sitting alone in the living room of the house on the rue de Verdun, Philippe de Montclair began to understand.

What if it had not been an accident at all, but Stanley Williams's ticket out of existence? What if Sarah's death had been caused by a deliberate action on his part? What if she had not taken him up for that run around the lighthouse? What if it had been Jeannine Allard or Helen Rosinski? What if, what if, what if . . . The questions hammered round and round in his brain until they drove him out in search of Eric.

Philippe found him in the third bar he tried—one that the four of them had sometimes sat at together, surrounded by dark polished mahogany and gleaming brass. Philippe wasn't sure what it meant that he had found Eric here, but he was determined to tell him: Sarah had died because of another man's suicide; her death had been needless. It might just wake Eric up.

Eric was drinking coffee. Philippe, so caught up in what he had come prepared to say, and thinking only about waking Eric out of his alcoholic stupor, assimilated that fact slowly. Yet here Eric was drinking coffee. There were books on the table in front of him. There was something happening here that Philippe didn't understand at first, but Eric eagerly supplied the details.

"You know, you're right," he said when Philippe approached, and he carefully marked a place in the book and put it aside. "There's still a lot to be worked on. The stability factor can't help but be crucial to future models."

Philippe raised his eyebrows but said nothing, and Eric took a swallow of coffee and eagerly continued. "There's the whole issue of weight and of properly balancing the craft before it even leaves the drawing board. But it's not insurmountable, don't you see? We'll get it stabilized from the start, then it won't matter what the people on board are doing." He paused, and withdrew a piece of paper from his book, sliding it across the table to Philippe. "And," he said softly, "we'll add these."

It looked to Philippe like the drawing of a lot of snakes. "What are they?" he asked.

"Belts," Eric said, still softly, with a bit of the glassiness back in his eyes. "Belts that would be attached to the seats in the airplane. They would close in front, just like the belts that we wear, with holes to adjust for different proportions. That way, no one ever need fall out of an airplane again."

There were tears in Philippe's eyes. "*Mon vieux*," he said, leaning forward to clasp his friend's hand, "I can't tell you how damnably sorry I am about Sarah—"

Eric waved his hand. "It's all right. It's all right." He smiled. "I know that I'm going to survive. And Aéroméchanique is going to survive. And she's going to survive, through both of us."

Philippe nodded, not trusting his own words, not trusting

his own emotions, and then Eric gestured towards the
packet of papers that Philippe still was holding, the *Leslie's
Weekly* account of the trials and times of Stanley Williams.
"What's that?"

Philippe started, then put the paper in his lap. "Nothing,"
he said. "Just a newspaper; nothing at all."

Having decided not to tell Eric about the newspaper reports,
Philippe told Amanda the whole story in a long letter that he
wrote just after the New Year, not knowing just what to say
or how to articulate feelings which were at best nebulous
even to himself. He wanted her, yet he feared what she
would do to his life. He needed her insouciance, her gaiety,
her love of brightness and pleasure; he feared her possessive-
ness, her temper, her inconstancies, and inconsistencies.

But more than anything, Eric's loss of Sarah had done one
thing to Philippe: It had crystallized for him the sense of
time being both short and precious. It was not only Sarah's
laughter which rang and echoed in the deserted rooms on
the rue de Verdun. Philippe, too, found himself aching for
what had been.

In a way, Eric had the advantage. Eric had a better-
defined grief; Eric had the solace of others' commiseration.
Sarah had not left him willingly; she had committed herself
to him and to their life together and would have stayed
forever.

Amanda, on the other hand, had run off with hardly a
backward glance.

For all that Aeroméchanique required of the two friends'
time and their energy, there was an emptiness, a wretched
longing for times past, that permeated the house they still
shared together. One night Philippe came home late and
drunk, bringing with him two prostitutes that he had
encountered downtown. Eric had met them wordlessly at
the door and had done what seemed to be expected. But
even the needed outlet of sex was tinged with longing and
regret, and left both men unsatisfied, bereft in a curiously
haunting way.

And then, late in March, as the winter was finally giving
signs of abandoning its hold on the capital, Philippe opened
the mailbox at the house on the rue de Verdun and found a
response from America.

March 16, 1913

Dear Philippe,

Well, I *must* say that you've been very faithful about
writing, which I have not, but then writing is such a
tiresome occupation when there are so many more
amusing things to be doing. I must conclude that you
have no amusements in your life.

I was sorry to read the clipping that you sent some
months ago, but I wonder why on *earth* you would want
to pursue such a thing. Sarah is dead, darling, and there's
absolutely *nothing* that you or anyone else can do to
change that. It's such a pity that the man killed
himself—*if* indeed that was what happened—but
there is no sense in making this go on any longer than it
already has.

Newport has hardly been amusing at all this winter.
All the people who are usually about are in New York,
or else have taken refuge in the Bottle or in Art—
they've just opened the Armory Show, don't you know,
and although it doesn't look much like Art to me I
suppose that's what it is, and terribly, terribly fash--
ionable, or so they say. (Haven't you *always* wondered
who that ubiquitous "they" might be referring to? I
have.)

Anyway, anyway, anyway, all this is to say that I just
might find it possible to go to France för a few weeks
this summer. I might go to Cornish, too, I don't know. I
don't want to make any *promises,* darling, we'll just
have to see.

All for now.

Loving regards,
Amanda

Amanda had sealed the letter tremulously, not knowing
what Philippe's reaction would be. So much time had
passed, and she had left him after she had already flung
herself into the arms of another man. What if he didn't care
for her anymore? What if he had already replaced her with a
more compliant French mistress? What if . . .

What if he realized how incredibly bleak and empty her
life had been without him?

There were so many things she would do differently, if she had only known: all her temper tantrums, all her demanding behavior and sulks, all her pettiness and provocativeness and complaints. . . . She hadn't realized how she felt about him. Her mother was right. For the first time, Amanda Lewis was in love.

And he had a wife. She had fought with him and against him about that, but it wasn't going to change, and she understood now why it wasn't going to change. If she had it to do over again, she would not waste her time worrying about his wife, but enjoying him and what they had.

Chapter Ten

Amanda worried herself sick during the entire Atlantic crossing.

She thought about the various ways in which Philippe might react to her presence, and she worried despite the fact that Philippe had responded to her letter, almost immediately, telling her that it would be absolutely terrific for her to come back. "We still have the house in Boulogne-Billiancourt, you see," he wrote to her, "and it's empty these days. Eric and I live here, but it's haunted by the ghosts of the good times that we all shared. Please come back."

It was a nice enough letter, but still Amanda had misgivings. She was afraid. She was always careful to avoid putting herself in situations that might bring her pain, or sorrow, or rejection. Since she was a little girl and had listened to her schoolmates repeat what their parents had said about Amanda Lewis's parentage, she had avoided people who might not accept her. Taking a risk such as this one, inviting rejection in order possibly to obtain something else that she wanted, was a very frightening thing for her to do.

Amanda was ill for most of the passage, which the crew soliticously accepted as seasickness and which she didn't tell them was actually nerves. She would get up in the mornings and walk around the deck, and then after breakfast sometimes sit outside in the pale April sunshine, wrapped in layers of blankets and with a hot water bottle clutched to her stomach. She watched people stroll by on their way to the shuffleboard games; fashionably dressed, wealthy people who could afford to travel first class across the ocean—people who were like her.

Amanda was realizing, slowly, that they were all a lot less amusing than she had always assumed.

She found herself sitting on the long deck chaise longues and unconsciously drawing her knees up under her chin in Sarah's characteristic gesture, encircling her legs with her arms and thinking about all that had happened: the days out at the Aeromécanique hangar, with Eric getting still another prototype ready and Sarah climbing up into the high seat to test-fly it; and the mud, no matter what season; Philippe with his hat at a rakish angle making sardonic comments when the airplane refused to fly, or flew erratically; Eric throwing his wrench and starting all over again; the dresses that she had ruined in the mud; and always Sarah, laughing at her for not having her eyes on the sky.

Amanda became conscious of tears in her eyes and dashed them away, impatiently, with the back of her hand. Best not to think of that. Best to think only of the future, of what was ahead of her. Sarah was dead and there was nothing that anyone could do about that, but life went on. And Amanda was increasingly sure that it was with Philippe that she wanted to spend her life.

Finally, the ship docked at le Havre and it was time to put all her fine resolutions and grand ideas into practice. Even Amanda knew that would be the hardest part.

Philippe welcomed her back with delight. Eric's eyes held reservations, but with a newfound wisdom Amanda knew that the reservations were not because of who she was, but because of the memories she represented.

Nothing had changed in the house. The first morning that she was back, Amanda walked through it, looking around her for alterations, wondering what the long months of absence had done. But it was all the same. The same stuffed velvet chairs; the same lead soldier collection; the same terrace with straggling flowers. They had never really put their hearts into that garden, Amanda thought, with unexpected regret. There had always been too many other things to be done. The portrait of Sarah's parents that she had had sent to her from America still hung in the front hall.

Philippe, walking up behind her, encircled her with his arms. "Nothing has changed," he whispered against her hair, with his same uncanny way of reading her thoughts.

"I know," she said aloud, and he let her go and turned her around to face him.

"I've missed you so much," he said. "I think that I understand why you left, but—"

Amanda put her arms around him and interrupted him with a kiss, a long, deep, satisfying kiss. "It doesn't matter," she said, at length. "It doesn't really matter anymore."

"No," he said, and pulled her closer to him in a sudden rough movement, his mouth on hers, obliterating all else but their pressing need for each other. Amanda stood and kissed him and felt all the familiar sensations wash over her: the roughness of his moustache against her face, the strength in his arms, and the odor of tobacco on his breath, mixed with the cologne he used. It all spoke to her, urgently, of the love and the desire and the delight she had always associated with being with Philippe.

He started fumbling with her jacket, and she gasped, "Philippe! No, darling, not here!" But he wasn't listening to her, and she laughed and responded in kind, pulling at his sweater and shirt and unbuckling his belt. "What if Eric comes home?" she asked, still laughing, and Philippe raised his eyebrows. "What happened to your sense of daring, *ma cherie*?"

She giggled at that, and they continued undressing each other as they sank to the floor, to the deep Oriental carpet that the antique dealer had brought back to France from Persia. Philippe's trousers and her petticoats were tossed aside with the same joyful abandon. They rolled over on the carpet, Philippe lying on top of her, her blond hair spread out over its rich hues. She was still giggling as he kissed her neck, her shoulders, the slopes of her breasts.

He straightened then, reaching for something beyond her line of vision, and she tightened her arms around him. "Don't stop, don't stop," she begged him in an undertone, and he laughed and withdrew from her altogether.

"Turn around," he urged her, and she complied, kneeling on the carpet. There, on her hands and knees, she saw what he had been adjusting: a full-length, mahogany-framed mirror.

"Oh, Philippe!" she squealed in excitement, and shivered as she felt his hands caressing her derriere.

"Watch us," he said to her, his voice slightly slurred with desire, kneeling behind her. "Watch us make love." And then he entered her, and she watched his face grow flushed

as he began to move, faster and faster, with all of the need
that he had held for her through the months of her absence.
She moaned and moved with him, pushing her backside
against his rhythm, and then soon, almost too soon, he was
gripping her and thrusting even faster, gripping her so hard
it hurt, but with the pain came mounting pleasure and it all
seemed to explode at once, with him grunting and her voice
joining his, crying out their love.

And then he pulled out of her and she lay down on her
side on the carpet, and he lay with her, both of them fighting
to regain their breath. Philippe reached over and traced her
profile with his finger; she playfully bit it when it touched
her lips. "I was watching you," he said. "You're beautiful
when you make love."

Amanda giggled and stretched luxuriously on the carpet.
"You're prejudiced. You think that I'm beautiful anyway."

"And you," he said, rolling over and propping himself up
on one elbow, and taking her hand to kiss it, "are too
modest."

She smiled. "I know."

In its own way, life continued as before. Change, Eric
thought ruefully, is part of it. Change is frightening, and it
takes away the security of knowing where everyone is and
what they're doing and why things are the way that they are,
but it is as inevitable as life. People make choices, and they
live with them. Sometimes, like Sarah, they die because of
them.

Eric was reading more and more that short hot summer of
1913. There were exciting things to be read, things that
everyone else in the business seemed to dismiss as pure
theory, but which Eric read with an eye to the future.

Philippe, when he could be dragged away from his
newfound infatuation with Amanda, agreed with him. "You
have to dream," he told Eric. "Dreams are the foundations
of Aeroméchanique. It's what distinguishes us from all the
others. They look and see what can be done, and they do it.
But you, *mon ami*, you from the first have dreamed of things
that couldn't be done, and you've learned ways of doing
them anyway. Keep your dreams."

As summer moved towards fall, Eric's dreams became
grandiose. There was a fellow down in Marseilles who was

writing about something called jet propulsion—a way of
moving objects through the air faster than ever before, faster
than anybody had ever dreamed of. "Imagine!" Eric said to
Philippe, his eyes glowing. "Imagine being able to fly
airplanes that fast. It would be only a few minutes to travel
over the whole of France!"

"But is it real?" asked Philippe, forgetting his own advice.
"Does the theory work?"

"I haven't worked it out yet," Eric admitted. "But I'm
going down there to see him—René Lorin his name is—
next week. He wrote to me—imagine that, to me!—asking
me to come and work on it with him. He's got the basic idea,
but it needs a lot of work, a lot of refinement. Make no
mistake, Philippe, it will be years before we can do anything
with it. But just think! What if it works? What if airplanes
can be moved by jets? The possibilities are incredible!"

"And Aeroméchanique will be the first company to do
it?" Philippe asked.

Eric winked at him. "No doubt about it. No doubt in the
least. With Lorin asking me to work with him, there's no
doubt. Wright and Curtiss and Blériot will all still be
paddling about the sky with propellers long after we're
leaving them in our wake."

Philippe grinned. "You're mixing your images, *mon
vieux*. That sounded decidedly nautical."

Eric returned the smile. "In our jet stream, then."

Philippe raised his eyebrows. "You really think that it will
come to that?"

"Mark my words," Eric assured him. "It will."

That September a Deperdussin monoplane broke the 100
m.p.h. "speed barrier," reaching a speed of 126.67 m.p.h.,
and Eric, not content with merely breaking records, left to
see the brilliant scientist in Marseilles to talk about jet
propulsion. Philippe and Amanda had the house on the rue
de Verdun to themselves. "Is it a good thing?" she asked
anxiously, "for him to be away on the anniversary of Sarah's
death?"

"A year already," Philippe said softly, staring out the
window, his fingers in a steeple. "It's hard to believe that
time goes by so quickly."

Amanda sat on the edge of her chair. "Sometimes, I
feel—" She stopped.

"I know," Philippe said, still without looking at her. "I know."

There was a long silence. Finally Philippe cleared his throat. "Marie-Louise has been writing to me," he said at last.

"I know," Amanda said. "I've seen the letters in the mailbox."

He glanced at her, then looked back over his fingers to the gray rain falling outside. "She thinks I should be spending more time with my son."

Amanda stood up abruptly and went to the window, staring out over the ruined flowerpots on the terrace. She hadn't done anything with them this summer, either. "Why don't you say what she wrote?" she asked quietly. "It's not just your son that she's been talking about."

"You've been reading my letters from Marie-Louise?" Philippe's temper flared for a moment, and then subsided almost at once. What else had he expected? Amanda would always be Amanda, and it was her childish irresponsibility that was part of her attraction.

She kept her back to him. "Of course I have," she said calmly. "You mustn't think that I like any of this any more than I did last time, although I must say that I've been nicer about it, on the whole." Hadn't he noticed, she wondered unhappily. Hadn't he realized how she had restrained herself? She had wanted to burn those letters, to tear them up and throw them down and stamp on them. She was trying so hard to be the perfect mistress for Philippe: passionate and undemanding. The latter was not her nature. But she was trying.

He stood up and walked over to her, his arms automatically encircling her slender waist. "I know," he said softly.

Tears came, hot and burning behind her eyelids, and she blinked furiously, determined not to cry or give in to the flood of sadness. She would not be weak. "She knows about me," she said, struggling to keep her voice level.

"I know," he said again, feeling helpless. Amanda was crying, he could feel the tremors in her body. Sudden guilt shot through him. What right did he have to do this to Amanda? Marie-Louise's sarcasm had burned through the pages of her letters. "I know that your little whore is keeping you fulfilled," she had written. "But I am staying chaste for

the sake of our family and for the sake of your son. The least
that you could do is come to see him from time to time so
that he knows you exist. Or would you prefer that I tell him
his father chooses to spend his time with an American slut
in Paris?"

Amanda had read that, and Amanda had not mentioned
it. That, too, was a change. He was beginning to understand
the price her pride had paid in coming back to him from
America, and how she was struggling to adapt to the kind of
life that was required of her here. He remembered the small
wedding in the ancient parish church nearby where Sarah
and Eric had spoken words of promise to each other, the
promise that Sarah had kept for such a very short time. Life
was short and life was unpredictable, and he was spending
his feeling guilty for the situation forced upon him, and the
unhappiness of the two women in his life.

And yet . . . And yet. Philippe de Montclair had been
raised a certain way, raised by nobility to be nobility, and
there was a lot more to it than simple class-consciousness.
He had been brought up to believe that the nobility was a
class set apart to act as a model for the rest of the
people—an icon, the priest from Angers who said Mass at
the estate had called it. Something to look up to for support
and inspiration. And, because of that, he had an obligation
to live a certain way. It was not a choice. It had never been a
choice.

Divorcing one's wife to marry an illegitimate American
commoner was not an acceptable manner of behaving.

He winced. Marie-Louise. His father and hers had been
friends forever, had been in the same hunt. Marie-Louise's
home in Brissac was similar to Philippe's in Angers: a castle
nestled on an estate, with acres and acres of woods and
rolling fields, with horses and stables and a whole subculture
of people who lived only to serve her family. In return, her
family supported those people, and behaved in a certain
manner.

Neither he nor Marie-Louise had ever questioned the
marriage plans when they had been announced, although it
was clear to both of them when they saw each other at the
hunt or at dances that there was no attraction present.
Philippe's mood was gay, energetic, fun-loving; Marie-
Louise was withdrawn, choosing her prayer books and her

rosary over any male company. She would have preferred to
enter a convent, she told Philippe on their wedding night
when, frustrated at arousing no passion in her, he fell back
on the pillows and asked what was wrong. She had always
wanted to be a nun, but she obeyed her father's wish, which
was to join the de Bousquet family of Brissac with the de
Montclairs of Angers. It was what he had wanted, and it was
done.

Philippe didn't blame her. How could he, having himself
agreed to his own father's marital plans? It *was* what was
done. One did not marry for love. That was what the
commoners did. The nobility was different—more refined,
more restrained. One made suitable marriages, and, if love
followed, that was a bonus. Not a prerequisite.

Marie-Louise knew that there had been women before
her. That was done, too—the young count playing the field
while he still could. And Philippe—usually accompanied by
the farrier's son, which really *wasn't* done—had had more
than his share of conquests, even resorting once to the
family law firm to help him disentangle himself from a
difficult situation, involving a husband and a possible
pregnancy. . . . But that was all right, because in the end he
did what was expected of him. And if there were other
women, afterwards? As long as he was discreet . . . Marie-
Louise deplored the women just as she deplored his sexual
urges, but she did what was correct, too. She was the
Countess de Montclair, and had a role to live out. She rode
in the local hunt and produced a son who would in turn
inherit the estate. She went to daily Mass at the castle chapel
and prayed for the soul of her wandering husband. She
graciously attended the local fair once a year and consented,
at Christmastime, to be photographed with the mayor of
Angers. It wasn't her fault that life hadn't given her what she
wanted, any more than it had given Philippe what he
wanted.

Philippe had, in fact, never known what he wanted. Not
until now. Fulfillment had come in the shape of a small
airplane company called Aeroméchanique, and love had
come in the shape of a beautiful American commoner, a
wealthy society woman who flaunted her lack of respect for
rules and regulations, who announced to the world her
disregard for how things were done. How could he blame

Amanda for her frustration? And how could he, in all honesty, blame Marie-Louise for her behavior?

He pulled Amanda closer to him. "I know," he said again, helpless and hopeless. There was no way out. They were, all of them, trapped in a game that they had never wanted to play. Somewhere, someone was moving them all around into predetermined spaces.

Philippe wondered what the next move would be.

They went out dancing again that night, and, as always in public, Amanda reverted to her society self, that part of her personality that would remain forever shallow. "Philippe, darling, there's such a recherché new place to go on the Champs-Elysées, it's called La Pergola, we absolutely must be seen there!"

He agreed, and they went, and as always when he was out with Amanda he forgot about everything but the gaiety that seemed to envelop her. The lights were glittering on the Champs-Elysées, sparkling with promises that one could only dream of having kept, and the air was alive with excitement. Philippe knew that it was not the night, nor the lights, that made the real promise: It was Amanda.

Amanda danced like she made love, like no one he had ever known before, graceful and fluid. While everyone around them struggled to learn the steps to the newest rage, a dance called the fox-trot, he was only too aware of how many eyes followed them as he and Amanda moved boldly across the floor.

The drama of the dance suited Amanda. Her cheeks were glowing, her blue-green eyes sparkling. Philippe drinking champagne, dancing with her and kissing her, knew that such pure pleasure had to be the best thing in the world.

La Pergola was everything that Amanda had heard it to be. The dazzling dance floor was filled with elegant men dressed in tuxedos. Women in long, slinky dresses with short sleeves exposing powdered arms and bangle bracelets, wore turbans and short bobbed hair; pearls, chokers, and diamonds glittered in the light. Sly remarks could be overheard at every turn. There were dinner tables there as well, raised well above and away from the dance floor but placed so that the diners could watch and enjoy the drama being acted out below them. Amanda glowed in the heady atmosphere, which was only partially due to the profusion of hothouse flowers in gleaming silver buckets lining the floor.

Friends of theirs were there, people they had met the year before, in London, and one or two that Philippe didn't know. A heavyset man with a monocle and a diamond pinky ring sat down next to him at the small table littered with empty glasses and bottles while Amanda was in the powder room. "Do you mind, old son?" he asked politely, and Philippe shook his head. "Not at all." The man was older than he was, with the pasty coloring that comes with excess weight and too much time spent indoors. His hair was brilliantined and combed carefully back, and he was dressed with meticulous care in exceedingly correct white tie and tails. He had, in all, the air of a shortsighted penguin.

"Splendid place, this, what?" he asked vaguely, looking around the room.

Splendid it was indeed, with its massive bird cages filled with exotic plumages, with its dance floor extending off into the distance, with its expensive prices for drinks. Philippe smiled. "One wonders," he murmured, "how long it will last."

The man turned his monocle on Philippe. "What an observant chap you are," he said. "Do I know you?"

"Possibly not," Philippe said smoothly, extending a hand. "Philippe de Montclair, at your service."

The Englishman took it in his own pudgy fingers. "Marcus Copeland," he said. "Delighted to meet you."

Philippe raised his eyebrows. "Marcus Copeland?" he asked. "Of Copeland Industries?"

"Yes." The voice was vague, the eyes behind the monocle were not. "And, as we're on the subject, you must be the Count who is involved with Aeroméchanique, aren't you? We supply most of your steel, I believe. I've seen you on the letterhead. We correspond with your associate, chap called Beaumont."

Philippe opened his mouth to answer, but then there was a flurry of movement and Amanda emerged from the powder room, laughing with two other women beside her. She was dressed in black. The skirt fell gracefully to the floor, its silk moving with and against her body. The dress

was a foil to her light complexion and flaxen blond hair, but
most dramatic was the low-cut back which revealed an
expanse of milky white skin never seen before in public. The
dress had caused quite a stir, and Amanda was reveling in'
the attention. She was meticulously made up, too, with blue
liner glittering around her eyes and spots of pink on her
cheeks. She wore pearls entwined in her long hair as well
and three strands of pearls around her neck, a present from
Philippe. Marcus Copeland adjusted his monocle again. "I
say," he breathed. "What a perfectly ravishing girl!"

Philippe was feeling expansive. "Would you care to meet
her?" he asked, diffidently, and the monocle turned to him.
"You know her?"

Amanda didn't give Philippe any time to respond. She
flounced, rather than walked, over to the table and addressed him directly. "What a tiresome old fuddy-duddy
you look! Do come and dance with me."

"Of course." Philippe stood up, and, with him, Marcus
Copeland. "Amanda, wait a moment, I'd like you to meet
someone." He watched her gaze travel past him and settle
politely on the Englishman. "Miss Amanda Lewis, Mr.
Marcus Copeland."

"So pleased," Amanda murmured, allowing her hand to
be kissed; and then, almost at once, she turned back to
Philippe. "*Now* can we dance?"

As they moved out onto the floor, neither of them was
aware of Marcus Copeland staring after Amanda, sheer
adoration in his eyes.

Christmas, 1913. Philippe, torn and unhappy, went home to
Angers and Marie-Louise and little Pierre for the holiday
season. Eric, with the excitement of his Marseilles trip still
sparkling all around him, took Amanda to London for two
weeks.

During a dance at a friend's estate, Marcus Copeland
appeared at Eric's elbow. "Beaumont, old man, I see that
you have Miss Lewis with you."

Eric turned to him in surprise, taking his hand out of his
pocket to shake Marcus's hand. "Marcus! How nice to see
you. I didn't realize that you were acquainted with
Amanda."

"We met, once." The gentleman in the monocle turned to

her for a moment, laughing, and as usual the center of attention, and then back to Eric. "It seems that Aeroméchanique would have a monopoly on beautiful women."

Eric inclined his head, accepting the tribute to Sarah behind the words, and then sipped his champagne. "Bit cold, wouldn't you say?"

"Devastatingly cold, old man, devastatingly cold." Marcus cleared his throat, adjusting the collar of his tuxedo. "Look here, old man, I know that it's damned forward of me, but do you think that I might ask her to dance?"

"Amanda?" Eric lifted his eyebrows. "Don't ask me, ask her. She makes up her own mind, you know." He hesitated. "But, Marcus—"

"Yes?"

"Don't go falling for her, or anything like that. She'll break your heart."

"I daresay," the Englishman replied heavily, "that she already has."

Philippe shook out the newspaper, trying to see it all. This was difficult with Amanda sitting in his lap. "How can I keep up on current affairs if you're in my way?" he complained good-naturedly.

"Why are you always reading that silly paper, anyway?"

"I like to know what's happening in the world," he explained patiently. "Besides, you'd like this bit. The Caillaux woman's been acquitted." He looked up to Amanda's uncomprehending stare. "You know, the wife of the Minister of Finance; she shot the owner of *Le Figaro* to prevent damning documents to be published. Aren't you interested?"

Amanda bit his ear. "I'm more interested in you."

Frowning, Eric looked over from across the room. "Keep it down, you two, won't you?" he asked.

"Eric," Amanda said to Philippe, "never reads the newspaper."

"Eric isn't interested in keeping up with the times," said Philippe. "He's only interested in the future."

"The future of airplanes," Amanda corrected. "Which is tiresome."

"It's more interesting," Eric rejoined, "than anything the

newspapers have to say." He stood up. "I have to go into the city. What's it like out?"

"Aha!" Philippe responded with a smile. "He doesn't read newspapers, but he still wants to know what's in them. Here we are: Wednesday, sixth of June, nineteen-fourteen—fair and sunny. There you are."

"Does anybody want to go with me?" Eric was already pulling on his sweater, an indication of his mistrust in newspapers and forecasts.

"Does it look like I do?" Amanda asked. "I'm trying my best to seduce the Count de Montclair, but it's an uphill battle, I assure you."

Eric glanced over at Philippe, who shrugged. "Mademoiselle Lewis is very persuasive," he said, and Eric smiled.

"I'll see you later, then," he said.

"*Much* later," Amanda said, tossing the newspaper on the floor.

Eric was still smiling as he stepped out the door. There was a letter in the mailbox, addressed to Philippe from Marie-Louise. He frowned a moment before putting it in his pocket. He would give it to Philippe later, he decided. Better let them have their time while they could.

He stopped at the post office on his way down the street; he had his own correspondence to mail—a letter to René Lorin, in Marseilles. They were still doing work together on the jet propulsion idea, although they had hit upon some snags. An order to Copeland Industries for more lightweight steel; another letter to a fellow in Germany called Hugo Junkers, who had written to Eric asking questions about design and wondering if he could visit Aeroméchanique's laboratory. And then, finally, he had composed a letter to Sarah's parents in California—the long-delayed, put-off letter. It had been months since he had written to them last, sending a card from London wishing them a happy Christmas and New Year.

He put the letters in the box and continued down the street, walking briskly towards the taxi stand near the park. What was there, after all, to say to the Martins? That the grief of his loss had dulled with time? That sometimes he had to close his eyes to conjure up the image of their daughter before him? The letters had been easy at first, filled with the sharp pain in which they had all taken refuge. Easy to fill the pages with his grief, his tears, his desire for darkness and death.

Now he had lived through his second Christmas without her, and she was an ache, a pain inside him, something that he carried with him always. Mrs. Martin had told him that he had to get on with life, that it was time for him to start a new family. He knew that there could be no other. That was not the issue. The issue, for Eric, was that he had emerged from the blackness of despair into a gray world of nothingness. Even the sharp horrible pain, the racking sobs, the sense of abandonment had been better than this. Even the anger at Sarah for leaving him had been better than this. This was nothing; this was limbo.

This, Eric reflected, was what purgatory must be. Long, gray days filled with neither happiness nor despair, the ache of loss without the comforts extended to the newly bereaved. How could he talk to her parents about that? How could he talk to anyone about that?

The sun was shining brightly, but to Eric, sitting in the taxi and staring morosely at the scenery passing by, it was as though the gray twilight would never end.

Eric wasn't home when Philippe and Amanda ate dinner, served politely and efficiently by Annie, and he wasn't home by the time they decided to go to bed. "Maybe he met someone," Philippe suggested with a smile, and Amanda turned to him.

"You're right," she said slowly, as though the thought had only then crossed her mind. "What Eric needs is a woman."

"I don't like that look," Philippe said, taking off his clothes across the bed from her. "If he does, he's perfectly capable of choosing one himself."

"Don't be silly," Amanda said, turning down the linen sheets. "He's not. He's got his head in the clouds all the time with all of his silly notions about Aeroméchanique, and he doesn't even notice things. It's up to us to introduce him to somebody suitable."

"Somehow," Philippe said, getting in bed, "it seems to me that 'somebody suitable' sounds pretty dismal. Sarah's a hard act to follow, you know."

Amanda turned down the gas lamp and crawled into bed with him. "People can love again," she said. "It would be good for him."

Philippe put his arms around her and kissed her neck. "Mmm," he said into the darkness. "Let's not worry about Eric now."

She smiled and reached down under the sheets. "Ooh!" she cried in mock surprise. "*You're* certainly not thinking about Eric now."

"No," he said, moving on top of her. "And neither should you."

Amanda woke up long before Philippe did, which was unusual. The sky was only faintly streaked with pink. It took an instant to realize why she was awake, and she almost didn't have enough time to run the long corridor to the bathroom.

She knelt on the cold tiled floor, throwing up into the bucket, her forehead covered with sweat. At last she was done, and slowly cleaned up after herself. She splashed cold water on her face. In the early dawn, she looked gray and drawn.

She tiptoed back to her room, and Eric's door opened, the door to the bedroom he and Sarah had shared and where he now slept alone. "Are you all right?" He asked in a whisper, looking at her face, and Amanda nodded. "Too much to eat last night," she whispered with a small smile, and he nodded and closed his door again.

Philippe was still asleep. She slid under the covers and replaced his arm over her and listened to his even breathing, and all the while her heart was hammering with fear. She stared up at the ceiling and watched the sunrise reflecting on the mirror that Philippe had placed there, and the fear and nausea churned and churned inside of her.

Amanda didn't talk about her fears for a long time, as though not talking about it would somehow make it less real.

She knew, of course. A few women do: Some mysterious inner voice assures them that it is so, and they don't think, or count, or wonder—they just know. They perceive movement before there is movement, life before there is life. They listen to their bodies and their inner changes, and they know. Amanda knew almost at once. It didn't take the early-morning dashes to the bathroom to tell her about it; she knew, with a certainty that was as terrible as it was absolute.

But still she pleaded flu symptoms or food poisoning whenever Philippe or Eric would observe the time she spent being sick. Uncharacteristically, she didn't complain and she didn't talk about it at all.

She made love with Philippe at night and would lie awake long after he had fallen asleep, one arm draped over her, his moustache tickling her bare shoulder. Sometimes terror would grip her and she would have to cover her mouth to keep from crying out, to keep from waking Philippe and telling him about it so that he could make everything all right. Philippe always made everything all right, somehow.

Even Amanda knew that Philippe wasn't going to be able to make this all right. So she lay awake and looked at her own terrified image in the mirror over the bed, and thought terrible fear-filled thoughts. The cold, clutching hand in her stomach clawed at her, tighter and tighter.

And still she didn't tell him. If she didn't talk about it, then maybe it would go away.

Chapter Eleven

By July of 1914 even Eric was showing some interest in what was being written in the newspapers.

One couldn't not notice, after all: Everyone, everywhere, was taking an interest in what was happening in the Balkans, and talking about very little else, which Amanda, as usual, found distinctly "tiresome."

Philippe seemed to be aware of it all from the start. He read about the assassination at Sarajevo, the murder of the Archduke Ferdinand and the Countess Sophie, and spoke of it one evening at dinner. It was one of the "little soirées" that Amanda loved so dearly, when they would invite a few people over to eat and drink and talk and listen to Amanda play the piano, at which, surprisingly, she had become almost accomplished, and she was immediately angry with Philippe for bringing up politics.

"Who cares, anyway?" she demanded at once. "Philippe, darling, it's not as though he was such a very distinguished person, don't you know." She giggled. "Actually, I always thought he looked a little silly, with that horrid uniform and that great drooping moustache."

"And Sophie," added one of the guests, the wife of the under secretary to the British ambassador, who suffered under the inauspicious name of Prunella, "is hardly a heroine. You'll have to cast your characters better, Philippe, if you want to make a melodrama out of this one. You know, of course, what they told her when she married Ferdinand."

"No, what?" asked Amanda eagerly, and Lady Prunella leaned towards her, dropping her voice dramatically. "My dear, she wasn't even royalty, and her children can't inherit. She couldn't even be seen in public with her husband!"

"Well," Eric said absently, looking into his wineglass,

"she was in public with him at Sarajevo, it would seem, and it cost her her life."

"I wonder who will succeed, then, if their children can't," Amanda mused.

Philippe looked around the table and shook his head. "You don't know what you're talking about," he said, explosively. "This isn't just an isolated incident, the murder of two obscure people. Something terrible is about to happen."

"Come now, Philippe, old man," said Prunella's husband comfortably, between mouthfuls of roast duckling. "A minor member of Austrian royalty gets killed. That happens, you know, and more often than you think. No need to make an international incident of it, what?" He chuckled. "Amanda, dear, have you seen that Charlie Chaplin film playing at the Odeon? We've been meaning to make an evening of it one of these days and take it in, what?"

"I'm not the one making an international incident of it," Philippe said doggedly. "Vienna is going to do that quite nicely, you mark my words."

Eric looked up at him. "Why do you think so?"

"They've been panting for a reason to go to war for months now. Just a nice little war to let the Serbs know who's in charge, and to show off their nice uniforms that have been gathering dust all these years."

Amanda sighed. "Such an obsession with uniforms. The Archduke was always wearing one, even without a war in sight."

"Well," said the under secretary to the British ambassador, leaning back and wiping his mouth with the linen napkin, "even if there is a lovely little war between Austria and—who did you say, old chap?"

"I didn't," said Philippe evenly, looking at him over the rim of his wineglass.

"Er. Quite. Well, in any case, even if there is a war, there's no reason to expect it to involve France! Just a minor disagreement, what?"

Philippe sighed and downed the rest of his wine in a single gulp. "Let's hope that you're right, Lord Charles. Let's just hope that you're right."

But there was no hope in Philippe's voice.

* * *

Eric was corresponding regularly with Hugo Junkers, the German airplane manufacturer who wanted to perfect a fighting airplane: one that didn't simply drop bombs on targets, as had the Aeroméchanique planes of the Tripoli war, but one that would actually fire on a target, perhaps even another airplane. Eric had been interested in the problem from the start. The prototypes he had set up at the Aeroméchanique hangar all encountered the same difficulty: to fire forward meant firing through a turning propeller, which more often than not deflected the bullet back onto the hapless pilot. Henri was complaining about the results, even with the imitation ammunition that they were using for the tests.

"It's all a matter of timing, if we can just work out the timing mechanism," wrote Hugo.

"Soon. I'll have it soon," Eric responded.

Philippe came out to the hangar frequently that summer, sometimes accompanied by Amanda. She wasn't feeling well these days, kept complaining of back pains, and sometimes spent an entire day just laying on a sofa, which wasn't like Amanda at all. He watched Eric work and talked with him, but when he saw the letters from Hugo he frowned.

"He's German, isn't he?"

"Right. From Düsseldorf originally, I think."

Philippe grabbed a chair and, turning it around, sat down on it backwards so that he could lean his elbows on the back. "Eric, that may not be such a good idea."

"What are you talking about?" Eric was studying the formulas on the papers in front of him. The answer was in the timing. Somehow the firing of the bullets and the rotation of the propeller had to be synchronized.

Philippe took off his straw boater hat for a moment and scratched his head. "Because Germany's getting involved with the war."

"On whose side?" Eric asked flippantly. He really didn't care.

"Do you really think that you can spend all of your days out here working on airplanes and never think about what they might mean to people? Fighter-airplanes, that's what you're building. Well, fighter-airplanes don't exist in a void, *mon ami*. They've got to be fighting somebody. Have you ever thought about that?"

Eric sighed and looked up from his calculations. "Now you're sounding like Sarah. Philippe, I'm not a politician, and I don't pretend to understand what is happening in the world. If I stop and think about it at all, it scares me to death. That's not my business." He took a deep breath. "My business is building airplanes. Good, safe, sound airplanes that will do what the politicians and the world want them to do. Hugo Junkers and I have become friends. Do you want me to end that friendship just because the government of his country—over which, I assume you will grant, he has very little control—has decided to get involved in this thing in Serbia? Or should I stop studying and perfecting my craft just because someone that I don't know and that I don't control might choose to use it in ways I wouldn't like?" He mopped his forehead.

"It's just not that simple, Philippe, or that clear. You're so damned determined to see the world in black and white, in good and evil, in right and wrong. Well, let me tell you, *mon ami*, I wish that it could be that simple. It's only simple for the politicians, the men in Vienna, who have the luxury to sit back and think thoughts of war. The rest of us, we're too busy living to be able to think simple thoughts like that."

Philippe opened his mouth to say something, and then closed it again. He watched Eric for a moment and then stood up. "You're right, of course," he said heavily. "And it's a luxury that will catch up with us all eventually, I'm afraid." He walked to the door of the hangar and looked out over the field, parched with summer. "God, Eric, I'm so scared."

Eric looked up in surprise. "Scared? About the war?"

"About the war. About the changes. About everything." He turned back to face Eric and leaned against the hangar door, standing in the precise place where Sarah had stood when Eric first met her. "It feels like it's moving too quickly, like things are happening too fast. One moment we're all here, being regular people, living normal lives, and now Sarah is gone and Amanda is sick, and downtown they're talking about mobilization."

"Mobilization?" Eric's eyes widened. "Mobilization in France?"

"If Germany does enter the war, it's not Serbia they're out to get," Philippe said. "It's France."

Eric stared at him for a moment, then shook his head and turned back to his work. "It doesn't really matter, does it?" he asked. "They'll never get past the eastern border. The French Army is too good for them."

"Perhaps. Perhaps not. That's the kind of nationalistic pride that sometimes does people in."

Eric shook his head. "There's no pleasing you, is there? First off, I don't have enough nationalistic pride because I associate with a German, and then I have too much nationalistic pride because I believe in our army. I don't know what to say to you anymore." He worked for a moment in silence, unaware of the brooding expression darkening Philippe's face. "Cheer up, Philippe. Even if there is a war, it'll be over by Christmas."

"Yes," Philippe said, his voice hollow. "It'll be over by Christmas."

Amanda finally told Philippe.

She approached him tremulously, not knowing how to find the words, how to convey the truth. She wondered if he would blame her, or, worse, if he would hate her for it.

Philippe was sitting in the living room of the house on the rue de Verdun and staring at the newspaper, an activity which had become more of an obsession of late: reading the newspaper, and thinking for hours about what each piece of news meant. Amanda and Eric had agreed that there was very little they could do if a war did indeed erupt in their midst. In any event, it wouldn't be such a long and terrible war, or so everybody said. But Philippe seemed to take it all very much to heart. He went and listened to the politicians and their speeches, and he read all of the posters that were suddenly appearing around town, and he came home and read the newspapers. He didn't seem to like anything that he saw or heard or read, and neither Eric nor Amanda could understand why he was so obsessed with it all.

When Amanda told Philippe her news, the sun was blazing in the window, hot and oppressive. The only really happy creatures in the house those days were the potted plants, stretching their leaves to the heat and sunlight. Amanda was sleepy and lethargic: She had taken to smoking opium in the mornings because it made her less nauseated, but combined with the heat it made her tired all the time. Long, hot days stretched out into longer hot evenings, most

of it spent lying down and reading or sleeping, the haze of
the drug and the haze of the summer blending into one.

Philippe seemed irritated this particular day, which
wasn't an auspicious beginning.

"I wanted to talk to you," she said softly, hesitantly.

He looked up from the newspaper, anger in his dark eyes.
"They're going to war, and there's no reason for it," he
said.

"I don't want to talk about the war," Amanda said, softly.
"Please, Philippe," and she went over and sat next to him
on the sofa, curling her body up next to his, like a cat. Her
closeness and the sultry fragrance of her perfume washed
over him, and there was a part of him that wanted to
respond, that wanted to hold her, to recapture the intimacy
they had shared not so very long ago, before the summer
and the assassination and all the talk. But the world was
moving too fast and his thoughts were moving with it.

"The Germans are demanding that Russia demobilize,"
he continued. "I think they'll declare war within the week,
and we won't be far behind."

"Philippe, for God's sake!" Amanda exclaimed impatiently. "I'm pregnant!"

There was a long moment of silence, and she bit her lip.
She hadn't meant for it to come out quite that way, but it
was too late to take back the words. The silence stretched
on, interminable and unbearable, and then Philippe slowly
lowered his newspaper and turned to look at her. "You're
joking, of course," he said at length.

"I'm not joking." Amanda's eyes started to fill with tears.
"I'm pregnant."

He looked at her and then looked away, letting the
newspaper fall to the floor of its own accord. He put his
elbows on his knees and his forehead in his hands. "Oh, my
God," he said softly. "Oh, my God."

She moved uncomfortably. "I'm not happy about it,
either," she said. "I didn't mean to do it, Philippe." The
tears came, burning and painful, and she cried until, after
what seemed to be a long time, he turned back to her and
put his arms around her and rocked her back and forth, back
and forth, as though she were a child in his arms. "It's all
right," he whispered. "It'll be all right."

But he didn't know how.

* * *

Philippe went downtown almost every day, and listened to what people were saying, at his bank and at the law firm of Beneteau and Giroux, which handled the de Montclair estate.

It was upon coming out of the law offices one day that he heard the news he had been most fearing. Over at the post office, a great crowd of people, mostly men, had gathered and Philippe instinctively walked over to join them. He couldn't hear, however, and with a few apologies elbowed his way to the front of the group.

And then he knew. He could see it in their faces. The few women present were crying, and the men looked tense and drawn, all of them listening intently to the speaker and exchanging hurried glances with each other. One young man towards the front of the crowd had taken off his neat straw boater hat and was, very quietly, shredding it in his hands. Philippe looked at him for a long moment before moving on.

It was a military man speaking, he realized as he moved closer to the front of the crowd. Unrecognizable, but wearing the dapper uniform of France and standing with that stiff ramrod posture that bespeaks the career military officer. Philippe took a deep breath and held it in and tried to listen, but there was still too much noise. He turned to the man on his right, a fellow about his own age, a student who wore the scarf of the Sorbonne. "What is he saying?"

The young student looked as shocked as Philippe felt. "General mobilization," he answered, his voice low and cracked. "General mobilization of all French citizens. Effective today."

Philippe turned back toward the speaker, whose voice was now carrying over to them somewhat better. ". . . We cannot have the Huns marching into our city! We must defend ourselves."

There was a question shouted from the crowd: "Will it come to that, General? Should we tell our families to flee Paris?"

The man in uniform stiffened perceptibly. "Absolutely not! We are French! They will never cross our borders! We will be marching in Berlin long before they get in sight of Notre Dame!"

Someone else shouted, "How long can we expect the war to last?"

"A few months, my boy, a few months. We will win it in no time at all. You'll all be back home for Christmas!"

There was a ripple of approval through the crowd at that, and the mood of fear seemed to lift, magically, from almost all of the men. One or two people elbowed their neighbors, and jokes were passed. Smiles broke out on faces, and only one or two people like the student and the young man shredding his boater shook their heads. Someone else spoke up, "It sounds like a lovely little war, General," and there was another ripple of approval at that.

Philippe didn't share in the smiles. He turned abruptly and fought his way back through the crowd, suddenly needing air. The women were still crying. *They know*, he thought. The women always know the truth. They don't delude themselves with the little games that we play. The women know. . . . Oh, God, Amanda. Amanda, lovely, laughing Amanda. Amanda was pregnant, and the war was beginning, and there seemed to be precious little he could do about either of those things.

And if the prevailing mood was to accept the war as some sort of lark, a way of showing "once again" French superiority, a game to demonstrate virility and courage, then there was nothing that he could do about that, either.

He would soon be off to war.

Robert Beneteau at the law firm had made Philippe's position clear. "We'll do our best to arrange a safe place at the front for you, Monsieur le Comte, but please understand that it is your duty and your obligation to march off with the rest of them. A bit of noblesse oblige, like it or not. It's times like these that the people look to you to set an example."

"And," Philippe had said softly, "if I disagree with the policy? If I think that this entire war is sheer folly? If I believe that we are entering it for no other sake than a damaged and guilty national pride?"

The attorney had sat down across from him and refilled his glass of brandy. "Then, Monsieur le Comte," he had said carefully, "you still go. No matter how others behave—and that includes personalities in the government. Don't get me wrong, I'm not defending them or their foreign policy—but no matter how others behave, you have an obligation to do the right thing. It comes with the territory, I'm afraid. You are a de Montclair. That name carries a certain responsibility with it."

"In that case," Philippe said heavily, "I must write another will."

"Of course, Monsieur le Comte," the lawyer said smoothly. "That would be entirely proper."

"Not necessarily," Philippe said, with a glint of humor in his eye. "Wait until you see some of the provisions I want in it."

"I am sure that you have made and will continue to make the right decisions." Beneteau glanced at the clock on the mantelpiece, a handsome antique with chased-gold hands and blue enamel figures. "Perhaps we could begin now?"

"Yes," Philippe said, after a moment of hesitation. "Let us begin."

The changes had been made. He was back at the house he felt the most comfortable in, with the woman he had come to love above any other, and his closest friend in the world nearby. Now was the time for peace and serenity and happiness.

Now was the time for war.

The men in France left for the war, proclaiming, "Long live the tomb. Death is nothing!"

Philippe departed Paris at the end of August, to spend a week at the estate before leaving with the cavalry for the front.

The de Montclair family had always been cavalry. And Philippe de Montclair would carry on that tradition.

The night before leaving, he stayed at home with Amanda and Eric. Amanda quietly curled into the crook of his arm, her head on his shoulder. None of them remembered, later, what they talked about; it wasn't what they said, in the end, that mattered. Only that he was leaving.

Eric would not be going to the front. The government valued his work with Aeroméchanique above any contribution he might make in the field, and he had been instructed to stay in Paris—which he did, willingly. Eric had no more desire than had anyone to go off and fight in a war that seemed to be, at best, futile. The politicians, the newspapers, the public was calling it a "lovely little war," but Eric was making the airplanes that were going to be fighting in that war, and he knew that it would be anything but lovely. The timing mechanism he had placed on the artillery was working, and the fighter planes would be completed and ready to be sold by the end of October at the very latest, according to Eric and Hugo's calculations.

So the three of them had sat and talked, as though nothing in particular was happening. That night Philippe and Amanda made passionate love in their bed under the mirrors, and she cried when he entered her, because already she was afraid that it would be the last time.

Then he was gone, to Angers and then east, where the fighting had already started on the Belgian border. After the door closed behind him, Amanda turned to Eric and put her arms around him and cried and cried on his shoulder. She would stay with him, they had decided. Until the war was over, and the baby born, Eric would take care of her.

A week later, Eric opened the mailbox and found a letter from Philippe awaiting him.

31 August, 1914

My friend,

Well, here we are. Hard to believe that this is good-bye. But I'm quite sure of it, you know. It's going to take a lot more than a few of us shedding blood on some hopeless battlefield somewhere to win this war—much less to convince people that there's absolutely no reason to be fighting it in the first place. But we all have to live up to what's expected of us, somehow, and this seems to have become my lot.

I'm not coming back, Eric. You can grin and act cheerful and talk about Christmas until you're blue in the face, but it won't make any difference. I know it, I can feel it in my soul, a cold clammy hand inside of me lateatnight,inthedarkness.I'mnotcomingback.Lorraine will be my first battle, and my last. And God, it's hard to leave just now, with Aeroméchanique doing so splendidly and Amanda pregnant and all. I suppose that I couldn't have chosen a worse time to go and die. I suppose that she'll hate me for it. But you understand, don't you, why I feel as though I have no other choice?

Listen, *mon vieux*. I've made some arrangements, and I want you to know about them. You're my friend, I trust you with my life and my soul, and God knows with my assets. Marie-Louise would muck everything up hopelessly if left to her own devices, and in any case I don't want her knowing any more than she does about Amanda. It will be hard enough for her, and for little Pierre, too, as it is, without knowing that my mistress is expecting my child as well. You'll see to it that no one talks to Marie-Louise, won't you? She'll be fine, in time. All that she ever wanted was to do what was proper. I only had time to give her one child (though thank God it was a son). She may remarry eventually, and have more children, and be someone else's correct wife. It really doesn't matter much to me anymore. Nothing seems to matter to me much anymore.

God, but I'm tired.

All right. I've made all these arrangements through Beneteau and Giroux. They can be trusted to take care of things properly, but I want you to know exactly what the lay of the land is, so to speak.

I'm leaving my family money—or most of it, in any case—to Marie-Louise and Pierre. Marie-Louise will expect it, and it's only proper that she should have enough to care for herself and for little Pierre, and live in comfort at the chateau. She'll probably use the money wisely. She's that type. Conservative. No risks and no adventure.

I'm keeping out 25 percent of the de Montclair estate money for Aeromćchanique—for you, *mon ami*. I don't want our dream dying just because I'm going off to get myself killed in some quest that I don't even begin to understand. The company has to go on. If nothing else succeeds in this life, Eric, I want that company to live. It's the only really significant thing that I've done with my life.

God, do you remember that night? Back on the estate, at the chateau, when we were first starting out, and drunk as roosters, sitting with the bottles all around us in the shed and you under that motorcar with grease all over you. It feels as though it was just last night. I gave you your wrench that night, *mon ami*, your lucky wrench. We drank and pledged that we would stay together and would write our names on the sky.

Well, my name's going to be blazing across the sky in spurts of artillery fire somewhere in the east, so it's going to have to be you, now—you, and Aeroméchanique. Don't forget that night, Eric, and for God's sake don't forget the dreams. We were going to reach for the stars, *mon vieux*. And soon I'm going to be up there with them watching you, and waiting for you to do it for us both.

I'm taking care of Amanda and the baby, too. I'm giving her stock in Aeroméchanique—all my stock, in fact, or almost: 49 percent for her; 2 percent for the lawyers to keep them going; and, of course, you have the other 49 percent, so there it is. In trust for the child I'll never know. The money from the estate will keep the company going if you should fall on hard times, and the company will keep her baby going. That's the best that I can do for her. I love her, and I want to be sure that my child doesn't want for anything. Frankly Amanda is so scatterbrained that she might not think about taking care of it. Keep an eye on her for me, won't you, Eric? She'll be all right in the end, but I'd like to think about you staying close to her, and staying close to the child, too.

God how I'm going to miss her—her mischievous laughter, and her bright eyes, and her devil-may-care attitude. She was all the sunshine, all the light that I could ever ask for in my life. I know you understand. I saw the way that you and Sarah loved each other. I only wish that we had had your courage—to seize the moment while it is at hand, and not to worry about all the rest.

Time proved you right and me wrong, *mon ami*, with Sarah getting killed in that god-awful crash and now me, off to die in some forsaken wilderness. I wish . . . oh, there are a thousand things that one wishes at times like this, aren't there? And we can't fill our lives up with 'if only's,' as you know only too well.

So tired . . . It's getting hard to write, and morning's not far off now. The sky's getting gray in the east. The east . . . oh, God. I'll give Sarah your greetings. Take care of things, Eric. Hold on to the dreams. Aim for the stars. And someday walk across the poppy fields and think of me lying there beneath them.

Yours in friendship and admiration,
Philippe, Count de Montclair

Chapter Twelve

*E*ric didn't show Amanda the letter.

It was much too personal, for one thing. It contained things that she couldn't understand, all the references to the early days before Sarah and Amanda had walked into their lives. Things that only he could understand. Things that he wasn't sure that he wanted Amanda or anybody else reading. He still found tears in his eyes every time he opened it and looked at it. That was his: They were his feelings; it was his pain; Philippe was his friend in ways that Amanda would never be able to understand.

As for the rest . . . well, if it happened, Amanda would find out about the terms of the will in due time. Eric himself wasn't convinced that Philippe was going to die. It could all be nothing but the emotion of the moment, which, granted, was running high and fast, and sweeping everyone up in its path, but it could well be that in a few months Philippe would be coming back.

He would, Eric told himself. He *would* be coming back.

Amanda, in the meantime, withdrew even more into herself. She smoked opium in the mornings, and slept or went for long walks in the afternoons. Even to herself, the days and weeks following Philippe's departure seemed to be lived out in a haze, where night and day were at best fragilely connected. Hours flew by and minutes ticked ominously.

She thought a great deal about the baby she was carrying. It was difficult not to. She could feel it moving, a distinct separate entity within herself that she found a little frightening. The nausea had left her, but the sense of heaviness— even though one couldn't yet discern her pregnancy by looking at her—remained.

She thought, too, about what it would be like when

Philippe returned. He had a child already, the son of his wife, who would stay forever at the estate outside of Angers and one day inherit it. She knew that the child she carried would have no such claim. And to be unmarried and with a child would not be easy—even in liberal France. Her status would change. If she were able to marry, even to someone who was obviously not the baby's father, then everyone could pretend and she and her baby would be accepted. But marriage was impossible.

And yet it was might not be such a bad thing. She had confided in Philippe her fears, and simply sharing them with him made them seem not so bad. The war was going to be over by Christmas, everybody was talking about it, and the feeling of optimism remained in the air. Philippe had spoken of the futility of it all, but Amanda wondered if that was so very important. It was not for them to decide. It was reality. They were at war with the Germans. She herself had never met a German and was quite prepared, as were most people she knew, to believe the worst of them. The French army was far superior because, as the priests were constantly reminding them, God was on the side of the French, and would route the Germans at once. Surely Philippe would be back by Christmas.

They would spend the winter ensconced here, made cozy in the big rooms by blazing fires. They might even have a small party or two of special friends, Amanda mused, to celebrate the end of the war and their imminent child. The snow would fall outside the wrought-iron gates. She wondered what it would be like to make love once she was quite pregnant and thought that, on the whole, it might be something delicious to explore. They would most certainly find out.

And then, in the spring, the baby would be born. In March, she thought, although she had not yet seen a doctor to confirm her suspicions. And they would go on living here, in this house that had seen so much love, so much caring, so much happiness and friendship. . . . It was here that she wanted to raise the child, in this place where the people were family to each other in ways that neither blood nor marriage could duplicate. This was the place, more than New York, Newport, or Cornish, where she wanted her child to grow and learn and live—with a father.

Philippe would still have his times at the estate in Angers,

of course, and there might even be another half sister or
brother; Amanda knew that, and knew that her own needs
could not dictate reality. It was a reality that she was willing
to accept, however, because she knew the other reality
within that one, the truth within the truth, which was that
Philippe's heart would always be with her on the rue de
Verdun, and he would always come back to her.

Eric did not share Amanda's hazy sense of peace, and as
the air became more brisk, his worry deepened. The Germans were drawing closer to Paris itself—only 30 kilome-
ters away and many were leaving Paris for the countryside
and the seashore. The fighter airplanes were almost completed, and already he had signed contracts with the French
government to produce them for the war. Nor was he
dealing solely with the French. The new Royal Air Corps in
England was eager to use them and had commissioned a
series of airplanes from Aeroméchanique, to be delivered in
the new year. Never mind that the Europeans were predict-
ing a quick end to the fighting: The English were far-sighted
people and assured Eric that, whatever happened, they
would follow through on their order. This was itself an
ominous sign.

Hugo Junkers, in the meantime, was subcontracting with
the Germans for the same airplanes. Aeroméchanique
would produce them, and he would pass them through his
fledgling company, putting a German manufacturing mark
on them, and thence on to the German Army. Eric felt guilty
about that. "They probably won't have the faintest idea
what to do with them, my friend," Hugo wrote to Eric, "but
one has to give the appearance of fighting for the 'cause.'
None of us, here, have yet figured out what the cause is, by
the way. Have you?"

"It seems to me," Eric wrote back, "that the war has been
conceived and planned by old men fighting for old ideals.
Which means, of course, that they're doing nothing but
leaving us all a legacy of hatred."

Sometimes, out at the hangar, Eric looked longingly into
his battered old file cabinet, and at all the folders he had
filled with his and Voisin's work on jet propulsion. There
was no time for that now. There was no time for anything
but production. He had had to hire an additional twenty
workers to keep up with the contract demands, and was in
the middle of constructing another factory as well. There

was no more time for visions, no more time for dreams, no more time for plans. There was nothing but production, production of the deadly little machines that were advancing the war.

Once in a while he could hear Sarah's voice, and her concerns. "God, Eric, it's another world up there. It puts everything in perspective, don't you see? We're all so small and insignificant, and so are our problems, and so are our quarrels. There's really nothing worth fighting over. Nothing." Yet he took her beautiful airplanes and turned them into war machines, and wondered, guiltily, what she thought of it all.

In late September, he opened the mailbox and found a letter from Marie-Louise de Montclair addressed to himself.

He held it for a long time, unopened, staring at the neat, correct penmanship and feeling the words within burning through the envelope onto his hand. Marie-Louise writing to him. The Countess never would correspond with the farrier's son. Not unless . . .

And then he ripped it open and looked at it and started to cry.

The air in the living room was hazy with smoke, a heavy, scented smoke from the water pipe Amanda had found somewhere up at Montmartre, where the opium dens were. She was sleeping, curled on the overstuffed velvet sofa, under the portrait of Napoleon. Appropriate enough, thought Eric grimly.

He had not shown her Philippe's letter; this one he could not hide.

He touched her lightly on the cheek, and she stirred and smiled in her sleep. God, he thought. Why do I have to do this? Why does all of this have to happen? It's not fair, it's not fair . . . If only they could just go back in time, and change things: Sarah would be here still, and Philippe, and they would all be laughing. . . .

Amanda woke slowly, surfacing reluctantly from a dream filled with airplanes and babies, Sarah was laughing and telling her to stay out of the mud, and Philippe was there, too, pulling her upstairs to the mirrored bedroom. And then she realized that Eric was shaking her shoulder, and talking to her. She moaned softly and opened her eyes.

He looked concerned. "Amanda. Amanda, are you awake?"

"Barely." She rubbed her eyes sleepily. "What is it?"

"Wake up first." He hesitated. "Would you like me to make you some tea?"

"No." She could feel the tendrils of sleep still clinging to her, and she tried to push them away. In her dream, Sarah had loomed over eight feet tall. She wondered if the drug weren't distorting things just a little for her. Eric was sitting on the edge of the couch, holding a letter in his hands and still looking worried. "What is it?"

He helped her sit up, and then went and fetched a rug to wrap around her. "Are you all right?"

"Yes." She focused blearily on him. "What time is it?"

"Nearly four o'clock." He hesitated. "I think that you need to read this letter."

She glanced at the envelope in his hands, and then looked back at his face, sudden certainty clutching at her stomach. "No."

He understood, and slowly nodded his head. "Yes."

She turned her face away from him, burying it in the heavy blanket Eric had brought her, the cold clamminess in her stomach slowly spreading over all of her body. Curious, a detached part of her mind noted; curious, that I'm not crying. "Tell me," she said finally, her voice muffled.

Eric cleared his throat. "He's dead, Amanda. He got killed in Lorraine, on the Belgian border, by artillery fire." He touched her shoulder, awkwardly, not sure how to ask for or give any comfort.

A shudder ran through Amanda's body, but her voice stayed calm. "How is it that his wife found out?"

"They sent someone. The army did, that is. That's the procedure, I think. They brought her back his uniform and his medals." He hesitated. "She only wrote to me because that was his parting request, and she felt compelled to honor it." His voice was grim. "She said that I am, of course, still welcome at the estate if I wish to visit my father." The words had been cold, stilted. It was clear that Marie-Louise never wished to see Eric again. She would have to, he thought, if the will held up.

Amanda wasn't thinking of Eric, or of the de Montclair estate. She wrapped her arms around her legs in the posture she had adopted, unconsciously, from Sarah, and still she didn't look at Eric. "I'd like to be alone, please," she said softly. After a long moment she felt him stand up and heard his footsteps on the rug.

The door closed behind him. And it was then that she started to cry.

Amanda waited until she was quite positive that Eric was asleep, waited until the house was coal-dark and there was no noise except for the occasional clatter of a carriage or motorcar on the street outside. She waited until she was as absolutely certain as possible that she would be alone and uninterrupted, and then she slid into Philippe's old, voluminous bathrobe and slipped down the corridor, locking herself in the bathroom.

She had taken some wire from the antique dealer's closet, the cupboard where he kept the things he used to display his artifacts, and this stiff wire was there, ready to hang a heavy portrait or suspend a lantern. Amanda had secreted it in the bedroom, waiting until nightfall with sobs of grief and fear for the only way that she could see out of the sudden imprisonment into which the news of Philippe's death had plunged her.

She sat on the edge of the large claw-footed bathtub in the candlelight, and slowly, resolutely straightened the wire. This was the only way. This was the only way, she repeated. The phrase was like a talisman against the act that she was about to perform: This was the only way.

Amanda had never thought of herself as particularly brave. She was not a Sarah Martin. She would never fly, or write, or do any of the great things that she had so admired her friend for. And even this, she knew, was the act of a coward, of a woman unable to face, alone, the consequences of her acts.

Bearing a child out of wedlock with Philippe beside her was just possible. Bearing an illegitimate child to a dead man was unthinkable.

She took a deep breath, and lowered the wire, slowly spreading her legs and feeling it enter her where she had so often welcomed Philippe, feeling the metal hard and cold and piercing. She gritted her teeth together and forced it in further, and further still, and the pain was too much, too intense, as she moved and forced it in, forced it to where the child was living and where she would kill it. She could not bear this child. She could not bear this child.

The pain was heat, intense and burning, too sharp entering the most vulnerable part of her body. It was too much. She struggled to force the wire inside and around, trying with all of her strength to kill the child she carried, and the pain spiraled up and up, inside her and around her, rising higher and higher and burning bright and hot and intense. When she knew she could not do it any longer, when the pain was far too much for her to bear, the red-hot coals inside of her too piercing and sharp and agonizing, the world suddenly turned black and dark and blessedly cool.

She never even felt it when her head hit the cold white tiles of the bathroom floor and she fainted, falling into a pool of her own blood.

She awoke, slowly and fuzzily, to a world of white.

She was in her own bed, the mirrors overhead reflecting her image, pale and small and wan with puffed eyes and a bandage on her head. There was a woman's voice somewhere off in the distance, but she didn't recognize it at first and thought that it must be Sarah.

Eric came into the room some time later, and, seeing her awake, sat down gently on the edge of the bed. "How are you feeling?" he asked, his voice soft and subdued. She shook her head.

"It's Wednesday," he said, his tone conversational. "You've been asleep since Saturday. We've been concerned."

"How—" Words, she found, were difficult to formulate.

"Annie found you early Sunday morning when she got in. I was asleep, still." He hesitated. "I—I've been feeling terrible, that you were doing that and I just slept. I find it hard to forgive myself."

She moved her head on the pillow. "It wasn't your fault." Her voice sounded low and hoarse.

He cleared his throat. "We've had the doctor in, of course. Several times, in fact. He says that you'll be quite all right before long. Just need a lot of rest, and we've got to take special care against infection."

"What about—" She couldn't finish the sentence.

Eric looked away for a long moment before turning back to her. "The baby is safe, Amanda. He can hear the heartbeat."

The world was closing in around her again, and she found that she was having trouble breathing. No. She could not. It was too much to ask. It was far too much to ask.

Eric was looking at her with concern, and she reached for him, her hands closing around his arm. "Help me," she begged him, her eyes filling with tears. "Please help me."

"What do you want me to do, Amanda?" There was pain in his voice.

"Help me. Take me to someone who will do it for me."

A spasm crossed his face. "I cannot," he said, unhappily.

She clutched at him with all of her strength. "You must. Oh, Eric, if you have any friendship for me at all, you must help me. I cannot bear this child. I cannot."

There were tears in his eyes. "My friendship for you," he said, quietly, "is exceeded only by my friendship for Philippe. Don't you see that I can't help you kill his child?"

She let go of his arm and fell back on the pillows, exhausted. "Will no one help me?" she cried, and then the tears came again. She turned and buried her face in the pillow, sobbing inconsolably. Eric reached over and touched her shoulder, but she shook his hand from her in a violent movement. "Go away," she sobbed. "Go away."

He stood, and made a helpless gesture with his hands, and finally left. And Amanda stared into space for a long time until sleep finally overtook her. This time, she had no dreams at all.

Eric noticed time passing, now, solely by the production of his airplanes. There were the fighters bound for the front and the fighters bound for England, and there was very little else.

He had not received any word from Hugo Junkers for nearly two weeks.

He spent most of his days and some of his nights out at the hangar, leaving Amanda alone in the house on the rue de Verdun to convalesce with Annie in attendance. That was all right, he reasoned. Amanda had scarcely talked to him since the day he had refused to take her for an abortion, and she was probably relieved to have him out of the house. Poor

Amanda, life wasn't shaping up according to her expectations. They were two bereaved souls living with ghosts: his Sarah, and her Philippe. But instead of comforting each other, they only found reasons to turn against each other, and the big house echoed not with their words but their silences.

He came home unexpectedly one afternoon to find Amanda dressed elegantly in a black suit he had never seen before, a chic hat on her head, and packing a suitcase. He hesitated, and then walked into the room.

"Where are you going?"

She whirled around at his voice, and dropped the clothing in her hand to the floor. "Eric! What are you doing home?"

"I came to collect some designs." He picked up the shirt she had dropped and handed it to her. "Where are you going?" She looked beautiful, better than he had seen her in months; and her slim figure in the tailored masculine suit gave no clue to her pregnancy. Her skirt was shorter than he had seen before: That was the fashion, to show the ankle and part of the calf. Sarah would have looked smashing in it.

Amanda turned back to the suitcase. "This place is becoming so dreary," she said, folding dresses and sailor shirts into it. "Like a morgue, which positively won't do. I deserve more fun than this place."

Eric leaned on her dresser and pulled a packet of cigarettes from his pocket. "So," he inquired, lighting one before passing the packet across to her, "where is it that you intend to find this fun?"

She shook a cigarette loose from the packet, lit it from his, and sat down on the bed, puffing rapidly. "London."

"You're going to London?" The shock of it went through him like a knife. He had assumed that the original plan would still hold: that Amanda would stay here, that the baby would be born in due course, and that he would look after both of them as he had promised Philippe. The thought that Amanda would leave him had never crossed his mind.

"Well, yes." She inhaled and held the smoke in for a few moments, then blew it out slowly, directly towards him. "You're a busy boy, Eric, don't say that you'll miss me."

"When are you coming back?"

"Coming back?" She looked at him blankly. "Eric, darling, that's rather the point, don't you see? I'm not coming back. Oh, it was all a lot of fun in the old days, but one simply cannot live in the past forever. One has the future to think about."

"Why do you think that your future is in London?"

"Well, I don't." She stubbed out the cigarette in an ashtray and went back to her packing. "I just know that I can't stand this horrid old house anymore." Her voice sounded defiant. "They're here, you know. Sarah and Philippe. Around every corner, down every corridor, up every staircase. I can't get away from them. And they're always laughing at me." She shivered. "I have to get away."

Eric was feeling a considerable amount of panic rising inside of him. He hadn't expected this. "Look, Amanda, we don't have to stay in this house. We can go somewhere else." He cleared his throat. "And if you're worried about the baby—well, I've been meaning to say this to you for a while, I guess that I've just gotten too busy." He rubbed out his own cigarette. "If you'd like—if it would make you feel better—I could marry you. I mean, we wouldn't be really married, not in the sense that Sarah and I were. But it would give the baby a name, and offer you a refuge, perhaps, if you'd like."

She stopped her packing a moment but still would not look at him. "Eric, darling, how biblical of you. Almost like marrying the brother's widow, isn't it? Well, no, thank you. I'm quite capable of looking after myself, and I don't want to stay in France."

"We could go someplace else."

She tossed the last few items in the suitcase and clicked it shut, her gestures bespeaking finality. "Eric, don't you understand? Don't you know why I was trying to leave before you got home? I don't want to be around you, not anymore. Don't take it personally, or anything. It's just that you're in my past. You and Sarah and Philippe. They were lovely times, Eric, and I'll cherish the memory of them. But it's time to move on."

"You don't really believe that. You're running away."

"And what of it?" Amanda said angrily. "That's my right."

He sighed and tried a different tack. "They haven't even read Philippe's will yet. Shouldn't you stay long enough to hear that?"

She looked at him directly. "I don't think so, Eric. I'm already pretty clear about what Philippe has left me, aren't you? If not, just wait around five more months."

He followed her downstairs, still arguing, still with the feeling of dread in his stomach. Philippe had told him to look after Amanda, but how was he supposed to do that when Amanda wasn't being cooperative?

A taxi was waiting for her outside the wrought-iron gates, a yellow Mercedes motorcar with its engine running. Eric followed her to the door and stood there, flanked by the stone lions that Sarah and Amanda had named one fine spring afternoon, back in those halcyon days when everything was still all right. Amanda never even looked back. She put her suitcases on the back seat of the car and got in next to the driver, adjusting the chic little black hat, and the Mercedes-Benz roared down the street in a cloud of petrol fumes. She was gone.

Eric stood for a long while in the empty doorway, as though by refusing reality he could change it, as though by denying Amanda's departure he could make her come back again. It didn't work, of course. He finally, heavily, closed the big door and went back into the living room and drew the heavy velvet draperies against the coming evening. Pouring himself a generous brandy, he went and sat in front of the cold empty fireplace.

God, how he missed Sarah. Sarah would have known what to do. Sarah would have reasoned with Amanda, or laughed at her, or somehow persuaded her to stay. Sarah would have found the words that escaped him, the compassion that he couldn't bring to the surface, the kindness that Amanda needed.

Sarah. She had been a shooting star, blazing across his sky with a brilliance he had never dreamed existed, leaving trails of white clouds in her wake. She had been a shooting star, and the sky was empty when she left it. It was all over. Sarah was dead, Philippe was dead, and Amanda was running away. It was all over.

"Is that all, Rodgers?"

"No, sir." The clerk cleared his throat discreetly. "There's a young lady to see you, Mr. Copeland, and she has no appointment. I have already told her to go away, but she insists."

"What is her name, Rodgers?"

"A Miss Lewis, Mr. Copeland, sir. A Miss Amanda Lewis."

Marcus Copeland drew in his breath sharply. This was totally unexpected. The last time he had seen Amanda was at that dreary dance over Christmastide, although he occasionally asked young Beaumont for news of her. She was in love with that other Aeromécanique chap, the Count de Montclair. Whatever could she be doing here?

He went, himself, to the door of his opulent office and found her sitting in the anteroom, elegantly dressed as always, fanning herself and looking bored. Even such a glimpse was enough to make feelings stir inside of him. He cleared his throat. "Miss Lewis?"

She looked up, then, and smiled, her eyes bright and her cheeks flushed, and the entire room lit up with her. "Mr. Copeland." She stood up, extending a hand to be kissed. "I do hope that you do᠁᠁᠁t too presumptuous of me to come and see you?" Her voice trailed off delicately, and he shook his head.

"Not at all, Miss Lewis, not at all. A pleasure, I do assure you, a pleasure. Won't you come in? Or perhaps I could take you to dinner someplace in the city?"

She smiled again. "Dinner would be lovely," she murmured. "But do let's talk first, shall we?" Her scent as she passed him was heady, intoxicating, and he found himself suddenly short of breath in her wake.

"A brandy? Or a glass of sherry? What can I offer you?" He took refuge in the formalities, and Amanda smiled again, draping herself against his desk ornamentally and preening herself. "Sherry," she said, her voice low, "would be marvelous."

"Done, then," Marcus said briskly, and occupied himself with glasses and decanter. "I can't think why sherry seems to have gone out of fashion these days," he continued. "It's a fine wine, discreet and genteel. I'm rather afraid that the cocktail has superseded it in the national palate, which is a great loss, as far as I am concerned. Ah, there you are, my dear Miss Lewis." He handed her the glass, feeling somewhat flushed, and she smiled again.

"Mr. Copeland," she said, her voice still very sweet and very light, "I have come to ask you to marry me."

There was a moment of silence. Marcus was holding in his

breath. I am an old fool, Marcus thought sadly. I am an old fool, and I'm about to become more of one.

He exhaled. "Very well, Miss Lewis. I shall be honored to marry you."

Amanda raised her eyebrows and sipped her sherry, laughing at him over the rim of her glass. "What? No questions? No reservations? Aren't you wondering why I should be coming to you like this, out of the blue, and proposing to you?"

He sat down in the large leather armchair behind his desk. "I must conclude that you have your reasons, my dear Miss Lewis. I'm not totally sure that I want to hear them." He paused, looking down at the amber liquid in his glass, and then raised his eyes to hers. "But I am too great a fool, and too totally besotted with you, not to seize this opportunity when it presents itself. I am forced to conclude that your relationship with the Count de Montclair is not entirely satisfactory?"

She turned away from him, sliding gently off the edge of the desk and walking over to the leather couch. "Philippe is dead," she said, her voice flat, like a bell with a crack in it. She sat down, tucking her feet in under her skirt, and smiled again, reaching for the mocking gaiety she had displayed earlier, the mocking gaiety with which she had always defined herself. "Besides, Paris is so gloomy, don't you think? Time to move on, don't you know?" She smiled brightly. "I do hope that you're pleased that I've moved on to you."

"My dear Miss Lewis . . . my dear Amanda. I can think of nothing that would so please me as to become your husband. Please don't think for a moment that—"

"Well, there it is," she interrupted briskly. "I'll arrange things, as we really ought to get on with it." She glanced at him. "How soon, Marcus?"

"I can get the license tomorrow." His voice was sad.

"Oh, darling, that's marvelous!" She walked over to him, almost diffidently, and put her arms around him. "Marcus, darling, I can't tell you how glad I am about this." She reached up and kissed his cheek, gently, and then disengaged herself. "I'm staying at the Saint-George," she said cheerfully. "We can talk over the details tomorrow. Good night, Marcus, dear, and thank you."

Rodgers, his clerk, came in after Amanda had left, clearing his throat and trying to seem as though he had not been listening at the door. "Will there be anything else tonight, sir?"

"I'm going to marry Miss Lewis, Rodgers," said Marcus.

Rodgers cleared his throat again. "Very good, sir."

"I expect," Marcus said heavily, sitting down and finishing off his sherry, "that she's gotten herself into some sort of trouble, and is getting out of it this way." He took a deep breath and shook his head. "Well, Rodgers, never mind. We all use people, sometimes. And to pass up the chance to marry a girl like that . . . I'm a fool, and I know it, but I'm going to do it."

"Yes, sir," said Rodgers, his face expressionless.

Marcus sighed. "Still," he mused, "I do wonder what happened in Paris to send her running off to me like this. I do indeed wonder."

Chapter Thirteen

Well, it's quite clear that we have more money at stake here than we thought we would."

Robert Beneteau, of Beneteau and Giroux, turned away from the window where he had been inspecting the rue Saint Suplice below him and frowned at his partner. Trust Giroux to belabor the obvious, he thought sourly, and reached into his pocket for his snuffbox. He delayed answering until he had consumed its contents and delicately sneezed. Knowing that Marc Giroux hated waiting, he took a deep pleasure in making him do so. At length he replaced the box in his pocket and folded his handkerchief. "So," he said, finally, "what is it exactly that you're proposing?"

The other man, younger, more heavyset, poked absently at the dead coals in the fireplace. His forehead was creased with anxiety. Beneteau had noticed that continual state of anxiousness when he first was thinking about taking the young Marc Giroux into partnership with him. Early ulcer, Beneteau's experienced eyes had predicted. But he knew how good Giroux was, too, and the partnership had benefited both of them. The firm had grown and flourished, and the offices hummed discreetly with the business of several very old, very moneyed, and very well-thought-of aristocratic families.

So far Giroux had kept the ulcers at bay.

Family solicitors, that's what the firm of Beneteau and Giroux were. Nothing difficult ever came their way; nothing unexpected. Even the death of a client caused no alarm. Clients were supposed to die, eventually. Condolences were offered to the family and friends, the appropriate will which had been appropriately filed was dealt with in the appropriate manner, and that was that. On the whole, it was a comfortable living.

There was, of course, young de Montclair; he had caused shifts in blood pressure in the office from time to time. There was, notably, the affair of that young girl back in —1907, was it, or 1908? It didn't matter. They handled that, too, with tact and discretion, and everyone was pleased with the transaction. Everyone was invariably pleased with Beneteau and Giroux's transactions.

But now, the war that was supposed to be over by Christmas was still dragging on, and the prospects looked increasingly bleak. It was February, and the invincible French forces were showing that their forward-approach-and-damn-the-enemy plan wasn't working very well.

Pity about young de Montclair, of course. A fine young man, upstanding, they had told his widow when the news came through from the front. Heroic death, and all that. Most appropriate. She had seemed distraught, poor girl. But those things happened in wartime, and de Montclairs had been fighting for their country for centuries. All very sad, and all very understandable.

But Philippe de Montclair had left them with quite a headache.

There was the American girl, for one thing; she wasn't being cooperative in the least. Taking off for London, just like that, and then suddenly married to one of the English industrialists before anyone knew what was happening. Unfortunate. It was clearly more difficult to keep track of her—and of the child that she carried—with her off and running around like that. And the Count had been very exact on that point: His lineage, bastard or not, was to be protected. Most distressing, the entire thing, but there one was.

As for that little company that he and the farrier's son had started—quite extraordinary partnership, that. It was really doing quite splendidly. He had a head for his business, had young Beaumont, there was no question about that, for all his coming from such dubious stock. He seemed to know precisely what he was doing, with those metals and those engines and so on. His airplanes had been quite the rage during the Tripolitan conflict and now were making an increasingly steady profit in this business against the Germans.

They had, in point of fact, recently engaged an accountant to come on board with the firm, simply to manage the Aeroméchanique money, and that was satisfactory indeed. Irregular, the arrangements in the de Montclair will, most irregular indeed, with so much of the stock dividends being tied up in trust for the Lewis (no, Copeland it was, now) child; but there you were. Clients could be eccentric. There was an old woman once who left her entire estate, and a large one at that, to her toy poodle. It had been done, so one had to be grateful for whatever small favors one had. And one couldn't say that young de Montclair had been anything but rational. Nevertheless, they were strange arrangements.

Moreover, as Giroux had just noted, the amount of money being made was really quite extraordinary.

Beneteau brought himself back to the present with an effort. He permitted himself one last delicate sneeze before pocketing his snuff and addressing his partner again. "What exactly do you have in mind, Marc?"

Giroux remained silent, lost in his own thoughts, poking at the dead coals, and Beneteau continued to talk. "It is a large sum of money. But nothing irregular. Everything is accounted for."

Giroux stirred. "I should think that Madame Copeland would be able to find some use for the trust fund. She does have access to the dividends. But she hasn't withdrawn any; hasn't even acknowledged its existence."

Beneteau frowned at him. "It is not our place to say what our clients should and should not do," he reminded his partner. "Madame Copeland has her own family money, as well as having recently married one of the wealthiest men in England. I should think she is managing to get by. And I need not remind you that we are responsible for managing the overall affairs of Aeroméchanique, and should be more interested in that than in what Amanda Copeland chooses to do—or not to do—with her portion of it."

Giroux shrugged. "All right. Let's talk Aeroméchanique, then. Forget Madame Copeland. I have concerns, you know. Me, I think about these things." He poked at the coals for a moment longer and then swung around to face Beneteau. "I think that Aeroméchanique should relocate."

"Relocate? Surely you are joking."

"I am not." Giroux motioned towards the window. "There is a war out there, and it's getting closer and closer every day. What would happen to us if Aeromécanique were to fall into German hands? It is not a ridiculous proposition."

"This is absurd." Beneteau's voice was brisk. "There is no viable alternative. Aeromécanique is as safe in Paris and Angers as it would be anywhere else in France."

"I wasn't thinking about France."

The older man sat down on the leather couch across from his associate. "You have gone mad," he said. "What can you be thinking?"

Giroux withdrew a letter from his pocket. "This came last week, when you were in Angers," he said. "Read it. Read it, and you will see that I am right."

Beneteau took the envelope, looked wonderingly at his partner, and slowly drew his spectacles from his pocket. Fitting them snugly on the bridge of his nose, he opened the letter and began to read.

February 12, 1915

Edward M. Buchanan, Esq.
154 Central Avenue
Los Angeles, California
USA

> To: Law Firm of Beneteau and Giroux
>   15, rue Saint-Suplice
>   Paris, France

Dear Sirs:

   It is in your capacity as representatives of the company Aeromécanique, Inc., and of its general manager, Mr. Eric Beaumont, that I have the privilege of addressing you. Even in what must seem to you Europeans as the wilds of the western United States—to wit, California—we have heard of the outstanding work that Mr. Beaumont has been doing on the design and production of airplanes, and I assure you that we are very interested indeed in the progress he is making.

   So interested, in fact, that we would like to issue a proposition. The United States Army Corps is currently contracting major work in the field of aviation from one Johnson Aircraft and Tool Co., Inc., a subsidiary of Johnson Industries, Inc. I am very sorry to inform you that Johnson Aircraft and Tool Co., Inc., is manifestly inept at the production of said airplanes, and it is only the nearsightedness for which our government is famous in such matters that manages to keep them gainful-ly employed at all, not to mention dinners on the tables of their employees.

I propose to reverse the fortunes of Johnson Aircraft and Tool Co., Inc., of the United States Army Corps, of Aeroméchanique, of Eric Beaumont, and—not altogether incidentally—of myself with one bold and brilliant move. I propose that Aeroméchanique relocate to the United States, specifically to California, where most of this sorry work is taking place. Mr. Beaumont could then subcontract work from Johnson—who I assure you will be only too happy to have a professional on 'oard, if such a nautical term may be permitted in reference to the production of airplanes—and, not incidentally, save himself should things turn nasty in your part of the world, as my spies inform me may well happen, I am sorry to say.

Do mull this over, gentlemen, and let me know of your decision.

Best wishes,
Edward M. Buchanan, Esq.

Beneteau read it through carefully, twice, and then folded the letter and took off his glasses. "Colorful character," he murmured.

"What he says makes sense," Giroux responded.

"Do I understand, then, that you are proposing seriously to consider this idea? We would need to investigate this American company. We would need to consult with Monsieur Beaumont."

Giroux shrugged. "We can do those things."

Beneteau shook his head. "I don't know, Marc. It's an extraordinary idea. It's—it's extraordinary."

"Yes," said Giroux, and smiled.

Amanda's screams were echoing up and down the corridor at the house in Cornwall, and all of the servants paused as

they went about their duties and shook their heads. Amanda
Lewis Copeland was giving birth, and the house itself
seemed to shiver with her pain.

The doctor was there, and the midwife. Marcus Copeland
had thought of all the necessary details when he learned that
his wife was pregnant. He had smiled sadly when she gave
him the news, just as he had smiled when she asked him to
marry her. He knew, of course. In their few months of
marriage he had not failed to be enchanted by this exquisite
creature, had not stopped being fascinated by her, had
continued to be consumed with an all-powerful love for her.

But he had not once been able to make love to her.

They had tried. Amanda, hoping to be able to at least
make an attempt to convince her husband that the child she
carried was his, frequently issued sensuous invitations. She
insisted on long massages and strange positions, coaxing
him and caressing him and, in the end, pleading with him.
She bought oils and mirrors and lacy lingerie, and she kissed
and licked and carressed until she was exhausted. Marcus,
for his part, was more than ready, the fire burning hot and
lustful inside of him. But something stopped him, every
time, the excitement died and he was unable to do anything
but hold Amanda with tears in his eyes and murmur, "I'm
sorry."

It was Marcus who always gave up, Marcus who always
shook his head and called himself an old fool for wanting
her, an old fool for loving her, an old fool for letting himself
be used by her.

Once she told him that she was pregnant he didn't even
try anymore. He gave Amanda her own bedroom, both in
the chic townhouse in London and on the estate in Cornwall. He remained attentive, and was still hopelessly, fatu-
ously in love with her, but he stopped trying to make love to
her. There was no need. He understood, at last, the reason
that she had married him and he gave her her distance
because of it; but he could not stop loving her.

His love for Amanda had been hopeless from the start. It
would probably be hopeless forever.

He wasn't with her, in Cornwall, when she retired there
early in March to give birth. He wasn't there to watch her
move around the house, heavy and awkward, to see her
make tea and sit by herself, staring out the windows at the
slate-gray ocean as it dashed itself against the rocks, nor to

watch the tears that came so frequently. He didn't know
who she talked to, or what she talked about. He couldn't:
For Marcus Copeland, in his turn, had been called by his
country to serve, and he could not refuse any more than
Philippe de Montclair had felt that he could refuse.

He had left a mere two months after their wedding, and
only an occasional letter indicated that he was still alive,
and fighting, somewhere in the east of France.

Amanda had ceased to care. Everybody she liked left her,
died, went off to do hopeless things in hopeless places, and
none of it made any sense. And this child, Philippe's child,
had no right being there. This child had no right being born.
She had tried to fight it, and now, as she started her labor,
she continued to fight it, not listening to the admonitions of
doctor and midwife who urged her to push, push. Amanda
lay and cried and screamed and fought against them, too,
not helping, not working, just crying and turning away
uncooperatively until, after several hours, they exchanged
worried glances and the doctor reached into his bag for
something to put Amanda to sleep.

She didn't want to have anything to do with the child. Not
now; not ever.

Eric put the letter down and slowly turned to face the two
lawyers who were watching him so expectantly. They didn't
say anything, and he automatically reached into his pocket
for cigarettes. Lighting one, he let the match burn down
nearly to his fingers before tossing it into an ashtray. He sat
down on the long leather couch and inhaled deeply on the
cigarette, his mind racing behind the deliberate actions. Go
to America? The thought was extraordinary.

Giroux glanced at Beneteau and, apparently receiving
some sort of encouragement from him, rubbed his hands
together slowly and looked at Eric. "We feel that it would be
in the best interests of Aeroméchanique to accept this
offer."

Eric raised his eyebrows. "And my best interests?"

"We do not represent you, Monsieur Beaumont. We
represent Aeroméchanique, and in fact are stockholders in
the company. When we address the issue of—"

Beneteau broke smoothly into his partner's conversation.
"It would most decidedly be in your best interests, Mon-

sieur Beaumont. We are, perhaps, correct in assuming that there is nothing more that ties you to France? You have never been close to your father, and your mother, we understand, is long deceased. On the other hand, there is much opportunity in America. You would, most of all, be safe, something which we can no longer guarantee here in France." He cleared his throat delicately.

"I don't know," Eric said. What would happen if Amanda decided to return? What if she divorced her Englishman and came back to the house on the rue de Verdun? What if he was no longer there to await her? He had made promises to Philippe, promises that he was bound to keep. Somehow, he had to look after Amanda and her child, the little girl born on the estate in Cornwall. He had received the news just the week before. Caroline, Amanda was naming her. How could he possibly look after them from America?

"And then," Beneteau continued, as though Eric had never said anything, "you do have a tie in California. Your parents-in-law still reside there, as does your brother-in-law, a Mr. Peter Martin, who I believe has taken over the management of the family business. Er—hardware, if memory serves. You would doubtless welcome this opportunity to be closer to the family of your wife."

Eric looked at him sharply. "You certainly know your business." There was that, of course. California, where Sarah had grown up. The newspaper where she had first worked. The streets where she had walked. The beaches where she had dreamed. He would be close to her there, to the girl she was before he had known her, to the family that he had never met. Her mother had been kind to him when Sarah died, he remembered. He could go and visit her grave.

He looked at the lawyers speculatively. "What makes you think that Aeromécanique is in danger if I remain in France?"

Beneteau raised his eyebrows. "German airplanes have been flying over Paris," he said, mildly. "You know that as well as we do." He sat down across from Eric in one of the leather chairs and leaned forward, his voice dropping in tone if not in intensity. "Monsieur Beaumont, please understand our position. The will of Count Philippe de Montclair stipulates that we are to look after the interests of both Caroline Copeland, his daughter by Amanda Lewis

Copeland, and of Aeroméchanique. We have considerably less control over Mademoiselle Copeland, due to the fact that her mother is resistant to interventions on our part. We have some control over Aeroméchanique, and, I may add, considerable interest in its fortunes due to our being the possessors of two percent of its stock." He gestured towards the letter in Eric's hands. "It is a generous offer, Monsieur Beaumont. An entrée into the American industrial scene. We hope that you will give it serious thought."

Eric stood up. "Is that all?"

The two lawyers exchanged glances once again. Giroux, the younger, said merely, "For now, Monsieur Beaumont, yes. For now."

Amanda stared out past her writing desk, through the window, to the ocean beyond. She had been trying for hours to write to her mother, and page after page had been crumpled and thrown into the wastebasket at her side. There was so much to say, and there was nothing to say.

She was, herself, a mother. How could she write to her own mother, who lived in the midst of propriety and reasonableness, and tell her about her granddaughter? What was there to articulate that had not already been demonstrated through her actions? How could she say what her mother would intuit to be the truth, that Caroline was not Marcus's daughter at all, but the child of a handsome French count? How could she express the misery, the deep depression which was settling over her now, a melancholy as fine as the gray drizzle off the sea, as enveloping as the mists on the cliffs that towered over the house? Was it proper to tell one's mother that ever since bringing another life into the world she had walked those cliffs alone, a cloak wrapped around her against the wind and sea spray, and thought about ending her own life?

It was silly to try. She herself had been born out of wedlock. Her mother was, if nothing else, forthright. She had not contrived to marry someone merely to give her child a name. Amanda compressed her lips. Why did she think of that now, when there were so many other things to think about? It had been so simple all these years to push the unwelcome thoughts of her father and her mother's actions into the back of her mind whenever they surfaced; why bring them deliberately to the fore now? Margaret Lewis had never bothered to marry her baby's father, nor any other man, preferring her own life, her own money, her own amusements to a life of sharing. And she had survived, merely by keeping her chin in the air and her determination strong. But Amanda was different. She could not live without society; she longed to be normal—well, not normal, but fully accepted by the class she had been born into. Amanda was—*face it*, she whispered to herself, *the word is frightened*. Frightened of all the gossip, all the talk, all the nasty speculation. And she didn't want anyone knowing how deeply she had loved the one man who was not anxious to marry her.

Her mother had said something long ago, before she went back to France . . . what was it? About love making one do rash things. No: Make rash decisions, that was it. Had she loved Amanda's father? Was her own "rash decision" the decision to bear Amanda? Had her mother been pleased or had she, too, been unhappy about her condition? Amanda thought of that horrible night on the rue de Verdun when she had tried to kill her baby, and shivered. Had her mother tried to do the same thing? If she had, she would never tell.

Amanda stirred as she heard a wail from the nursery, and the here and now took over her thoughts. Bless Marcus for providing her with all that she would need for the baby, including a nurse who cared for her night and day. Amanda herself had scarcely looked at the child. Caroline had Philippe's eyes; that much alone was apparent in the wrinkled and wizened little face, and that was enough to condemn her.

If there was one thing that Amanda didn't want to be reminded of, it was Philippe.

Nothing in Amanda's experience had prepared her for motherhood. All of her friends in the States seemed to spend most of their time avoiding pregnancy, and children were thought of in her circle as "simply too, too dreary, darling." She had named the baby Caroline because it seemed as good as any other name, but beyond that wasn't sure of either her feelings or her obligations. What on earth did one actually do with one of them?

And then there was Marcus. He wrote occasional letters to her, describing scenes that she didn't want to see and events that she didn't want to know about. He commanded a unit which seemed to spend most of its time in something called foxholes, firing at people who looked just like them.

That was Marcus's agony: that the Germans were not the abstract enemy he had been trained in London to hate, but people like himself, men with blue eyes, boys with exhaustion written across their faces. They were people with histories and families and hobbies and friends. He confided his uncertainty and guilt to Amanda, but all that she read in his words was cowardice. Philippe had been brave enough to face the enemy; why then did Marcus have to waste so much time and energy thinking of reasons why he shouldn't? That Philippe most probably shared the same agony was not something that she considered.

Marcus was less a person to her than Philippe had been. He was an abstraction, a husband she had been forced to take because it was expedient to do so. She didn't love him, and, frowning over his letters, she began to think that she didn't even particularly like him, which made all matters infinitely worse.

She read without sympathy his letters describing the blazing arcs of the flares at night, which lit up the landscape like a fairgrounds; his stories of the men in his unit and the fear and the dirt and the mud; and his questions concerning the morality of a war spent killing people who looked and acted and presumably felt very much like he did himself. She read them with some irritation, suppressing the reality of it all, trying not to think of the realities that had killed Philippe.

And then one day she read the letter from the Major who had been Marcus's superior officer expressing sorrow and distress that such a fine person as Captain Copeland had fallen in the service of his country.

He had stepped, it seemed, on an English mine—one of the mines that he and his unit had been busily planting in the fields. She could close her eyes and see the blinding flash of light, hear the roar of the explosion, know the darkness that followed and enveloped one in its soft cocoon of unknowing.

Like Marie-Louise de Montclair, Amanda was now an

official widow of the war. People would exclaim over her,
left alone with a small baby, to fend for herself in the world.
A dramatic and pathetic thought. Too real.

Of course, she had been left to fend for herself with
combined resources of the Lewis and Copeland fortunes to
keep her comfortable—and the Aeroméchanique money for
her child.

She sighed and crumpled the paper in her hand and
started on a new page.

March 29, 1915

Dearest Mamma,
    Well, the rumors that you hear are true. Things are
getting much much worse with the war. But, after all,
what a *dreary* topic, war. I remember when we all
thought that there was nothing to it, and that everything would be perfect by Christmas. Everything. And
now nothing is perfect and it is as though the world is
coming to an end.

No, Amanda thought; that would not do. Her mother
mustn't think that she was overwhelmed. She must see that
Amanda was in control, and sparkling, as she always was.
That was the only thing to do. She sat and nibbled on the
end of her fountain pen, and at length began to write again.

    Well, it's all such a *silly* thing, isn't it? And you'll
never believe this, Mamma, but Marcus has had the bad
taste to get himself killed, too, on top of everything else.
He stepped on one of his *own* landmines, which was a
tiresome thing to do, and I'm not proud of him at all.
    I'm going back to London next week. They're saying
perfectly *idiotic* things about there being danger, even
in London, but that's simply too, too *ridiculous* for
words. The Germans wouldn't *dare*. And it's getting far
too stuffy here in Cornwall, tied down to a nursery and
a nanny and a child, which is too *tiresome* for words, I
don't know how you *ever* managed, Mamma.

There. That was better. Make her think that it was all a
joke, that life was all a joke: Philippe, and Caroline, and
Marcus, and the war. Nothing was important. Everything

was a source of amusement. That way, she wouldn't have to
confront anything. Not here, on paper, with her mother; and
certainly not with herself, ever.

Anyway, anyway, anyway, I'll be up in London for
the Season, which ought to be *marginally* acceptable at
least; and then I might go back to America. I should
think that Caroline *ought* to be brought up properly,
don't you? And I can't *possibly* do it myself, there are
far too many *other* things to be doing. And you're so
good at it, Mamma, you've made all your mistakes
already, with me, so there you are. You can make her do
all the things that I *hated* when I was a little girl, like
sitting through those interminable sermons at Saint
John's in Newport, and learning to ride a horse like a
lady. Who knows, Mamma, perhaps Caroline will turn
out better than me, and you needn't think that you
wasted *all* of your time, after all.

Well, enough said for now. I will write you again
soon, Mamma—

Loving regards,
Amanda

Eric finally made his decision.

He was lying in bed with the sirens blowing outside,
urging everybody to run to safety because another German
airplane had been sighted. Laying in bed where he and Sarah
had made love, and where her ghost still lingered, gently
chiding him for his participation in the destruction going on
outside, he had decided.

He was going to go to America.

It was the only thing that made sense for him anymore,
yet the very decision felt as though he was tearing his heart
out of his body. He would have to leave this house where he
and Sarah had danced and talked and eaten and made love;
this house where they had been happy. He was giving up the
memories of her that were tied to this place. He was giving
up the continued presence of her ghost, laughing and crying
with him every night in his dreams.

He knew the price that he was paying: He was losing her.
He was losing the ability to reach out and touch the pillow
on which she had slept, to sit at the table where she had

eaten dinner, to unlock the doorway which she had so often walked through. He lay in bed and listened to the air-raid sirens and grieved for his loss of the immediate presence of her, here, all about him.

From now on, all that there would be was the Sarah in his heart and in his head, the Sarah that traveled with him, more abstract and yet more intense.

He was going to America; to California, Sarah's first home. To Edward Buchanan, Esquire, about whom he knew nothing at all. To a new place and a new life. And there was a fluttering of fear in his stomach as he thought of it.

And yet there was also a world of hope and promise.

Amanda bit on the end of her pen, and added a postscript:

> Oh, and Mamma, what do you think happened but *Eric Beaumont* of all people came to see me last week. Yes, and he was on his way to America. Some terribly *important* industrial tycoon there wants him to go and build his little hangars in California, of all the *impossible* places. Well, of course he's going to become so *depressed* just moping about and thinking of Sarah while he's there, I shall have to make it a point to go out and cheer him up when I've nothing better to do.

She sealed the envelope, dripping the wax on the back carefully and grinding the seal with its intertwined initials on it. The room smelled after that of the wax and the candle. And she thrust the letter aside as though she could no longer bear to look at it.

Eric had come to Cornwall with no invitation and no advance notice, just appearing one day in a rented motorcar. She had kept him waiting for a good thirty minutes while she sat in her bedroom and smoked cigarette after cigarette, afraid of confronting him after so many months, with so many words left unspoken between them.

Eric had waited patiently, which was in character; and then she finally went down to see him and he looked at her pale skin and her red-rimmed eyes and said, merely, "You're beautiful, Amanda. May I see her?"

She was angry with him for that, and angry, too, because of the way he had looked at Caroline, with a light in his eyes that she knew was not for her daughter, but for the father that the daughter would never know. He didn't say anything, just looked and looked, and even when Caroline began to cry (which she did, infuriatingly, all the time), he still held her and smiled. It was surely a trick of the light that showed up tears in his eyes.

And then he had told her that he had decided to move Aeroméchanique to California. He was sitting patiently in Marcus's huge living room, adorned with the heads of assorted beasts he had killed on safari in Africa. Eric was sitting directly below an enormous stuffed antelope, and Amanda found herself addressing the trophy rather than the man. It felt safer.

He lit cigarettes for both of them, and then continued calmly and quietly, ". . . on the advice of Beneteau and Giroux, Amanda, so you must admit that it makes sense."

"Must I?" She was pacing the room, nervously, drawing in on her cigarette in short abrupt puffs. Her hemline, only inches below her knee, he noted, was even shorter than the last time he had seen her in Paris.

"They are advising me in the best interests of the company. And of your daughter, incidentally."

"Oh, that." And she was angry again. "I don't want a trust fund for her, Eric, and you must talk them out of it. I'm perfectly able to take care of her myself, you know. I'm not exactly penniless."

He shifted his position uncomfortably. "I'm afraid there's nothing that they can do, Amanda. The terms of the will are clear. When Caroline turns twenty-one, she'll be equal owner, with me, of Aeroméchanique." He paused, looking not at Amanda but at the cigarette burning in his hand. "You really needn't be so concerned, Amanda. You can bank the dividends, or invest them, or whatever you'd like. I'm sure that Beneteau and Giroux would be glad to advise you."

"I don't want their advice!" She whirled from the window, where she had been once again staring out at the ocean. "I don't want their advice and I don't want Philippe's stocks or money or daughter!" She turned back to the window, hearing perhaps the harshness of her words echoing in the room, and her shoulders sagged.

Eric put out his cigarette and got up and walked over to

her, putting his hands on her shoulders and drawing her
back against him, her velvet dress against the coarse tweed
of his jacket. He still couldn't see her face, but he could feel
the tremors pass through her body as she cried. "It's all
right," he said, but felt the helplessness behind his words. "I
really do understand. I miss him, too."

"I don't miss him!" It was a snarl. Amanda had recovered
her poise with a venegeance. She pulled away and turned to
face him simultaneously. "I don't miss him. I don't want to
remember him. Why don't you just take your horrid little
company and go off to America and leave me alone? Why
doesn't everybody just leave me alone?"

"Because people care about you," Eric responded. "Because I care about you."

"You," she said coldly, "care about the promises that you
made to your friend when he died. You care more for his
daughter than for me. Go away. Just go away!"

"Amanda—"

"Get out of here." Her voice elevated, winding its way up,
higher and higher, on a thin thread of hysteria. "Get out of
here!"

The door opened and a manservant anxiously inquired,
"Is everything all right, madam?"

"No, it isn't." She drew in a deep breath, steadying
herself. "Myers, you may show Mr. Beaumont out."

"Very good, madam. This way, please, sir."

Eric hesitated. Amanda was making a show of sitting
down and lighting a cigarette, her back turned decisively
toward him. He shrugged his shoulders. "Amanda, if there's
anything I can do . . ."

"This way, sir." The manservant advanced towards him,
and Eric gave up and walked out.

Behind him, Amanda put down her cigarette and cried
and cried.

Chapter Fourteen

The wrench was the last thing he packed, the last thing still lying about, not crated up and carted off and taken away—the lucky wrench that Philippe had given him that night in the shed behind the de Montclair chateau, when they had gotten drunk and maudlin and promised each other the stars and the sky.

He reached for it now, picking it up gently, caressingly almost, as though it were a woman instead of an old and worn piece of metal. It had started him off, in those days of lying under engines and getting grease all over him and figuring out how they worked and how to make them work even better. It had stayed with him as he moved from the design of motorcars to the design and fabrication of airplanes, and now from the design of airplanes into the design and fabrication of the metals and alloys used to build them, and he was still never without it. He had changed, the world around him had changed, but that wrench remained his one constant.

He looked around the deserted hangar one last time. It seemed larger, suddenly, now that it was empty. Strange . . . it, too, held its ghosts. He felt as though he could turn around and see one of them standing there: Philippe grave and smiling, a bottle of beer in his hand; Sarah laughing and kissing him; Amanda, holding on to her hats. It was yesterday that they had stood there. It was a thousand years ago. It was easy to wonder if it had ever happened.

The wrench would remind him, would always be there to remind him of all that had happened, of what he had come from. In order to know where one is going, one must always be aware of where one has been. This he would always remember.

He walked to the hangar door, and stood there, breathing deeply, savoring the odor of country air and the remnants of grease and petrol. This small airfield, and this hangar that Philippe had bought with perfectly good drinking money so that he, Eric, could work toward his dream: That he would remember.

The mud that Amanda had complained of: He would always remember the mud. He looked ruefully down at his boots. A fitting farewell. No matter what time of year it was there was mud, clinging to boots and trousers and jackets, ubiquitous and pervasive. He leaned his head up against the doorjamb and closed his eyes, remembering. He recalled evenings long before Sarah had come through this door and into his life, evenings spent in bars with Philippe drinking themselves silly, and all the calculations whirling around and around in his head. No matter where they were, no matter what they were doing, still the numbers stayed with him. The women came and went, the drinks were drunk, and still the numbers floated around his consciousness. What if, what if, what if . . . The possibilities, then, were endless. What if. What if . . . lighter metals. Lighter combinations of metals. And then he would try them out here the next day, only to have still another thing go wrong.

The reports out of America about the Wright brothers had fueled his own mounting obsession to do as well—no, to do better. He knew already, even then, that he could be better.

And then Sarah, beautiful and elegant and fearless, came into his life, taking his airplanes up and his heart away. Sarah trying out his inventions, becoming his test pilot, then coming back and saying, "Yes, it was fine, but it still needs . . ." It always needed something; she was invariably right. She had been an excellent pilot. He would make the necessary correction and wait for the next problem to present itself.

Those were the days when anything was possible, stretching out into infinity. As though it could always be like that: him and Philippe, working and laughing and drinking together, and Sarah in some airplane appearing as a speck on the horizon, and the tightening of his stomach muscles as he saw her circling and knew that she would lie in his arms that night. And Amanda carrying them back into the gaiety of the city. The four of them together, popping champagne corks and laughing uncontrollably and making probable improbable plans for their lives together. In retrospect, it seemed as though the sun was always shining—on the airfield, on their love, and on their friendship. All of them young and bright and thinking that it could last forever.

Eric opened his eyes again and pushed himself off the doorjamb and felt around in his pocket for his keys. Nothing lasts forever. Sarah had fallen out of the sky and had ended the only real love he had ever felt. Philippe had gotten killed in that great war that was going to be the last war and wasn't even over yet. Damn it all.

He got into his motorcar and started the engine and drove slowly away from the hangar, up the narrow dirt track to the road to Paris. He had already sealed the keys to the house on the rue de Verdun in an envelope and addressed it to the antique dealer, who would now be the one to live with the ghosts, the whispers on the stairwells, and the phantom caresses in bed. Eric had stood this morning in the sunlight and said good-bye to the stone lions and to all the secrets that they guarded.

He put the wrench in his pocket and turned to the door, and towards his future.

The voyage across the Atlantic Ocean was uneventful. Eric was expected in California, but he went to Boston, first, standing alone out at Squantum Field and staring at the shallow mud-flats into which Sarah had fallen almost three years before. He knew that Sarah would have had other preferences: Sarah would have urged him to stop by the Allard Flying School and share a beer with Marc Allard, or take in a show with Jeannine, but then Sarah had never been as morbid as he. Nor had she lost anyone she loved. Her life, short as it was, was unmarked by the kind of tragedy that he had learned to live with.

Americans, Eric observed as he took the long train ride across the country, were a strange people. Their openness and friendliness were deceptive, and he could not help but wonder what lay beneath that jovial exterior. What did it mean, this custom of treating casual acquaintances like long-lost family members? How could they ever indicate that they treasured someone, if their first interaction was at that level?

The countryside, too, was different. It was flat, with miles

and miles of empty horizon and vast expanses of fields. As
the train wheels clattered across state after state, he began to
ache for the smaller, neater French countryside with its lush
green grass and hedges, its leafy trees. His people he had
known he would miss. That he could also feel for his
country as an entity was a revelation.

Eric sat in his seat and listened to the clattering of the
wheels beneath him and stared out at the scenery rushing
past, stared out with eyes that drank it all in and saw
nothing. Sarah had done this; Sarah had sat perhaps on this
very train as she crisscrossed the country in her newspaper
days, in her barnstorming days. An airplane appeared on the
horizon and he narrowed his eyes to look at it, thinking only
of its design. Sarah wouldn't have been thinking of the
design. Sarah would have been thinking of the power and
the passion of flight.

California was near and drawing dangerously closer, and
even Eric, preoccupied as he was with problems and solutions and engineering ideas, realized that he was embarking
on a new era in his life. If he was ever to give Sarah up, the
time was now.

He got off the train in Los Angeles, as instructed by the
lawyers, the conductor bellowing, "Last stop! Last stop!
Everyone off!" in his ear. He carried only one suitcase, with
all the personal gear that he needed; the rest would follow.
He wore his good tweed suit, with the new gold watch given
to him by Beneteau and Giroux before he left Paris, and his
jaunty boater hat and neat bow tie. Sarah's picture was safe
in the suitcase. It was all that he needed.

A portly man, dressed neatly and somewhat flamboyantly
in a suit with a loud checkered vest and a gold watch fob,
calmly scanned the faces of the descending passengers. He
looked briefly at Eric before moving over to address him.
"Mr. Beaumont? You are, one presumes, Mr. Beaumont?"

"Yes," Eric said, the English still feeling foreign on his
tongue. "I am Eric Beaumont."

The older man extended his hand. He could have given
Eric about ten years and twenty pounds, Eric thought, but
the weight added somehow to the air of florid authority. He
moved somewhat slowly, but the gray eyes assessing the new
arrival were anything but slow. "Delighted, Mr. Beaumont.
I am Edward Buchanan, at your service, and it seems that

you are in need of some at the moment. Service, that is. Let's go and get a drink."

Eric followed him through the crush of people, surrendering his ticket to the collector at the gate, and walked out of the train station into the bright California sunshine. Los Angeles. Even then, with the first impressions crowding in his mind and jostling with each other for space, he was aware of a sense of open space that he hadn't found in Europe or even in the eastern part of the United States. The city was mostly flat, the purple foothills fringing the city shimmered in the distance. The city itself was a hodge-podge of structures—some squat and stucco, others brown-stones with elaborate ornamentation. Interspersed throughout were a large number of frame bungalows. There was an openness about the buildings, too: sweeping porticos and massive doors, with glass windows—many of them of stained glass and of a size he hadn't seen before. The boulevards were wide, with ample sidewalks, and there were signs posted all around for some exhibition hall. Although there were masses of flowers everywhere, there were hardly any trees about, and those that were there were not the stately poplars he was accustomed to. They were smaller, exotic trees. Palm trees and banana trees, he learned later.

Edward walked briskly, unerringly, swinging a fashionable cane in his hand until they arrived at a bar, filled with shadows, nearly empty. Clem's Café, it said over the door.

"Two whiskeys, Keith. Doubles, if you would be so good."

"Right away, Mr. Buchanan."

Eric, feeling awkward, looked around him. "You're well-known here."

"Pays to be well-known, my boy. Well-known and well-connected, you can't go wrong, I always say. Ah, here are our drinks. To you, my boy, and to that little company of yours!"

Eric obediently raised his glass and drank, the whiskey stinging his throat, but gliding down smoothly nonetheless.

"So," Edward continued, patting his waistcoat pockets as though in search of something, "you're the French wonder boy who's experimenting with jet propulsion and alloys. You don't look all that impressive to me, I must confess."

It had never occurred to Eric that anyone besides himself would take any interest in what he was doing. "I didn't know until you wrote that anyone in America had heard of me."

"Of course we have, my boy, of course we have. Anyone who is anyone in aviation knows about Eric Beaumont. Got the inherent stability problem licked, from what I've heard."

Eric toyed with his drink. He felt angry without understanding why. "And you're someone in aviation?"

Edward laughed. "I'm someone everywhere, my boy. That's what my business is. For a percentage of yours, I'm going to make you very, very rich."

Eric looked up from his glass. "And just how do you propose to do that? Not much money in solving stability problems, I'm afraid. I've made more off manufacturing."

"There's always money in solving problems, my boy. Remember that. Your first lesson, we'll call it. There's always money for solving problems. The trick is to find out who has the problem, and how badly they need a solution. And, of course, how much they can afford to pay you to solve it. That's where I come in. We're sitting on top of a gold mine at the moment, and I don't want to lose a nickel of it."

Eric blinked. "Gold mine?"

"Precisely. Precisely." He laughed as Eric continued to look blank. "That great bloody war of yours in Europe, my boy! You've been producing airplanes for them to go and shoot each other out of the sky with. Well, that's all well and good, but you're wasting your potential. Can't stand wasted potential." He had continued patting pocket after pocket and now finally came up with a thick dark cigar. "Mind if I smoke?"

Eric felt bemused. "Not at all." He reached in his own pocket for his cigarettes and lit one before offering the matches to Edward.

"Good. Good. Now, where was I? Ah, yes, potential. Yours, to be precise. And mine, of course, which as of today is closely linked with yours. Our fortunes, dear boy, follow each other now. Yes." He puffed meditatively at the cigar for a moment. "The Army Corps has some interesting ideas. They've hired some self-important company to carry them out, which is typical of the Army—now there's a group about which to make a study in wasted potential, if ever I've seen one. As I was saying, interesting plans. You could do a lot with them, my boy, you and that company of yours. What is the damned thing called, anyway? I keep forgetting."

"Aeroméchanique."

Edward shook his head. "Won't do, my dear boy, simply won't do. We need something that people here can pronounce. Something catchy. Yes, that's the ticket, something catchy." He hummed under his breath for a moment, staring out at a point in space just above Eric's left ear. "Something that we can turn into initials, that would be catchy. It's all the rage, I understand. The trend, don't you know, my boy, and we have to keep up on trends. Let's see . . . airplanes, research, and design. Hmm . . . well, that's it, of course. Aviation research and design—A.R.D." He tapped the ash vigorously off his cigar and swallowed the remainder of his whiskey in one gulp. "No. No. Doesn't ring true. Doesn't sound right. Publicity titles—they have to sound right, my boy. I like the aviation research part, though. . . . Hmm. Right. Got it." He looked at Eric triumphantly. "Aviation, research, and mechanics. That's the ticket. A.R.M. Like?"

"I liked Aeroméchanique." The general manner, Eric thought, was one of genial bonhomie, but the eyes were shrewd and the mind was racing a thousand miles a minute behind the sleepy exterior. Edward Buchanan would either be Aeroméchanique's greatest asset or its greatest liability. He hadn't yet decided which.

"It's a splendid name, my boy. Resplendent with a French *je ne sais quoi*. Most appropriate." He leaned forward, suddenly more intense. "Do you want this goddamn company to make money or don't you?"

Eric blinked. "Of course I do."

Edward leaned back, a satisfied smile on his face.

"Well then, my dear boy, I suggest that you start trusting me. I'll leave the designs to you and you leave the rest to me. It's the only way that it will work." His manner became more relaxed, polished, urbane. "A.R.M. it is, then. A good day's work. Yes, my boy, a good day's work. Finish your drink, and I'll drop you by your hotel—just picked up a new motorcar myself, and can't wait to show it off in town. Have to see about finding you a proper place to live, too, of course. And a place to work, though Johnson might have something to say about that."

"Johnson?"

Edward nodded vigorously. "The aforementioned American firm, my boy. Johnson Aircraft and Tool Company, subsidiary of Johnson Industries. Though how they manage to call that group of utterly hopeless imbeciles a company eludes me altogether. You'll be subcontracting from them initially. We'll see what we can do after that, once you've established your reputation in this neck of the woods, so to speak, my boy." He stood up and tossed some bills on the table. "I do have a feeling that Johnson is getting more than they bargained for. We'll have to see just how astute they actually are. Not that I have any faith whatsoever in their degree of astuteness, my boy, or even that I'd lay even odds that they know the word. But it will be interesting to see if they recognize the future when it stares them right in the face."

"The future?"

Edward gave him a look, swift and enigmatic, and shook his head. "God help us, my boy, you don't even realize it yourself."

London was rainy and cold and dreary.

Amanda shook her head as she combed out her hair, which she had finally decided to cut short. Blond curls tickled the nape of her neck. It was decidedly more sophisticated, she thought, as she carefully adjusted the *aigrette* in the turquoise turban which matched so perfectly the color of her eyes.

She had thought to find some amusing people in London on her return from Cornwall and the dreary memorial service that she had dutifully held for Marcus—one didn't recover much of the body, the major had told her, when someone stepped on a mine. But everyone was in New York or Paris, or so it seemed. And Amanda needed people, though she didn't want to acknowledge that the need for the sparkle and glitter of others was to keep her ghosts at bay. Instead, it was easy to hide behind her old facade of superficiality and giddiness. But the emptiness was there, and the grieving; a sorrow as genuine as it was surprising.

Sarah was gone, Philippe was gone, Marcus was gone, now even Eric was gone in some intangible way, and she was left alone with a baby who served only to remind her that the happier times were over.

But she wasn't ready to go home.

Amanda did all the things that one did in London, but the gestures felt empty. She attended the theater and took in some films, admired the new Chagall that was on loan to the Museum and went to the dances that were still being valiantly held to help support the war effort. There was a tetanus epidemic in the trenches, earnest-faced nursing sisters reminded one at the entrance to each dance: Donate generously, so that the men don't have to die from two causes.

No, Amanda thought as she dropped coins into the proffered box each night, do let's just confine our dying to combat with the Germans. It's so much neater that way.

She met a man at one of the dances, a thin pale fellow with melancholic eyes. He hadn't been called up for service, he said, due to illness. He never specified what the illness was, just that it prevented him from active duty. He was thinking of perhaps volunteering to drive an ambulance at the front.

Amanda sat and smoked her cigarettes and listened to him talk patriotism for over an hour. She didn't ask his name; she didn't want to know his name. She didn't want to know where he came from, or what his family history was, or how much money was in his bank account. All that she cared about was that this man wasn't going off to war, wasn't going off to die like everybody else. He was here, he was real, he was alive. Never mind that she didn't like the way the hairs grew on the backs of his hands. He was alive.

She finally stood up while he was in the middle of a sentence about the recent British merchant shipping losses and said, abruptly, "Take me home, now."

"I beg your pardon?" He looked disoriented.

"I said take me home. Now," Amanda repeated, pulling on her gloves, hardly waiting for him to follow her. He was no Philippe, it was true. But Philippe wasn't there anymore.

They went back to Marcus's luxurious townhouse, past the closed nursery door where Caroline and her nanny presumably lay sleeping, past the empty rooms that Marcus would have liked to fill with children, happy children, children whose nursery rhymes weren't being interrupted by political speeches or more news from the front. She took the thin young man into the great bedroom where she and Marcus had tried so hard to make love all those long nights, and, silent and breathless, she undressed him with the lamp still lit. He lay back on the bed and watched her while she undressed, too, her clothes joining his in a heap on the floor, taking off everything but her lacy black garter belt and black textured stockings.

He didn't say anything as she moved over him, straddling his body with hers, moving her lips over his neck and his chest and his arms and down to his waist. He shivered a little when she touched his pubic hair, feeling her lips move over his penis, encouraging the erection that was already there, wet and soft and exciting, and she moved back up him then, gracefully, coming to kiss his mouth again and again and again, deep wet kisses that threatened to engulf them both.

Amanda sat up, still straddling him, the lamp flinging her shadow up against the wall. He reached his hands up and touched her breasts, hesitantly at first, and then with more assurance, rubbing her nipples with his thumbs until they were large and hard and swollen. She reached down, feeling for the hardness of his penis, holding it between her thumb and forefinger and sliding her hand up and down on it until he was moaning with desire.

She moved again, slightly, just enough to bring the tip of his penis to her opening, and then she slid down on him, all the way, his penis disappearing inside her, and he moaned again as she moved and kept moving, thrusting and rotating and tightening around him until he was gasping. His hands were still on her breasts, and he was pinching her nipples so hard that they hurt, and it was Amanda who was moaning, and he began thrusting with her until suddenly he cried out loud and went tense before collapsing and not moving at all anymore.

Amanda slowly disentangled herself from him and slid down onto the bed, the satin sheets that she had bought for Marcus tangled all around them. There was light shining in the window from the gas lamp on the street even after she put out the lamp on the bedside table. It had been a mistake to leave that one on. Here in the semi-darkness it was easier to feel closer to this man. She could pretend that he was anyone she liked, that she was anyone at all. Almost grateful for his anonymity, she put her arm around him and closed her eyes. He was already asleep.

She woke to the sound of screaming and of explosions going on all around her. Next to her, the man from the dance was sitting up in bed, and she could clearly see his frightened eyes by the flashes of light from outside. Amanda jumped to her feet, suddenly conscious, as she heard footsteps in the corridor outside her room, of how she was dressed. She started fumbling around in the room for something to put on. Finding her Oriental silk robe, she knotted it swiftly around her. "What's happening?" she demanded of the man in her bed, who still wasn't moving. "What in God's name is happening?"

"I don't know. I don't know." He seemed to be frozen to the spot.

There was more screaming outside, and Amanda jerked open the bedroom door and ran out into the corridor. A maid fled by, her nightdress and nightcap still on. Amanda clutched at her. "What is happening?" Wordlessly, the maid pulled away and ran down the stairs.

Oh, God, she thought: Caroline. She tore down the hall to the nursery, to find the nanny competently dressed and putting layers of woolens around the baby. "Mrs. Driscoll," Amanda gasped, "what is it?"

The older woman never even glanced up. "Some sort of bombing, mum," she said tonelessly. "From some great zeppelin, or so they've told Mrs. Davies." Mrs. Davies was the cook, and privy to the first rounds of gossip in the house. "The constable was by just now, telling everyone to go into their cellars, mum," she continued, lifting the baby in her arms. "We're all headed down, now. You ought to come, too, mum."

Amanda stood back to let the nanny pass through the doorway, and then followed her downstairs wordlessly. She spent the rest of the night huddled in the winecellar—one of Marcus's prides and joys—with the servants, two of whom were acutely hysterical throughout most of the time. At one moment, just before dawn, she watched a giant rat scurry across the floor not a foot from where she was sitting. Caroline cried and wet herself, and the smell of ammonia persisted even after Mrs. Driscoll had taken care of the situation.

Amanda sat huddled in a blanket and tried to stay calm. It had not escaped Amanda that in their mad rush to safety, and even with their consideration for her child, no one had stopped by Amanda's door to wake her and urge her to safety as well.

They would never accept her, she thought; the servants would never accept her as mistress of this house. They were loyal to Marcus, and there was probably not one among them that believed Caroline to be his daughter. They put on the appearance of it all, because they were good British servants, but appearance was all. There was no loyalty to Amanda.

The morning dawned, wet and miserable, and people flexed tired muscles and limbs. Amanda climbed slowly back up the stairs to her bedroom to dress. The room was empty. It was as though her companion of the night before had never been there. Pulling on blouse and skirt and sweater, slowly, like an elderly woman, Amanda made a decision. Before she even ventured out into the streets to see what damage had actually occurred, before she went to the American ambassador's office to articulate her plans and book passage on a ship, she had already made the decision: She was taking her baby, and she was going home.

Eric took the long train ride up the California coast the next day.

It was a ride of breathtaking beauty, with high cliffs soaring out over great waves dashing themselves against the rocks. The sky was more blue than he ever recalled seeing it—a piercing blue which somehow hurt the eyes. The trees, too, were different—green and lush but with leaf patterns he did not recognize.

He listened to the accents on the train, just as he had listened to the accents as he rode across the country, hearing the long flat a's and imitating them in his mind. The people were friendly and smiling here, too, and it was a wonder that any business got done at all. Everyone seemed to be on a prolonged holiday. If news of the war had penetrated into

California, no one that Eric could see was letting it ruin their day.

It was a pilgrimage of sorts, this ride up to Northern California, to the place where Sarah had lived as a child; time to see her places, meet her people. Perhaps, he thought, he would capture that part of her he had never known—and then, at last, be able to let her go.

He rented a motorcar in San Jose, and drove out to the house on Western Avenue. Flowers, he remembered belatedly, and drove back into town to stop at a florist's. Lilies; Sarah's mother liked lilies. Sarah herself always said that they reminded her of a funeral, and what cold flowers they were. She had preferred the warm vibrant colors of the wildflowers that they used to pick in the field behind the Aeroméchanique hangar.

When he knocked on the door, it was opened by a woman who looked like Sarah would have looked if she had lived twenty years longer. The same fine features, delicate upturned nose, smattering of freckles, the same rich auburn hair. There were wrinkles around this woman's eyes and mouth, and a sadness that he understood without any words being spoken. It was the same sadness he saw reflected in his own mirror every morning as he shaved.

The woman stared at him for a moment, the welcoming smile dying on her lips as recognition seeped in, and then another, deeper smile took its place. "Eric," she said softly, giving his name the American pronunciation. "You are Eric, aren't you?"

He nodded and offered her the flowers. "For you, Mrs. Martin."

She took them, and in a single sweeping gesture put her arms around him as well. "Eric," she repeated, and he could hear the catch in her voice. "Come in. Please, do come in."

She was alone, she explained; her husband still went down to the hardware store every day to give Peter a hand. "He fusses too much. I keep telling him not to, to enjoy his retirement and leave it all up to Peter, but he won't listen to me. What do you take in your tea?"

"Just a little lemon," he said, walking around the living room, and stopping to pause before a picture. "Is this Sarah?"

She looked in from the kitchen. "Oh, that old picture. Yes,

it is. She had just gone up in her first airplane flight, with that fellow—oh, dear, and I can't even remember his name, imagine that, it was all that we heard from her for weeks on end. Some foreign-sounding name, I know."

"Santos-Dumont?" Eric suggested.

"Oh, yes, that's it. She went up with him at a fair she was covering for the newspaper, and to tell you the truth, I don't think that she ever wanted to come back down again after that. She wasn't what I would call a very down-to-earth girl anyway, if you know what I mean, although fancy me telling that to you! She was your wife, after all." She came into the room, carrying a tray. "Here's your tea, Eric, dear. And tell me how long do you plan to stay? So kind of you to come all the way to California."

He sipped the scalding liquid. "Actually, Mrs. Martin, I've come here to stay. I've moved my company here, on the advice of the company lawyers. They were afraid of what might happen if France fell into German hands."

"Oh, my dear." She was genuinely distressed. "Such a difficult thing, to leave your home, although I do certainly understand and, when you put it that way, such a relief to have you safe. You must come and see us often. Sarah would have liked that, I think."

Eric thought so, too. He could not give Sarah up—never push her memory out of his mind—or his life. Later, as he went alone to the cemetery where she was buried ("You really can't miss her, dear, the town pitched in and bought the biggest stone they could find. It's actually a little much, but what can you say when people are being so kind-hearted . . ."), he thought of her smiling as he talked with her mother. Sarah's circle, he thought, was now complete.

Chapter Fifteen

Newport was exactly as Amanda had remembered it.

The big bridge still scared her when she crossed it, just as it had when she was a little girl, and the ships still stood docked, waiting to be loaded or unloaded, the openings into their holds like so many great caves. The town proper was bustling, people moving this way and that to avoid carriages and the occasional motorcar that sped down Main Street. And the drugstore where she used to buy penny candy still was on the corner.

She wondered, fleetingly, whether Caroline would one day purchase penny candy there as well.

The taxi took them in through the coast road where all the mansions stood, along the exclusive waterfront that was reserved for families who had money, and through the big iron gates and up the long sweeping gravel drive to her own estate. As she stepped out of the motorcar and felt the salt spray in her face and smelled the ocean, fresh and clean, she felt contented. After the zeppelin attack on London, all that she ever wanted now was to feel fresh and clean again.

Mrs. Driscoll had the baby wrapped up against the wind and followed Amanda into the mansion without a comment, without a backward glance, the same way she had agreed to leave England and stay on as Caroline's nanny without a thought to leaving her own country. Amanda didn't know why, didn't know what family and friends Mrs. Driscoll might have been choosing to leave—and, after all, the war was reason enough—and nor did she ask. Mrs. Driscoll's family was not her concern. Her own survival was. Despite the recent sinking of the *Lusitania*, the ocean crossing had been uneventful.

Jenson, her mother's butler, met them in the front hall as they came in, their footsteps echoing on the marble floor of the foyer. "Miss Amanda," he said politely, while she handed him umbrella and gloves and hat.

"Is my mother here?"

"I regret to say that Mrs. Lewis is summering in New Hampshire, Miss Amanda," he said blandly.

"I see," she said, and then, more briskly, "Jenson, this is Mrs. Driscoll. She will be staying here with us as my daughter's nanny. I trust that you will see to it that she is given a room and settles in adequately?"

"Of course, Miss Amanda."

"Good. Oh, and Jenson?"

"Yes, miss?"

"I ceased to be called Miss Amanda when I married Mr. Copeland in England. I trust that you will remember that?"

Not a muscle moved in his face. "Very good, Mrs. Copeland."

"Thank you. That will be all, Jenson."

Amanda waited until Mrs. Driscoll had followed Jenson upstairs, and then she walked through the foyer and out into the dining room, and from there, in turn, to the terrace. The ocean was as she had remembered it, cold and gray and harsh. Nothing had changed from the time almost three years ago that she had fled here from Philippe because she was too afraid of her love for him.

This will be a suitable place, she thought, for Caroline to grow up. Proper and correct. Philippe, in his own way, might even have approved.

She stopped herself at that thought. Philippe was no longer the issue. Marcus may well have known that this child was not his, but no one else knew. Marcus had carried the secret to his far-away grave. Only Eric knew, and Eric was in California.

Amanda straightened her back, stretching up to her fullest height. Caroline was Marcus's daughter. She was Caroline Margaret Copeland, and no one—no one—was ever to suggest anything different.

Edward Buchanan frowned and shook his head. Another new idea; he wasn't at all sure that he liked all the new ideas that young Beaumont was proposing. There was, after all, such a thing as moving too fast.

He patted all of his pockets, out of habit, and finally located a cigar, one of the rich expensive Havana cigars that he had imported exclusively for himself. There was nothing wrong with spoiling oneself, from time to time, especially if one had earned a little pampering. And Edward felt that he had.

Eric was sitting across from him at a small table in the dimly lit bar of Clem's Café where Edward had summoned him after his trip up the coast. Edward tended to do most of his business in bars; it wasn't such a bad way to work. People were more relaxed, let things slip, sometimes, that they wouldn't admit to in the sterile atmosphere of an office or board room—usually the best information, too.

Downing the rest of his beer in one gulp, Eric signaled to the waitress for a refill. "I know it's not what you want," he said to Edward, lighting a cigarette and extending a fresh match to light the other man's cigar. "But it's what I want, and it's not such a great concession."

Edward puffed on his cigar for a moment, waiting as the waitress brought Eric another beer and himself a whiskey. At length, he took the cigar from his mouth and responded. "Not what I want that counts, my boy. It's Johnson I'm thinking about."

"If Johnson needs me as much as you and they seem to think, then they won't care."

"Johnson doesn't like to be dictated to."

Eric sighed in frustration. "Look, Edward, I'm not asking them to do anything! I'm not dictating anything to them at all! I just want to locate my hangar and my offices and my workplace in San Jose. They can stay in Los Angeles—hell, they can go to the moon for all I care. I just want to be up north."

Edward drank a swallow of whiskey. "But there's nothing there, my boy! Decidedly unglamorous. And San Jose— such a sleepy little town. Not much to say for itself, if you catch my drift. Er . . . prunes, I think. Yes, that's it, they grow prunes there. All well and good if it's a laxative that you're manufacturing, but . . ." He allowed his voice to trail off and took another drink of the whiskey.

Eric, eyes narrowed, was studying the tip of his cigarette. "There's plenty of land to construct runways," he said. "That's all I need, for now. Transportation isn't a problem, there's the train. I'll bring in everything I'll need." He paused, inhaling swiftly on his cigarette, and then exhaling again, blowing the smoke out of the side of his mouth. "Edward, there are people there that I care about. People that I want to be close to. The only other person in the world that I have is my father, and we were never close, not even when we were living together. But Sarah's family is in San Jose . . . and they're my family, now, too. It's important to me to be close to them."

"Personal reasons. Never a good way to do business. It's not going to go over well in the industry, my boy. People want change, but they don't want it too fast, if you catch my drift. Makes people nervous."

Eric pulled a map from his pocket and smoothed it out on the table between them. "Look, Edward. Look at this valley. It would be perfect. It doesn't have to stay a sleepy little town forever, don't you see? Or we could expand over here, towards Palo Alto. No, stop, don't tell me: I know. Orchards. My father-in-law drove me up there. It's beautiful, Edward. We could start something there. And then all the other industries would move in to be close to us, instead of the other way around. We could make something out of this valley."

Edward puffed on his cigar. "Doesn't do to be too far ahead of your times, my boy. Doesn't do." He peered at the map. "Got your heart set on it, now, do you?"

Eric nodded. "They're my people, Edward."

Edward frowned and ground out his cigar in the ashtray. "You wouldn't be getting just a little obsessed with that? Your wife, I mean, and her family?"

"I can't get obsessed with her. She's dead." His voice was flat.

"Nonsense. I see your eyes when you talk about her. Hell, I see your eyes when you think about her. They light up." He sighed. "Very well, my boy, very well. The great valley it is, and Johnson can like it or lump it, that's the ticket."

Eric drained his glass. "Thank you, Edward," he said politely.

Edward signaled the waitress for another round. "You would have gone and done it, no matter what I said, wouldn't you?"

Eric met his eyes. "Yes."

Edward started laughing, and kept laughing as the waitress came and put fresh drinks on the table. "That's the ticket! That's the ticket, my dear boy! Courage of your convictions, and all that sort of thing. Always admired that in a man, I have. Very well. Very well." He looked meditatively into his whiskey, and Eric began thinking for a moment that he was seriously drunk. "Tell you what," Edward said suddenly, and Eric was sure in that moment that Edward was going to tell him something he had had no previous intention of saying. That Edward was about to disclose a part of himself that he would have otherwise left unrevealed.

"What, Edward?"

"Saw her once, I did, your Sarah. Lovely girl. Newspapers were all agog about her for the longest time, I remember. Called her nice things, I think."

Eric leaned forward eagerly. "You saw Sarah? Where? When?"

"Exhibition show in San Francisco. Back in nineteen-eleven at Selfridge Field if memory serves me correctly. Not my usual cup of tea, my dear boy, but I was with a lady who wanted to fly more than anything else in the world. Well, that was the idea that day, anyway." He gave a mirthless laugh. "She said that she wanted to be with me more than anything else in the world, too, but she gave up on both me and flying." A shadow of pain flickered across his face and was gone. "Can't seem to remember her name myself, and I'm sure that says something, doesn't it?"

"And you took her to an air show? When Sarah was flying?"

"Right you are. That was the ticket! Cotton candy and a brass band and airplanes all around and about in the sky. Charming events they were, I must say, though at first I couldn't see enjoying all the hoopla, don't you know. Short-term investment, hoopla. Your Sarah was part of a team—quite extraordinary, really, two girls and a man, or am I confusing her with someone else? Don't remember their names."

"The Allards," Eric supplied, and the name made his heart ache with the memory. "Marc and Jeannine Allard."

"Was that it?" Edward was beginning to show the effects of the whiskey. "Very well, then, the Allards. And your

Sarah, my boy, though of course that was before you met her, wasn't it? Lovely girl she was. The lady I was with, she was quite taken with Miss Martin's outfit. Very chic, I remember her saying, that silk suit and all. And of course she flew beautifully, and very dramatically, too." He took a gulp of his whiskey. "Tell you what, my boy, she was quite impressive. And we Californians don't impress all that easily. We tend to get very blasé about things." Another pause, and then he said, his voice definitely slurred, "She must have been quite a girl."

Eric stared into his beer. "She was," he said seriously, "a spectacular girl." And he wondered at how after all this time the tears came so readily to his eyes.

Amanda went to a party at the White Horse Tavern in Newport.

She went because she was dutifully going through all the motions expected of her, doing all the things that a wealthy society widow was supposed to do, and after all, one couldn't let a war interfere with one's fun. Her friend Gemma Robinson-Taft rented the Tavern for a birthday party, a party with a theme, which was all the rage. Gemma had chosen a haunting.

The Tavern was the right place for it, the oldest building in Newport, with probably enough ghosts of its own; but Gemma imported more, and all the guests were asked to dress appropriately. Sheeted ghosts and caped vampires were everywhere when Amanda arrived, clinking glasses and smiling at each other and flirting from behind their masks.

Amanda was dressed as a ghost, but an elegant one, a medieval queen with white powder on her skin. Caroline had shrieked when she went in the nursery to say good night, and Amanda decided then and there to have nothing more to do with the baby. Really, she was getting too, too tiresome.

She walked through the small dark tavern rooms and drank champagne and smiled and talked with people she knew until she had finally had enough and, needing air, walked outside into the chilly October twilight. Hugging herself against the cold, she wondered again at the emptiness she felt. Nothing was filling her aches; nothing.

The losses were too much, and neither motherhood nor the resumption of her gay society rounds of parties and dances was making any difference. Sarah and Philippe, gone . . .

"You look rather upset. Is there anything I can do?"

She jumped at the voice, and turned quickly to face the intruder. He was an older man—even with his mask in place one could tell that. Considerably older, but distinguished. In his late forties, she guessed, and seemingly kind as he invited her to tell him her troubles.

Somehow, Amanda found herself feeling better already. Accepting the proffered handkerchief, she dabbed at her eyes. "I'm sorry. I'm just a little tired."

"It's quite all right. Would you care to join me in a brief walk? We shall doubtless frighten the neighbors, but a little scare never did anybody harm."

She hesitated, and then took his arm, falling into step beside him. "It's so stuffy in there," she said, the explanation lame even to her own ears.

"Indeed it is. I don't believe that I've seen you about, or am I so obtuse as to have missed such a ravishing beauty?"

She blushed under the makeup. "I've been living in England. My husband was recently killed in the war, and I decided to come home after that."

"Home?"

She nodded. "My mother is Margaret Lewis."

"Ah, indeed? Then you must be the lovely Amanda. Your reputation lingered long after you. I am honored to make your acquaintance." He turned slightly to face her, offering his hand to be shaken. "I am Charles Osbourne."

Amanda raised her eyebrows. "Charles Osbourne? It is I who am honored, then. U.S. lawn tennis champion—what year was it?"

He laughed. "Further back than I care to remember, Mrs.—er—?"

"Copeland," she supplied. "But Amanda would do. Go on, when was it?"

"Nineteen-oh-one. Dear me, it has been some years now, hasn't it?"

"I remember Mamma talking about it. You were quite the ladies' man, as I recall. I think you may have had lunch out at our estate. Mamma was forever putting on parties for the tennis people when they were in town."

"As I recall, you were a pretty little girl with pink ribbons in her hair peeping out through the banisters on those great curved stairs of yours."

"You *do* remember!" she said, delighted.

"One can hardly forget the lovely Amanda Lewis. Amanda Copeland, now. Allow me to express my condolences on the death of your husband, my dear. My own wife died some years ago, so I am not unacquainted with the particular grief you bear."

Amanda inclined her head. "It is very difficult," she said.

"Most difficult indeed, I should think. Have you children?"

"A daughter," she said diffidently. "She was born in March. My husband never lived to see her. Have you any children, Mr. Osbourne?"

"But you must call me Charles," he protested, helping her negotiate her way around a great mud puddle. "There! Yes, I do, but I'm afraid not any I can see. My ex-wife—another marriage, you see—has custody. Divorce is such a messy affair."

"So they say," said Amanda, half of whose friends saw divorce as a pastime. "Oh! Here we are, already!" And she was surprised at the depth of her disappointment.

"And Gemma will think us such frightful boors. Dear Amanda, do allow me to call on you the next time that I am in town."

"In town?" she echoed. "Where do you live, then?"

"Well, New York City, of course. Where else? One cannot play tennis all of one's life. I live and work in the city. I am actively involved with the theater—a sort of promoter, if you will. Perhaps one day you will come down and see one of my productions."

"I should be delighted," she said, regaining her poise. What a silly thing, acting so besotted over a man twice her age, just because he made her feel better.

And yet, walking back into the Tavern and accepting another glass of champagne, and smiling blankly at the people all around her who continued to carry on their conversations, all she could think about was that, perhaps, just feeling better was all she wanted out of life. Just to feel better. No ghosts, no regrets. Just to feel better.

By autumn they had all of the major construction finished. A.R.M., as Aeroméchanique had become, was now based in San José, California; Beneteau and Giroux were pleased with the decision.

"After all," Giroux said, popping a peppermint into his mouth, "we don't want to be subcontracting from that American company forever. A little distance is just what we need to keep them aware of the fact that we are separate."

Beneteau smiled at his partner's use of the first person plural. "Quite right, Marc," he said. "Monsieur Beaumont appears to have things well in hand there. I was impressed with his last report."

"Which leaves only," Giroux added, "the question of what we are going to do."

"Which 'we' would that be?"

"Our law offices, of course." Giroux sounded impatient. "Do you want us to suffer the same fate that we didn't want to wish on young Beaumont?"

"What nonsense. The Germans wouldn't be interested in us."

"It is you who is speaking nonsense, Robert. Look at the facts. The war in the air is heating up nicely, isn't it? What are those damned pilots calling themselves now? Aces? What wouldn't anybody give for a piece of the major aircraft supplier to the war?"

"No one knows that Aeroméchanique even exists anymore."

"Somebody is making the Nieuports and the Fokkers and those silly English airplanes—remind me to talk to Beaumont about that. I have no idea what his English subcontractor is making, but it's not Aeroméchanique designs. And they know that somebody is making them with a vengeance. We know it's Aeroméchanique, now A.R.M., and if we know it, somebody else will know it, too, eventually." He paced the room, pausing to look out the window. "Robert, look at it this way. If the French government ever found out that we're playing both sides on this, they'd roast us alive. So would the English and the Germans. What is left?"

"I'm not moving to America." The older man looked truly alarmed at the prospect.

"I'm not suggesting that you do. But someplace else, someplace nice and safe and neutral. I was thinking Switzerland."

"Now who is talking nonsense? We all have seen what good neutrality did for Belgium, didn't we? How many atrocities have the Germans committed on the civilian population of Belgium? How many rapes? How many executions? The whole country's become a scene of bloody carnage!"

"That's Belgium. I'm talking about Switzerland."

"And what's to say it will be any different there?"

"And what's to say it will be any different here? Face it, Robert. France isn't a match for the Germans! And win, lose, or draw isn't going to matter for us once they find our connection with A.R.M. For God's sake, man, let's get out while there's still time!"

There was a sudden silence in the room. Beneteau sat hunched over on the leather couch, holding his head in his hands. Giroux stood by the window, feeling rather than hearing his words echo in the small office. The clock with the chased-gold hands slowly counted out the minutes into the emptiness.

Finally, when the silence became unbearable, Beneteau looked up. "I suppose that you may be right," he said heavily. "You were right about young Beaumont, and you may be right again. My wife will hate me for this, but we will move to Switzerland."

Giroux moved away from the window as though released by his partner's words. "Mine will hate me, too," he said cheerfully. "But it's the only thing to do. Zurich is becoming an international capital of world finance. We could find a niche for ourselves there, you will see. All will go well."

"I hope that you are right, Marc. I only hope that you are right."

Eric bought a house in the city where Sarah was born, and took on a subscription to the newspaper for which she had worked, and began to build an industry of which she would be proud.

Johnson Aircraft and Tool Company were everything that

Edward had said they were—and more. Their engineers brought Eric problems, and he realized that it would have taken a decade of education before they could even begin to work out the problems themselves. Aviation might have begun in America, but there it seemed to have stopped. The patent wars between Curtiss and the Wrights and the others had halted progress. And even now there was no understanding of the needs of pilots in wartime.

Eric never stopped to ask himself how he knew, or why he knew. He wouldn't have been able to articulate an answer. It was Sarah's voice inside of him, talking to him about controls and wind factors and cloud cover; Sarah's voice reminding him about velocity and speed and resistance. He had only been up once in one of his own creations, and still, in her own way, she had taught him to fly.

Edward was by his side, supporting him, negotiating for him, speaking the corporate language which Eric had never learned to speak. Edward Buchanan, who had appeared from nowhere to guide Eric's star to America . . . Edward would never take Philippe's place, but already Eric felt an affection for him that once he had thought was reserved only for Philippe.

"Who are you?" Eric asked him one day as they sat in Edward's favorite bar while Edward made telephone calls and Eric ran projections in his head. "Who are you?"

Edward glanced at him in a friendly way. "Do you mean that figuratively, literally, metaphorically, socially, intellectually, philosophically, or psychologically, my boy?"

Eric got flustered. "I mean—where do you come from? Why are you so interested in all of this?"

"I told you. I'm a professional problem-solver." That about said it, too, Edward reflected. He wasn't just being cryptic. He had always tried to solve problems, even as a child in the Pacific Heights mansion in San Francisco where he had grown up witness to his parents' constant fighting. His older sisters all cried during their parents' stormy battles, but Edward had tried to intervene, had tried to solve their problems so that they would stop shouting at each other. It hadn't worked, of course. One day his mother had packed two suitcases full of clothes and walked resolutely down the front steps and out of his life, to disappear into the mists of Portland, Oregon. He had learned then that when he couldn't solve problems he got hurt.

His father didn't waste time in replacing his mother. He went out to the local saloon one night soon after and got drunk and somehow persuaded one of the bar-girls there as well as a justice of the peace that what he really wanted to do that night was to get married again. The next day Katie, his stepmother, was sitting in all of her bright red finery at their breakfast table. Edward's sisters served the breakfast in silent, cold disapproval, but Katie wasn't such a bad sort, only a little loose. Two months later, for his eleventh birthday present, she took Edward down behind the mill pond, where the grasses grew high, and gave herself to him.

After that, being at home presented a new problem, as it became patently obvious that he both wished to and couldn't share his father's wife. So Edward solved that problem by leaving, first to live with some of Katie's ex-colleagues in a big house next door to the saloon, and then to attend school when his father couldn't stand his disgracing the Buchanan name any further.

At boarding school he solved problems by financing his social life through doing other people's homework. He was able to get by on the most brains and the least amount of work. It was all a game, Edward discovered—learning what was expected and then finding ways to get around it. School was a game; relationships with girls were games, too; and, undoubtedly, the business world would prove itself to be a game as well.

There was never any doubt in his mind that he would be successful. He started out in a bank, as was proper. He learned the ins and outs, the power structure, in his first two weeks; seduced the vice president's daughter in his third; received his first promotion in his fourth.

By dividing his free time between analyzing the bank's problems and trying to deal with them so that he would get noticed, and making love with Vanessa, he earned more promotions, until he was an assistant vice president himself at the age of nineteen. Pregnancy and marriage followed in short order, but his joy at his son Lionel's birth was as nothing compared to his excitement at taking over the new branch in Los Angeles. When Lionel died ten years later of meningitis, Edward had a difficult time remembering what he looked like.

Vanessa scolded him about his obsession with his work and the amount of time he spent away from home, and he solved that problem by giving her the divorce she kept hinting that she wanted. He had left the bank and was working as a consultant to a number of large corporations that could afford to pay him lavishly to come in and tell them what they were doing wrong, and how they could do it right. It was child's play; it was almost too easy.

By the time he was thirty, Edward had been through more companies—and more women—than most people saw in a lifetime. He wanted more; he wanted stability. He found it with his own company, and with an opera singer named Laura Corridan who refused to marry him—she was a socialist, she said, though he never quite figured out what her politics had to do with marriage—but who lived happily with him when she was not on tour. He knew that there were other men. Laura believed in impulsivity and open love, and for three years he managed to live with it, having his own flings when she was away but always aching silently as he thought of her in the arms of other men.

He came home late one night after talking through merger negotiations downtown. He was tired and needing a whiskey, a long bath, and a session of lovemaking, and he found that Laura had grown tired of waiting and started without him. He opened the bedroom door and found her asleep, her long red hair tangled and tumbled, the sheets down around the foot of the bed; the man sleeping next to her lay with his hand possessively on her breast.

In a daze of confusion and pain Edward went to the night table and took out his pistol and shot them both. Afterwards he burst into sobs, and the police found him in the room, clutching the sheets. Edward stood trial for murder.

It didn't help his case that Laura was a famous and well-liked performer. It didn't help that her companion was an avowed socialist, active in local politics, and incidentally the son of the editor of the *Los Angeles Tribune.* There was very little debate; the jury sentenced him to life imprisonment, and the general sentiment was that he had gotten off lightly.

Ten years later a lenient governor decided to pardon

Edward's crime of passion and return him to society, but Edward himself would never be the same. Ten years in prison changed a man. One could start afresh, but one could never really start over. There are certain experiences which are inscribed too indelibly on the human soul.

He began consulting again, this time to the United States government. He began dating women, like the one he had taken to the air show to see Sarah Martin and the Allards. Times had changed; it was apparent that soon there might be a war on in Europe, and people like Edward were useful. People had forgotten Laura Corridan. People had forgotten what had happened.

Only Edward remembered Laura, and only Edward still had nightmares, waking up sweating and shouting, seeing again the bedroom, himself moving in slow motion over to the night table, picking up the gun, raising his hand, squeezing the trigger . . . It was all too real, even now.

And then he started reading about the young French genius who was doing extraordinary things with airplanes, and all the gears in his head clicked into place. This was the beginning, he thought. This was the chance, the only chance that he might ever have. Miss this, and it would be all over.

The old excitement came back, as he negotiated eagerly with the French lawyers, as he made plans for the relocation and the subcontracting. He wasn't going to muck it up this time. He even cut back on the heavy drinking to which he had become accustomed; he wanted to be well-prepared for this chance of a lifetime.

And now, here sat Eric, asking him about where he had come from, and he knew that Eric might well understand. But he would wait. If there was to be a time of revelation, it was not now.

Edward smiled and said, diffidently, "Don't look a gift horse in the mouth, my boy. Just trust me. We'll be very good for each other."

Christmas, 1915. Amanda had gathered all of her courage and invited Charles Osbourne to the estate house in Newport, and to her surprise and delight he had accepted. She had seen him again in New York twice, but she was particularly anxious about this meeting.

They sat together under the Christmas tree, Amanda's

mother having chosen to remain in Cornish for the holiday, opening each other's presents and laughing and exclaiming over each package. Amanda giggled and drank warm spiced cider, and wondered at the warm flush of relaxation and well-being. It had been a long time since she had felt like this.

And then Charles handed her the smallest of all his presents, a small box with a satin ribbon. She opened it quickly, with the eagerness of a child, and when she saw what was in it her smile faded and she turned to look at him.

"What does this mean?"

He reached over and took the box from her, and withdrew the heavy diamond and ruby ring within. "This means," he said softly, "that, if you'll have me, I'd like to marry you. What will it be?"

She stared at him for a long moment, waiting for her heart to speak; but it was silent, and she sighed and decided to simply listen to her feelings instead. Which were warm and relaxed and happy. "Yes," she said, simply.

Charles took her hand and slowly slid the ring on her finger. "There you are, my dear," he said, kissing her.

He was more like a father than a husband, she thought; he was much older than she, confident, established, secure— but kind. He could give her the things she had never had—he was a man devoted only to her. The thought twisted inside her for a moment, painful, unwelcome. The man who had engendered her, her father, had never been a part of her life. The decision that her mother had made in the heat of passion had left her this legacy.

That wasn't going to matter at all, not anymore. She would never again think of her absent father with regret or longing. Charles would be him, for her. Charles would make her happy. That was all that mattered. Once married, she would no longer think of Philippe. Charles would banish all the ghosts.

Running barefoot into the kitchen, she returned with a bottle of cold champagne and glasses, watching him with adoring eyes as he popped the cork and poured the bubbly wine. "Merry Christmas, darling," she said warmly when he touched his glass to hers. "Merry Christmas."

Chapter Sixteen

I hear," Eric remarked to Anna, Sarah's mother, "that all the European pilots are wearing scarves like Sarah's now. Especially the aces. It's become the fashion."

Anna looked up politely from her coffee and pastry. He had begun the habit of taking Saturday breakfast at the Martins', even more important now since New Year's, when Mr. Martin had sustained a stroke which six months later still incapacitated him. Peter, it was to be noted, was glad to be running the business on his own, but Anna was concerned and grateful for Eric's steady presence.

"It's a nice tribute," she said, now. "But what a pity that the war is still going on! Is there no end in sight?" There was a time when she wouldn't have spoken of the war, for that was not women's business, and she had always carefully kept to her place. But life had changed at the house on Western Avenue since New Year's eve, when Herbert had collapsed on his way home from a party and hadn't gotten up since. Sarah, Eric thought sometimes, would have liked her mother more now. They would have had more in common. Another regret.

"I'm afraid not," Eric said, sipping at his coffee, and marveling once again at a nation of people who could drink it so weak. "Heated up, if anything. Everyone's fighting over the Somme." Eric's business was doing well because of the war. More work was going into the airplanes that were fueling the fire, and Eric, anticipating America's entrance into the action, was stepping up production. Hugo Junkers was dead, Eric had learned, shot down in one of his own airplanes, but the French and the English—to keep pace with the Germans, were stepping up their orders for airplanes. Thanks to Edward, A.R.M. stock was soaring in value. Eric had given a percentage of his interest in the company to Edward, who had at last taken an official title: Chief Executive Officer. They were turning over more of a profit on their own business than they were on the Johnson subcontracting. A National Advisory Committee for Aeronautics had been established in America, and Eric was invited to join.

And still Eric spent all of his spare moments in the house on Western Avenue with the people who had become his own. That was where life counted, there, with the woman who looked like the daughter she had hardly understood, with the man who could no longer talk and the younger man who talked too much, and with Sarah's photographs smiling a benediction on him from every wall. Here, at last, was home.

Amanda readied the hot wax to be applied to the envelope, and hesitated a moment, deciding to reread the letter one more time before sending it.

June 20, 1916

Dearest Mamma,

I'm writing to tell you that I'm married. Please don't be angry with me for not inviting you, we just had a Justice of the Peace and there was no sense in you coming all the way down here just for that. And don't be angry with me for getting married again (for I know well your views on marriage), because it really is so *dreary* to be unattached. It was all right for you, I suppose. It must have been or you wouldn't have chosen all these years not to marry. But I'm different than you, Mamma. It *is* nice to have somebody around that you can take to church on Sundays and so on. It's what I want, and it's what I have, now.

Anyway, anyway, anyway, I've found somebody just delightful. You'd rather like him in spite of yourself. His name is Charles Osbourne—yes, Mamma, *the* Charles Osbourne, who used to be such a tennis champion, see! I *told* you that you'd approve. I met him at some party, ho-hum, Gemma Robinson-Taft and her crowd, and he proposed to me over Christmas, and we've exercised remarkable restraint in waiting until June to actually get married, don't you think so?

Now, Mamma, here are the plans, just so that you know. Caroline is staying here in Newport, at the estate. There are simply scads of servants just sitting around with time on their hands and nothing to do, poor creatures. Anyway, anyway, anyway, she will stay on here, and you can see her if you ever decide to come back to *civilization* from your dreadful, chilly New Hampshire. And I am off to New York. I think that it will be just so amusing to stay in the city, for a few years at least, and play.

Well, Mamma, if you need to see Caroline, you can either run down to the estate on the train, or send for her to go up to Cornish (though *why* you insist on staying there is beyond me, Mamma. Cornish is passé now, don't you know. It *might* have been amusing when Saint-Gaudens and Maxfield Parrish and their little entourage lived there and gave all those *naughty* little parties, but really, Mamma! Aren't you living just a teensy bit in the *past*?) Just please don't involve me. Jenson is still at the estate, and you know how much he *adores* hearing from you, Mamma, and how *helpful* he is in making all those *tedious* arrangements, I really don't understand how he does it. Such a clever man, and so clever of you, Mamma, to have found him in the first place. Emma Kirkland was telling me just the other day that she would *kill* to get Jenson for her place. Anyway, Mamma, you and Jenson can make all the plans for Caroline that you like; I just want some time away from her with my husband, which really doesn't seem like a *great* deal to ask, don't you know.

Now there is still another problem which is endlessly *dreary*, and I am becoming quite cross with the whole thing. I am *still* getting those stock statements forwarded from you, Mamma. You know exactly what I'm talking about—Eric's little company out in California, I've forgotten its new name (and why on earth did he change it, just as we were getting used to the other?). I keep putting them in drawers, Mamma, but there are just so many drawers that one can fill, *n'est-ce pas*? Won't you please please simply keep them? I wrote a letter to those lawyers—silly beasts, they've moved from Paris to Zurich, I can't *imagine* why and it is most inconvenient, changing addresses like that;

how can I be expected to keep up?—but they say that the stock is in trust for Caroline and there's *nothing* that they can do but keep sending the statements and the dividends.

Mamma, understand this. I told Charles that Caroline is Marcus's daughter, and I fully intend to keep things that way. I do not want this surfacing and ruining my reputation. It just wouldn't do. After all, Mamma, I've never been left by any man, except for Philippe, and all over that stupid blind patriotism of his. After all, another woman is one thing, but I simply *couldn't* compete with a whole bloody country. Anyway, anyway, anyway, I don't want Charles coming across those statements and asking awkward questions. He really is quite proper. So do keep them, Mamma, there's a good sport, and I promise that I'll be good and read them all, every single scrap, next time that I come up to visit.

Lovingly,
Amanda

She sighed, and went about the business of sealing the envelope. Her mother wasn't going to like it, of course. She would have old-fashioned views about motherhood. Whatever her reasons had been for bearing a child out of wedlock, one certainly couldn't say that she hadn't devoted herself to Amanda's upbringing. But Charles had offered Amanda an escape—escape from the mansion in Newport and all its memories, memories of the times she had spent here with Sarah, of the times she had spent here alone aching for Philippe, and escape, too, from the bright eyes of the baby upstairs who was looking more and more like her father every day.

She had grasped at Charles's offer with the fervor of a drowning person reaching for a lifeline. She would go to New York, and forget it all.

If the price she paid was marriage to an older man, a man who aroused little passion in her, a man who felt more like a father to her, then so be it. She could always find someone to sleep with. Finding someone to be kind to her was something different altogether. She sat for a few minutes in silence, and then picked up her pen again. She didn't want to write to Eric, didn't want to communicate with him. It was too much like ripping open old wounds, but he, too, would have to know how definitively she was sealing off her past. He would have to know that Caroline was protected by one man's name and another man's fortune, and needed nothing more.

An hour later she shook her head and threw away the last of her writing paper and changed her clothes into something a little more becoming—shorter hemlines were again the rage—and went downstairs in search of a drink. She couldn't tell Eric. Not yet; not like this. It would just have to wait.

Charles was sitting in the immense living room, reading the newspaper. Amanda went over to the sideboard and poured herself a large gin and tonic. "Would you like anything?" she asked him, and he shook his head.

"How is the letter writing coming?" He put the newspaper down to devote his full attention to her. She liked that about him.

"All right. Mamma won't be happy, but I've never yet managed to make her happy, so what else is new?"

"Will she mind about you leaving the baby here? We could take her with us to New York, you know."

"Charles, darling, don't even think of it." She took a long drink from the glass in her hand, and went to sit next to him on the couch. "Caroline will be perfectly happy here. I was, and she can do all those silly things that children do. And the sea air is supposed to be good, or so people say, although I myself have never quite understood why they say it." She rested her head on his shoulder and felt the comfort and assurance flowing out, peacefully, from his body into hers.

Charles put his arm around his bride's shoulders and hugged her closer to him. "Well, Mrs. Osbourne," he said, "how does it feel to be married for nearly five hours?"

"Delicious," Amanda said, and snuggled even closer to him. "How shall we celebrate tonight?"

"A quiet night at home?" Charles suggested. "We could put some records on the gramophone and dance, here, in the living room."

"Don't be silly, darling." Amanda laughed. "One simply cannot just stay home, can one? It just wouldn't *do*." She thought about it for a moment and then sat up straighter, sparkling again. "I know, darling! The casino! We'll go and pop some champagne and have a little flutter and listen to the orchestra and dance there. Oh, Charles, do say yes! It will be the most spectacular night!"

He smiled and ruffled her hair fondly. "Whatever you would like, my dear."

"Then it's settled," she purred. "Oh, Charles, life is going to be so divine together."

He kissed the top of her head. "Yes," he said, meditatively. "It certainly does look that way."

Eric heard about Amanda's marriage by chance. He had written obediently every quarter to Beneteau and Giroux in Zurich, enclosing a full report on the doings of A.R.M. and the subcontracting work with Johnson Industries, and listened in turn to the advice they gave him. Edward usually concurred with their advice. They were all in agreement, it seemed, when it came to business procedures.

The lawyers' letter that fall of 1916 was filled with news: They had begun a subsidiary company for financial consulting. "The war," wrote Giroux, "has certainly had a positive impact on the economy, unstable as the markets may seem. There seems to be a pressing need for some financial consultancy, and we have decided to set up a subsidiary to answer that need. Operating independently, of course, as Financial Management Services. We'll be sending all of your accounting work along to them, just so that you recognize the name on the letterhead."

Eric shook his head. He was banking his own dividends from A.R.M., but it was obvious that the lawyers were putting their two percent to good use. He almost didn't read the rest of the letter.

"We have heard," continued Giroux, "from Mrs. Copeland regarding the status of her daughter Caroline and the ownership issues of A.R.M. Mrs. Copeland, as you may know, is in fact no longer Mrs. Copeland but Mrs. Osbourne, having married a Mr. Charles Osbourne of New York City in June." Here Eric shook his head in disbelief. So Amanda, like a chronic alcoholic, had thrown herself into the arms of still another man in order to deaden the pain. When, he wondered, was she going to grow up enough to face it on her own?

Perhaps never. Perhaps that was Amanda's fate, to always keep herself a child, an enfant terrible, gay and carefree and never confronting the issues of life.

"Miss Copeland is currently living in both Newport, Rhode Island and Cornish, New Hampshire with an entourage of servants and presumably the grandmother, with whom we have also been in correspondence. It is our assumption that Mrs. Lewis will take a more active role in Caroline's life once Mrs. Osbourne is well established in New York. Perhaps you could arrange a business trip to the East Coast in the near future and ascertain for yourself that Miss Copeland is being well provided for."

Eric put down the letter. Damn Amanda. What was she up to now? Beneteau and Giroux had investigated Osbourne, it appeared, and found nothing in his past or present to contraindicate marriage to Amanda "with the possible exception," Giroux wrote, "of his age, which is considerably more advanced than that of his wife. However, this may serve to bring some stability into her life which would be much needed, as you can imagine."

Eric planned a trip immediately. Edward was capable of running things without him there, and he would be no good at the drawing board or even in the boardroom with his mind on other things. He wanted to be in Rhode Island before Christmas.

Before Christmas. There was an echo there: Amanda resting on the overstuffed velvet sofa in the living room of the house on the rue de Verdun, smoking her cigarettes and laughing at Philippe, sitting so earnestly with his newspaper. "I don't see what all the fuss is about," she was saying. "Everybody—but *everybody*—says that the war will be over before Christmas." Philippe didn't believe her, and Philippe had been right, and Philippe had died.

And now everybody's attention was on the Battle of the Somme, and the war seemed to be endless, with the casualty counts mounting higher and higher each day. When would it end?

This was one Christmas promise, Eric told himself, that he was going to keep. One way or the other, he would look after Philippe's daughter.

Eric arrived in New York in a snowstorm, with the wind whipping the frozen crystals all around him and the air he sucked into his lungs frigidly cold and wet. It took him some time, and two taxicabs, to locate the Greenwich Village address that the lawyers had given him.

He hadn't told Amanda that he was coming because he was afraid that she would say no, or else simply disappear. It was not the sort of thing that he would put past her. Amanda's flight from reality was too extravagant for her not to protect it as strongly as she could.

The front door was painted a dark green, and a maid answered it, looking disapprovingly at the snow swirling around him. "Yes?"

"I'm here to see Mrs. Osbourne."

"I shall have to see if she is here. Who may I say is calling?"

"My name is Eric Beaumont. We're old friends." This brought another frown. "Listen, let me wait inside, won't you? It's very cold out here."

"I'll have to see if she is in," she repeated as Eric put his foot on the doorframe so that she couldn't close the door. "That will be fine," he said. "But look at the weather. I'm only asking to wait inside."

The maid frowned at him, and then at the snow, as though it were somehow Eric's own doing, and then she relented. "All right, but just in the front hall here. I won't have you tracking things about on the carpet."

Eric took off his hat and coat, and stood and waited. Finally, he heard a flurry of footsteps on the stairs, and then Amanda was standing there, beautiful as ever, her cheeks flushed and her eyes angry. She was wearing a velvet dress, just below her knees in length, and cut low in front in a long V neck, strands of pearls wrapped around her throat and at her ears. She had cut her hair short, he noticed, the lustrous curls framing her delicate face. She was magnificent. She was also furious.

"What are you doing here?" It was a whisper, but the force behind the words was strong. "How did you find me?"

"I'm fine, Amanda, and how are you?" He was determined to avoid a confrontation.

She glanced over her shoulder. "Come in here," and she took his arm and pulled him into a small drawing room. Shutting the door, and leaning against it, she glared at him. "Why are you here?"

Eric looked around him, taking in the fringed lampshades and the velvet-covered furniture and the Persian carpet, the modern paintings on the wall. He sat down and eased a packet of cigarettes from his pocket. "You don't have to worry," he said. "I know that you're married, and I know that your husband doesn't know about Philippe. It's all right. I'm not going to say anything."

She relaxed slightly and went to sit across from him, reaching automatically for the cigarette he offered. "Then why, Eric?"

"I want to go see Caroline."

"Caroline?" Amanda exhaled and stared at him through the smoke. "Why on earth do you want to see Caroline?"

He shrugged. "I have an obligation."

"To him?" she asked, and then laughed. "Poor dear Eric, you do take things seriously, don't you? She's fine. I tell those silly little lawyers so every time they write."

"I'd still like to see her. You can tell your husband that I was a friend of Marcus's, if you'd like, but I want to see her from time to time."

"And me?"

The question took him by surprise. "It's been my impression that you wanted no part of seeing me, Amanda. I've stayed away to accommodate you, because I felt that you didn't want any part of me."

"Well, if you're not going to be difficult, I don't see why we should have to stay strangers. Actually, I always rather liked you, Eric, darling. We never had much to say to each other, but you've always been kind. That's something that I've come to value in recent times, you know. Kindness." She paused, and then went on, her voice almost diffident. "Of course, there's more to life than kindness. There's passion." She blew out some more smoke and looked at him speculatively. "I don't suppose that there's any hope of seducing you."

He was surprised, and didn't try to hide it. "I don't suppose so."

She sighed. "That's what I thought. Worth a try, though, anyway. It might have been nice to become lovers—after all we've been through together, it seems that's the only thing that we haven't shared. And I do think I owe you something. . . . You saved my life, that night in Paris. I hated you for it, then. But I'm rather glad of it, now, on the whole."

Eric wasn't sure what to say. Become Amanda's lover? Most men who met her would kill for the opportunity. Her lovemaking would no doubt reflect what she was in other spheres of life, he thought: creative, enthusiastic, coquettish, difficult, petulant. . . . Like a roller coaster ride. But he hadn't come here for a roller coaster, and, besides, he had become too wise. He had learned through his grief, and he knew why she was asking him to do this. "You know that you can't recover what you're looking for by going to bed with me."

A quick sharp glance. "What do you mean?"

He shrugged. "Oh, you know, after Sarah died and then Philippe died, I thought about it, too. About us staying together. About falling in love with each other. Of course I did, and you did, too—don't look at me like that. They had left us, and we were there together, and you were so beautiful and so vulnerable. . . ." He took a deep breath. "It seemed to make some sense. God, Amanda, a man would have to be blind, or crazy, or both, not to think those thoughts. Men dream about taking you to bed. And I knew that we could have tried to build something together. But I knew that it was wrong, too, though it took me a while to figure out why. I know why, now." He hesitated, not wanting to hurt her. "Amanda, I'd only be looking to you for memories of Sarah, and you'd only be looking to me for memories of Philippe, and it wouldn't work. It wouldn't be fair to who we really are."

She stretched out her hand, wordlessly, and after a moment he lit another cigarette and handed it to her. "I expect," she said at length, "that you're right." And she concentrated very hard at keeping back the tears. So sudden, so unexpected . . . She hadn't thought about Eric for so very long, except when she was trying to tell him about her marriage, and had given up for lack of words. And now here he was, so close, so familiar, so safe—and so undeniably attractive, masculine, and strong. He stirred her, inside, and she found herself mourning the loss of the desire as quickly as it had come.

Eric was still watching her. "What is it, Amanda? What is wrong?"

"I don't know!" she said, explosively, and he saw that she was very close to tears. "People tell me that I'm attractive, but . . ."

She was watching him, waiting for a comment. "You're beautiful, Amanda. You always have been."

She sat primly, looking a little lost and a little afraid. "Then what's wrong with me?"

"I don't understand, Amanda. Doesn't your husband love you?" What on earth have I wandered into? he wondered.

"He's—oh, Eric, he's kind and considerate, and he takes such good care of me. And I shouldn't ask for more, I really shouldn't. But he's so boring. He won't go anyplace, or do anything. And he won't make love to me. He just falls asleep."

Eric raised his eyebrows. "The ultimate insult."

"Well, it is, rather, don't you think? And it's not that I feel so very passionate about him myself, come to that, it's just that one really ought to . . ."

"Only if one wants to, Amanda, dear," Eric reminded her gently. "It's not something that you have to do. And don't do it so that you can try and resurrect Philippe."

She blew smoke out from her mouth. "Eric, darling, you're missing the point. It's so that I don't have to try and resurrect Philippe."

"Quite so," he said, not really understanding. "Well, Amanda, you're still as beautiful as ever, and your husband is a fool not to think so—or not to take advantage of it. How is Caroline?"

"How is Caroline? What sort of question is that?" Amanda asked, irritably. "I expect that she is well. My mother is with her in Newport, taking care that she is raised correctly, I suppose. My mother is always correct." She glanced at him. "She's only two years old, Eric."

"I know." And what was that supposed to mean, he wondered. Was Amanda afraid that he might talk to Caroline and tell her the truth? It was a reasonable fear, but he would hardly address a two-year-old. That could wait.

There was a noise in the corridor, and the door opened, revealing a tall man with a ruddy complexion, graying hair, and twinkling blue eyes. "Amanda? I'm sorry to interrupt—"

Amanda had sprung to her feet. "Charles! No interruption at all . . . Please . . ." She was wringing her hands in nervousness, and Eric wondered about that, and decided to help her. He stood up and walked over to the door, his hand already out. "Hello. I'm Eric Beaumont. I was a friend of Marcus Copeland's, and happened to be in New York, and thought that I'd pay my respects to Amanda."

"Well, of course!" The older man beamed, pumping Eric's hand up and down. "My name's Charles Osbourne. Delighted to meet you! And splendid of you to drop by, especially in this weather. Amanda, dear, see if Mr. Beaumont won't stay to supper."

"Thank you," Eric said smoothly. "But I think not, tonight. I'm really on my way out of town, going up to Boston on some business. I was hoping to get permission to stop off and see Caroline on my way." He shrugged. "Just a gesture, you see. Marcus was so looking forward to her birth."

Amanda was staring at Eric as if he had gone mad. Charles nodded and beamed at him. "I understand perfectly, old man. Tragedy that he never got to see his own daughter. Tragedy." His voice didn't sound tragic in the least. He casually put his arm around Amanda's shoulders. "What business is it that you're in, Mr. Beaumont?"

"I do subcontracting work in California from a firm called Johnson Industries. Perhaps you've heard of them?"

"I have indeed. That war in Europe seems to be helping their business, I'd say. Judging from your accent, you must come from Europe yourself."

Eric nodded. "France. I decided that it didn't pay to stay around with the war going on, though."

"Makes sense to me. Perfect sense. Don't want to make yourself the sacrificial lamb, I suppose . . . Well, we won't keep you, then. Amanda, why don't we just give Jenson a ring and tell him to be expecting Mr. Beaumont? He could spend the night at the estate and proceed to Boston tomorrow."

"Well; I—" began Amanda.

"I'd be most grateful," Eric said, and Amanda closed her mouth.

"Splendid," said Charles, warmly, and began walking Eric to the door. "Beastly weather. Can't think of the last time it snowed like this in the city. Ah, thank you, Mildred. Here's your coat. There we are." He waited while Eric put on his coat and hat and muffler. "Good luck to you, Mr. Beaumont."

"Good-bye, Eric," said Amanda distinctly, standing behind her husband.

Eric looked at both of them for a moment, and then nodded and let himself out. It wasn't what he had expected; he wasn't sure exactly what he had expected. But there were changes happening in Amanda's life.

There was a new thought, he reflected as he rode north on the train. He had many changes occurring in his own life, but he expected, somehow, for Amanda's life to simply sit still. He wanted her—the most changeable creature on earth—to stay steady for him. He wanted no change where there had to be change; he found he resented her for it. Put in that perspective, one could really do little more than smile.

He returned to San Jose early in January, having found Caroline not in Newport, after all, but at the Lewis house in New Hampshire.

Mrs. Lewis was a forbidding woman who knew at once who he was and why he had come, but she softened over tea and scones in her long kitchen which overlooked the Connecticut River. "You've got more sense than Amanda, at least," she snorted after they had been talking awhile. "Did this Philippe fellow have sense, too?"

"More than me," Eric said, half truthfully.

"Well, then. It is a pity about him dying. Shan't tell the child yet, though." Her steely blue eyes met his and dared him to contradict her.

"Not yet," Eric agreed. "Later, though."

She nodded. "Later."

He gestured towards the child, playing nearby with Mrs. Driscoll. "She's beautiful."

"She's got more than her share, yes. Same as her mother."

Eric looked up. "Same as her father."

"That may well be. I haven't much use for men, myself. They were mostly a bother, all of them. I prefer to spend my time with women. They can be catty, Mr. Beaumont, but they're seldom senseless. The 'Mrs.' in my name is purely a courtesy. I was born a Lewis and will die a Lewis, you see. I never bothered to marry Amanda's father; the man had no sense at all. Just like him, she is. And all this nonsense about that trust fund . . ." She peered at him. "Is it such an important thing?"

Eric shrugged. "The dividends hardly equal your family fortune yet, no. We'll have to see what happens in the future."

"There's something that you're not saying, young man. What is it?"

He shook his head. "Just that there's more to it all than

money, than dividends. Edward Buchanan—that's my chief executive in San Jose, the business end of the company if you will—Edward thinks that not now, and not for a long time to come, but someday the company might be very powerful. I don't know myself. If that happens, then the stock Caroline holds would be worth a great deal."

She thought it over. "What kind of power?"

"Edward says that the aeronautics industry is the driving force behind politics. Philippe de Montclair thought that, too. They may be right."

"You're giving me other people's opinions, not yours. Why do you distance yourself from all that?"

Eric shrugged again. "It's not of any interest to me. All I care about is designing airplanes. If the war ever ends, I want to do work in jet propulsion. I don't care much about politics, and the ins and outs of the business world aren't particularly interesting to me, either. I'd rather leave it to people like Edward who speak the language."

"Nonsense. Your English is more than adequate."

He grinned. "It's not English that we're talking about, Mrs. Lewis."

She returned his smile, vivid and unexpected. "Ah, well, there you are, Mr. Beaumont. And now it is time for my nap." He stood up with her, and she smiled dismissively. "It has been a pleasure, Mr. Beaumont."

He shook her hand. "I assure you, Mrs. Lewis, it was all mine."

She turned at the door. "Mr. Beaumont?"

"Yes?"

"Come and see my granddaughter whenever you wish. You're less a fool than most men. I can even talk to you, sometimes. You seem to have some sense, and that's what the child needs in her life. You might even do her some good." And then she was gone.

He found himself whistling as his feet crunched on the packed snow on his way out to the motorcar he had rented in Boston. He had very little doubt but that Mrs. Lewis would, in her own way, do Caroline a great deal of good as well. Funny, though, that Amanda could have a mother such as Margaret Lewis.

He returned home to rainstorms and a dismal note from Edward. "Happy New Year. We have problems. Get back to work!"

"What is it?" Eric hadn't bothered going downtown to the office; he merely telephoned as he sifted through the rest of his mail. A card from Mrs. Martin. He smiled.

"Eric, my boy, Johnson's getting irritated. It doesn't do to irritate them. Not this early in the game."

"Irritated about what?"

"Oh, nothing major, my boy. Just the fact that you've cost them three of their best engineers since December."

"I don't know what you're talking about, Edward," he said blankly, reading Mrs. Martin's invitation to Sunday dinner.

"Eric, my boy, wake up and smell the coffee! They've defected. Joined the enemy camp." Eric could hear him sigh. "They've come to work for us, my boy! Shows remarkable sense on their part, I can't say that it doesn't. They see a winning venture when it's staring them in the face, but in the meantime! The powers that be are not happy, my boy."

"So to hell with the powers that be."

"I'm not so very sure that we can be that cavalier at this particular point in time, my boy. We haven't gotten ourselves a name yet. We still should be subcontracting."

"If they don't like my work then to hell with them. If their people think it's more interesting working for me, then that's fine. Edward, for God's sake, let's just make airplanes!"

There was a pause, during which Eric could imagine Edward working on his cigar. "Well, my boy, you might have a point there. You know, of course, that the demand has stepped up?"

"Yes." The newspapers in New York and Newport and Boston had been screaming at Eric for weeks. Wilson had run on an antiwar ticket but was now seriously considering entering the fray in Europe. The U.S. Army had already started putting their orders in.

"So why don't we start competing with Johnson?" Edward spoke up. "I'll talk it over with the firm in Zurich and let you know."

"Whatever you like, Edward. I just want to do my work, all right? I don't want to get involved in bickering. That's what you're there for."

"At my level, my boy, we don't call it bickering. We call it negotiations."

Chapter Seventeen

Eric still didn't realize that he held the key to the future in his hands.

All that mattered to him was the work. And he went at it doggedly, creating and thinking and living out the vision that he and Philippe had promised each other on a faraway star-drenched night when dreams seemed as close and real as the horses moving restlessly in their stalls nearby.

All the while, he pondered on how to make things better, better, better, and all the while he held the key in his hands.

The key, Edward had said, was locating the problem. Solutions are a dime a dozen, my boy. Find the problem. Solving it would be a piece of the proverbial cake.

Well, it had been easy to locate the problem with Johnson Industries: a lack of imagination, a lack of skill in determining needs—a lack of everything, actually, except money. As Edward said, there was a war on, "and there is nothing like a nice hot war to generate a lot of nice cold cash." Edward said it in glee. He was picking up a percentage of the A.R.M. profits. Eric didn't care. All that mattered to him was his work.

Locate the problem, and then find a solution. He had found another problem, and by the winter of 1917 Eric was sure that he had found the solution: Boron.

It had been in front of him all along, of course, only he was too tired or drunk or whatever he happened to be at the time to notice. His father had used a derivative of it at the de Montclair estate, for Christ's sake. And he hadn't even noticed.

He could see it now, by closing his eyes and remembering:

his father at the smithy, with his huge leather apron and the fires glowing blue and hot, and Eric sitting nearby, chewing on a blade of grass or drinking a beer, talking, and—with his mind on something else altogether—watching. He watched his father pour the white powder on the metal and heat it, talking casually all the while about one of the estate horses or the wager going on in the village over the paternity of the Menusier girl's new baby, and the powder effervesced and bubbled on the metal the whole time through. Eric watched it, and never made the connection.

Boron was there in the damned gramophone needle, too, when he and Sarah cranked up the old machine she had saved up for, and listened to the music and danced together, her scent in his nostrils and her body warm and sweet and supple against his. It brought him his first livelihood, and it brought him his most special times with Sarah, and he never realized the importance it would have in his future.

It was simple. Airplanes now were being designed for war—for battle. In order to achieve speed and carry heavier loads, the airplanes had to be light, but they also had to be strong enough not to fall apart when subjected to high velocities, or much tension. The British "quirk" airplanes were falling apart all the time. Too much strain on the frames of airplanes was producing dead pilots. In combat situations, the last thought on a pilot's mind was how fast he could go before his airplanes fell apart. He was more interested in how fast he could go before he would get caught by the airplane pursuing him. And the answer had been there all the time.

Alloyed with aluminum, boron produced a strong, hard, light metal. Eric worked the calculations over and over again, late into the night, the numbers and ideas and possibilities filling his head. Smoke from the pipe he had taken to smoking since Mrs. Martin had made him the gift of one for Christmas filled the room and empty bottles accumulated by his worktable. Finally, one night he pushed back his chair. Sarah's photograph smiled a benison over him, and he winked at her. "We did it, *cherie*," he said, raising his glass just a little. "We did it."

Edward, to his dismay, was less than wildly enthused about the idea. "Boron? Never heard of it," he said briskly.

Eric was undeterred. "Well, why would you?" he asked reasonably. "You're not a chemist, or a blacksmith. But it's going to work, and we need it."

"Where do we get it? How much does it cost?" Always practical, that was Edward. He puffed at his cigar, and then leaned forward. "Who knows about it?" he asked, suddenly.

Eric sucked in his cheek and considered. "Anybody who's interested in ironworking probably knows about it. It's an integral part of the process. I don't think that anyone's thought of applying it to the manufacture of airplanes, though. I'd be surprised if anyone did. It took me most of last night to work it through."

Edward thought for a moment, and then nodded. "Anything to help the flying machines. It's a great idea. Got to keep the lid on this, my boy. Think of something brilliant, and everybody's quick to jump on the bandwagon, if you catch my drift." He clapped Eric on the shoulder. "Splendid work, my boy. French wonder, that's what you are. All right. Down to the fundamentals. Where do we get it, how do we get it, and how much is it going to cost?"

Eric didn't meet his eyes. "It's in the desert, Edward."

There was a pause, during which time Edward removed a gold watch from his pocket, peered at it, and then looked up at Eric. "In the desert? Lying about, you mean?"

"Not quite. It's a derivative. It's taken from ulexite and colemanite, and it's found in deposits in the desert." He paused. "In Death Valley, to be precise."

Edward frowned. "That's not exactly our backyard, you know. You absolutely need this stuff, my boy? Sounds expensive."

"Yes, I absolutely need it, and yes, it's expensive." Edward wasn't going to like this, he thought. "Seven hundred and eighty dollars a ton," he said, softly.

"Seven hundred dollars a ton?" He sounded strangled. "That's highway robbery, my boy! Highway robbery."

"Seven hundred and eighty dollars," Eric corrected him. "And I need it. They bring it in on alternate Tuesdays. By mule trains." He took a deep breath. "And I absolutely do need it."

Edward's face was bright red, but his mind hadn't stopped. One could almost feel him running projections. "We'll just see about that, my boy. We'll just see about that."

He frowned at the glowing tip of his cigar. He was all ready to be off and fighting, the same spark in his eyes that always showed up whenever he felt pushed or challenged. Eric smiled.

"Just get me my boron, Edward. That's all I ask."

"Boron you want, and boron you shall have, my boy. Seven hundred and eighty dollars a ton! I ask you! We'll work on it, my boy; we'll work on it. Keep this little project under your hat, though, that's the ticket."

Eric smiled. In his mind, the creation process was already completed. If only, he thought, he could simply sit back and work on the bloody stuff. He knew what he was doing, and he knew that he was doing good work, but everybody was constantly making other demands on him. Even Edward, who certainly had his best interests at heart, made demands on him: Tell me more about your process. Document it, document it, my boy. But be very careful. Can't let people know what we're up to. Do this, do that, but be very careful. Above all, be very, very careful.

Eric sighed. Secret documents and shady deals were part of the new world he had entered, this world of businesses and corporations and people who would as soon spit on your grave as say good morning to you. He understood all of that, but it was still hard to accept, to become accustomed to. His old world was more familiar, much safer, much easier. It had been much easier to be on the airfield with Philippe and Amanda and Sarah.

That train of thought was not getting him anywhere. He roused himself and brought his mind back to the project at hand. Expense was Edward's primary concern, not his. So it was expensive pulling boron out of the desert by mule train; he still had to have the boron.

Eric didn't tell anybody about the process, of course. There was really no one to tell. Frankly, he kept to himself too much. But Johnson, it soon became evident, knew that he was trying to get boron out of the desert. There had been some not-so-subtle hints dropped, some suggestions, all of which he ignored. He was fulfilling the subcontracting work which Johnson had hired A.R.M. to do. It was quite simply none of their business if he decided to do other things as well. There was no exclusivity clause in the contract.

But Johnson knew that the French brainchild was hauling boron out of the desert—and for a hefty price tag, too—and they were determined to find out why. They couldn't. Edward had seen to it that the secret was well-guarded; there was nothing for them to find out. So they did the next best thing.

Eric took a deep breath. They say that the husband is always the last to know, he reminded himself. He wouldn't know; his wife had never been unfaithful. But he was married to his work as well, and he knew in this moment, even before walking into the conference room, that he had lost her.

Johnson was claiming a patent on the processing of boron from the ulexite and the colemanite found in Death Valley. Monsieur Beaumont and A.R.M. could continue to manufacture boron, of course, and do whatever they pleased with the boron—but they were going to have to pay a fee to Johnson Industries each and every time that they did.

Edward was livid.

"It won't do, my boy. It simply won't do," he said furiously under his breath. "There has to be a way around it. There has to be."

Eric was resigned. "We lost it, Edward. Admit it. We're just going to have to make enough money to make up for the loss of the patenting process."

"That's not good enough! That's simply not good enough!" He puffed furiously at his cigar. "It won't work. We'll sustain more losses than we can manage. I don't know if you realize this, my boy, but there is a very fine line in business between the black and the red, and I greatly fear that we are treading dangerously near that line at this moment. We can't afford it."

Eric spun his glass around on the table at Clem's Café, where whenever they were in Los Angeles he and Edward sat night after night, drinking and devising wild plans—some of which even came true. Or might. Or could. He looked up at Edward. "I have to have the boron. I can't possibly work without it. You don't understand. The possibilities of use are . . . staggering."

"How staggering?" The drink had not dimmed the shrewdness in Edward's eyes, nor slurred the sharpness in his voice.

Eric sighed. "I might be dreaming, Edward, but I think—I think that if I had some good chemists, and some good engineers working for me . . ." His voice trailed off and Edward prodded him.

"Yes? If you had them, what then?"

Eric looked up and said softly and very solemnly, "The stars, Edward. I want the stars."

"You are speaking, of course, figuratively."

"I am speaking as literally as I know how. Later, when the war is over, and I get back to working on jet propulsion . . . There are other things, too, industrial uses. We could make a lot of money, Edward. But if we can fly, why not fly as far as we can?"

Edward chuckled. "You, my boy, have flying on the brain. You should have been a bird."

"I loved one, once." There was silence for a moment, and then he looked up and said in a normal voice, "Edward, I'm not giving up on the boron."

The other man lit a cigar and puffed pensively. "And I, my boy, am not giving up to Johnson Industries. I think that their usefulness for us has come to an end."

"You mean that we should stop subcontracting?"

Edward's eyes glittered. "I mean, my boy, that I want to take them on."

There was a moment of silence, and then Eric spoke into it, his voice soft. "You're insane. They're mammoth. They *are* the bloody industry, Edward."

"Right. And so are we. You aim for the stars, but you don't even have the vision to see three feet in front of your nose. I find that mildly disturbing, my dear boy. Mildly disturbing. A.R.M. is the industry, too, and if Johnson wants to play, then we'll show them just how hard we can play."

Eric shook his head. "It's David and Goliath, Edward. It'll never fly."

"Remember when they said that about your little attempts at airplanes? Leave it to me, my boy." He patted Eric's back. "Leave it to me."

Everyone but Amanda, it seemed, was going to France.

The Americans had finally entered the war, and with a vengeance. Everywhere, but everywhere, one walked one

saw posters urging young men to sign up for the Army or the
Navy. Amanda tried to ignore them, but it was difficult. One
gray afternoon when Charles was indisposed—and Charles
was so often indisposed—when she had taken in a news
film, she emerged into the street to find it raining. She ran
for shelter under an awning and found herself examining
recruitment posters while she waited for a taxi to rescue her.
The Sword Is Drawn: The Navy Upholds It, exclaimed one.
Join The Air Service and Serve In France. Do It Now!
declared another.

Amanda turned away from the bright colors, hugging
herself, feeling faintly nauseated. They all made it sound
like a game, like something fun, like something to do as a
distraction. A Wonderful Opportunity for You, one of the
posters read. She had seen what that wonderful opportunity
was. Her daughter's father had been killed responding to
that wonderful opportunity. Her dreams, or so it seemed
lately, were haunted by arcing tracers and airplanes dropping bombs on cities, by screams and moans of pain,
because of that wonderful opportunity.

And yet Americans were responding to it in droves. "Over
there," they all sang gaily. It was something exciting and
romantic. Women in the streets giggled over the men's
uniforms, and men gave them passionate kisses to last until
they came home.

How many, Amanda wondered dully, would actually
come home at all? And how many would die and be buried
in shallow unmarked graves in the poppy fields where her
Philippe lay? How many? How long?

But when the taxi came, she got in and forced herself to be
gay. That was the only way to cover the dull ache inside that
came from tears still unshed for all of her losses, losses that
she sometimes felt she could no longer bear. Longing for the
house on the rue de Verdun and the careless happy days
when she had lived there with Philippe and Sarah and Eric
persisted. So did anger at the violence that had torn
everything and everyone that she had loved away from her.

She blinked hard. Charles was supposed to keep her from
feeling the ache. That was what she needed: people to fill her
house, to fill her days, to fill her life so that she wouldn't
have to be alone and feel that unbearable pain. Charles
wasn't doing it by himself.

Soon she was going to have to go looking for someone who would.

Robert Beneteau frowned and went over the report a final time, peering at the paper through his pince-nez, his thumb drumming absently on the edge of the table. The other men in the room stayed absolutely still, waiting, patient. There are times when fortunes can turn on a word, so to speak, when money can be won or lost in a matter of moments. Those who wish to acquire fortunes wait and speak very softly indeed on such occasions.

Marc Giroux was watching his partner's face. Intent, with more lines than it had ever had before, his own was a caricature of intensity. Almost without noticing it, his hand strayed to his pocket and brought out a roll of white antacid tablets. Absently, he placed one in his mouth. The ulcer had not stayed at bay forever.

The other three men in the room continued to wait with patience. One of them smoked a cigarette; another carefully removed his glasses and cleaned them thoroughly, an exercise in futility since they had been immaculate to begin with. Nervous tics, all of them. They were conscious of the power which they were holding, the power to decide and advise one way or another. And the choice had to be correct.

Above all, they could not make any errors. Not at this stage in the game.

When Beneteau and Giroux had moved to Zurich, they began to take on additional partners—there were now five of them in all—and they began to expand, to acquire subsidiary companies. The two percent stock of A.R.M. was serving them very well, and the quiet dusty Paris days were long over.

Beneteau finally looked up, first at Giroux, and then his gaze traveled over the three younger partners. They had not hired family lawyers; they had hired young hardened attorneys who specialized: corporate law, international law. There were no senile old ladies leaving estates to toy poodles, here.

"What do you have to say about this report?" Beneteau's voice was dry, and he reached for the glass of water he always kept near him these days.

Giroux spoke first, as was his right as senior partner. The

others deferred to him. "If Monsieur Buchanan is correct—and we have no reason to believe that he is not, he has been thoroughly investigated—then the time is right. The opportunity is right. A.R.M. has a chance of becoming a major force—not just in the industry, but in the world. I say that we should not pass up such an opportunity."

"Please explain what you mean, Marc."

The younger man gestured. "*Voilà.* The war is going to end soon, it can't go on forever, and then there will be a slump in production. We do not need to be affiliated with an industry standard which made its mark in wartime. People want peace."

"War is what makes money," the corporate lawyer, whose name was Rousseau, commented drily. The youngest of the lawyers, Rousseau was also the most cynical. Having come of age during the war, he insisted on viewing it with dispassion.

Giroux nodded. "Of course, of course. And it has made us a great deal of money. But we are not at a place yet where we can decide upon who goes to war and who does not. What we can decide is whether or not we want people to have confidence in us."

"So you are saying that a break from Johnson Industries would inspire that confidence?"

"Of course it would. We are ready to move on into peace, into rebuilding the world, into promoting the values that everybody's been fighting about all these years: the war to end all wars. Some people actually believe that, you know."

Beneteau cleared his throat. "Our Monsieur Beaumont does not seem to have invested a great deal of energy into this plan."

"Our Monsieur Beaumont is a genius. He is also—like most geniuses—very nearsighted. He cannot see what this would mean for his company."

Beneteau looked at him sharply. "And precisely what would it mean, Marc?"

Giroux sat forward on the front of his chair and began to talk very rapidly, very excitedly. "*Voilà.* Monsieur Beaumont is experimenting with alloys. He says it's to make lighter, stronger planes that are well balanced. *Moi,* I know nothing of such things, but I know he has succeeded. Bravo, Monsieur Beaumont." He took a deep breath. "But there is more. He is interested in rockets. He is interested in jet propulsion. There will be another war, gentlemen. There is no question about that, I believe, in any of our minds. There will be another war, and when it comes, whoever has superior weaponry will vanquish. And whichever industry is manufacturing the superior weapons will have the government dependent upon them." He looked around. "Do I make my point?"

"So the sooner that we become independent, the sooner the lines will be drawn within the industry," said De Mornay, the expert in international law.

"Yes, Monsieur de Mornay. That is it."

Beneteau said, "There is logic in what you have to say, Marc. Me, I would support it. But we cannot do this alone. The fact still remains that Monsieur Beaumont is not as interested in this particular business transaction as we might like."

Rousseau cleared his throat delicately. "Well, monsieur, I think that I can perhaps be of some assistance in this matter. The matter of Monsieur Beaumont, of course."

"Of course." Beneteau and Giroux exchanged looks of amusement. "Pray enlighten us."

"I have—er—taken the liberty of going through the files on Monsieur Beaumont. It is common knowledge within these offices that he was married to one of the first women pilots, Mademoiselle Sarah Martin, and that she died tragically, to his deep distress—is it not?" Assenting nods all around. Beneteau added, "There are those who believe that he has not been the same since her death."

Rousseau nodded. "Just so. And it is also common knowledge that Mademoiselle Martin died when she and a passenger fell out of the airplane that she was flying in Boston?" He paused. "I did some research, messieurs. The gentleman passenger who fell first, a Mr. Stanley Williams, thus upsetting the balance in the airplane and causing it to flip Mademoiselle Martin to her death as well, was manager of a company in the Midwest"—he consulted his files— "called Williams Tool and Die Company, which was going bankrupt. His wife was long dead, but the woman he had been seeing of late had recently left him for his partner, and together they absconded with what they could get of the remaining company funds. It was very clearly suicide, messieurs. A note was found, later, written to his daughter, telling her of his plight and of his plans." Another pause. "He killed Mademoiselle Martin in the process, of course, and the suicide note never became public for various political reasons. But, more to the point for us, messieurs, the company in question was a subsidiary company of Johnson Industries, Inc., and could quite conceivably have been saved financially had Johnson decided to do so. Mr. Williams did apparently turn to them for financial assistance. They did not choose to give him any, and wrote the company off as a loss. And so Mademoiselle Martin died." He looked around. "What more do we need?"

"You can prove this? You have documentation?" Giroux asked excitedly.

"Absolutely."

"In what form?"

"Company records. A copy of the note, hand-copied by the daughter in question and with a signed affadavit saying that it was indeed in her father's writing and that he had handed it to her personally before leaving for the exhibition in Boston. An article from the Kansas City *Sun-Times*—his hometown paper—telling of his financial plight, that of his company, and its affiliation with Johnson Industries, with the request for funding; another article telling of his death."

Beneteau was brusque. "Very well. We send the articles anonymously to Monsieur Beaumont. If that doesn't get him out for blood, nothing will. Johnson Industries will be called upon to act as scapegoat for its unfortunate subsidiary." He allowed himself a brief smile. "Nothing, of course, could suit us better. Agreed, gentlemen?"

Of course they agreed. The playing of the game was all that counted now.

Eric got drunk over the newspaper clippings. He had thought about the accident often in the ensuing years, but then A.R.M. had begun to fill the void in his life, and he had lived. He had begun to reach for the stars, as he had promised Philippe. His debt was paid.

And now, five years later, here it was again, as fresh and painful and unnecessary as it had been back in 1912. The man had killed himself deliberately, the newspaper clippings said; as did the letter to his daughter and the company reports. He had killed himself deliberately, and in so doing had—just as deliberately—killed Sarah.

And he had worked for Johnson Industries.

Johnson could have saved Williams's company. They could have underwritten a loan, pulled it into the black, paid for the air show which had cost Eric so dearly. They could have done so many things, but Williams Tool and Die was a small subsidiary, meaningless, best to be written off as a loss. No one at Johnson Industries, Eric was willing to wager, had lost any sleep over the incident.

They could have saved Stanley Williams, and saved Sarah, and they hadn't. She could still be there today, alive and vibrant and laughing and warm. She wasn't, and she wasn't because of Johnson Industries.

It was no longer a matter of paying too much to haul boron out of the desert. He stared morosely into his glass of beer—he had never shared Edward's taste for Scotch and had given up on trying to drink American wines—and thought about how he would cut the throat of one of the largest industrial firms in the world.

When he had it figured out, finally, he smiled. And that night he slept.

Chapter Eighteen

*I*t's still not going to work."

Edward hadn't realized that he was speaking aloud until Eric, sitting across from him at the huge mahogany table in Eric's office, looked up. "What was that?"

"What was—hmm? Oh, sorry, my boy. Preoccupied, and all that. Didn't mean to think out loud."

"What isn't going to work?"

"Cash flow problems, my boy. Nothing to trouble yourself with. My problem entirely."

Eric frowned. "I thought that we were doing all right. We've been expanding—we've got those buildings off the new road south of San Jose. How did we construct them without any money?"

Edward leaned back and began patting his waistcoat, searching for the inevitable cigar. "Ah. There it is, my boy—the joys of capitalism. You don't need actual money in order to get what you want, you simply have to know who will do things for you on the strength of future assets."

"Future assets?"

"Projected future assets, then, there's the ticket." He had located the cigar and now lit it with some ceremony. "Ah. Much, much better. Assets. Well, you see, my boy, the fly in the ointment, if I may be permitted so gauche an expression, is still and forever our friends at Johnson."

"I thought that we were free of them now."

"One is never free of one's nemesis, my boy. And you didn't exactly endear yourself to management with that plan of yours, either—luring all their finest engineers away to A.R.M., tut, tut. Not good diplomacy, my boy. Not good diplomacy." But he was smiling.

Eric returned the smile. "Yes, well, they're happier now. We're much more progressive than Johnson."

"A snail is more progressive than Johnson, my boy. A snail. However, you are very clever, and I expect that they'll work out well here. Still," and he puffed on the cigar, "they're still being tiresome with that boron deal. Johnson, that is, not your clever little engineers. Got to find a way around that, and we'll solve all our problems."

Eric sighed and walked over to the window. The ocean was there, the great Pacific Ocean, bright and sparkling in the morning sunshine, and once again that familiar longing welled up inside of him—the longing for Sarah. "I hate them," he said suddenly, explosively, without turning back to face Edward.

"So I've gathered, my boy. So I've gathered. Though you've never made me aware of the details of this particular obsession of yours—"

"It's personal." Eric sat down again and started to play with his lucky wrench lying on the table. "What are the options?"

Edward sighed and shook his head. "Personal," he thought, read Sarah. She was the only personal aspect of Eric's life. Everything else, all his energies and passions and ambitions, belonged to A.R.M. It wasn't healthy, but there it was. "I'm thinking that we should go public with some of our stock," he said levelly.

"Go public with A.R.M. stock?"

"There, there, my boy, don't panic, no need to panic. Not all of it, my boy, not all of it. Just enough to get us a little more on the black side of the ledger, that's all. Used to play the stocks, I did, when I was younger than I am now. Know a little about them. Stock, that's the ticket. It should sell like hotcakes."

Eric shrugged; this was Edward's domain, not his. Research and development for A.R.M. was his whole life now; even the occasional woman he escorted never intruded on his work. Or on Sarah, living on in his mind. He had lost Philippe, and he had lost Sarah; it was up to Edward to see that he didn't lose his company.

The war was over.

The war to end all wars was finally over, and people

seemed to believe all the promises that said the peace would last. They gathered in the streets, huddling in their warmest coats against the November chill, and listened to news of the signing of the Armistice. The newspaper headlines all screamed promises of peace forever now that the one Great War had been fought and won. One newspaper ran a photograph taken somewhere near Verdun of six or eight airplanes thrown together in a heap for burning. Over thirteen million had died. There would never, they were all saying, be another war. Four years later, the war that would be over by Christmas was finally over.

Amanda shook her head over the newspaper stories, but she was willing to simply accept it all for now. The war was over, and that was all that mattered. Besides, she had just been given some stunning new earrings by Charles. . . .

The racetracks were opened again, and she immediately bought a box—it didn't do not to have one's own, after all—and began entertaining parties there. The theater, somber for some months, blossomed with works such as *Exiles* by James Joyce, Jerome Kern's *Rock A Bye Baby*, and Lawrence Langner's New York Theater Guild, and Charlie Chaplin reigned supreme at the movies. All of New York, it seemed, had caught onto Amanda's mood of frivolity. Life was beautiful, life was far too short, and those who had not been killed were intent on celebrating for a good long time.

Once in a while she remembered her obligations to her home and to her daughter.

December 19, 1918

Dearest Mamma,

Well, the war is *finally* over, thank heavens, such a dreary thing, wasn't it?—and people are beginning to show some signs of life again. Even Charles has been quite lively . . . He took me over to *Harlem*, of all places, last Saturday, there is the most darling little recherché place there called the Cotton Club, filled with sweet little colored girls just dancing their hearts out. . . .

Mamma, I *do* appreciate your taking care of Caroline, and of course it's lovely of you to invite me up for Christmas, but it's just too, too much to ask of me just now. With the war ending, and all, don't you see that I'm far too busy to get involved with a *child*? So do be good and tell her that I send my love. I'll have her down to New York for Christmas sometime, that ought to make it up to her. I *know* that I'll never be the mother to her that you are, Mamma, darling, so why don't we each simply concentrate on what we do best?

People *are* coming back to the city, and life seems to be getting *fun* again. Remember how it used to be, Mamma? The races, with Gerald talking about silly things and Freddie running up and down the stands with our wagers, and riding about on that unicycle of his, and we were all so afraid that he would fall on his head? It's like that again, only Gerald is still in Washington, which must be *awfully* dreary. I can't imagine why he should have gotten interested in a political career, and of course dear Freddie *did* fall on his head, but that was in the Ardennes, and just too, too sad to think about . . .

Oh, Mamma, just take care of things, won't you? I simply can't face it all . . . and you're so good at facing things. Kiss Caroline for me . . .

> Lovingly,
> Amanda

She sighed. Superficial, of course, but what did people want from her? She had always been superficial. She had no intentions of changing now.

Still, there was something decidedly missing. Charles was a peach, but he wasn't the youngest man she had ever been with—and, well, frankly, he didn't satisfy her. Not the way that others had done. Not the way that Philippe had done.

She leaned over her dresser and watched her reflection in the mirror as she carefully applied her lipstick. That wouldn't do at all, thinking about Philippe. She had gone for almost a week this time without thinking about him, and then her mother had to write to her from New Hampshire and remind her. If only Caroline hadn't been born, if only all that silly stock wasn't tied up in her daughter's name, if only people would forget, then perhaps she could, too.

"Amanda!" Charles's voice boomed up from downstairs. "Are you ready, dear?"

She inspected her lips and then pulled on the tight-fitting sequined cap that matched her blue sequined dress. "Yes, darling!" she called brightly. "I'll be right there!"

Searching inside her purse for compact and keys, her hand stopped for a moment on her address book. Eric Beaumont was in there, but he had been silent for so long. It was a year, now, since he had so suddenly appeared on her doorstep in that awful blizzard, resurrecting old ghosts and demanding to see her daughter. Dear Eric. Just what she needed, and just what she didn't need.

She wondered, as she ran down the stairs to allow her husband to wrap her in the mink coat he had recently purchased for her, if Eric would show up again this year.

Edward had been right about the stock: It sold as soon as it went on the market, bought—interestingly enough, Edward thought—by a French bank, the Banque de la Sécurité. Edward rubbed his hands gleefully over double whiskeys. But it still wasn't enough. Eric kept making demands on him. Chemists, Eric wanted now, chemists and physicists— the best chemists and physicists. They argued over it interminably.

"You're the one who always says that we have to get the best of everything!"

"I had no idea, my boy, that sour old professional types could command such high salaries, or I should have become one myself."

"I need them. I'm ready to start testing rockets, Edward. Rockets that will penetrate the stratosphere. Have you any idea how important this work is?"

"Have you any idea how costly this work is?"

"I don't care. Just get me the damned money, Edward!"

"Don't slam the door on the way out, my boy. Makes a fearful racket." Edward shook his head and opened the letter that had arrived in that morning's mail.

8 February, 1918

Law Offices of Beneteau and Giroux
23 Blvd. Saint Germain
Zurich, Switzerland

                    To: Mr. Edward Buchanan, Esq.
                        A. R. M., Inc.
                        1647 Poplar St.
                        San Jose, California, USA

Dear Mr. Buchanan:
  We are in receipt of your letter of 16 January, and
indeed are distressed that the company once again is
finding itself in need of funds. The stock sale combined
with the income derived from the remaining stocks in
your control constituted, we had hoped, a viable option. Now, of course, it is time to examine other such
options.
  You suggest in your letter a loan on the strength of the
forty-nine percent of A.R.M. stock owned and controlled by Mrs. Amanda Osbourne. While this does
indeed present interesting possibilities (and of course
the income from said stocks is very substantial and
would in all likelihood solve the solvency problem
being currently experienced by the company), it is our
misfortune to inform you that it is not our privilege to
make any decisions concerning Mrs. Osbourne's fi-
nances. She has chosen to distance herself from all
contact with both this office and with A.R.M., and we
do not anticipate any change in her attitude. You may
of course wish to approach Mrs. Osbourne on your own
and make your request directly to her. We will, in the
meantime, continue to pursue other financial oppor-
tunities.
                    Yours for the firm of Beneteau and Giroux—
                    Marc Giroux

Eric was skeptical about the idea from the start.
  "I don't think that Amanda wants to see me just now," he
said, signaling the waitress for a beer. "What are you
drinking?"

"Whiskey. Make it a double, my boy." Edward was morose.

"She's married. There's something about the marriage that's all wrong, but I don't know what it is, and neither does her mother. Just a feeling. But Amanda's making it clear that she wants to be free to live her own life, so we're letting her do that."

"We?"

"Mrs. Lewis and me. Amanda's mother." He lit a cigarette, blowing smoke from the corner of his mouth. "Don't look at me like that, it's no conspiracy, Edward. We correspond from time to time, mostly to talk about Caroline. She's a lot more willing to talk than Amanda."

"So what has this to do, my boy, with my modest proposal?"

"Amanda's not taking proposals from me, Edward. She doesn't want anything to do with me."

"But this is business, my boy. A different proposition altogether."

"Not in her mind." He took a swallow of beer. "Edward, Amanda's a very confused person. She loved Philippe and I think now she hates him for making her love him. Caroline is the worst reminder of a past she would kill to have again. If that doesn't make any sense to you, then that's fine. It probably doesn't make any sense to her, either. But what it all adds up to is that she doesn't want me in her life. Period."

"Perhaps," said Edward judiciously, looking into his glass, "it's her husband who doesn't want you in her life."

"I don't think that's the issue," Eric said seriously. "Amanda's always done what she wanted with men, anyway. She wasn't even faithful to Philippe, for God's sake, and he was the only man she ever loved. No, if she wanted me, she'd do what needed to be done, and no husband would stand in her way."

"So. She would not be unwilling to be seduced."

Something in Edward's tone made Eric look up sharply. "It's not me you want to go ask her for the loan, is it?" he asked slowly. "It's you."

"If she won't respond to you, my boy, then we'll have to give her something that she wants. Then perhaps she'll give us something that we want."

"And how can you be so sure of what she wants?"

Edward drained his glass and stood up. "I've known women like your Amanda before, my dear boy. We all have pasts, don't you know, and those pasts dictate our needs now. Free psychological advice, my boy: free, gratis, and for nothing. Look at a person's past and you'll see what they need now. Supply and demand, my boy. Locate the problem, and find the solution."

Eric shook his head. "Something tells me that it's not that easy."

Edward tossed some bills on the table. "Life never is, my boy. But as long as we hold the illusion, we manage not to drown in hopelessness. I think that I'll go and have a chat with your friend Mrs. Osbourne."

"It won't work, Edward." Eric looked up at him from where he still sat. "She won't advance us any money. She doesn't care about A.R.M. She doesn't care about us."

"Of course not, my boy. Haven't you learned anything yet? I know what your Amanda cares about. See you around." And he was gone.

Amanda was more beautiful than Edward had anticipated.

He had, after all, cast her in the role of villainess—there was hardly any other option, as Eric had been the one to describe her, and Eric, even with his compassion for her conflicts, felt a great deal of anger toward her. Perhaps, Edward speculated, because she had survived—and Sarah and Philippe hadn't.

"An opportunist," Eric said. "That's what I thought of her, at first. Always complaining about stupid things— weather, for God's sake. She made it sound as though we had bloody invented bad weather. I never understood for the longest time what either of them saw in her."

"Either of them?"

"Philippe and Sarah. He was in love with her, and Sarah liked her. They were friends, though I never understood why. Amanda was charming, of course, but it was fashionable to be charming. Sometimes, though—" He stopped, frowning, as though pursuing an elusive thought just beyond his grasp.

"Sometimes?" Edward prompted him.

Eric shrugged. "I don't know. Sometimes, maybe, I

thought that we were seeing her at her best. That she was most real, most genuine when we were all there together. I don't think that she's improved with time."

"She's in the society pages quite a lot."

"She is?" Eric shrugged it off. "Well, if you go for that kind of thing, I suppose she succeeds at something. I still liked her better when she came to watch our planes take off." He smiled at the memory, and Edward knew what was going to follow. "Amanda and Sarah—you should have seen them, Edward. All dressed up—Sarah in silks, and Amanda wearing the silliest hats I've ever seen—and traipsing around in the mud and the rain and the wind. Amanda was always holding on to those great big hats of hers. And Sarah . . ."

But nothing that Eric had said prepared Edward for Amanda Osbourne's sheer breathtaking beauty. No matter what the faults of her character were, nothing showed on the outside: no anger, or avarice, or age. She was dressed in a blue dress of some material that shimmered as she moved, and made her eyes bluer than any sea or sky. But the beauty was in her graceful fluid movements, in her laughter that sparkled all around her like droplets of water flung from a fountain. She seemed, somehow, more alive than any other woman in the room.

Edward paused. It had taken a lot of time and favors to obtain an invitation to this Westchester lawn tea party—if that was what it was called, some silly affair for some obscure charity—and this was his first glimpse of Amanda. Amanda splendid and in control—in her element.

He observed her for a few minutes, talking and laughing and sipping champagne from the high fluted glasses, joining first this group and then that one, the perfect guest. He watched her, and eventually, as he had known that she would, she began to watch him watching her. She paused in the midst of a conversation, her laughter still part of those around her, her eyes meeting his across the terrace and the people who stood and talked and laughed between them. Edward smiled gravely and raised his champagne glass in a silent tribute to her, and she responded with a slight inclination of her head. It was a small gesture, it was nothing, but Edward had known women like Amanda before.

He wandered, aimlessly it seemed, into the dining hall which opened onto the terrace. A manservant came to refill his glass; it was when he began to admire some of the paintings on the wall that he heard the faintest rustle behind him, smelled the perfume drifting on the air. He smiled to himself.

"Do you like the Impressionists?"

He turned politely. "It's a style that I have often admired, though I must confess to having little actual knowledge of the genre. Perhaps you could provide some—enlightenment?"

She smiled, and the blue-green eyes began making promises. "I expect," she said, "that I could, at that." She smiled again at her own double entendre, then changed tack slightly. "I don't believe that I've seen you before."

"Possibly not. But one can't be everywhere at once, can one? So tiresome."

"Of course one can't. Of course, so very tiresome." She murmured, pausing long enough to bestow a bright smile on an elderly man passing by. "But of course one must do what one can."

He lifted his glass again, a mock salute. "Of course. One must always do what one can."

Amanda sipped her champagne, watching him over the rim of her glass. "You don't live around here, do you? I thought I knew all the amusing people in New York."

"Ah. But all the amusing people don't live in New York, do they?"

She giggled, suddenly, and turned away from the rest of the room so that her fit of merriment was for him alone. "I expect not. Who *are* you?"

"Well." He adjusted his cuffs, fastidiously. "A subject upon which we could, of course, spend hours. However,"—Edward paused delicately—"it seems that other places and times might be more"—here he raised his eyebrows slightly, and receiving an answering smile, continued—"opportune for such a discussion."

Amanda was not to be deterred, though, and as she drifted—apparently purposelessly—from one group to another throughout the afternoon, he saw her asking questions. Discreetly, of course, but she was asking questions all the same.

She received no answers, and an hour later Edward smelled the already familiar perfume, deep and floral, like jungle flowers, next to him. Her smile was bright, coquettish.

"Have you plans for the remainder of the evening?"

He inclined his head slightly. "As a matter of fact, no. I am, as the expression goes, entirely at your—er—disposition."

She was watching some other people, pulling on her silk gloves. "You could drive me home, if you wished," she suggested, the intensity of her voice belying the bright casual look that she scattered around the room. Whatever the outcome of her latest flirtation, Amanda Osbourne was covering all of her bases. No one, later, could accuse her of flinging herself at her newest conquest.

That he was to be her newest conquest was an absolute certainty in her mind.

Amanda took him to her home, an hour's drive back into the city, in Greenwich Village. "My husband," she explained carefully, "is in Chicago for business."

Edward nodded noncommitally.

She had undressed before he even thought to touch her, undressed with the slow, almost nervous, ingenuity of a child, revealing white lace and then, underneath, black undergarments: a brassiere with delicately shaped cups, a garter belt supporting black silk stockings, and—most importantly—a body which could leave men breathless.

And even once he was undressed, and touching her—hesitatingly at first, for something about this woman made him careful—she was not willing to simply go through the accustomed movements, the time-honored motions, the skills that Edward had perfected over the years and through all of his dalliances. She wanted more excitement and mystery and thrills beyond those usually experienced in the bedroom. She wanted . . . Edward wasn't sure precisely what it was that she wanted, but he was content to allow her to take the lead, to guide him into her world of games and play.

They were games, the ways in which she made love to him. Games complete with mirrors and toys; games in which she assumed different roles: the courtesan, the nun, the lady, the whore. Edward tolerated them at first, but then, slowly, subtly, found himself being drawn into them, again and again and again. . . .

He awoke with the sunshine streaming across the bed and pieces of string still tied around his wrists. She was next to him, still sleeping, her hair tangled and a bruise on her upper arm. He shook his head, slowly, and tried to extricate himself from the covers. He felt old beyond his years.

But his price for the night before was there, on the night table, the paper he had asked her to sign, the agreement allowing A.R.M. to borrow money from the interest accumulating on her stocks. Amanda had signed it blindly, not knowing who he was or what she was agreeing to. She would probably never find out; she wasn't interested in her A.R.M. stocks; Edward had no problems with his conscience.

He dressed quickly, sliding the precious paper into an inside pocket of his jacket. Behind him, on the bed, Amanda stirred. "Are you leaving?"

"I was thinking about it," he said easily, already patting his pockets, searching for his cigar and matches.

She stretched and purred. "It was a lovely night. Do you have to go so soon?"

He sat down on the edge of the bed. "Afraid so, my dear, can't help it. California awaits."

She pouted prettily, and he marveled at how good she looked, even after such a night. "Will you do one thing for me?"

"Of course, my dear."

"Tell me your name."

He smiled, and patted her hand in as avuncular a fashion as he could manage after the intimacy they had shared. "Edward Buchanan, my dear. You'll hear great things of me."

"I already have." She smiled flirtatiously. "Go now, Edward Buchanan. I will remember you for a few days."

And that, he reflected as he left, was probably a significant compliment from Amanda Osbourne. The best that he could hope for, in any case.

But it was not Amanda's compliment that was making him smile as he booked passage back to San Jose. It was the paper she had signed, heavy and significant in his pocket; the paper that would save A.R.M.

Edward smiled. This had been the most unusual corporate bargaining in which he had ever engaged. But he knew in his heart that, given the chance, he would do it again. She was many things, Amanda Osbourne, but there was a strange, strong attraction that she held for men.

And then he dismissed her from his mind and turned towards the West, and the future.

The Arts of Peace
1922–1932

Chapter Nineteen

New York, Christmas, 1922.

When Caroline was seven years old, her mother arrived one cold winter morning, sweeping down on the estate in Newport with a parade of several motorcars, any number of maids, and a special present for Caroline. "You're coming to spend Christmas with us in New York, darling, isn't that simply too marvelous?"

With glowing eyes, Caroline ran to kiss her grandmother good-bye, not seeing—not caring to see—the storms brewing under the old lady's icy exterior. Caroline slipped her small hand into her mother's velvet-gloved one, and went happily into the elegant leather interiors of her mother's vehicle.

Mother looked wonderful, Caroline thought, and a thrill of pride rushed through her. She herself had never felt pretty—Grandmother always said that she was beautiful, but added that beauty didn't count—so Caroline was amazed by her mother. This beautiful lady, with the becoming cloche hat and the sapphire-blue velvet coat that opened to reveal a skirt fashionably, daringly above the knee: this lady was her mother. *Her* mother! She shivered with the joy of it and thought only of the holidays ahead. Mother had promised her two weeks!

Caroline's earliest memories were of her grandmother's big house in Cornish, with the Connecticut River shining out beyond the paddocks and horses whinnying in the frost-laden, snowy New Hampshire mornings.

That was Caroline's first real home; she liked living on the estate with her grandmother and her grandmother's entourage, wealthy ladies who gossiped gently over teas until, one by one, they lay peacefully beneath headstones in their respective family plots. She learned how to be polite to those old ladies, and they, in turn, fussed over her and brought her chocolates and wondered aloud to each other about how Amanda's girl had turned out so very well, after all.

Grandmother was—well, it was hard, after all, to define Grandmother: strong and tall, even as she grew older and her servants had to do more and more for her. Every morning she rode out into the dawn, dressed impeccably in a velvet riding suit, her big bay gelding tossing his head, his breath puffing out white in the frosty air. Caroline sometimes went with her on these early excursions, her own gray pony jiggling and dancing with the sheer joy of the morning gallop after a night spent shut up in a barn. On these mornings she felt her whole young being at peace with the world, Grandmother's world.

Grandmother's world extended beyond Cornish, too, to the great stone house in Newport where she eventually sent Caroline when it was time for her to attend school. Here, too, her bedroom overlooked the water, not the fast-flowing Connecticut River, but the ocean itself, the Atlantic. And, Caroline knew, somewhere off on the other side of that ocean was the country where she had been born: England.

Grandmother spoke to her of it sometimes, once Caroline was old enough to realize that most girls didn't grow up with their grandmothers and with an elusive dazzling figure of a mother who popped in long enough to let her daughter smell the richness of her perfume and then was gone. Grandmother, who of course knew everything, explained it all: how Caroline's father had been killed during the Great War, how he had been brave and strong to the end, how he had belonged to one of the finest families in Great Britain. Caroline ought to be proud of him, Grandmother said.

She was less effusive about Caroline's own mother. She had to understand, Grandmother explained, that the death of Caroline's papa had been a great shock to her mother, and that it was important for her to spend time on her own, rebuilding her own life. She lived in a city to the south called New York City, and was married to a nice older man, and sometimes, when she could, she would come and visit Caroline. But it was important for Caroline not to expect this too much. Caroline sensed rather than understood the criticism implied in her grandmother's explanations.

As a young child Caroline didn't mind. She had never experienced her mother as a consistent presence, so she couldn't miss her when she was gone. In the meantime, of course, there was Grandmother, and Clea, who had taken Mrs. Driscoll's place when Caroline turned five and who dominated those parts of Caroline's world which were not already defined by her grandmother.

The estate in Newport was, if anything, even grander than the one in Cornish. At night, it sparkled with lights, looking like an enchanted castle from some fairytale. Caroline made up stories about it when she was left to sit alone in the bedroom which was far too big for her, and her grandmother lay in bed with one of her vapors, and the halls and stairwells were hushed and quiet. She imagined it as it must have been when her mother lived here, filled with music and the glitter of lights, and people. She couldn't imagine her mother alone. There would always be people around her; attractive, amusing people who would make her laugh— that beautiful laughter which sounded like a bell ringing. . . .

Caroline grew up "properly." She was driven places in the long black car, even though she would have dearly liked to take the trolly, noisy and dusty and teeming with the kind of people she would never meet in her grandmother's drawing room. She was privately tutored at first, and then eventually driven to school on the other side of town when one of the doctors her grandmother was forever consulting offered his opinion that the child was becoming too withdrawn and that the company of other children might do her good. She was taught how to dress and how to move and what to say to the various foreign dignitaries who had become her grandmother's latest amusement.

She learned it all, and always said, "Yes, Ma'am," to her grandmother. Even Clea was heard to remark to the scullery maid that Miss Caroline was the easiest charge she ever had.

During the trip to New York, Caroline's face had been pressed eagerly against the glass window of the big black car, taking in all the grime, all the sootiness, all the wonderful magic of the city which her grandmother always clucked her tongue at. And now, at long last, she was here!

Mother and Mr. Osbourne—it was hard to call her

mother's husband Uncle Charles, as he urged her to do—
lived in a lovely four-story house in Greenwich Village,
which was still, as Mother assured her, "quite the place to
be, darling, don't you think?" Caroline didn't know what to
think, but she was ready to accept whatever her mother
chose to tell her, and she nodded in eager agreement. She
would have agreed with anything that Mother said.

They did marvelous wonderful things, like driving over to
visit the newly opened Madison Square Garden, and looking at the Statue of Liberty, and riding the Victorian
carousel in Central Park. Mother was nicer than Caroline
had remembered her—she was very frantic, rushing about,
and laughing rather too much and, even though she wasn't
sick, taking all sorts of pills that Caroline didn't recognize,
but she was kinder than Caroline had remembered.

Mr. Osbourne was a lot older than Mother. He seemed
ancient, though Mother seemed to like him well enough,
and he smoked horrible foul-smelling cigars and liked to put
his arm around Caroline, which made her want to wiggle
away. He would sometimes stay home in the evenings—
Mother never stayed home in the evenings—and play
records on the bright new phonograph. His favorite was
"Show Me the Way to Go Home," which he played over and
over again until Caroline knew it by heart.

She stayed home with him during those evenings, of
course. Mother, bright and pretty in her fine clothes, would
sweep into the room with her perfume all about her, and
kiss both of them on the foreheads, and say gaily, "Well,
darlings, I'm off. Have a simply marvelous evening, won't
you?"

Caroline would simply sit and stare, unable to speak. She
longed to be invited to accompany Mother, but she knew
that it would never happen. Whatever Mother did at night,
she didn't want either her husband or her daughter along for
it. Caroline knew better than to ask, so mostly she sat still
and silent, smiling and praying that her mother would give
her just one more kiss before leaving. Without knowing
why, she had been suddenly accepted back into her mother's
attentions and affections, back into the charmed circle of
those upon whom she bestowed her glitter and warmth. As
an infant Caroline had slipped out of her approval for
reasons that she couldn't understand, and had been ban-

ished to her grandmother's domain. Now she had slipped back in for equally mysterious causes.

She was afraid that if she said or did anything wrong she would be exiled back to Newport and Cornish, and to the long quiet evenings when her grandmother played canasta and Caroline sat and read quietly by the fireside. So she said nothing, and stayed safe.

Mr. Osbourne—Uncle Charles—would laugh it all off. "She's young, she has to have her flings," he would explain, but Caroline never quite understood what precisely that meant. All that she knew was that Mother dressed up nicely and disappeared into the night, and that she, Caroline, stayed home with Uncle Charles and listened to his records on the phonograph player and talked to him about Newport, which was where he had lived as a boy, and where, indeed, he had met her mother.

He had told her that story many times, every night that Mother went out. He would pour her a glass of lemonade, and then fill his glass with some amber-colored liquid which he called his "little tipple" and which smelled terrible, and he would put the record on. The scratchy music would fill the air around them, and he would talk about Mother. Caroline sat still on the rich Oriental carpet which adorned the sitting room, and she would sip her lemonade and listen politely, even though he said the same things over and over again. He spoke about how lovely Mother was at some silly costume party in the old White Horse Tavern (she could close her eyes and see it, standing alone at a corner in Newport; her friends at school told her that it was haunted), and about how he couldn't keep his eyes off her, and how her laughter had echoed in his mind for days afterwards. Caroline nodded: It echoed in her head, too, that lovely warm laughter.

One night—just three days before Christmas, it was, and five before she was due to be taken back to Newport—Uncle Charles poured her a second glass of lemonade and came to sit beside her on the carpet. He lowered himself to the floor with much ado, because he was, after all, rather old and more than a little overweight, but he managed it at last. And he took one of her hands in his, looking closely at the ring on her finger, the one that Grandmother had given her on her sixth birthday, a red ruby glinting in the lamplight.

"It's a pretty ring, Caroline."

"Thank you," she said politely, and tried to pull her hand away from him. His fingers were fat, and his hands moist, but she didn't want to be rude.

"Very pretty." He kept looking at it, as if he wasn't aware of her trying to squirm out of his reach. "Did some little boy give this to you?"

"No, sir. It was a gift from Grandmother." The only little boys she knew were the neighbor, who was away at school in England most of the time, and the gardener's son, a detestable brat named Timmy who threw pebbles at her window.

Uncle Charles transferred his gaze from the ring to her face. "Oh, Caroline, come now, don't tell me that all the little boys aren't just crazy about you. You must have a lot of admirers at school."

"No, sir." She didn't like the feel of his warm breath on her face, and she couldn't see where this conversation was going. She found herself suddenly wishing with all her heart that the drawing-room door would open and that Mother would appear, snowflakes on her coat and that strange brightness in her eyes, and rescue her from Uncle Charles. How could Mother have married him, Caroline wondered.

"I don't know why not. You're a very pretty little girl, Caroline." As he said it, he let go of her hand altogether, and moved his pudgy fingers up to touch her on her neck, under her hair. She stiffened, but short of being rude and getting up she didn't see what else she could do. And Grandmother would be mortified if she was rude.

Uncle Charles didn't say anything for a moment, he just kept touching her neck, and it started to feel good to Caroline: a slow, rubbing movement, not unlike what Clea did for her at home when she was sick with the flu or had a fever. Then he said, in an odd sort of voice which didn't sound like his at all, "Caroline, I want you to do something for me."

It seemed as though she was waking up, so hypnotic had been his hands rubbing her neck. "Yes, sir?" she asked, dutifully. Behind her, the record finished and started making scratching noises.

"I used to have a little girl like you, did you know that?" She shook her head, and he went on. "When my wife—my wife before your mother, you see, dear—and I decided to stop being together, my little girl went to live with my wife. And now I can't see her anymore."

Compassion rose in Caroline's heart. No wonder he was so silly, sometimes, with his lemonade and long stories: He just missed his daughter. She wondered if Mother ever missed her the way that Uncle Charles missed his little girl. It was a comforting thought. "I'm sorry, sir," she said awkwardly, thinking that perhaps he was a nice man, after all, and Mother had been right to marry him. Perhaps Mother understood how much he wanted to be with his little girl, and that was why Caroline had been invited here for Christmas. Perhaps, if she made Uncle Charles very happy, happy enough to forget his daughter, Mother would let her stay here forever.

Uncle Charles looked at Caroline again, and she saw tears glinting in his eyes. "Yes, I sure do miss her," he said, softly. "It would help if I could pretend that you were my real daughter sometimes, Caroline. Would you pretend that with me?"

She nodded, intent. "Oh, yes, sir."

He nodded, too, as though a pact had been made between them, and then he held out his arms to her—awkwardly, because he was still sitting on the floor. "Caroline, little girls like to hug their daddies."

She hadn't thought of that—she didn't know what it was like to have a father, and hugging was never part of Grandmother's repertoire—but she thought how pleased Mother would be, so she moved closer to Uncle Charles and felt his arms come together around her. He smelled even worse close up. She took a deep breath and slowly, uncertainly, put her arms as far around him as they could reach.

They stayed like that for a few moments, motionless, with Uncle Charles holding her close against his chest, so close that she could feel his heart beating, which was a very strange feeling indeed, and then at last he released her. "Caroline, that felt very good. Did it feel very good to you?"

"Yes, sir," she said dutifully, hoping that he would now dismiss her and say that he would see her in the morning, as he had every other evening. Instead, he was still talking. "It feels good for a man to be close to his little girl. There are a lot of ways of being close, Caroline. Did you know that?"

"No, sir," she said, wondering what he was talking about.

She had never felt close to anything or anyone, except perhaps Cricket, her gray pony at the estate in Cornish. She had forgotten until this very moment how much she missed Cricket, and began to wish strenuously that Uncle Charles would leave her alone so that she could think about her pony instead of this awful man.

"I'd like to show you some ways that we could be close, Caroline. Sometimes it's hard for me, with your mother dashing off to spend time with other people. I miss my own little girl and I miss your mother, and I get very lonely here. I like to feel close to somebody."

Caroline didn't say anything and so he reached for her again, not this time to smother her in a hug, but to touch the brooch she had pinned at her collar. "This is very nice, Caroline, but I think that you'd look even prettier without it."

She stared at him. She was really confused now. What was he talking about?

Uncle Charles was doing something with the brooch, and in a minute it fell to the carpet, rolling away from her, twinkling in the lamplight. And then his hands were on her shirtwaist, and on her skirt, and to her amazement he was taking her clothes off. Finally she found her voice again.

"Please don't do that. I don't want you to do that." She wasn't even sure exactly what he was doing—why would anybody take her clothes off—but she knew that it didn't feel good. Grandmother had always taught her to be modest. She didn't even undress in front of Clea.

Besides, she was getting cold.

"Caroline, my dear . . ." His voice sounded even stranger, now. There was a slurred quality to it that she had never heard before. "Caroline . . ." His hands were moving over her body, touching her in places she was sure were places that he shouldn't be touching her, his fingers on the tiny points of her nipples on her chest, moving down over her belly to the space between her legs. It felt horrible.

She pushed him away, finally, and struggled to get to her feet. "Don't," she pleaded, and there was fear in her voice, even she could hear it, echoing hollowly, and she had a wild mad desire to go back in time and never ever start this whole conversation with Uncle Charles at all.

He had let go of her, but now in horror she saw why: It was

so that he could take off some of his clothes, too. His legs were hairy and at the place where they joined the rest of his body there was something more horrible still, a sort of stick of flesh, more pudgy even than his fingers.

It was pointing straight at her.

He pushed her now, back, until she was lying on her back on the carpet, spilling her lemonade and not even noticing it. "Caroline . . . Caroline . . ." His voice was panting, as though he had just been running, and the fear rose in her again as he began to lower his body onto hers.

She screamed, then, and he sat up abruptly, and his voice was cold, just like Grandmother's when she had done something wrong. "Stop that," he ordered, and she sat up, too, her eyes wide with fear. "Listen to me. We can do this my way, or we can do it your way. My way is nice. Your way will make me hurt you. You don't want to get hurt, do you, Caroline?"

She shook her head, mute with fear, and he continued. "We're going to do something that will feel very good, and then you can go to bed. And you'll never ever tell your mother about it, because if you do I will hit you very hard. Do you understand that, Caroline?"

She nodded again, silently, but with tears streaming down her face. This was surely the most terrible thing that had ever happened to her in her whole entire life, worse than when they had burned her most precious doll because she had been with Caroline when Caroline had been very sick. This was worse than losing Esmerelda had been. This was worse than anything.

"All right," Uncle Charles said, and his voice was kind again, without that hard edge of command. "Now do just as I say, and everything will be all right. I want you to lie down on your back."

So she did as he said, and he lowered his big body on top of hers, and he started kissing her, though they were not like any kisses she had known before. Grandmother kissed her on the cheek, sometimes, but her lips were thin and dry like paper, and they felt like leaves in the fall. Mother's kisses were light butterfly kisses on her cheek or forehead, laced with perfume. But these kisses were long and wet, and Uncle Charles made sucking sounds when he kissed her, and he kissed her in all sorts of places—on her mouth, and on her neck and shoulders, and on the tiny peaks which hadn't yet become the breasts that other ladies had, and down . . . down there, in a place unmentionable and terrible and mysterious.

Caroline closed her eyes and started thinking about other things. There had to be something that she could think about, something beyond this lovely Oriental carpet and this big horrible man who was on top of her, something somewhere that was clean and shining and good. And she thought about Cricket, and the sugar that she used to feed him, flat on the palm of her hand, and the jumps that Grandmother coached them over in the near paddock—the one that overlooked the river.

Uncle Charles had moved again, and was doing something between her legs, forcing them farther and farther apart. Suddenly there was a dreadful pain that obliterated Cricket and every other thought from her mind, that made it impossible to know anything but this terrible hot searing feeling between her legs. A pain like broken glass, sharp and insistent and horrible.

Uncle Charles was panting and gasping, and he had his hand down there, and then the pain got worse. When he moved his hand away, she realized with horror that he had somehow put his stick inside her and that was what hurt so much. He reached up and took a fistful of her hair in his hand, and he pulled at it until her head hurt, too, and he kept moving the lower part of his body in a terrible awful rhythm, pounding her until she thought that she wanted to die. Please God let me die, anything to have this stop, anything.

And then he cried out, loudly, and pulled even harder on her hair, and thrust harder into her, and his whole body started shaking. At last, he stopped. A minute later he got off her, and, without looking at her, said in a cold, toneless voice, "Get up, Caroline. Put your clothes on and go to bed."

But when she moved—slowly, because it hurt—she realized with horror that she was bleeding. She looked at the bright red blood on her fingertips, and looked at Uncle Charles, wonderingly, and he said, impatiently, "It's nothing, girl. Just mop it up. It'll stop by itself. It just means that you're a big girl now."

Tears streaming down her face, she put her clothes on, mutely, thinking that becoming a big girl was a terrible thing to do. At the door, he called her back. "Remember—not a word to your mother, or I'll really hurt you."

Caroline didn't say anything, just crept up to her room. That night she had a dream that would haunt her for years, a dream of going into a deserted house on a beach and finding a man waiting for her there, a man like Uncle Charles, large and forbidding, with the same red vest he wore so frequently. The man asked her to give him the ring on her finger, and she said, no, it was hers. He walked over to her and, taking a knife, cut off her finger so that he could take the ring.

She woke up in a cold sweat, the same cold sweat which would terrify her for years to come.

Long after Caroline had gone upstairs, Amanda came home and saw the blood on her precious carpet. She came into Caroline's room, and while Caroline pretended to sleep, she sat next to her, not saying anything. She held her hand, and gradually Caroline felt herself falling into a peaceful sleep. And then a sob escaped from her mother's lips and she ran out of the room. Caroline was awake again.

The next morning over breakfast Mother had changed back to what she was before: She was the Ice Princess once again. Caroline had fallen out of favor. She would, after all, have to spend Christmas in Newport with her grandmother.

Caroline didn't understand exactly what had happened, but that didn't matter: She never did. And she didn't understand why her mother was so angry with her. She only knew that she had to continue to be very, very good, so that perhaps somehow she could make up to Mother for what had happened that night.

Eric had spent the early-spring Saturday morning as he spent all other Saturday mornings, eating breakfast with Sarah's mother. No one else was there. Mr. Martin had lapsed into a coma about a year after his first stroke, and had died a few days before the anniversary of Sarah's death.

Peter had finally moved out of the house on Western Avenue, deciding that it was time to strike out on his own, an endeavor at which he was not particularly good. He was out at the A.R.M. offices at least once or twice a month to ask Eric for advice, or a loan, or both. Edward shook his head after one such visit. "Never make much of himself, will he?"

"What do you mean?" Eric was protective of his brother-in-law.

"Can always tell a slacker. You should, too, by now, my boy. Never amount to anything. Greedy eyes, but not the brains to go out and get what he wants."

Eric shook his head, but Edward seemed to be right. More and more, Peter was content to sit back and let his hardware store be run by his employees, and boast about his connection to A.R.M. Edward narrowed his eyes when he heard about that one. "Loose lips sink ships," he intoned.

"The war is over, Edward." Eric had laughed.

"Same principle applies, my boy. Same principle applies."

Anna Martin only made helpless gestures every time that Eric talked to her about Peter, and so, quietly, he had set about helping his brother-in-law. He bought the young man a house; he offered him an education—anything to keep Peter away from the quiet house on Western Avenue and his mother, whom he upset so much.

And still, every Saturday, Eric and Anna had breakfast together.

Eric drove back to his house early that afternoon with little on his mind except Mrs. Martin's fluffy pancakes and the idea of a booster rocket that he had been toying with for some time. He lived on the outskirts of San Jose, close to the A.R.M. offices, in a rambling frame house that tried to look Victorian but only succeeded in looking old. It didn't matter to him; it was a place to live. A wide front porch encircled the house, and near the front steps was a swing where he sat at night with a glass of beer and looked up at the stars or out at the palms, oaks, and willows lining the street.

Today, Amanda Osbourne was sitting on it.

Eric killed his car engine and sat there for a few moments, silent, thinking. It had been nearly four years since he had last seen Amanda, and, although he had religiously inquired of her mother as to her health, he had not spoken to her in all of that time. The truth was that he was so engrossed in his work that the passage of time meant little to him.

He walked slowly up the front steps and she raised her face and looked at him. Her eyes were rimmed with red, and there was a pinched look about her, a paleness he had never seen before, a pain fresh and immediate and real. He didn't think about what he was doing; he simply opened his arms to her and when she stood up and came over to him he enfolded her, holding her close to his chest and saying all the words that he used to say to her, once upon a time, in the happier days of the rue de Verdun. "It's all right. . . . there, there . . . Don't cry, silly Amanda. . . . It'll be all right." And her body shook with sobs.

Eric took her hand and led her inside, noticing with part of his mind how stunning she looked, in a short, blue embroidered dress with patterned stockings and a three-cornered hat. She must be about thirty, he thought. She'd never looked more beautiful—or more unhappy. They sat in his living room, a few chairs and sofas grouped around the cluttered worktable that he used. Amanda wordlessly pulled a packet of cigarettes from her handbag, shaking her head when he offered her coffee. "If you have anything stronger, Eric, darling, now's the time."

He looked around his kitchen but couldn't come up with anything but beer and whiskey—Edward's brand that he always kept around. He splashed some whiskey into a glass and added a little water before bringing it out to her.

Amanda was recovering her poise. Already she had straightened, and was dabbing at her eyes with a lace-trimmed handkerchief. She accepted the whiskey from him and downed half of it in one gulp before finally speaking, her voice shaky. "Well, Eric, since you're so good at dropping in on me unannounced, I thought I'd return the favor."

Eric lit a cigarette of his own, shaking out the match and dropping it in an ashtray. "You know you're always welcome here."

"Hmm. Quite the bachelor, still, are you?"

He met her eyes, wondering why she needed to mock him. "Still a widower."

She played with her cigarette for a moment, and then finished off her whiskey. "How about another one?"

"How about telling me why you're here?" he countered.

Amanda sighed and stood up and walked over to the window which looked out over nothing more interesting than his front lawn: grass, trees, hedges. "You're so domestic, Eric, darling. Sarah would have loved it here."

Eric winced. "What is it, Amanda?"

She turned suddenly, leaning against the windowsill with the light at her back so that he could only really see her in silhouette. "Caroline came to New York for Christmas."

"I'm glad to hear that." And it was March, now. Why had it taken her so long to tell him about this?

"Well, she didn't actually stay for Christmas. I sent her home early." She took a deep breath. "Eric, I don't know what to do. I don't know how to tell you this. I think—I think she was molested by my husband."

The whole earth seemed to have gone red all of a sudden. "What did you say?"

"Well, I can't be sure, of course. He denied it, but she's being such a frightened little rabbit, and there was blood on the carpet. . . ."

"Charles Osbourne raped Caroline?" Eric thundered.

"Oh, Eric, rape is such a horrid word, isn't it? Perhaps he was just too affectionate. There was no way for me to stop it, don't you see? I was out. How was I supposed to know? There had never been any hint of anything being wrong. How was I to know that my husband found my daughter more attractive than me?" There was pathos in her voice, but Eric was too angry to hear her.

"I'll kill him."

She moved away from the window, formless anxiety hovering all around her. "Eric, dear, surely you're not serious."

"Surely *you're* not serious! She's your daughter, Amanda! Have you no feeling for her at all?"

"She's my daughter," she said, tonelessly. "He's my husband."

"Jesus Christ," Eric said, with feeling. "Can't you understand anything, Amanda? Who the hell is this that you've married, anyway?"

"What do you expect?" Amanda burst out. "He didn't have Child Molester written all over him when we got married!" But that was why he was never allowed to see or visit his child by his first wife, Amanda thought, the dull ache turning into a throbbing pounding in her head.

Eric sat down heavily on the sofa. "All right," he said, as calmly as he could. "Where is she now?"

"Caroline?"

"Well, of course, Caroline! Who else would I mean?"

"She's with my mother. In Newport or Cornish, I don't know which."

"All right," he said again, willing himself to be calm. "What are you going to do about Charles?"

"What do you mean?" Amanda asked, blankly. "What can I do about Charles?"

"God, Amanda, I don't know. Divorce him. Bring him up on charges. I don't know!" He took a deep breath. "If I had my way, I'd kill the bastard."

"He's my husband. I can't do that."

"She's your daughter, God damn it, Amanda. She's just a little girl, for Christ's sake. She needs you to protect her more than he needs you to protect him."

"But there would be a scandal." Her voice was faint.

"So what?"

"So what? I'll tell you so what . . . ." She paused. "None of you ever really understood—not ever. Sarah and you and Philippe, you all had other things. Sarah had her writing and she had her flying, she had ways of defining who she was. Things that she was good at. And Philippe had his respectability, he had his title, and he had Aeroméchanique. He was the Count de Montclair and nothing could ever take that away from him. And you—you had your planes and you never cared anyway. You always had your own way of defining yourself because you weren't rich from the beginning and people didn't expect you to behave in certain ways. And you didn't care—you can live without people! So none of you could understand." She was crying.

"Understand what?" He tried to make his voice a little more gentle.

"I don't like to be on my own, alone. I'm nothing. The only way I have of defining who I am is by what other people say about me. That was why it was so important to me to marry Marcus and give Caroline a name, don't you see? Because that's all I have. I'm not anything else—I'm not a writer or a pilot or a businessman. I don't do anything. What they say about me is who I am. What would they say if they knew that my husband raped my daughter?"

Eric took a deep breath. He hadn't ever thought much about Amanda's life. He had seen the emptiness, the lack of purpose, the voids, but he hadn't known that she had been struggling with these things all the years. He didn't know that she had seen them. And, in a way, he understood.

But, even understanding, he could not condone. Philippe had asked him to look out for Caroline. It was time he started taking that promise more seriously. He had certainly done a splendid job of it to date, he thought with a stab of guilt.

Eric turned to face her. She was wiping tears from her eyes again. "Amanda—Amanda. I'm sorry, you're right, I didn't understand. I'm not sure that I do now. I'll try to help you, but you'll have to do some things as well."

She hiccuped on a sob. "What?"

"I want Caroline to come here, to California, for a while. I'll work out the details with your mother, don't worry. Don't look at me like that, I don't mean *here*. The last thing that she needs is to stay alone with a man. I'll have her stay with Sarah's mother for a while. A few months, maybe a year, time to be away from everything."

"What else?"

"You have to do something about Charles, or I swear to you, Amanda, I'll see to it that this gets smeared in every newspaper from here to New York City. What you do with him is your decision. Get him into a hospital, or divorce him, or whatever you need to do. But you can't see Caroline again until you do something about Charles."

"You have no right to threaten me." Her voice was subdued.

Eric stood up. "You're right, Amanda. I don't. Let's go directly to the newspaper, now, shall we? I know the editor of the San Jose *Chronicle*. He's an old friend of Sarah's. Let's start with him."

"No!" It was a shout.

"Then you'll have to do as I say."

Amanda looked up at him, resentment and gratitude mingling uncomfortably together. "All right. All right. I will."

He nodded. "Sit back down, then. We have a lot of planning to do."

She sat down again, her expression meek, but he knew that he had, if anything, worsened things between them. Still, there was nothing he could do about it. He owed

Philippe, and it was time he started paying on that debt.
Caroline would have to be protected.

Caroline was hesitant about the entire venture, at first.

Her misgivings made all the sense in the world to Eric.
Caroline had been betrayed already by one "uncle;" there
was no reason at all that he could give her to trust another.
Only time would heal that particular wound, if indeed it was
ever to heal. He wondered, fleetingly, if it ever would.

He met her at the train and recognized her at once: small
and frightened and tired, but with Philippe's dark vibrant
eyes and Amanda's lustrous blond hair. He looked at her
gravely, and she looked back at him shyly. He put out his
hand.

"Hello, there. Do you know who I am?"

She nodded, equally grave. "You're Mr. Beaumont."

"That's right." He shook her hand, formally, seriously,
and then asked, "Do you know why you've come to California?"

Her gaze never wavered. "My mother says that it's
because I should see the country. My grandmother says that
it's so that I'm far away from Mr. Osbourne."

"I see. And which do you believe?"

"My grandmother."

Eric nodded, as though confirming something, and picked
up her suitcase. She followed him silently, never looking up,
neatly negotiating her way among the people who cluttered
the railway station. Eric helped her into the motorcar and
then sat in the driver's seat and started the motor. "It will be
different here from anything that you're used to," he cautioned her. "Mrs. Martin isn't as wealthy as your family."

"Will Mr. Osbourne ever be here?"

"No." Eric shook his head. "I promise you that Mr.
Osbourne will never come here."

"Then that's all right." She settled back into the cushions
and he drove her out the long road to the house on Western
Avenue where Sarah's mother was waiting for them with her
own kind of peace.

Chapter Twenty

*E*ric spent most of his weekends and some of his evenings at the redwood frame house out on Western Avenue, sitting at Anna Martin's kitchen table and watching Caroline grow up. Caroline had eventually accepted Eric as part of her landscape, accepting his explanation that he had been a friend of her father's and begging him to take her to the beach to fly the kite he had given her for her ninth birthday.

Caroline had spent her ninth and tenth birthdays in California. She had played on the streets that Sarah had played on—doubtless, Eric reflected, with children of the children Sarah had played with—and she went to school at the big noisy brick building down on the corner of Harrison Boulevard, and she wrote careful, neatly penned letters back east to her mother and grandmother.

But she never talked about them.

Shortly after Caroline had arrived, Eric had received a letter from Amanda. "Darling Eric, this is such a wretched thing that you're making me do, and you're really quite *horrid*, but I'm divorcing Charles. See! Are you happy? He keeps on telling me that I'm making an awful mistake, and so I probably am, but there you are. And there's *nobody* else interesting on the horizon, either, which is *dreary*, and I'm not as young as I used to be. Imagine, Eric! I just turned thirty-three, which is a *ghastly* age. Do kiss Caroline for me, won't you?"

Despite Amanda's compliance with Eric's ultimatum to do something about Charles, Amanda never wrote Eric requesting her daughter's return. During the first three years, Amanda had visited only on two occasions, each time on her way out to attend movie premieres in Los Angeles.

The low-waisted filmy dresses in pastels and whites and small cloche hats she wore suited Amanda's ethereal beauty, and Caroline would regard her mother with a combination of awe and shyness. Yet Caroline, who in her early adolescence was a bit precocious, didn't hesitate to point out to Eric—with implied criticism—that her mother was exactly like a heroine in that novel by the wonderful new writer F. Scott Fitzgerald. Amanda, Eric thought, held a certain romantic appeal for her daughter, but the part of Caroline that was grounded in reality, that needed a mother, couldn't accept her mother's behavior. Eric knew also that Caroline's grandmother's health was fading, so on each birthday everyone agreed that Caroline's stay would continue for another year.

Now in 1926 as Caroline's eleventh birthday approached, Eric realized that it was likely that Caroline, who looked more and more like her father, was likely to be his charge until she was an adult. The thought pleased him. With Philippe's daughter and Sarah's mother he felt he truly had a family.

"When will you tell her the truth?" Anna's words at breakfast that day startled him from his reverie.

He looked up from his coffee. "What?"

Anna sat down comfortably across the table from him. "About her father. Are you going to go on protecting her mother's reputation?"

He shared her smile. "Hardly. But not yet. She's too young."

"You're too overprotective," Anna admonished.

"Probably." He looked out the window to where Caroline was swinging on the wooden swing he had hung from the big elm tree in the backyard of the Martins'. "But she deserves a childhood. God knows she's got a lot waiting for her."

"Meaning what?"

Eric shrugged. "The company, I guess. She's got forty-nine percent of the stock waiting for her when she turns twenty-one, plus my shares when I die. That's a great deal of responsibility."

Anna shook her head. "Don't be so sure," was all that she would say. "Don't be so sure."

The money Eric needed was there, at long last. It provided him with the means to make the expansions he so desperate-

ly wanted, to hire new employees, to outdistance Johnson
again and again.

Eric spent his days working on plans to outwit Johnson
and ruin them for destroying his life. He spent his nights
sitting in front of Sarah's picture. Fourteen years now since
she had been killed, and she was still alive to him, every
night of his life, when he retired to this room with his bottle
of beer and her picture, and closed his eyes.

With his eyes closed, he could still manage to summon her
back from the grave to a time in a small hangar with a small
field when a young girl came out to try his airplanes for him.
He was no longer making those airplanes with his own
hands, and she was no longer flying them: But that didn't
matter anymore. Sarah lived on.

He was no longer the young man who had courted her and
loved her, but she was still, in his mind, that young girl, and
always would be.

He never considered it an abnormal way to live. The
work that he had always wanted to do—that Philippe had
encouraged him to do—and the memory of the woman he
had loved were enough for him. Caroline was here, now.
There was a family for him out on Western Avenue. He was
doing what he had promised Philippe and Sarah that he
would do. For Eric it was a happy way to see out the rest of
his days, but, for Edward, it was just the beginning of
something bigger.

"My boy, my boy. I sometimes despair of your business
sense."

"I have no business sense." Eric laughed. "That's why
you're here."

Edward sighed, and automatically began his search for a
cigar and matches. "Someday, my boy, that won't be
enough. Someday you might find yourself at the helm—yes
thanks, got them—the helm, as I was saying, of this great
ship of ours, my boy, and you just might have to steer her."

"What are you saying? You're not leaving A.R.M., are
you?"

"Leaving a good thing when I see it? Nonsense, my boy,
utter nonsense. I am speaking figuratively, of course—such
a splendid thing in our material world, isn't it, to be able to
speak figuratively?—meaning simply that you haven't got
the whole picture. A danger, that, my boy, a danger not to
see the whole picture. Narrow-mindedness, and all that.

Can't have that happening, no siree. Must give you the whole picture."

"I'm not interested in the whole picture, Edward. I just want to do my work." He leaned forward eagerly, across the table, searching the older man's face. "I'm working on rockets. I've been experimenting with liquid-fuel rockets, engines that will put us farther into the air than we've ever dreamed of going. How can I take time off from that to worry about the whole picture of some little company?"

"That company is hardly small anymore, my boy. And it's your company. You should show a little more interest, I should think."

"I'm interested, Edward, I'm interested. In working," Eric protested, stubbing out the cigarette he had been smoking and leaning back in his chair. "You don't seem to understand. You're the financial genius. You're the one who has made A.R.M. into more than a little company. You brought us to America, for God's sake. Don't start talking to me now about the whole picture, Edward. It's a little late for that."

For Caroline's eleventh birthday Eric gave her a ride in an airplane. He didn't fly it himself, of course. He never had learned, never had even been up in one since that one exhilarating, breathtaking flight with Sarah. One of his test pilots had taken her up, had helped Caroline into the airplane, strapped her in, and lowered the glass cover which was Eric's newest invention: a shield and shelter for the passenger. No longer would they have to contend with the noise and cold of the slipstream.

Caroline was excited beyond words. Eric and Anna stood and watched as the airplane taxied to the end of the runway and sat there for a moment while the pilot did the final check and revved the engine. And then the noise of the motor rose from a snarl to a high whine, and the airplane was hurtling down the runway, a blur of gray as it passed them, whipping their clothes all around.

Eric shielded his eyes against the sun as he watched the airplane climb. It was a monoplane, one of the newest in A.R.M.'s aircraft division, sleek and graceful, with none of the boxiness that had so often characterized the airplanes that Sarah had flown. It swept by them and headed out towards the ocean. Eric's pilots told him that the view was spectacular. He smiled and turned back to Anna. "Coffee?"

She sat in the hangar waiting room and drank bitter coffee that Eric had sent from France, and listened to him. "There's no reason, if she likes it, that in a few years she can't take a few lessons, here and there."

"And if she doesn't like it?"

He glanced at her while shaking a cigarette loose from the packet. "Don't even *think* that. It's sacrilegious around here."

Anna laughed. "And what happens then when she goes back east? Will she go to the Allard's flight school, too?" She watched his face, stretching the moment out, taut and filled with feelings that could never find words. Anna took a deep breath and reached across the table to cover Eric's hand with hers. "You know you can't make her into another Sarah, Eric. She has to be able to live her own life."

"She's not going back east." His voice was stubborn.

"Who are you to say? Mrs. Osbourne has a perfect right to her, if she wanted. She's divorced that animal; it would be quite safe."

"I don't want Caroline waking up to find somebody new in her mother's bed every morning."

"There's the grandmother. *She* might choose to raise Caroline. Or maybe nothing will happen, that's not for us to say. Oh, Eric, just listen to me. You can't own Caroline. Don't hold on to her too tightly. You don't—"

Anna broke off as the door burst open, and Caroline rushed into the room, filling it with laughter and sunlight. She ran to Eric, throwing her arms around him in an exuberant gesture, and giggling as he spun her around him. "Eric! Eric! It's wonderful! It's the most wonderful thing I've ever done in my whole life!" He put her down and she ran to Anna, nearly upsetting her coffee cup. "Oh, Mrs. Martin, you wouldn't believe what it's like up there! Everything is so bright and shiny and clean. . . . You can *see* things! Like the ocean, you can see where it's deeper, and where it's more shallow, you wouldn't *believe*!"

"I take it that you had fun," said Anna, smiling indulgently.

"Fun? Fun! Oh, Eric, let me learn to do that! Please let me learn to do that!"

He sat down and pretended to consider. "I don't know, now. You can't do your homework if you're up there with your head in the clouds. . . ."

"Oh, Eric! I'd be sure to do all my homework." She wrinkled her nose. "I'll even eat liver and onions, and not complain. Not *ever*. Oh, please!"

Eric and Anna smiled at each other over Caroline's head. Just remember, her eyes cautioned him. I'll try, his responded.

And Caroline danced around and around and around.

Flying had renewed the interest in life that Charles Osbourne had taken away from her.

She had learned to be good, and played the part of the obedient daughter dutifully, never questioning her mother's decision to send her back to Newport, and never questioning her grandmother's sudden fierce protectiveness and her decision that Caroline should go live in California for a while. Caroline didn't argue and didn't question other people's decisions. She had learned her lesson well: Hope for something, and your hopes will be dashed. Dare to love, and that love will slap you in the face.

And then she went to live in California and found that love could take many varied and unexpected forms. She felt love for Mrs. Martin who, in her plain clapboard house out on Western Avenue, talked with her and listened to her and was as pleased with her accomplishments as Caroline herself, but without blaming her, either, for her failures. There was the love she felt for Eric, who had been her father's friend and who opened up the skies to her. And now there was the love, the great love that she had found at last as she was taken up in those wonderful airplanes and shown the world from another perspective altogether. "Eric, did your wife ever take my mother up flying?"

He was startled by the question. "I don't think so. I don't think that your mother was all that interested. Why do you ask?"

She shrugged. "I just wondered. Maybe if my mother had ever gone up flying, she wouldn't feel so very lonely."

There were still shadows in her life. California sun and the excitement of flight couldn't banish all the horrors from her life, and, try as he would, neither could Eric. There was a part of Caroline that understood at a level deeper than either Eric or Anna could reach that life was not innately good, that there were terrible things afoot in the world, and that they could touch one's life, suddenly and without warning. It was as though there were two Carolines: the happy, sunny young girl who wanted to be a pilot and who giggled over chocolate cake with Mrs. Martin; and the fearful, withdrawn child who knew that there were always shadows beyond the sunlight.

At Grace Episcopal Church on Sundays, Caroline sat and listened to the priest talk about forgiveness, and she thought about her mother and Uncle Charles and wondered how she could forgive. She had forced herself to feel cold and dead inside whenever she thought about them, because it was the only way to block out the feelings of pain. The priest was young and intense, and seemed to know what he was talking about, but secretly Caroline wondered: What had been done to him, in his pristine life, that he would have to forgive somebody for? And as she knelt with the rest of the congregation to take Communion and say the words that everybody else was saying and speak to this God "whose property is always to have mercy," she wondered why He hadn't seen fit to be merciful with her.

It didn't matter, she finally decided. God did what was best from His point of view, and if people didn't agree with Him, it wasn't really their place to say so. She had so much to be grateful for, as Grandmother had always reminded her—a warm home, and more than enough to eat and wear, and a good education. Mother didn't matter. Uncle Charles didn't matter. The man who had stepped on a mine in England and blown himself out of her life forever didn't matter. None of it mattered.

And then she shook off those feelings of hopelessness and begged Eric for one more ride, please, just one more ride in the airplane. When she thought about flying, things were different—as though a breath of fresh air had blown into her life, scattering out the old dead leaves of her past, blowing clean and cold into her soul.

She began to look more closely at the photographs of Sarah Martin on the walls and in the scrapbooks at the house on Western Avenue. She spent long hours listening to Mrs. Martin or Eric talking about her. It seemed Sarah had never been afraid. And whenever Caroline started feeling frightened or lonely or panic-stricken, she learned that she could summon the images of flight, of soaring out over the ocean and the countryside, and make herself feel better.

Every night, Mrs. Martin would come into her room and tuck her in and say her prayers with her—even Clea, at the estate in Newport, hadn't done that—and find just the right teddy bear to nestle with her. "Are you all right, pumpkin?"

"Yes, thank you. Mrs. Martin?"

"Yes, dear?"

"I wish that Sarah was my mother, instead. Then we'd all live here together, and Eric would be my father, and we could go flying."

Mrs. Martin kissed her forehead. "You can go flying, anyway. Good night, Caroline."

Eric was enthusiastic about Caroline's newfound passion, and as summer deepened into fall he began to encourage Caroline to go up more and more often on test runs, to ask his pilots questions. Years before she ever took the controls, she knew as much about airplanes and air currents as Sarah ever had.

"I don't understand."

Louis du Terlong of Financial Management Services was sitting under the awning of a café in the outskirts of Zurich, talking on a telephone which had been brought to his table when the call finally came through. Three empty coffee cups and a littered ashtray on the table before him attested to the length of time he had been waiting there. The younger man, who had only recently joined him, sipped pensively at a Pernod.

"Well, yes, of course. No, we didn't know. Yes—yes." A pause. "I think that our research facilities are adequate. No, we weren't aware of that. Yes, of course. Yes, sir. We'll deal with it. Yes, sir. Good-bye, sir."

The younger man, Raoul, sipped his Pernod. "A problem from the main office?"

"So it would seem. The firm is not pleased."

"Ha. Nothing would please them. Beneteau and Giroux think that if they don't do something themselves, it doesn't get done right."

The older man turned on him, viciously. "In this case,

Raoul, they happen to be right. We haven't held up our end of the business."

"And what is our current transgression, then?"

"The company stock that went public—Monsieur Beaumont's stock, you remember?—was bought up by the Banque de la Sécurité."

"I know. We all knew that. What's the point, Louis?"

He sighed and snapped open the briefcase lying on the chair beside him. "Look at this. Look at all the research that we did into the financial status of the Sécurité. We put Catherine Roualt on it, she's our brightest new researcher, and here it is—pages and pages of reports. We gave them a clean bill of health, and the sale went through. And now they own twenty percent of the company."

"I don't understand. What's the problem? The Banque de la Sécurité has been around for years. I used to bank there myself, when I lived on the other side of the border. What's the issue?"

Louis swept the papers off the table and back into the briefcase. "During the Great War, the Banque de la Sécurité went into a financial crisis. You're too young to remember that, but me, I remember. I saw the headlines."

"And so?"

"And so they survived. Nearly over the edge one day, surviving the next. No one knew how. It was assumed, I think, that some wealthy benefactor had helped them out— incognito, of course. Everything was incognito in those days, and we were all too concerned with the battles going on in our own backyards to pay too much attention. Besides," he finished, as though this alone were explanation enough, "it was in France."

"And?"

"And we were right. Somebody helped them out." He slumped back in his chair. "Somebody named Johnson Industries."

There was a moment of silence as Raoul absorbed this information, then he shook his head. "And how much control do they have now over the Sécurité?"

"Enough. Enough that when Johnson says frog, the Sécurité jumps." Louis passed a weary hand over his forehead. "There's more."

"I was afraid of that."

"The company—A.R.M.; that is—still has loans outstanding—chiefly in the United States. All of them were
taken out before the lady signed the note and freed up her
assets to be used for the company. Nothing much." He
cleared his throat. "Except that they've all been bought up
by the Banque de la Sécurité within the last eight months.
And we never even noticed. We never even made the
connection."

Raoul was staring at the older man as if he had gone mad.
"You mean—a takeover?"

"Seems clear, doesn't it? Buy up stock under another
cover, buy up loans, and *voilà*. And now we have to figure
some way out of it."

"We do? Why us?"

"Because, you imbecile, we're supposed to be the financial
geniuses behind all this! The world might not know that
we're connected to Beneteau and Giroux—though Johnson
may well know; they seem to know just about everything
these days except what we had for breakfast this morning—
but the law firm knows that we're supposed to be working
for them, and we seem to have botched things up pretty
thoroughly."

"It wasn't entirely our fault." Raoul sounded sullen, like a
child who had been scolded. "The firm's supposed to be so
all-out clever, why didn't they see this?"

"They did, you imbecile. They did."

Another silence, then Raoul ventured, "How much did
the loans amount to?"

"More than you or I will ever see in a lifetime, that's for
sure." He threw some bills on the table and stood up. "I
want you back at the office, now. Get Catherine to figure out
why we didn't find out about Johnson's connections to the
Banque de la Sécurité. And see if there's anyone we can
place inside the bank to get us information. I want to see you
in my office at four o'clock, and I'll be expecting some
answers."

"Anything else?"

"Just remember: We're very vulnerable just at this moment. Very vulnerable. We could all lose our jobs as it
stands." He tapped the empty glass on the table. "I'd lay off
the Pernod during working hours if I was you, Raoul."

"Is that an order?"

"Just call it advice. They haven't become the most powerful law firm in Europe by being nice to anybody. Least of all a junior employee in a subsidiary that hasn't been fulfilling its function."

"I'm not exactly junior."

"That's what you think. Four o'clock, Raoul. Answers."

Louis set off, walking briskly in the opposite direction from the office, heading towards the park. One couldn't be too careful: that was why the telephone call had come to this café, rather than his office; that was why he met with Raoul here, just two old friends enjoying a drink on a pleasant spring day.

Many things were happening that spring of 1927, things that excited Edward far more than the first steps in aviation by a twelve-year-old girl. Eric's new radial air-cooled engine had been selected by Charles Lindbergh for his imminent flight from New York to Paris in his airplane, *The Spirit of St Louis*. Already, the engine was being proclaimed by the aeronautics community as the breakthrough of the decade. But as usual Eric's sights were set even higher. For months he had been closeting himself with a select staff of engineers and scientists talking and planning. The rockets, Eric assured Edward, were going to work, and the applications were astounding. The military prospects interested Edward the most. "Just the ticket, my boy, just the ticket!" he exclaimed in delight. "Economy's going all to hell in a basket anyway. Work on your rockets, and then we'll see what we can do about stirring up some action to use them in."

"You can't be serious." Eric was shocked and confused.

"Of course I am. As I've said, my boy, there's nothing—nothing!—like a nice little war to get things moving. We'll see what happens when the time comes. We'll see. We'll see my boy."

It was neither Eric's rocketry nor the thought of another war that was occupying the law offices of Beneteau and Giroux that fall. They were more than occupied already with the final report filed by Financial Management Services, the subsidiary that they had spent so much time and money nurturing. This subsidiary, Giroux was now being assured had failed to live up to its hard-earned reputation for being the brightest and best in the business. Financial Management Services was bringing them treacherously close to the brink of ruin.

"It seems clear, then," said Giroux, with his usual gift of overstatement, "that we're looking at the possibility of a takeover of A.R.M. by Johnson Industries."

"I still don't understand how this happened," Beneteau said from his position in front of the mantelpiece, where a little clock with chased-gold hands marked out the time in that quiet room. "How was it that this was missed?"

"We don't know yet, monsieur. Not completely. But it seems that—"

"I *know* what it seems," Beneteau broke in, his voice heavy. "We may have lost A.R.M. and Monsieur Beaumont to Johnson Industries."

"He will not work for them," Rousseau said briskly. "He couldn't. He will resign and begin a new company, perhaps—"

"There will never be another opportunity to have a company such as A.R.M.," Giroux said gloomily, searching in his pockets for antacid tablets. "Monsieur Beaumont is no longer as young as he once was. And A.R.M. has already established its reputation in the field, thanks to the hard work of both Monsieur Beaumont and Monsieur Buchanan. There are two giants: A.R.M. and Johnson. If there is but one, it would take decades to build up another company to challenge it. We do not have decades, gentlemen." He coughed discreetly. "Also, we have shares of A.R.M. That company is our only hope."

"So, we need a solution." Beneteau looked around the room. "What is it going to be?"

No one knew. No one knew, and they dispersed silently, each to his own office, to mull it over. But Beneteau and Giroux remained, talking until the shadows deepened on the walls and the chased-gold hands of the clock crept around the face three and a half more times. They were the veterans; they were the ones who had started the firm: They had the most to lose if they lost A.R.M.

Chapter Twenty-one

*B*y the time Caroline was fourteen, she spent most of her spare time out on the airfield.

She was too young to do any of the things that Eric was permitting her to do, but no one dared say no to him, and so she was barely more than a child when she flew. Not only did she fly, but she learned, piece by piece, each part of every airplane that Eric allowed her to get near. "Sarah was like that, fastidious about safety. That's how I want you to be, Caroline. I want you to be careful. Check every bolt and every wire, check that your engine is clean and your propellers oiled. I don't want you even getting into the cockpit until Matthew's watched you check everything."

"Oh, Eric," she would sigh.

But Eric only wagged his finger at her. "Everything, Caroline. I mean it."

A.R.M.'s airfield in 1929 was a good bit more sophisticated than the little Aeroméchanique property outside of Paris. It included several large hangars, a laboratory, a tower, and several long and well-kept runways. They were still developing airplanes, and Sarah wouldn't have recognized those, either. Eric's sleek new all-metal designs with covered cockpits and a mass of instruments in front of the pilot had been among the first in the industry. Caroline's flights were a great deal safer than ever Sarah's had been. Not that she was the better pilot—Eric would never admit that anyone could rival his Sarah—but the airplanes were safer and easier to control.

Still, there was something that tugged at Eric, a whisper of memory, a rustle in the back of his mind, whenever he looked out and saw Caroline stepping up into one of the small single-engine airplanes he was letting her fly. There was something about the slender girl's figure, the long silky hair, the bright clothes. Sometimes he almost found himself saying Sarah's name out loud, or walking over to the door to hail her.

Caroline had turned into a beautiful young woman in the years she had lived in California. At fourteen years of age, she had none of the awkward gawkiness of her friends. She was quieter, more assured than her schoolmates, although her teachers complained that she was a bit of a dreamer. Sometimes, when Eric was at the Martin house for dinner, he would look across the table at Caroline while she was engrossed in eating or in telling some story, and see Philippe's dark sparkling eyes, and he ached for him, too. His daughter was becoming very beautiful. Tall and slender like Philippe, Caroline's hair had remained as golden as her mother's, and her carriage and graceful movements were more than an echo of Amanda's dancelike grace. Eric wondered, fleetingly, what had become of the other child, Pierre, Philippe's legitimate son. He would be seventeen years old now, a young man, possibly with marriage plans. Somewhere on the other side of the ocean there was a boy who must look just as Philippe had looked—if Caroline was anything to go by.

Eric was seeing less and less of Edward these days. Edward had listened with rapt attention to the news outlined to him by the lawyers, something to do with a possible stock takeover, and he had launched himself into the plan they had devised to save A.R.M. Eric hadn't really paid too much attention to it all.

Edward was pursuing other ventures on his own: women, primarily. He always seemed to have a new one on his arm—and presumably in his bed, as well, although Eric never asked Edward any questions about that part of his life. He liked women dressed in short fringed dresses with yards of pearls around their necks, women with rolled and gartered stockings and short shingled hair and heavily made-up eyes and tight-fitting cloche hats. Edward was always humming these days, "Tiptoe through the Tulips," "Singing in the Rain." Eric noted his friend's euphoria with amusement.

"Sounds like a wonderful world out there."

"It is, my boy, it is. You really ought to crawl out into the sunlight from time to time. Sit up and take notice, all that sort of thing." Edward pulled out a cigar and went through the ritual of lighting it. "There! What was I saying? Ah, right, sunlight. Lovely ladies around, too, my boy." The girl with him tittered nervously, and Edward reached back and pinched her behind. "You ought to try one, sometime, my boy. Time to get back into circulation, what?"

"I'm not interested, Edward."

"This lad," Edward said to the girl, "is trying out to become a monk." She giggled again, and Edward turned to Eric. "Tell you what, my boy. Virginia, here—such a lovely name, Virginia, first American state and so on, splendidly patriotic and all that—Virginia would be happy to show you a little of what you're missing. Wouldn't you, my dear?"

Virginia pretended to pout, but she was watching Eric out of the corner of her eye at the same time. He smiled, but shook his head. "Thanks, Edward. But I'm just not interested."

Edward peered at him. "You're not turning queer on me, my boy, are you?"

Eric smiled again. "I think it would be easier for you to understand if I were," he said, quietly. "But I'm not. I just don't want to be unfaithful to Sarah."

The girl named Virginia took out a piece of chewing gum and put it in her mouth. It made a loud clacking sound.

Edward said, "Sarah has been dead for seventeen years, my boy."

"I know, Edward," he said. "Give me another seventeen before I can think about anyone else."

Edward was following the stock market those days as avidly as he was following the fortunes of A.R.M. and the short skirts of his lady friends. "Nothing like it, my boy, for excitement," he explained to Eric. "Need a little excitement in life, what?"

Eric looked at the long columns of figures and letters on the newspaper. "I just don't understand."

"It's a game, my boy. Just like life. Everything's a game." He lit a cigar and sat back, waving it in the air to punctuate his points. "Don't you see, my boy? Just another problem to be solved."

Eric sat down across from him. "And what problem is that?"

"Making money, how to." Edward looked at him with a

satisfied smile. "Oh, not A.R.M., my boy. We're doing splendidly. Absolutely splendidly. Thought we were in trouble back there two years ago, but there's a nice little coup being worked out on our behalf in Europe, don't you know. But we needn't bother with that, the firm is handling it all."

"The firm?"

"Beneteau and Giroux, of course. And company. They're right on the money, my boy, right on the money. Trust those lawyers with the shirt off my back, I would. No, this is merely a lucrative private venture of my own, don't you know. A nest egg, so to speak. So that the cruel ravages of time and eventual retirement need not gnaw quite so fiercely, nor the wind howl, et cetera, et cetera."

Eric wondered if Edward had been drinking. "So what are you doing?"

"Market manipulation, my boy. Market manipulation." He gave a great sigh. "Haven't I taught you anything? It's as simple as can be, so follow me closely: I whisper some information in a few well-connected ears, and they whisper the selfsame information into a few more well-connected ears, and then, to borrow one of your phrases, my boy— *voilà*!"

"What information?"

Edward waved the cigar airily. "All sorts of information, my boy. Concerning this company, and that company, and where there is likely to be growth, and where there is not; that sort of thing, don't you know. As I said, all sorts of information." He smiled. "Some of it, from time to time, is actually true."

Eric shook his head. "So you're dealing in rumors."

"Rumors, my boy, have received decidedly bad press. Useful things, rumors. Civilization wouldn't be where it is today without rumors, don't you know. More important than sex."

"I don't believe I heard you say that." Eric shook his head. "The great Edward Buchanan thinking that something is better than sex!"

"More important, my boy. Not better. More important. Sex cannot thrive without rumors, don't you know." He winked broadly. "But don't get me started on the ladies, my dear boy. Don't get me started. There's money to be made in rumors, as long as they're well-placed."

"So what happens?"

"So what happens, he asks. Lord love a duck. It's true. I have failed thee as a father, McDuff." He inhaled deeply on the cigar, and surrounded himself with smoke as he exhaled. "What happens, my boy, is that certain stocks decrease in value, allowing yours truly to snap them up at disgracefully low prices. Disgracefully low. And then, a few rumors later, those same stocks are soaring in value, and before you know it, I am able to sell off quite a substantial little packet. All in a day's work, my boy. All in a day's work."

Eric shook his head. "Seems to me that people would get wise to you, and stop believing the rumors."

"Never stop believing rumors, my dear boy. They're gold dust."

"I'll settle for the real thing."

Anna Martin frowned and looked across the kitchen table at Caroline, who was playing with her spaghetti. "If you don't eat that, it will get cold."

"I'm not hungry, anyway." Caroline carried her plate to the sink. "May I be excused, please?"

"Do you have homework?"

Caroline wrinkled her nose. "I suppose so."

"Then I suggest that you get to it." She paused. "And not the books that Eric gave you!"

"Why not? That's studying, too!" Caroline's voice was rebellious.

"It's not going to get you anywhere in life. Your studies will."

"Not going to get me anywhere in life?" Caroline leaned against the doorframe. "It's the only thing in life that matters, don't you see?"

Anna sighed. "What I see is a young lady who is much too taken with the romance of flying and far too little taken with the reality of life. Even Sarah did more than fly, you know. She had a career."

"I'm going to have a career, too. I'm going to be a pilot."

"And who is going to pay you to fly? You can't count on Eric providing you with free airplanes for the rest of your life, you know."

Caroline's chin jutted out defiantly. "I'll fly the mails,

then. They're doing that all the time. Using airplanes instead of trains."

"Don't be silly," Anna said automatically. "It's dangerous. Only men fly the mails."

"There's nothing they do that I can't," Caroline said stubbornly. "I'm learning to fly and I'm going to be very very good at it. And then they'll realize how good I am and they'll hire me."

Anna had a fleeting image of the mail pilots, with their tight schedules and their hazardous routes, and of Eric's reaction to such a decision on Caroline's part. Over his dead body, she thought, and decided to humor Caroline. "Well, that's fine, dear. You do that. But you're not flying anything, anywhere, unless you pass your examinations. Eric has said it, I've said it, and that's that. So you might as well study for now."

She watched the girl's retreating back with a sudden twinge of memory: Sarah announcing her decision to move to New York and write for *Leslie's Weekly*. They had the same stubbornness, the same determination. It was strange sometimes to realize that this wasn't Sarah's child, but Amanda's. . . .

Edward sat down heavily on the large leather chair behind his desk, and looked worriedly around his office. Chief Executive Officer, it said on the brass plate on his door. It was a fine office, a place to fill with hushed voices and beautiful women and the smoke from expensive Havana cigars, which was, of course, what he usually did.

Today, though, he sat hunched over the telephone, staring with glazed eyes at the figures on the papers in front of him, feeling the tiny claw of fear tightening in his stomach, knotting and unknotting, a beast awakened from its slumber and starting to move ominously about. Fear. He had known it before, of course, known it intimately. But there was a kind of finality this time to the feeling.

For the last year Edward had been playing with high stakes, and now he had lost. In disbelief and panic, he realized that his speculations had ruined him. A.R.M. hadn't been affected; Edward had been careful to keep A.R.M. money out of his speculations, but A.R.M. would

have to survive without Edward, because he had played too
heavily this time. The stock market manipulation had
started as a small thing, a game on the side, a word
whispered here and there into an accommodating ear. But
he had already spent a considerable amount of money which
didn't belong to him, and which he could no longer return.

There was no turning back; there was no way out.

Carefully, neatly he assembled the papers that Eric would
need, all the A.R.M. documents which he normally kept
locked away in his desk, and he placed them on top, in plain
view. Taking a blank sheet of letterhead paper from his top
drawer, he toyed with his pen for a moment—strange how a
man who had never been at a loss for words could suddenly
feel himself trapped by such an oppressive silence—before
finally beginning to write. He wanted to compose a short
note to Eric—a good-bye, that was all.

When he was finished, he got up from his desk, heavily,
and, going over to his office door, slowly turned the key,
locking himself in. He poured a large tumbler of whiskey
and drank it down, fast and straight, trying desperately to
stop the cold claw raking his insides, the claw of fear, the
claw of despair, the claw of failure.

And then, finally, he walked purposefully over to the
window, opened it, glanced out briefly from his tenth-story
office at the panoramic view of the factory and the ware-
houses and the hangars and the runways he had helped to
create, and then, without further ado, he stepped out.

Eric, running up the stairs two and three at a time, fairly
bursting with news that only Edward would be able to
interpret, found that he had to use his key in Edward's
door—not so unusual, that, when Edward was entertaining
he often locked the door—before bursting in. "Haven't you
heard?" he gasped, not realizing at once that the room was
empty. "Haven't you heard? The stock market crashed this
morning!"

Amanda Osbourne took her newspaper with her tea in the
afternoons. It had already been several days since the awful
event at Wall Street, but it was still very much in the news.

An article on the second page caught her eye. Wasn't that
Eric Beaumont's little company, the one with the tiresome

lawyers in France or Switzerland or wherever they were? Somebody from the company named Edward Buchanan had killed himself by jumping out of a window all the way out in California.

For a moment she frowned slightly, as though permitting herself in that one instant to feel something for someone other than herself, or perhaps searching her memory for the connection her mind assured her was there. . . .

Another loss. That was how Eric saw it, in those long dreary days and weeks after Edward's funeral: another loss. He was a sort of dark King Midas. Anyone he loved, anyone he cared about, anyone he needed died. First Philippe and Sarah, and now Edward; he imagined, whimsically for a moment, that they were off doing whatever it was that people did once they died, and they were all together, while he was alone again.

Sometimes, when he really thought about it, he realized that this was his destiny: to be alone and to stay alone. It was partly because he wasn't like other people—he had come at last to recognize and believe in his own brilliance—and it was partly because the people he loved were not like other people. There had never been anything ordinary about Philippe de Montclair or Sarah Martin or Edward Buchanan, and that was why they were gone, burned out like meteors in the night sky, fast and brilliant and brief.

And Eric remained, because he still had work to do, things to create, a world to build. But it was hard; sometimes he was very tired and wished simply for it all to be over, so he could finally go to sleep and rediscover his youth and his loves.

The lawyers in Zurich sent one of their own, Jean-Luc Rousseau, to live in San Jose and begin to teach Eric some of the things that Edward had wanted him to learn. Eric dutifully listened and paid attention and learned how to run this company of his. All throughout the bleak dark days of the Depression that was to follow, Eric worked on his projects and learned the ins and outs of international corporate management.

Eric wasn't aware of the way he changed after Edward's death. It was a change so subtle, so gradual, that no one around him noticed it until the metamorphosis was complete, and by then it was too late to remark upon it. Caroline only noticed a light that was gone from his eyes, a bruised look about him, a sadness that nothing—neither her laughter nor her tears—was able to touch. Eric had become more remote, though he was still devoted to Caroline and Anna. It would be years before the two women realized how completely he had changed.

Everyone he cared about left him. So Eric ceased to care.

Eric didn't even realize what was happening. He did know that the increased tensions and stresses of his work—tensions and stresses that had begun when Rousseau had arrived and compelled Eric to assume more management responsibilities—were giving him new habits. He was drinking more than ever in the evenings, and now—to his own surprise—he sometimes brought women home with him.

They never stayed more than one night, of course. He wasn't looking for involvement, or caring, or love. But more and more of them came, as the long months following Edward's death stretched into years, until they all became a blur of bodies and faces and voices. And he didn't care.

His mind kept returning to the same thought: He had loved Sarah, and she had left him. He would never love again.

Caroline alone was his light, his brightness in a gray and terrible world. Caroline still held him rooted deeply to the world. She was fourteen, still so young that she could not live in California if he were not here to look after her, and the last thing in the world that he wanted was to send her back east to Amanda. Caroline was still bursting with the joy of discovery of the sky, and she somehow assured him that there could again be life, and light, and perhaps, in its own way and its own time, love.

"The situation appears to have resolved itself."

Robert Beneteau was speaking to the gathering in the conference room. He had gathered the partners, with the exception of Rousseau, who was still in California, and all the other young, energetic lawyers. All were ready to face the challenges of the next few decades. That they would be momentous decades nobody thought to question.

Marc Giroux shifted in his chair and adjusted his hearing

aid—a bother, that, but more and more necessary in these recent years. "What was that?"

"We have a report. From Financial Management Services. Louis du Terlong is more astute than we had, perhaps, given him credit for being."

"His research department left something to be desired, surely?"

Beneteau made an impatient gesture. "We've been through all that, Marc! There is such a thing as beating a dead horse."

"One cannot be too careful. That was a major error. It could have cost the company enormously. I still don't see, in fact, how it *isn't* going to cost the company enormously."

Beneteau cleared his throat. "That is what I am attempting to outline. Marc, gentlemen—oh, yes, ladies—" This was in deference to the two newest members of the staff, Françoise Duroc and Marie-Chantale des Ebernieres, who despite their law diplomas still found themselves, more often than not, in charge of the coffee. In this moment they exchanged wry looks. "—here is the Financial Management Services report. I am sure that you will find it entirely satisfactory." He cleared his throat again, appreciating the moment of drama in the room. "As we all know, F.M.S. has in the past several years been establishing a reputation throughout Europe as an aggressive and forward-looking firm. We have, of course, groomed them to obtain just such a reputation, and it has now proved to be the correct route to have taken."

He could gloat over that one. Giroux—and others in the firm—had felt that Financial Management Services was becoming too large for a subsidiary company, too independent, too well-known. It was he, Robert Beneteau, who had pushed for their independence and their reputation. His decision had finally paid off.

Beneteau paused long enough to take a drink of water, and then continued. "In any case, in recent months the Banque dé la Sécurité has finally decided to call in the loans still outstanding on the A.R.M. account—quite a number of them, by Louis's reckoning. They thought, of course, to take advantage of the disastrous financial situation in the United States in order to push the company over the line into bankruptcy, and thereby regain for Johnson full control of the industry. Or majority control of A.R.M., which would, of course, amount to the same thing in the end."

He had them now. There was absolute silence in the room. Perhaps, after all, he should have gone into criminal law. There was no question but that he had a flair for the dramatic. "Well, we still have the blanket agreement which Monsieur Buchanan obtained from Madame Osbourne, and the assets in her account are, of course, extraordinary. A loan was made on the strength of those assets, and A.R.M. simply paid off the loans to the Banque de la Sécurité."

The spell was broken: There was a sudden babel of voices, with questions and comments and laughter. Beneteau raised his hand. "Wait, there is more. Apparently—as you can imagine—Johnson was angered by their inability to manage a takeover of the company, and they demanded that the Banque de la Sécurité investigate the source of the money used to pay off the debts. The Banque de la Sécurité has no such investigatory wing, so they hired a firm to investigate for them."

"Let me guess." It was Giroux, a light in his eyes showing that he was appreciating the situation, even though he had initially guessed wrong. That was what people liked about Marc Giroux: his ability to laugh at himself. "They hired Financial Management Services?"

"Well, they tried to do so," Beneteau admitted. "But, as we had discussed, F.M.S. didn't take the contract. Too busy, not that Johnson was to be deterred. So we—er—sold them F.M.S."

"What?"

"We *sold* it?"

"Quelle surprise, alors!"

Beneteau held up his hand another time, and waited for silence, but Giroux was still smiling. "Please hear me out. Louis brought this plan to our attention months ago, and the partners discussed its feasibility at that time. As I said, Johnson was not going to give up, so they offered to buy out all the F.M.S. stock in order to control the investigations. The major stockholders"—and here he coughed discreetly, for under various covers the firm was the major stockholder —"found the offer difficult to refuse, particularly after it increased a number of times. I might add that the resources provided by this buyout more than compensates for the money borrowed against Madame Osbourne's account, which happily leaves the company once more in the black, even in this time of great financial distress nationally."

"Then what of F.M.S.?"

"Ah. Well, they did in fact conduct the investigation, at some considerable expense to both the Banque de la Sécurité and to Johnson, I am sorry to say." He didn't sound at all sorry to say it. "They found in the end, of course, that they were investigating themselves, which is a sad waste of time and effort, but so it goes."

"Then Johnson now knows that we owned F.M.S."

Beneteau shrugged. "And if they do? It doesn't really matter, does it? It's theirs, now. One or two employees have asked to be transferred to other subsidiaries within our network, but by and large I expect that it will be business as usual."

Françoise ventured a question, her first. "Don't we need F.M.S. as a subsidiary?"

"Not particularly. Louis and one or two others are coming to work directly for us." He coughed deliberately again. "In any case, losing a subsidiary seems less important than the loss of money and face experienced by Johnson and the Banque de la Sécurité. Wouldn't you all agree with me?"

Of course they did.

There was going to be another war.

Eric Beaumont knew it, and knew intuitively that this war was going to be dramatically different from the last one, that it was going to require new weapons, new methods of warfare, a new attitude about fighting. And he knew what kind of materials were going to be needed: tube alloys.

He had bought out an American company that had been experimenting with the alloys, and he was already seeing the possibilities. People were learning how to split the atom: To most it was an intellectual exercise, but Eric could see the practical uses, and he could see what was going to happen.

He knew because he was going to make it happen.

Chapter Twenty-two

The trouble started with a great clanging noise, just as the textbooks had said that it would.

There was a time when Caroline would have identified the problem instantaneously. She used to pore over her flight and engineering books at night with a flashlight under the covers, so Mrs. Martin wouldn't know that she was still awake. But she hadn't looked at a textbook for some time, and she was exhausted, nearing the end of a very long flight indeed.

Caroline had, just in time for her seventeenth birthday in March of 1932, flown across the United States.

She had flown across the continent. There was nothing in those words that could adequately encapsulate the feeling. Others had done it before her. Unlike Sarah, Caroline was not setting a record; she was content merely to do what felt right for her, and she had decided that flying solo across America was what she needed to do. It would be a time to be alone, to rely solely upon herself, to find what it was that she really wanted out of her life.

Eric had been against it, of course. That was part of the problem. Eric was set against anything that had to do with her growing up. He wanted to keep her safe and secure in the old house out on Western Avenue. Flying was all right, of course, as long as she was supervised by A.R.M. people. Anything, for that matter, within reason was all right, as long as she was supervised by A.R.M. people. Caroline was getting more than a little tired of being constantly followed and supervised by A.R.M. people.

Well, she was flying an A.R.M. airplane, but it was her own, the gift Eric had given her for her seventeenth birthday. The all-metal plane with retractable landing gear was one of the most advanced planes designed for private use. And Caroline was delighted to own a plane that she knew was the object of envy among pilots everywhere. She had decided to celebrate her birthday by taking three weeks off from school and flying across the country.

It was wonderful. It was the closest she had ever gotten to ecstasy, pure and unadulterated. She was alone, truly and totally alone, for the first time in her life. No one was following her, or telling her what to do and how to do it. She was mistress of her own destiny. Eric had helped her plot the course and had marked all of her charts for her, but Eric was thousands of miles away. If she chose another course, that was her choice. If she chose to stop at one place rather than another, that, too, was her choice. She could eat and sleep when and where she liked, and no one—no one—was looking over her shoulder. Freedom had become a very precious commodity indeed.

She had done all the right things, of course: She had made a correct, polite visit to her grandmother in New Hampshire —her mother was away, no one knew exactly where — and she listened to her grandmother tell her what to do about her future and resolved to ignore all of her advice. And she had signed a great many autographs, for it was still an unusual thing for a young woman to fly so far by herself. But she had done all of this in a hurry, the sense of eagerness always crowding in. She wanted to be away from people and up in the air again—to soar with the eagles. . . . And then, finally, she had flown back, the vast expanse of the country spreading itself out flat and rugged beneath her wings, with the shadow of her sleek airplane flitting over it all as quick and deft as a bird.

The plains and the mountains, the cornfields and the hillsides, the industrial cities and the factories and the smokestacks, the vast mirrored surfaces of lakes, the rivers winding their sinuous paths to the sea . . . they all felt as though they belonged to her, as though she were becoming part of her country in ways that she had never even thought about. Caroline knew, with absolute certainty, that she could never feel the same way about America again.

She watched her instruments, the altimeter, the airspeed indicator, and the compass, and assured herself continually that she was still on course, maintaining the correct height, still on the right heading. The air around her changed as she flew west, too. Soft and pliable at times, it could suddenly become hard and sharp, buffeting her about with turbulence that made the ocean tides look like nothing at all. Air never failed to interest Caroline. Compared to Eric, she knew little about its composition, or why it did the things that it did, but she had learned about it from a purely practical viewpoint—and she knew never to take it for granted.

If there was a golden rule about flying, it was never to take anything for granted.

And until now Caroline's luck had held. There had been a minor gas leak back east, when she was still in Pennsylvania, and she had landed without further ado and had it seen to. The mishap delayed her by a few hours, no more. There was some bad weather over the Rockies, with wicked air currents that banged on her fuselage and tossed her about with the strength of a Titan, but she clung resolutely to her course and rode them out. There was rain, but rainclouds were made to be risen above, and she never lost her sense of wonder at climbing high into stormy clouds and emerging beyond, into a world reserved for a select few, a world of brilliant sun and sky and a carpet of white fluffy clouds.

Now that she was almost home, her thoughts turned to her welcome.

She was already in California, though still considerably north of San Jose, when the sudden explosion pulled her from her reveries—mostly concerned with a very long, very hot bath and, if she could talk Mrs. Martin into it, a cold beer—and forced her back to the present. The explosion took her by surprise. The airplane shook and shuddered in its wake, and black smoke started trailing out from the front of the airplane. It came from the engine, from the nose, directly in front of her. . . . She started to cough before she even started to think.

The engine pitch rose to a wail before stopping altogether. The silence that followed was deafening.

Mother of God, Caroline thought. This is it. I missed something, somewhere. I was careless, or I was unlucky, but somehow I missed something. One always pays the price; Michael the flight instructor had taught her that in his safety lectures, over and over again. One always, in the end, paid the price.

The propellers were still spinning, but that was because of

the airstream, not the engine. The engine was, in fact, quite dead.

I must have thrown a rod, she thought wildly. Nothing else could account for that terrible noise and this terrible silence. I must have thrown a rod.

She was going to have to find a place to land, and quickly. The smoke was billowing out all around her, reducing her visibility. There would be no thought of resuscitating the engine if she was correct in her diagnosis. Pity that this hadn't happened twenty minutes ago, when she was above the desert, a great landing place. She was going to have to find someplace else, and she frowned as she looked at the trees and town below her. A road: If she could only find a road, she might be able to land. Michael had told her that airplanes were persona non grata on roads, but an exception would have to be made this time.

She banked around to the right, her knuckles white as she clutched the yoke. Panic was already beginning to pluck at the edges of her stomach and her mind was wildly running projections. It was then that something on the ground caught her eye, flashing through the black smoke which was continuing to pour from the engine's dead cylinder: It was the wonderful sudden gleam of sun on metal—an airplane.

It was parked near a small hangar on an equally small airfield, just one or two runways, and neither of them paved. But there was a brightly colored windsock flying like a pennant, and it was simple after that to find the runway that would bring her down into the wind. Simple to find, but with her airspeed dropping it was going to be a miracle if she managed to get over to it and down in one piece.

Caroline dampened her lips. One pass: That was all that she was going to have, and it was a short runway. She had gotten spoiled, learning to fly on the huge A.R.M. installation. She was accustomed to a precise landing pattern and enough runway beneath her to touch off and come around again if anything went wrong. There were going to be no options here.

She had swung around as far as she could, and she lined up on her final—and only—approach. She still wasn't quite parallel, but she was as close to it as she was going to get. Her airspeed was dropping, and all of the instruments on the panel in front of her were going haywire, the needles on the gauges swinging wildly back and forth. Now, she thought. It's now or never, and she forced the nose down, down, and then the wheels had touched and bounced up again; she held steady and they touched again, and she applied the left rudder and the brake simultaneously and the plane screeched as it slowed and swerved in a great arc until it had almost turned completely around. Then, at last, it stopped.

Caroline sat still, her hands gripping the yoke between her legs, her breath coming in ragged gasps, her heart thudding painfully in her chest. She was alive. She hadn't crashed, she had brought her airplane down, she was alive. That was all that really mattered.

Gradually she started to move, flexing her arms and legs, unsnapping her leather helmet and pulling it from her head. She unfastened the safety belt and slid off the seat, opening the small cockpit door and sliding out onto the ground. Her legs buckled as they touched the ground, and she touched the plane to steady herself. Hardly a jaunty descent, she acknowledged to herself with a wry smile, but she was hardly feeling in a jaunty mood.

She was still getting over the fact that she was, miraculously, alive.

She brushed off her flying suit, more out of habit than need, a small reassuring ritual gesture which assured her that she was indeed still there, and she turned back to the cockpit to try and locate her map. She was going to have to find a telephone and call Eric and let him know where she was; and she wasn't precisely sure that she knew where to tell him.

When the hand touched her shoulder, she screamed.

The young man jumped back immediately, as frightened as she was. "I'm sorry. I say, I'm frightfully sorry. I didn't mean to scare you. . . ."

Caroline steadied herself against the side of her airplane. She had had more than enough surprises for one day. She looked at him. The man who had touched her was in his early twenties, tall and broad-shouldered, with gray eyes, a strong jawline, wavy brown hair, and a moustache. Part of her mind was thinking, irrelevantly, that he had the whitest teeth she had ever seen.

She brushed hair out of her eyes. "That's all right."

He looked from her to the airplane. "Engine trouble? I saw you coming in. You looked like a disaster, with all that smoke. . . . That was a very nice piece of flying."

"Thank you. Is this your field?"

He smiled. "It is. I'm glad that it could be of some use." He extended his hand, a little timidly. "My name is Andrew Starkey."

She shook his hand. "Caroline Copeland. Listen, do you have a telephone I can use? I'm going to need to organize a ride home, and someone to come and get the airplane. . . ."

"Yes, of course. There's an office in the hangar, why don't you come over. And I can offer you a cold drink, as well, if you'd like."

The radio was crackling in the office, repeating once again the story that Caroline had been hearing all over the East Coast: the kidnapping of the Lindbergh baby. Andrew glanced at her and saw her listening, and said softly, "Isn't that awful? It's been in all of the headlines."

"Yes," Caroline said, and wondered why she suddenly felt so cold. She didn't know them personally, although Eric had often consulted with Charles Lindbergh. Still, they were her idols. To have such a perfect marriage, and to be able to fly together like that, and then that lovely baby. . . .

Andrew reached over and changed the station. A tinny voice started singing "April in Paris." "Now," he said briskly, "about that drink. Is beer all right?"

Caroline smiled. "Beer would be perfect," she said, and watched him open it for her and pour it in a glass, cold and amber and refreshing. He poured one for himself as well, and touched her glass with his, his gray eyes, heavily fringed with lashes, gazing on the bright gold of her hair. "Happy landings."

"Happy landings." She drank half the glass in one swallow.

"Well, the telephone's there. But, you know, I'd be happy to drive you home myself."

She almost laughed. "You don't even know where I live!"

He met her eyes. "I don't care where you live."

There was a moment of silence. Caroline thought about Eric, and how concerned he would be, not as much for the airplane as for her safety. And she'd have to wait here for hours. . . . On the other hand, Andrew Starkey was young and undeniably attractive, appeared reasonably sensitive, and . . . "San Jose," she said, suddenly.

"Fine," he said calmly, still watching her.

"That's got to be hours away from here!"

He smiled. "Not enough hours," he said.

Caroline was suddenly aware of a certain warmth engulfing her, a tugging at her stomach, a feeling fresh and new and terribly exciting. She looked consideringly at Andrew Starkey, and then she smiled. "All right, then. Thank you."

"Great." He was looking at her as though he was aware of the wave of strange feelings inside her, and she realized belatedly that her cheeks must be flaming. She turned away from him, drinking the rest of her beer, and tried to seem casual. "What is it that you do here? I mean, is this all for business or pleasure?"

"Entirely pleasure." He made it sound wicked. "I manage a restaurant in San Francisco for work. But I've always loved to fly."

She turned to face him, nodded in shared excitement. "Oh, I know, I know! There's nothing like flying!"

"Even after a mishap like today's? You might well have been killed, you know."

Caroline shrugged. "Anybody can get killed at any moment," she said, and thought of her father stepping on a landmine and of Eric's wife falling out of the sky and of Mr. Buchanan jumping out of a window. Life was too filled with mystery, with uncertainty, to live it in the shadow of what could be. Even people who were careful weren't safe, not in the final analysis. Maybe especially people who were careful weren't safe. "I'd rather know my risks," she said, more firmly.

Andrew Starkey raised his eyebrows. "A noble sentiment," he said. "And now, Miss Copeland, if you would be so good as to drink up, we can start our trip."

"Are you sure about this? I can call. . . ."

"Entirely positive. The pleasure, I assure you, will be all mine."

She put down her empty glass. "All right, then. But only if you'll call me Caroline. Miss Copeland sounds so stuffy and formal. Not like me at all."

"Done. Caroline it is. Shall we be off?"

Later, when she thought about it, she wondered which road they took north. She wondered what sort of motorcar Andrew drove. She wondered at all the scenery that flashed past as the afternoon sloped into dusk and the sun set on their left. She didn't remember any of it, not ever.

What she remembered, in the end, was the warmth and the excitement. She felt so comfortable with this man who shared her passion and enthusiasm for flight. Everything about him was new and wonderful, each element of his personality something to be explored and examined and filed to think about later, in the long stretches of solitude until she could see him again.

That she was going to see him again was never at any point a matter of doubt.

"Eric, I need to talk to you."

"I should say that you do." He was leaning over the angled drawing table set up in front of the window in a corner of his office, and he had barely looked up when Caroline came into the room.

"Oh." His tone had been cold, and she hesitated before going on, anxious first to please him. "Are you angry with me about the airplane?"

"Was there anything that you could have done to prevent that accident?"

She shook her head. "No. It was the engine. And I kept the airplane intact when I landed."

"Then I don't suppose that I'm angry with you about the airplane."

There was a moment of silence, during which Caroline half-sat, half-leaned against his big mahogany desk. It had been Edward's, once. She carefully brushed an imaginary piece of dirt off her gray trousers—Eric hadn't approved of these, either—and bit her lip. "But you're angry with me about something, aren't you?"

He studied his design for a moment and then slowly and deliberately put down the pencil and pulled a packet of cigarettes from his pocket. "What gives you that impression, Caroline?"

She looked at him sharply, to see if he was being sarcastic. "Oh. You *are* angry."

Eric lit the cigarette and flicked the match out. It gave him time to think. He wasn't sure, actually, precisely what it was that he was feeling. The young man who had driven Caroline home last week had aroused a lot of emotions in Eric, not all of them pleasant. Jealousy? Surely not. Protectiveness, certainly. Caroline was too young to be driven home by some young cad, especially somebody who owned a restaurant and flew airplanes as a hobby. . . .

Anna had laughed at him. "She's growing up, Eric," she said. "You have to let her be."

"No, I don't," he replied, aware of how unreasonably stubborn he was being and yet still unable to change it. "He's not right for her."

"How could you possibly know? He hardly said three words," Anna remonstrated. "Besides, who says that he has to be right for her? Was Sarah your first girlfriend?"

"That's different."

"It is precisely the same thing. You're simply being difficult."

Now he sat down behind his desk and smoked his cigarette and looked speculatively at Caroline. She had become so beautiful. At seventeen, she had fulfilled the promise of her background, of Philippe and Amanda together. Amanda's flaxen blond hair shone on her daughter as elegantly as it had shone on herself at that age. But Philippe's dark, enigmatic eyes were there under the fringe of short hair—for in the last year Caroline had taken to looking just like that Earhart woman, favoring men's trousers and short hair. She would probably grow out of it, but the phase was disturbing nonetheless. The high Lewis cheekbones were there, too, and the tall, slender build that characterized the de Montclair family for as far back as Eric could remember. Caroline was, physically, the very best that Amanda and Philippe together had to offer. Perhaps that was the danger.

Eric exhaled a stream of smoke. Was Anna right? Was he just being difficult? He wanted nothing but Caroline's happiness, and safety. After that animal her mother had married, any man was a likely abuser in Eric's eyes. Maybe this Starkey fellow was all right, after all. . . . He did seem to do something to the girl, something that she liked. Anna said that he called her on the telephone every night, and that Caroline spent all of her time giggling and chattering. "I think it's good for her," Anna said.

"No," Eric said at length. "I'm not angry with you."

She looked at him, still with some apprehension in her eyes, but decided to take his statement at face value. There was a silence before she said, "Eric, do you believe in love at first sight?"

Did he believe in love at first sight? He considered the question, but he wasn't thinking about Caroline and Andrew. Suddenly Caroline and the office and indeed all of California vanished, and he crept back in his life, back to the moment the back door to his small hangar opened and Sarah stood there silhouetted against the sky. Did he believe in love at first sight? His mature mind said no, but his young man's heart had leaped when he saw her standing there. Did he believe in love at first sight? He had loved Sarah in that first minute he saw her, before she spoke a word, before he had even risen to his feet to greet her.

"I think so. I think that a lot of feelings can happen at different moments, maybe even when we least expect them." At least that was honest.

Caroline was silent for a few moments, tracing some imaginary design on the top of the desk with her fingertip. "How can you tell if you're in love?"

He shook his head. "Caroline, it's been a long time since I was in love. Why don't you ask Mrs. Martin about all this?"

She met his gaze. "Because she never ever was in love. She said so."

Eric cleared his throat, embarrassed at so honest an expression. "Yes. Well, I suppose that it's just something you know."

"Did you know, when you fell in love with your wife?"

Here at least he was treading on familiar ground. "Yes," he said, and even to himself the pain and hollowness was clear in his voice. "Oh, yes. I knew."

Caroline sighed. "That's exactly how I feel," she said.

Eric told himself that he was being overprotective. He told himself that he was meddling in someone else's affairs. He told himself many nasty things, and then he did what he felt it was his duty to do.

He wrote a long letter to the lawyers.

"Is she really serious about him?" Beneteau's voice was anxious.

Rousseau stretched and took his coffee cup over to the window with him. "She thinks so. Monsieur Beaumont thinks so."

"She's so young," Giroux interjected.

"She's seventeen, Marc. Your wife was younger than that when you got married."

"My wife," Giroux said primly, "is from another generation."

Beneteau, reflecting on the situation, reached for a glass of water. "Do we know anything about him?"

"There are a lot of Starkeys in California. It would take weeks to obtain a complete dossier."

"Well, I suggest that we obtain one! We can't afford another mistake like Osbourne."

A ripple of agreement went through the room. "Caroline Copeland has to be protected."

"Do we have a sense yet that she's going to be able to take over the company?"

"God knows. Beaumont is doing fine for the moment. There's no need to rush things."

"No, we can't rush things. He's doing well, and she's showing a healthy interest in the airplanes. But we've got to be very careful about who she associates with."

"And who she marries," Rousseau said.

"She can't be that serious?"

"God knows. But the money and the company ownership go straight through to her child, too, so we'd best be careful about what genes she mixes in with hers."

"She's only seventeen, for Christ's sake!"

"Marc, will you leave off with the 'she's only seventeen' crap, please?"

"And will you two stop arguing?" Beneteau asserted his authority. "Let's just stick to investigating Starkey, all right? If he's all right, then we don't have anything to worry about."

"And if he's not?"

"Then we have something to worry about."

Andrew kissed her for the first time on the deserted airstrip where they had first met.

She had thought that she would be afraid. Night after night as she talked with him on the telephone, and laughed, and felt the joy pouring from her, she knew that something like this would one day happen. And, night after night, she lay in bed and stared at the ceiling and worried. Charles Osbourne had kissed her, and now ten years later Andrew Starkey was going to kiss her, and it conjured up all the old hatred and fear and resentment. She was afraid that these feelings would make her turn away from him in revulsion. She couldn't stand that. She couldn't stand the thought of hurting Andrew.

Nor could she tell him, either, of that horrible Christmas. He would think terrible things of her. He would realize that she wasn't a nice girl anymore. There were words for women like her, women who had had sex like that. Andrew would never want her, not if he knew. She was damaged merchandise.

So she lay in bed and struggled with her dilemma, and then Andrew called and asked her to fly down for the day. A picnic, he promised. It would be so good to see her again.

Breathless with excitement, almost forgetting her fears, she went.

Eric had replaced her faulty engine and had had his people overhaul the new one completely by then, so that her airplane was once again safe to fly. She wasn't at all nervous. She daringly went out over the ocean on her way down, skimming over the waves like a sea gull, feeling the masses of blue and green water rush under her. The sun sparking on the waves was blinding.

And then she banked and worked her way inland to the small airfield that had once already, she was certain, saved her life. She flew towards the young man who stood near the hangar with bright eagerness in his eyes and promises in his heart.

She tipped her wings to him once she saw him standing there, and then she went carefully into the landing pattern she had been taught, watching the windsock to tell her which runway to use. There it was, and she turned again for the base leg of the landing and turned in once more for her final approach.

Caroline set down lightly and taxied evenly to a stop. Mrs. Martin had told her that the airplanes Sarah had flown had no brakes, and that she often flew in circles to lose momentum before burying her propellers in bales of hay. The good old crazy days, Caroline thought, wondering how Sarah had found the courage to fly those simplistic machines they called airplanes.

She sat for a moment in the airplane, flicking off switches, assuring herself that everything was in order, and trying to gather her courage. After her last mishap, Michael had given her a rabbit's foot to hang in the cockpit. "Can't be too careful, Miss Copeland," he observed, and now she took the hard little object in her hand and squeezed it. When she finally reached up and slid back the bubble of glass which enclosed the cockpit, she felt how hot the sun was.

Andrew was still standing by the hangar, watching her. She shook her hair out of the flight helmet and hopped down on the dirt runway, automatically dusting herself off before turning to walk towards him. And he was walking towards her, and then he was running, and she was, too, breathless with the feelings that were beginning to churn in her stomach, once again. He caught her and soon was swinging her around and around before setting her down on the ground once more. Slowly, his hand came up to her chin and he tipped her face up to his, looking long and seriously into her eyes, leaning forward until he was closer, closer, only a breath away, and Caroline closed her eyes for no other reason than that it seemed the thing to do. Andrew's lips were on her, kissing her gently, sweetly, and she tightened her arms around his shoulders and responded to him, kissing him with her own gentleness and her own need. Leaning against him, she could feel his heart beating through the cotton of his shirt.

Caroline's stomach was churning. She had expected to be repulsed, and she was excited instead. She had anticipated wanting to draw away from Andrew, and, rather, she wanted to be closer still.

He wrapped his arm around her shoulder, casually, as he led her away from the airplane and out of the sun into the shade of the few trees allowed to grow near the hangar. In that shade his motorcar was parked, and in the rumble seat of the motorcar was the picnic.

Later, she could close her eyes and recite the menu. The picnic had taken on, in her mind, a totally different significance: a betrothal feast, perhaps. After all, Andrew had kissed her.

They had wine, a cold, crisp, dry white wine of the sort that California vineyards were starting to make and which rivaled their French counterparts. There were grapes, cold and fresh off the vine, dipped in sparkling crystal sugar. They ate sandwiches made with sourdough french bread and filled with cheese and ham and chicken and lettuce. There were mushrooms, stuffed with some spicy mixture of cheese and crab. They finished off with pastry, sweet and runny and sticky, and Caroline sat entranced while Andrew licked her fingers clean.

She was in love. She knew it. She had known it that first night, and she had known it all these weeks, weeks filled with letters and telephone calls and wakeful nights spent staring at her ceiling. She was in love, and everything was perfect. One day Andrew Starkey would marry her, and then because he loved her, he would make love to her properly, not like horrible old Uncle Charles. And they would have children who would learn to fly, and they would settle down here, near Eric, and live happily ever after.

When Andrew finally pushed aside his wineglass and the remains of the picnic lunch, and gathered her in his arms, she smiled and closed her eyes. This was the way it was supposed to be.

She had earned this peace, she thought, as he bent to kiss her again and she tasted the warmth of his mouth. She had earned this happiness. After that horrible episode in New York . . . after her servitude to her grandmother's whims and her terror of her mother's . . . after living in the shadow of the Dresden China Aviatrix in the house on Western Avenue . . . this, at last, belonged to her. At last, at long last, she had the sun and the sky—and a love that could fill her life.

Chapter Twenty-three

I think that we have a problem."

Eric automatically took a cigarette out of his gold cigarette case—a Christmas gift from Caroline and Anna—and lit it. Inhaling, he coughed and frowned at the cigarette before transferring the frown to Rousseau, the French lawyer who sat so gracefully in the chair in front of his desk. Thank God for Rousseau, who had been there and pulled him out of his slump after Edward's death, and damn Rousseau, who thought he had all of the answers.

Eric drew in on the cigarette, exhaling slowly, blowing smoke out of the corner of his mouth. "Which is?"

Rousseau tapped his foot in the air. "Monsieur Starkey."

Eric looked at him silently for a long moment, and then stood up and walked over to the window, turning his back on the lawyer and still puffing on his cigarette. "Please be more specific."

"Monsieur Beaumont, you must know that the firm takes a very lively interest in Mademoiselle Copeland's well-being. It was a mere matter of procedure this past spring, when she first became involved with Monsieur Starkey, for us to investigate him. Routine, do you understand?"

"And?"

"Monsieur Beaumont, Monsieur Starkey's business credentials are impeccable. He attended Stanford and opened his restaurant on money borrowed from a bank, and he has that loan very nearly paid off, despite the fact that he has been in business a mere three years. For a young man not yet twenty-five, these are good credentials. We were pleased." He paused, possibly for effect, before continuing. "Alas, Monsieur Beaumont, his family history is not as impeccable. His father, one Bernard Starkey, is a well-respected member of San Francisco politics. He is, in fact, bruited to be the next mayoral candidate and may very well win the election. His campaigns have been supported by money supplied by his wife's family, a well-established and certainly successful industrialist family in Southern California. I expect that you could at this point hazard a guess as to the wife's maiden name."

Eric expelled a long stream of smoke in the direction of the window. "Johnson."

"None other than."

There it was again, that hated name, the people who had killed Sarah. And Caroline had been seeing one of them. He was a Johnson. All the beautiful flowers, the telephone calls, the dinners, and the long flights together out over the redwoods—and the new airplane, Eric thought with a sudden lurch to his stomach, the airplane that Andrew had ordered from A.R.M., and Eric had thought it was just a way for Andrew to get closer to him. What a fool. He was a Johnson. All the time he had tricked and manipulated Caroline . . . had used her to get closer to A.R.M., for God only knew what purposes.

Johnson had found a way to get to him.

The law firm had neatly foiled Johnson's attempts at a takeover and made them lose face in the process. Now all they wanted was revenge, and here was a ready-made way to get it—through the one human being that Eric loved more than any other, for whom he felt responsible. If they couldn't get at him through A.R.M., then they would go through Caroline. The bastards.

Eric's window overlooked part—only part—of the vast A.R.M. compound. The company was stretched across hun-acres of land, now, with laboratories and hangars and runways and factory buildings spreading out in all directions from this, the main office building. Here was Eric's office, here also was Rousseau's, for the times that he was in America to advise Eric; here was Accounting, and the business office, and Sales, and even a fledgling Public Relations office. There was Security, now, too. That had been Rousseau's idea. The entire compound was fenced in and patrolled with men and dogs belonging to A.R.M.'s own security firm.

Eric stood and smoked his cigarette and looked out over the compound. Johnson wanted all of this, and, failing to get in by devious business practices, they were choosing to get in through devious personal relationships.

Well, it wasn't going to work. They weren't getting A.R.M., and they weren't getting Caroline. And that was that.

He turned his back to the panoramic view and faced Rousseau. "All right. What do we do?"

The lawyer shrugged delicately. "The situation, Monsieur Beaumont, is not as straightforward as it may seem. Monsieur Starkey is indeed the son of a member of the Johnson family, but he has no connection other than that with Johnson Industries. Oh, his uncle arranged the loan that started him off in the restaurant business, of course. And I expect that his little airfield was also financed and supported by the family. But that is all on a purely personal level."

"What are you saying, exactly?"

Rousseau cleared his throat delicately. "Our investigations have been very careful, Monsieur Beaumont, and we are quite convinced that Monsieur Starkey himself is unaware of any of the machinations which may or may not take place around him. Monsieur Starkey is, in point of fact, somewhat of an innocent. We are quite convinced that his relationship with Mademoiselle Copeland is nothing more than a natural mutual attraction. To him at least, there is no plot behind it."

Eric shook his head. "Of all the men she could meet . . . it has to be more than coincidence!"

"How? Did Johnson Industries tamper with her airplane, last spring? Did they cause her to experience engine problems at that particular place and that particular time, so that she could meet Monsieur Starkey? Think of what you are saying."

Eric stubbed out his cigarette in the ashtray on his desk. "So it was a happy coincidence," he said, his voice sounding anything but happy. "But it would have happened, then, someplace else, some other time. Christ, Caroline is so young, so vulnerable. Of course she fell in love with him. Of course. They knew that she would."

Rousseau held up his hand. "You're overreacting. Wait a minute. I do not seek to underestimate the danger here, but you need to know that we are quite convinced that Monsieur Starkey is on no devious errand. It is, as you say, a simple and strange coincidence." He took a deep breath. However, it could become far more than that. Monsieur Starkey is in debt to his mother's family, and they may decide to give him some options for payment. We don't know. You see, the reality is that we don't know exactly what Johnson knows. We don't know if they have the full information about the contents of the will of Count de Montclair, and we don't know if they know that Mademoiselle Copeland is his daughter, and we don't know if they realize just how powerful she might, in time, become. If they do know, then she is already in danger. If they don't, then she is all right. Either way, she must end the relationship with Monsieur Starkey immediately. It carries with it far too much risk."

"So, they shall separate." Eric said it coldly and almost as a statement of fact. Rousseau looked at him sharply.

"She may have something to say about that."

"That's nonsense. She's only seventeen. She'll do as I say."

"Hmm." Rousseau took a pipe from his pocket and proceeded to fill it from a tobacco pouch. "We must take care not to let her know why. There's no sense in alerting Monsieur Starkey—and, through him, Johnson Industries—to our deep interest in Mademoiselle Copeland. If they don't know about her yet, it's best kept that way." He struck a match and started the lighting-up ritual. The pipe was an attempt to stop smoking so many cigarettes, but he hadn't quite gotten the hang of it yet. It usually took a full packet of matches to get one going properly.

Eric sat down heavily behind his desk. He knew what was coming next, and he wanted no part of it. He needed Caroline in his life; he needed her insouciance and her gaiety, her youthful energy and her exuberance. He needed the shadow that flitted across her face, too, from time to time, which was the same shadow he had seen so very often in her father's eyes. As Caroline got older, she became in so many ways more and more like Philippe. She was Eric's link, his tie with the past—Caroline, who had never even been to France, and whose voice echoed France back to him even clearer and surer than his own.

Eric, however, knew what had to be done. She had to be protected, at any price. Caroline was going to *be* A.R.M., someday. She couldn't be married to a Johnson. . . . They had killed Sarah. They were out to destroy him. Eric clenched his fists unconsciously at the thought. If she married a Johnson a merger would be inevitable. She was strong enough, in her own way, but she didn't have the strength to stand up to Andrew, and all the rest of them. She wouldn't be able to do it. It would be the end of the dream, Philippe's and his dream, and as though echoing that thought the words came drifting back to him: "If nothing else succeeds in this life, Eric, I want our company to live. We pledged that we would stay together, and write our names on the sky. . . . So it's going to have to be you, Eric, you and Aeromechanique. . . ."

He took a deep breath. That had to come first, before his own personal feelings and personal preferences. Over the years he had come to realize that he no longer existed as an individual: He was A.R.M. Until it could be safely handed over to Caroline, he was A.R.M. He had to remember that.

Rousseau was still struggling with his pipe. Eric watched him for a moment, and then said softly, "She will have to go back east."

The lawyer looked up and abandoned his pipe. "Yes, of course. We think that's the most appropriate action at this time. It's the only way to be sure. If Monsieur Starkey makes any problems, then we will have to get to him, we will have to change his mind somehow. But sending Mademoiselle Copeland back east is the first step. It would be most expedient."

"All right." Eric stood up and went back to the window, watching the people scurry around below him like so many ants. There was a test scheduled for later that afternoon, he remembered as he watched the activity. A liquid-fuel rocket. All the other rockets he had worked on had fallen over on themselves and ignited. But someday it would work, it *could* work, if only . . . And, with a start, he drew his mind back to the problem at hand. "I'll tell Caroline this evening."

"Very good." Rousseau stood up. "The firm will, of course, support you in every way possible. But it is the only solution."

"Yes," Eric said, and wondered at how hollow he felt inside. "It is the only solution."

* * *

Andrew and Caroline walked up to one of the high cliffs overlooking the ocean. It was one of Caroline's favorite places in the world, with a breathtaking view of the water as it dashed itself in giant waves on the rocks far below. The whistling wind was broken only by shrublike trees which stood sentinel on the tops of the cliffs. It was, she often told herself, the closest one could come to flying while still on the ground.

There were some boats out today, dotting the ocean— fishing boats, mostly. The small pleasure sailboats she used to see had all but disappeared. They were too expensive to maintain in these days of the Great Depression.

The Depression hadn't touched Caroline's life, not really. Although Mrs. Martin was frugal and careful, her life was made easier by the knowledge that Eric would somehow always see her through. In addition, A.R.M. was a giant, and had not been one of the giants to topple with the stock market; and Eric took care of his own. Of course, Caroline knew that one day she would be very wealthy. The Copeland fortune, waiting for her in trust, was immense. So it was that Caroline flew her new airplane with very little thought for the quiet desperation of the lives over which her winger shadow flitted.

Andrew, also, was doing well. The restaurant he owned catered to the more wealthy segment of San Francisco, the people who still had money to purchase an expensive meal, who fled the poverty and squalor of the streets to take refuge in a quiet, refined atmosphere of white linen tablecloths and expensive silver and fine wines. "My uncle helps out, sometimes," Andrew told Caroline, and she nodded in understanding. Her mother did, too, financially at least.

He sat down, and she snuggled against him, her head resting on his shoulder, and together they looked out to sea. "I wonder," Caroline said dreamily, "what's on the other side."

"Japan, I should think," Andrew said. "With the odd island in between, of course."

"Japan," Caroline said, savoring the foreign sound on her tongue. "I should like to go there someday."

"Whatever for, my dear girl?" Andrew had taken to calling her that, lately, and she liked it. It reminded her of somebody, but she couldn't quite place whom.

"I don't know. To see something different and strange, I suppose. To do something extraordinary. Everybody is always doing extraordinary things, you know. Everybody but me."

"Nonsense," Andrew said firmly, disengaging his arm from hers to root around in the large canvas bag he had carried up to the cliffs with him. "Only a few people ever do really extraordinary things, and they always get punished for it."

"That's silly." Caroline plucked at the grass on either side of her and flung tufts of it over the edge of the cliff. "Eric's wife was extraordinary. She was the first woman to fly across the Channel. And the others—oh, you know, the Lindberghs. And Amelia Earhart. She flew across the Atlantic Ocean this summer. Imagine that!"

"That's not so very extraordinary," Andrew said, pulling paints and canvas from his bag. He had recently begun painting, and it had quickly become his favorite pastime, particularly when he was painting Caroline. "They're simply doing what they planned to do. Anyone can make a plan, and work at it and work at it, until it happens."

"All right, if you're so smart," Caroline said, "What is it in life that's extraordinary? And what do you mean, about people being punished for it?"

"The really extraordinary things," Andrew said, starting to sketch the outline of her face, "aren't the things that make people famous. They're small, local things. Like saving a child from a burning building. Or doing an act of kindness to somebody that no one else will ever know about. The things that happen not because of what we plan to do, but because of who we are. And the world doesn't take any too kindly to that sort of thing. People should all be the same. That way they're easier to control."

Caroline shivered. "Easier to control? That sounds ominous."

For a long time, he didn't answer. He sat and drew her face, coloring in the pink of her cheeks, the dark shadows in her eyes, the long windblown blond hair. At length, he finished the portrait and held it out to her; and it was then that he spoke. "You're right," Andrew said. "It is ominous."

Eric finally told Caroline. After the letters and telephone calls had been taken care of and he knew that his plan would be acceptable—long after all the arrangements had been made, he told her.

"What do you mean, I'm going back east? I can't!"

He glanced uneasily at Anna Martin, but she tightened her lips and said nothing. Caroline was pacing up and down the living-room carpet with more energy than he had realized she had. "Caroline, it makes sense. You're finished with school. It's time for you to think about what you want to do with your life."

"I *know* what I want to do with my life!"

"You think that you do. But you're still very young."

"I'm only a year younger than your precious Sarah was when you met her! What if there had been somebody there telling her that she was too young?"

"There was," Anna Martin said quietly.

"I am responsible for your welfare, and your mother and grandmother and I agree on this point, Caroline. You need to spend some time with them. You need to be able to make decisions about your life that are based on reason, not on emotion."

"So you've been talking to my mother? Great! And since when has she given a damn about my welfare?"

"Caroline, watch your language," Anna cautioned.

But Caroline lashed out. "She's a whore herself! The only thing she ever did was to bring me into the world, and even *that* she tried to avoid!" She caught Eric's look and went on. "You didn't think that I knew about that, did you? That she tried to abort me? Well, I know all about it. This is the person I'm supposed to have some sort of daughterly love for? No thank you!"

"Caroline—" Anna's voice was pleading.

"And," Eric said coolly, forgetting his best intentions, "did she tell you about your father?"

"Eric, no," Anna said helplessly, half rising from her chair.

"My father? My stupid father who walked over one of his own mines? Oh, right, I'm sorry—he was a *friend* of yours. I shouldn't speak ill of the dead, now, should I?"

"Eric, this isn't the time," Anna warned, ignoring Caroline.

"The time for what?"

Eric looked directly at Caroline. "Marcus Copeland," he said carefully, "was *not* your father."

There was a moment of silence. Anna was holding her breath, biting her lip, watching Caroline. Caroline herself had stopped in mid-stride, almost in mid-sentence, staring at Eric with her mouth open. He took advantage of the quiet to continue.

Eric began softly. "Before you give me any more of your misplaced rage, let me assure you that I am not your father, either. I wouldn't want you jumping to any conclusions. This is not, as Mrs. Martin seems to be trying to communicate, the best possible time for me to tell you this, but it seems to be dictated by circumstances. Would you prefer to sit down?"

Caroline sank silently into the nearest chair at hand, the one that Mr. Martin had sat in in the old days.

Eric pulled out a cigarette and lit it. "All right. Your mother and Sarah came to France together, in nineteen-eleven. Sarah was flying some exhibition shows there, and your mother came along because they were friends and because she wanted to see France. Sarah had heard of Aeroméchanique, which was just starting up in those days. She wanted to see our airplanes." He risked a glance at Caroline, but she was sitting as still and rigid as a statue, and he went on. "I would never have been able to start that company on my own. I was the son of the farrier on an estate in France—the Chateau de Montclair, near Angers. We—we French live in a very stratified society, Caroline. I was interested in engines, and would probably have become the estate mechanic if left to my own devices. But the son of the count was my age, and we had played together when we were children. We played at battles, we were knights together, we did everything together. To him, it mattered less what I was than who I was."

He paused, and the ticking of the clock on the mantel-piece suddenly became very loud. Anna was carefully avoiding his eyes. Caroline was still sitting straight and prim, her full attention focused on him. Now she dampened her lips and said, "Go on."

"We grew up together. We got drunk for the first time together, out behind the barn where my father shod the horses. We had our first girlfriends together. When his father died suddenly in a hunting accident, and he became the Count de Montclair himself, we just continued being friends. It never ever bothered us that we came from different places in society."

He closed his eyes, the better to see the past. "My friend—Philippe—knew that I was interested in engines. He used to sit and talk with me while I tinkered under motorcars—the estate cars, junk cars, anything I could get my hands on. And when there were things that I didn't understand, he sent off for books so I could learn. He hired people to teach me things. We had this dream together, you see. We were going to start a company, and we were going to make airplanes."

Caroline made a noise that sounded like a moan, and he opened his eyes to look at her, but she hadn't moved. After a moment he continued. "Philippe put up all the money. He had to, I didn't have two centimes to my name in those days. Funny, isn't it, how times change. He financed the whole operation. We rented an office in Angers, and some land outside of Paris. It was closer to the factories, you see. We figured it would cost less that way to transport materials. We built a hangar and cleared out a field, and we started working on airplanes. Well, *I* started working on airplanes. Philippe sat around and drank beer and watched me, and talked, mostly. And that's what we were doing when Amanda and Sarah came over one day, to see the airplanes."

Anna stood up, abruptly, and went over to the windows to draw the curtains against the darkening sky. She lit a lamp on an end table near the sofa, and sat down again, but still she said nothing.

"I met Sarah that day, and you know all about that. But Amanda met Philippe then, too, and though I've never completely understood their relationship, I think that, in their own way, they fell in love then, too."

"He was my father."

Eric looked at Caroline. "Yes. Philippe de Montclair was your father."

She drew in a deep breath. "I see. What I don't understand is why he didn't marry her, then. You married Sarah." A sudden thought occurred to her. "Where is he, now?"

Eric held up his hand. "One question at a time. First of all, he couldn't marry her, though I know that he thought about it. He was already married." He watched the pain flick across Caroline's face, a fleeting shadow, and he felt sad for her. For a moment he saw the pain in Amanda's eyes. "It was an arranged marriage, Caroline. Their parents had made all the plans when they were babies. They didn't have any choice. When Philippe first met Amanda, his wife was already pregnant with their child."

He watched her assimilate the presence of a half sibling and went on before she could ask any questions. "Philippe and she shared something—something special, something unique. She's never recaptured that feeling with anybody else, to the best of my knowledge. It was almost too real for her. She couldn't play with Philippe, the way that she plays with other people. She knew about his wife, and she knew about his son. He was always honest with her."

"I see." Caroline's voice was small and tight. "Where does my brother live?"

"At the Chateau de Montclair. He's the Count de Montclair now, though his mother is still pretty much in charge of things there."

"I see," she said again, tears welling in her eyes. So her father was dead. How could she cry for a man she didn't know? A few minutes ago he hadn't even existed for her. "Please go on."

"We all rented a house together—a place in Boulogne-Billiancourt, which is a district of Paris. It was a beautiful old house. . . . It belonged to an antique dealer, and every room was filled with things he had brought back with him, from all over the world. It was an enchanted place. And we were all very happy. Philippe went down to Angers sometimes, to visit his wife and son, but mostly he stayed with us. It felt as though it would last forever. Sarah and I got married, and your mother—I think that your mother got scared. When Sarah went back to America to fly the exhibition at Boston, the exhibition where she was killed"—he risked a glance at Anna, but she was looking at her hands folded neatly in her lap—"Amanda went with her, went back to her house in Rhode Island. I think, at that time, that she would have married Philippe if she could. But she couldn't, so she left."

Eric was tired and thirsty and reached for the lemonade next to him. It was warm, but it helped his throat anyway.

"She came back, though. Philippe wrote to her and told her how much he missed her, how much he loved her, and I can only guess that she felt the same. She came back, and then there were three of us living at the house in Boulogne-Billiancourt. The company was doing well, we were beginning to do some fairly major—major for those days—expansion into manufacturing."

Careful, he told himself. Focus on Philippe and Amanda, not on the deep depression that Sarah's death had plunged him into, not on the long dreary days and sleepless nights that those weeks and months had meant for him. This was Caroline's story.

"Philippe and Amanda were very close, Caroline—very close. But terrible things were happening in Europe. Since then I've realized that Philippe understood them better than any of the rest of us did. He knew that there was going to be a war, and he knew that it was close. And then Amanda found out she was pregnant with Philippe's daughter. With you, Caroline."

He took a deep breath. "Although your mother was scared, I think she wanted you. But almost immediately, the French Army began to mobilize. And your father went off to war. He didn't step on one of his own mines, Caroline. He was in the war for barely a month. He was shot by the Germans at the front, somewhere in Lorraine. They buried him there, with all the others who died in his outfit. You'd be horrified by the number of people who died . . . all of them young. Old men made the decisions that sent young men to their deaths."

"Was that when my mother tried to abort me?"

Eric wrenched himself back to the present. "Yes. She couldn't endure it, Caroline—your father getting killed, and her all alone. There was no one to take care of her, except me, and I never was much of a support in her eyes, I suppose. Maybe I should have worked harder at it, I don't know. I guess I was too caught up in mourning all the deaths—Sarah's, Philippe's—and I let go of everything but my work." He spread his hands palms up, and looked at them, laughing mirthlessly. "I even offered to marry her. Me! To make her feel more respectable. To make her feel as though it wasn't such a bad thing, after all. But she turned me down, and she went to England. She always had had admirers, you know. It wasn't hard for her to find one willing to marry her."

"Marcus Copeland?"

"Marcus Copeland. He had always wanted her, from the first time he met her. God, it had been years that he had loved her, from afar, unrequited."

"Did he know she was pregnant?"

"I think so. I don't think it made any difference. He was willing to take whatever she was willing to offer him. A few months after they were married, he was called up and did, in fact, step on a British mine and get killed. He wasn't such a bad sort."

"And everyone thought that I was his daughter."

"And everyone thought that you were his daughter. Except that you look so very much like your father—"

"Do you have a picture of him?" she interrupted.

"Yes, of course. At my house. I'll give it all to you—the pictures, and the letter he wrote to me the night before he set off for the front. He knew about you, Caroline. I think it was one of the greatest griefs in his life never to have known you."

She swallowed. "What did the letter say?"

"It said that he knew he was going to die, and would never see any of us again. It said that he had some regrets. And it said—" He glanced at Anna.

"It said?" Caroline prompted.

Eric took a deep breath. "He talked about the arrangements he had made to take care of you. He left you all of his stock in the company, Caroline—Aeroméchanique, as it was called then. It's now A.R.M. You're the majority stockholder, or will be when you turn twenty-one. Until then it's in trust for you, and is controlled by your mother."

Her face looked bruised, he thought, as though someone had hit her. It was a lot to assimilate at once. He took another careful drink of the lemonade and waited for her to speak.

"What," she said at length, "does this have to do with my going back to Rhode Island?"

"Because it's important that you stay safe, Caroline. And that seems to be a safer place for you, just now."

"Are you talking about Andrew?"

"In part." He sighed. "Caroline, there's a company that's out to get A.R.M. I could explain to you about all the whys and wherefores, if you would like, but for now just take my word for it. They're called Johnson Industries. And Andrew's family works for them."

That got her. She jumped out of her chair, was suddenly in the middle of the room again. "How dare you? How dare you suggest that Andrew—"

Eric stood up, too. "Calm down," he said flatly. "I'm not suggesting anything at all about Andrew. I'm assured that he has no idea about the competition between the two companies, and probably not of your status within A.R.M. And I need to ask you not to tell him, because he might—without meaning to—tell the wrong person about you. You are in danger, Caroline, because of this legacy. As long as they don't know who you are, you're safe. But if you marry Andrew—no matter how innocent he happens to be—they will know, Caroline, and they will try to control you."

What was it that Andrew had said to her, a few weeks ago, up on the cliffs? Something about controlling other people. Maybe, after all, he was right. But it wasn't fair. Other people got to love, and she didn't. It wasn't fair.

"I need," she said, shakily, "to think about all of this. May I please be excused?"

Eric and Anna exchanged worried glances. "We need to decide—"

Caroline lost her temper. "You can decide whatever the hell you want!" she cried. "But just leave me out of it all! If this is what it means to be an heiress, then I don't want it." And she whirled and ran up the stairs to her bedroom.

Eric pensively walked over to the wall and took the phone off its hook. "Just for tonight," he said, seeing Anna watching him. "We can talk some more in the morning. But I don't want them talking tonight."

Wordlessly, she nodded. From Caroline's room, all they could hear was the sound of sobs.

Chapter Twenty-four

"Good morning, Miss Copeland. Won't you sit wherever you feel the most comfortable?"

Caroline eyed with suspicion the man in the tweed jacket and baggy trousers. He seemed far too young to be a psychologist. She had been expecting a gray beard and glasses, and instead she was confronted by an appealing young man with twinkling eyes. "Aren't I supposed to lie on the couch?"

He smiled. "Traditional psychoanalysts use a couch, yes. But that isn't my orientation, and I prefer to be able to interact more directly with the client. Would you have preferred to lie down?"

She shrugged. "I don't really care. I'm not here because I wanted to come, you know."

"Yes. I understand that you were referred by your . . . grandmother, is it? With some reluctance on both her part and yours?"

Caroline chose a tweed-covered chair that looked like his jacket and sat down. "She thinks that psychologists are a waste of time and money. But the rector at the church told her that it would be a good idea, and she does everything he tells her to."

"And do you think that psychologists are a waste of time and money?"

"I wouldn't know. I don't particularly need one."

"I see." He sat down in a chair across from her. "Why do you think the rector recommended that you see me?"

"I guess because I'm sad most of the time."

He sat back and looked at her. "Any particular reason?"

"No," she said sarcastically. "I was raped by my stepfather when I was seven years old, and I just found out that

344

instead of being the legitimate daughter of an English industrialist, I'm the illegitimate daughter of a French count who left me interest in a company that I don't care about, and because of that I've had to leave the only man I ever thought that I could love and marry, and I'm back here in Newport living with my grandmother who is a holy terror. That's all. Nothing to be sad about." Caroline primly folded her hands in her lap and returned the doctor's gaze defiantly.

"I agree. You don't sound sad. You sound angry."

"Well," said Caroline explosively, "why shouldn't I be angry? They took away everything I wanted and gave me something I don't want. . . ." Her voice trailed off and she retreated immediately. "Oh. I'm sorry. I don't really mean that. Eric is so good to me—and Mrs. Martin. They took care of me and Eric taught me how to fly. He gave me an airplane. . . . It's just that now I wonder if he did it for me, or if he did it because I'm his friend's daughter and will someday inherit his company."

The psychologist leaned forward. "Well," he said, his voice reasonable. "Let's look at that, then, shall we? . . ."

Amanda folded the last of her nightdresses slowly, pensively, and put it neatly in her suitcase. That was it. That was all. Everything that she would need was ready.

She sat down next to the open window and lit a cigarette. This was the correct decision. She was sure of it. Eric had told her that Caroline now knew the truth, so there was no use continuing to maintain a facade. Anyway, it was becoming more and more difficult as the years went by. She was no longer young: forty-two this year. Forty-two. It rang in her head like a death knell.

She had decided what to do and was going to follow through with her decision—probably, in retrospect, the most sensible plan she had made in her entire life.

First, however, she would have to visit with Caroline and see her as she was now. The child was eighteen, a beautiful young woman, or so Amanda was told. She sighed. There would be questions, and accusations, and undoubtedly a scene, and Amanda wasn't entirely sure that she could cope with a scene. Still, it would have to be. She had put it off for too long. No, she corrected herself, I've never even faced it.

Finishing her cigarette, she looked out over the city from

her Sutton Place apartment. She would not see New York again—or at least not for a very long time. It was a painful thought, and yet one she had long ago confronted.

Nevertheless, as she turned away and back to her room, she wondered at how frightening it all felt.

Caroline sat in the sunny room that her grandmother liked to call the verandah, for reasons best known to herself. It was a long room, with any number of windows, all of which looked out over the rolling green lawn. The grounds were meticulously kept by a platoon of gardeners according to her grandmother's specifications. The room was nearly always bright and this effect was enhanced by having one entire wall mirrored.

Caroline had been sitting here for over half an hour, waiting for her mother who, as always, was late. She hadn't particularly looked forward to this interview, but Dr. Hargrove had assured her that it would be beneficial.

"Until you confront your mother with some of this anger," he had said, only last Tuesday, "you'll carry it with you and seek out other people to vent it on. It belongs to her."

That, Caroline thought, was easy enough for him to say. He didn't have to be the one to face her mother. She did, and she wasn't looking forward to it.

Noise near the door alerted her to Jenson's appearance in the doorway, looking stiff and formal and correct as ever. As a child, Caroline had teased him unmercifully, trying in vain to elicit a smile. Now, she simply accepted him as she accepted the heavy old polished mahogany furniture. He was part of her grandmother's world.

Behind Jenson stood Amanda Osbourne.

Caroline hadn't seen her mother since she was twelve, and she wasn't prepared to see Amanda look so—different, Caroline said later to Dr. Hargrove.

"Different?" he asked.

"Older," Caroline acknowledged, whose image of her mother was soft and fuzzy.

Amanda took a deep breath and looked closely at her daughter. So many years . . . After all that had happened in her life, she was finally prepared to call them what they were—wasted years. She might have, in a different world, in a different time, come to know this child of hers, if she had not been so blind in her need to run away from Philippe.

That Caroline looked like Philippe was unquestionable. Her mother's flaxen blond hair she might well have, though Amanda's, now, was showing streaks of gray, but in every other way she was more his daughter. She had the same high cheekbones and hollowed cheeks, the same dark shadowy eyes, and tall slight build.

When Amanda walked hesitantly into the room, Caroline looked at her with rapt attention. Her mother seemed small, brittle. That was not Amanda's way. Amanda normally took possession of the rooms she entered, and of the people within them. Amanda's mischievous flirtatious control was her hallmark. Caroline stood politely, and waited until Jenson withdrew before speaking.

"Hello, Mother."

Amanda approached her daughter and, instead of offering a scented cheek, as she once might have done, extended her hand. She wasn't altogether sure of how to approach this adult daughter of hers. "Hello, Caroline. You're looking very well."

"Thank you." They stood like that for a moment, awkwardly, before Caroline indicated the grouping of sofa and loveseat and chairs, covered in floral chintz, which her grandmother liked to call her collection. "Let's sit down."

Amanda moved as gracefully as ever, and Caroline couldn't help but notice, looked as extravagant and gay as ever. Her Schiaperelli dress was accented with the color that the designer had made all the rage—"shocking pink," Caroline thought it was called. But there was a faint tracing of wrinkles around her eyes and mouth, and a wary, tired look in her eyes that Caroline had never observed before.

"I've asked Jenson for tea," Amanda said with forced gaiety. "I don't expect that he'll be any too quick about it, though. He never was."

"I know," Caroline agreed. "Sometimes I think he's as old as this house."

"At least," Amanda said, and they shared a smile for a moment. Now or never, Amanda thought resolutely, and dampened her lips. "Caroline, Eric tells me that you had a conversation before you left California, a conversation about your father."

Caroline looked at her intently. "About my real father, you mean," she said softly.

"I see." Amanda paused. "I suppose I'm glad you know, though I would have preferred to tell you myself. Still, I'm glad." She hesitated. "Were you frightfully disappointed?"

"Disappointed?" Caroline frowned. "In what? In my father being who he is?"

"I suppose," Amanda said carefully, "in your being illegitimate."

"Oh." She hadn't thought much about that aspect of things, with the exception of wondering about her brother. Thoughts of Philippe—of trying to get to know him, in retrospect, as it were—had been foremost in her mind. "I expect that it's not such an awful thing. No one really knows about it, anyway, and I think that if it ever mattered it would have mattered when I was growing up." She managed a smile. "I suppose I should thank you for protecting me from that."

"It wasn't you I was protecting." Amanda shook her head. "It was both of us, but mostly myself. I'm afraid that I've been very selfish for a great deal of my life, Caroline."

Caroline shrugged. "I wouldn't know. I never saw enough of you to be able to tell."

There was a silence, and the words seemed to take on a life of their own and echo around the room. Into the silence marched Jenson, silver tea tray in hand and the eternal frown on his face. "Tea," he announced, "is served."

Caroline watched him put the plate of cream cakes and the teapot and cups noisily on the low table. "Thank you, Jenson," she said coolly, while Amanda looked out the window.

"I see that Mamma is still cultivating roses, Jenson," Amanda said.

His face remained impassive. "I really couldn't say, Mrs. Osbourne. Shall I send for the gardener?"

"No, no, of course not." Her voice was irritated.

"That will be all, Jenson," Caroline said.

He inclined his head. "Very well, Miss Caroline."

Caroline, feeling a small sense of triumph, poured the tea. "He never changes," she said, offering a cup to her mother.

Amanda shrugged. "Just as well. It seems that everything else does." The tea was scalding hot and she sipped at it tentatively. How did she begin to talk to this adult child of hers? How did she bridge the gap of all the years and all the neglect, all the things she should have said and done that had been left unsaid and undone until it was far too late to address them anyway? Their love was like a flower that had stayed too long in the sun until it wilted on its stem: still tied together, but with nothing to touch but dryness and death.

Now, when it was perhaps too late to speak, there were words that needed to be spoken. Amanda had always done what she wanted, but now what she wanted was, perhaps, beyond the realm of possibility. She wanted Caroline to love her, yet she knew in her heart that it was too late for that: too late to give back the kisses that should have been there when Caroline fell and skinned her knee; too late to give back the laughter they should have shared, the bedtime stories she should have read, the counsel she should have given her daughter, the truths that ought to have been told. Too late, too late, too late . . .

Now she could only look at Caroline, curiously, with a mixture of affection and hopelessness, and wonder: When Caroline herself had children, how would she think of her mother? With understanding and forgiveness? Or with hatred and cynicism?

Amanda cleared her throat. She had been trying to think of how to talk to Caroline during this long trip up to Newport, thinking for once not of her looks or the fashions around her, not of her own comforts, but of the young woman who was waiting for her. Amanda knew only too well how she had failed Caroline. And this one last gesture, this catharsis, might well have meaning only for her. For Caroline, it might be too little, and far too late.

Caroline was watching her, waiting. Amanda cleared her throat again. "I'm sorry," she said, slowly, painfully, "that I haven't been honest with you about your father. It wasn't fair of me. I'm glad that Eric told you, I'm glad that you know."

Caroline stirred her tea, looking into the depths of her cup for guidance. What did she say now? Of course it wasn't fair. Of course it had been a rotten thing to do, hiding her, shielding her from the truth. But what good did it do to let all of that go, all of that out? Her mother had said it. They both knew it. It made more sense, somehow, to go on. She looked up and met her mother's eyes. "Tell me about him," she suggested, her voice low.

Amanda was taken aback. She had expected anger; Caroline's low, small voice was anything but angry. Tell her about him? For so long she had refused to even think of him, and already the years had closed in, blurring the memories, moving him back into the shadows of her past. She took a deep breath and summoned him back, accepting the pain that came with it, cutting through her like a surgeon's scalpel. She had come here resolving to do whatever needed to be done. Philippe, she thought silently, Philippe, and suddenly, astoundingly, there was laughter again in her soul.

She looked up and watched his daughter as she spoke. "He was young, and he was serious—intense and serious, except when he started drinking. Then he laughed and laughed. . . ." Her voice trailed off and she smiled. "He would drink any kind of beer, but he was very particular about his brandy. And his horses. Give me good horseflesh and a good brandy, he used to say, and I'll be all set."

Caroline smiled, imagining. "What did you talk about?"

"Good heavens, what a question. We talked about the company, of course, and society things . . . and politics, Philippe was always one for talking politics, though to tell you the truth I simply wasn't interested, and made him stop whenever I could." She caught her daughter's eye. "Well, I never understood politics properly, I expect, and it made me feel insecure to hear him talking about it, that was why I never let him go on for very long. And we talked of other things . . . travel, and the theater, and art. He loved art." She glanced away for a moment. "Mostly, though, we didn't talk. We *did* things—went dancing, or to a show, or to the races, or to parties. . . . Sometimes we went out drinking and dancing until dawn and would take a carriage back through Les Halles, with the morning mist and chill still in the air, and we'd stop and buy hot roasted chestnuts and eat them all the way home."

Caroline felt herself relaxing. This was what she needed, not a litany of statistics, nor some dim image of a shadowy man, something real and concrete, something that would make him seem closer to her—more real. "What about his family?" she asked softly.

A shadow flitted across Amanda's face. "I never met his wife," she said, clearly. "Nor his son. I know that he cared for them. It hurt me more than I was ever able to admit to him."

Caroline leaned forward. "Tell me," she said, "if he hadn't been married already, would you have married him?"

Amanda put her teacup down in the saucer with a rattle. "In a heartbeat," she said, the simple words sounding like the tolling of a churchbell.

"Why couldn't you tell her that you were angry?"

Caroline took the throw pillow from the couch next to her and held it on her lap, almost as a shield from the probing questions. "I don't know," she said, unhappily.

Dr. Hargrove frowned. "You can do better than that."

"No, I can't!" She seemed surprised at her own vehemence, and shook her head. "I really don't know. It just didn't seem to make sense anymore. She had said that she was sorry, and I believed her. She seemed to be so unhappy. . . . I almost felt sorry for her."

"Let me remind you of a few facts, Caroline. This woman you're feeling sorry for abandoned you, kept silent after her husband raped you, never saw you for years on end. . . . And it didn't make sense to get angry with her?"

Caroline met his eyes. "She's my mother."

"Lucretia Borgia was somebody's mother, too." He sounded exasperated, and Caroline frowned. She wasn't pleasing him. She tried to summon some anger to parade in front of him. "It felt good that I was the one receiving her, in her own house. The butler listened to me, not her. That was getting back at her, a little bit. It was enough for a start."

"So you're willing to wait and get your revenge in bits and pieces? Does this remind you of anything else?"

She hugged the pillow to her stomach. "I don't know."

"What else did you get in bits and pieces in your life?"

She bit her lip, concentrating. "Her. My mother. I saw her from time to time, at her whim, when she felt like it."

He nodded. "Good. All right. And who was it that decided on this meeting, you or your mother?"

"She did."

"I see. So once again she was giving herself to you in her own time—in bits and pieces. Do you see how you reacted against that?"

Caroline blinked. "By taking control of the situation?"

"Maybe. But what I see you doing is responding in the same way, by giving yourself back to her in bits and pieces.

She says, 'Caroline, I want to have this talk with you; I want
to say I'm sorry; I want you to forgive me.' In her own time.
And *you* say, 'All right, talk to me, but you're not getting
everything back in a neat package when you want it. I'm still
dealing with this, and I'm getting my revenge on you a little
at a time.'"

"How?"

"By making her feel awkward in front of the servant. You
said yourself that was a start. Did you do anything else?"

She frowned, trying to remember. "No. She—she kept
me off balance."

"How?"

"All this new information—all these decisions. Everything. I thought that we were just going to talk about my
father."

But they hadn't just talked about her father. As Caroline
sat and sipped her tea, Amanda had continued to talk.
About Charles Osbourne's recent death and about her own
decision, reached after months of·reflection, to leave the
country.

"You're going on a vacation?" Caroline asked, bewildered. Since when had Amanda felt the need to notify her
daughter of her traveling plans? And Amanda's expression
was so intense.

"No, not on a vacation, darling," Amanda chuckled. "I'm
going to move out of the country."

"To France?" Caroline asked.

"Oh, no, of course not. I may want my memories back,
but I'm not going to join them. I could not face Paris. Oh,
no, I'm going somewhere else altogether. Your father would
laugh." She smiled suddenly, the memory lighting up her
face. "Escape without pain, Caroline. I want to get away and
yet I'm not willing to give it all up—or to face it. It's a
struggle."

"I see," repeated Caroline, completely bewildered. "Well,
Mother, if that's what you want . . ."

"Well, darling, I'm glad you see it that way," Amanda
said, briskly. "Because it really does seem to be the answer.
One always need to know when the correct moment is for
retiring from the party."

"Quite," said Caroline, feeling lost. "Mother, what are
you talking about?"

"Well, dear, if you were listening . . ." Amanda stopped herself in time. She was turning over a new leaf. She had asked Caroline for this interview; she was going to try and heal some of the hurt that there had been between them. But the child was still so obtuse. . . . She sighed. "I'm going up to Boston next week, and I'm buying a house. I need a place to keep my things, a house that doesn't belong to my mother or to some husband, something that will be all mine. But I'm not going to stay there, not really. I'll be off—of course I'll come back to sign over all those tiresome papers to you. I'm sure that you'll do so much better with all that money than I ever did. But I'm leaving for Africa. Traveling, don't you know. I'll be out of everybody's life—good riddance, your grandmother will say."

There was a moment of static silence in the room, during which Caroline wondered whether to burst out laughing or not. Of all the impossible ideas . . . "Mother," she said carefully, "Africa? On Safari? Isn't that—roughing it—just a little too much?"

"Nonsense, darling. The British have made great strides in civilizing the place, and I have friends in Kenya. Roger Auchincloss is out there on a plantation. With his wife, of course, and there are others. . . . It's really quite romantic, don't you think? And it might be amusing to see what society life there is like, and I'm really so very exhausted from all of this. Maybe I'll buy some land, raise zebra or whatever you do there. Anyway, anyway, anyway, that's my plan, so you see, darling, I'll be quite out of your way. You won't need to think about me. And I'll always have the house in Boston if things become really tiresome out there."

Caroline nodded noncommitally. "Mother, are you going to be happy in the wilderness? I would have thought that you might prefer to remarry."

"Well, darling, I suppose that I thought so, too, but there are only so many men that one can love, don't you know. And to tell you the truth I'm getting a little tired of it all." Amanda was silent for a moment, pulling a cigarette from a packet and lighting it. "No, of course that's a lie." She inhaled deeply, leaned back and blew the smoke out of her nose, and then looked directly at Caroline. "The truth is that I'm tired of looking for someone to take your father's place. There isn't anyone really. And I'm *glad* that you know about your father now, or you'd never understand any of this. I loved him, Caroline. I loved him as I've loved no other man in the two decades since he died. I loved him with all my heart and all my soul, and I've never stopped missing him. I tried to fill the emptiness with all sorts of other people and all sorts of other things, and it simply hasn't worked."

Caroline was shaken by her mother's honesty. "So now you're trying to fill it by running away."

"It's all that's left. And it does make sense; it's the only thing that makes sense to me." She smiled again, brightly, artificially. "For now, anyway, darling. It's really quite the thing to do, don't you know, and something different. It will be an adventure. One can't simply sit about and brood for the rest of one's life, can one?"

So that's it, thought Caroline. You're feeling guilty, and you want to run away from the feelings. Nothing had changed, in the end. Nothing.

Now Caroline looked at Dr. Hargrove and shrugged. "I reacted, more than anything else. I let her control the conversation. How could I keep her from controlling the conversation?"

"Does that remind you of other things that she has controlled in your life?"

She made an impatient gesture. "God, yes. Everything. She or my father; between them, that is."

He had a puzzled expression. "Your father? I thought you only recently learned who he is."

"Yes, of course. But now that I know. . . . He made Eric promise to look after me, so Eric's looked after me. He left me the controlling stock in A.R.M., so now I have to do certain things and behave in certain ways because of that company. And I'm so—jealous—of my mother, because no one ever told her what to do. She always did whatever she wanted, and now that it's all over she's making this one last grand gesture of going into the wilds of Africa so that she doesn't have to get old and listen to us telling her what to do. Or maybe it's so that she can flit back into our lives whenever she likes and tell us what to do again. But I've never *not* had anybody telling me what to do."

He nodded. "It sounds as though you're getting closer to your anger."

Caroline shrugged. "What good does it do? That's what it all comes back to, isn't it? I can get as angry as I like, but it's not changing anything. I'm still stuck with this damned company."

"It sounds like you don't want it."

"Of course I don't want it. I'd give anything not to have it. I don't want the responsibility, and I don't want to always have A.R.M. people trailing around after me, and I don't want to have A.R.M. making all my decisions for me."

He looked out the window for a moment. "But you like airplanes, and this company manufactures airplanes."

"I like to *fly* airplanes; I don't care how they're made. Eric's made airplanes for years and years and years, and only once in his life has he ever gone up in one. That's not the kind of life I want. I wish that I could live more like my mother." Her voice caught on a sob.

The young psychologist nodded. "You envy your mother's freedom."

"Yes! Yes! At least, if she didn't end up with the man she loved, it was because of some stupid war . . . it wasn't because some stupid company told her that it would be bad for business!"

"While you . . ." He paused delicately.

"While I had to leave Andrew. Eric said that it was dangerous for me to stay there, in California, and stay with Andrew, because the people who financed his restaurant are the same people who are in competition with A.R.M. It's so unfair. It's so unfair."

"Well . . . What would have happened if you had chosen to ignore Eric and stay in California, with Andrew?"

Caroline frowned. "It wouldn't have been fair to Eric. He's worked so hard—and my father did, too—to build that company. It wouldn't have been fair to him."

"So you chose to put Eric's needs before yours."

"I suppose." She frowned. "Or my father's. I'm not sure which." She wrinkled her nose, thinking. "Eric wasn't giving me all that much choice."

"You could have run away with Andrew."

That was true. That was what Andrew had proposed when she told him why they were sending her back east. He suggested they run away together, forget Johnson Industries and A.R.M., and simply be together. "We could fly the mails, Caroline. We wouldn't be rich, but we would survive. And we'd have each other."

"Yes. Yes." She had been breathless with excitement, his

breath in her ear, his body so close to hers. She felt an overwhelming desire for him and an overwhelming need to be with him, now, forever. Andrew was her love. She couldn't give him up, not for the sake of some stupid company. Eric could keep the company. She had her own life to live.

"Tomorrow." Andrew looked into her eyes. "Tomorrow we'll leave. We'll go to Los Angeles. There's a mail run out into the Rockies, out to Colorado. They're always looking for pilots to fly the Rockies."

She wrapped her arms around him and kissed his cheek. "Tomorrow."

But the next day she had waited for three hours at his small airfield for him to come. She had stolen out of the house on Western Avenue at dawn, leaving behind her a scrawled message for Mrs. Martin to read, and she had bicycled out to the A.R.M. complex, her prized possessions and clothes in a small suitcase balanced on the back of her bicycle. No one had stopped her as she hastily checked her airplane. No one said anything to her as she taxied out onto the runway and lifted off just as the sun was beginning to rise over the hangar. Even her radio was silent.

She landed at Andrew's little private airfield and waited for him to come. They would take both of their airplanes, they had decided. They would be of more value to the small companies which subcontracted from the Postal Service if they could provide their own planes, as well. She made coffee on the small primus stove in his office and waited. Finally, her hands shaking, she used his telephone to call a taxi to take her into San Francisco.

His restaurant was crowded with the people who came for breakfast, and she had to fight her way back to the kitchen. "Hey, Caroline, come to help?" asked one of the cooks, and Caroline stepped out of the way of a hurrying waitress to respond. "No," she said, a little breathlessly. "Is Andrew here?"

"Haven't seen him all morning," the cook replied, flipping an omelette. "Pass me the pepper, would you, honey? Thanks. Have you been out to the airfield? He's usually there when he's not here."

"Thanks," Caroline said hollowly, and turned back to the door. The taxi was still waiting, and she went out to the

Victorian house on Clay Street he still shared with his parents and younger sisters. "Starkey," said the brass plaque on the door. She traced it lightly with a finger before ringing the doorbell.

A woman she didn't recognize answered the door, frowning at first Caroline then the watch she had pinned to her blouse. Calling hours were in the afternoon. "Yes?"

"I-Is Andrew in? Andrew Starkey?"

"Who shall I say is calling?"

"Caroline Copeland." She hoped that her voice was steady.

"Just a moment, please." It was much longer than a moment, and Caroline found her hands trembling harder and harder the longer she waited. Finally the door opened again. "I'm sorry," said the woman. "Andrew is not receiving guests today."

Caroline stared at her. "But he must!" she exclaimed. "I have to talk with him!"

The woman's expression indicated clearly what she thought of young women insisting to see young men with such adamancy. "I'm sorry," she said again, sounding not in the least sorry, and shutting the door.

"Wait!" Caroline's hand flew to the doorframe. "Can you tell me—when will he be able to see me? When will he be going back to the restaurant?"

"I'm sorry," the woman said again, and closed the door very firmly in Caroline's face.

She cried all the way back to the airfield, her mind searching for explanations, for excuses, and she cried as she strapped herself into the airplane and took off into the brilliant blue sky. She went back to the house on Western Avenue where Mrs. Martin waited for her with sadness and wisdom in her eyes. "Andrew called."

"He did?" Hope flared again in her heart. There was some reason, some terrible and logical reason for his having abandoned her. He would explain, and it would be all right in the end.

"He said," Mrs. Martin recited carefully, her worried eyes searching Caroline's pale face, "for you not to go back, because he won't be there. He said that it's all over."

Caroline pushed a hand through her unruly hair. "I don't believe you," she said unsteadily.

Mrs. Martin shrugged. "Call him yourself."

She did so, her fingers nervous on the new dial that had been recently installed on their telephone. No longer did one have to speak through Nelda, the operator in San Jose who listened to all and sundry on the telephone. "Andrew?"

"Caroline? I left you a message."

"What happened? I don't understand."

A silence on the other end, then, coldly, harshly, "It's all over, Caroline. Go back east the way they want you to do. It's the best thing."

"No! Andrew, no!" She started to cry again. "Andrew, I love you! Please don't do this to me. . . . I want to be with you."

His voice was muffled. "I don't want to be with you anymore, Caroline. I've met somebody else."

There was a tearing feeling in her stomach. "You've met somebody else? But last night you said . . ."

"Last night," he cut in brutally, "I said what I thought would work. But it won't. I love her, and I want to be with her. So go back east and forget me."

"Andrew, no—"

"Just get on with your life, Caroline! Good-bye!" There was a crash in her ear and the line went dead.

Mrs. Martin was watching her with sympathy. "Did you say anything to him? Did you tell him anything?" Caroline spat the words at her.

Mrs. Martin moved toward her protectively, her arms wrapping around her. "No, Caroline. I only told him how sorry I was that he had decided to end your relationship."

"Well, you needn't have lied." And then she started crying again, a flood of tears so overwhelming that she thought that surely she would never recover. Life would never be the same again. The sun might shine, other people might go about their business, but inside of her there would always be something cold and very, very dead.

Now she looked at Dr. Hargrove, and the same dead expression was on her face. "I could have run away with Andrew," she said in a monotone. "But he wouldn't let me. And if you'll excuse me, Doctor, I've done more than enough talking for today."

· 4 ·

Towards the Future
1936–1938

Chapter Twenty-five

The law firm of Beneteau and Giroux was very worried indeed.

Everything was working out well, it would seem, for A.R.M. The economic Depression into which most of the United States seemed to be submerged had not done much to affect the company adversely. The firm was learning to think more globally than they had done in the past. Individual people were less important in the long run than the company itself. Monsieur Buchanan's death was a loss, *bien sûr,* but he had served his usefulness, perhaps, and could be replaced by a more knowledgeable, more involved Monsieur Beaumont. And Eric certainly seemed to have changed his attitude in the past few years. He was far more aggressive now and far more concerned with the company's prosperity, though he was still committed to his creative dreams and designs.

Eric had taken A.R.M. from a small airplane company to a major manufacturer, a solid supplier to the airlines of the larger airplanes that were now becoming popular, the ones that took passengers from one place to another so much faster than the trains did and, of far more importance, to the United States military. Eric had taken the company from a small pasture outside of Paris to a conglomeration of buildings and hangars and runways, stretching out over hundreds of acres of the Santa Clara Valley, surrounded by fences and patrolled by men with dogs and guns. Eric's fertile mind, which never rested, continued running the projections that had first brought him success—what if, what if, what if . . . And the ideas found their way from his brain through his hand onto paper, into models, into real engines and turbines and rockets.

Eric kept learning. In his late forties he wasn't content to leave the new theories and formulas to the younger man. When he didn't know the answer to something, he hired someone to teach him. His fascination with physics had grown to the point where, though he held no college diploma, he was rivaling the brains of the great universities. He held visions of wonder and horror in his mind, and turned them over into profits for A.R.M.

Johnson Industries remained on the edges of his company and his consciousness. Years earlier, they had failed at their takeover bid through the French bank, the Banque de la Sécurité, but he knew that they were merely biding their time before they decided what to do next. Before A.R.M.'s success, they had been the undisputed leader in the industry. Now they were a close second, and determined not to stay there forever. Eric knew in his heart that they would ruin him if they ever found the chance. But he cared less and less, for he was going to ruin them first.

And yet the partners of the law firm of Beneteau and Giroux worried. Because in a scant few months—it was already January of 1936—Caroline Margaret Copeland would turn twenty-one years old, and would legally become the majority shareholder in A.R.M. She would have the option, then, of taking over the company as its chief administrator. The lawyers were increasingly convinced that Amanda and Philippe's daughter was not strong enough to provide the leadership that the company needed.

Eric continued to assure them that the world was headed towards another war, and they had no reason not to believe him. The signs were all there. It would probably start with Germany, again. Already compulsory military service had been reintroduced in Germany and there were rumors of troop movement here and there. Zurich largely ignored the rumors; Switzerland was, as always, a neutral state, but the law offices of Beneteau and Giroux were very much attuned to them. There was going to be another war, a war that would lift America out of its Depression and provide a rallying cry for the politicians of the world. Quietly, behind the scenes, A.R.M. would be enriching itself by providing the weaponry for the war.

It made sense, Eric argued to them, Edward's words echoing in his mind: "There's nothing like a hot little war

for generating a lot of cool cash," and A.R.M. needed a cash
flow. Eric had dreams, and dreams today could only be built
with money; so he encouraged the war effort. He wrote a
letter, personally, to President Roosevelt, assuring him that
should the hostilities which seemed to be lurking around
and about erupt, he would be able to supply the United
States military's vast needs. He received an answer virtually
by return mail, thanking him for his thoughts and assuring
him, in turn, that in all probability the United States would
not enter any European conflict. "But it is heartwarming to
see that our shores are protected by your vigilance," the
President wrote to Eric. "I should be pleased to shake your
hand in person should you decide to come to Washington."

Eric never stopped to think about what Sarah's opinion of
his actions would be.

Beneteau and Giroux worried about Caroline. War was on
the horizon, and A.R.M. was potentially going to come
under the control of a girl who was more interested in her
own love life than in the fate of the industry, whose only
interest in aviation was her own airplane and the joy she
experienced flying, who was very confused about her feelings and her needs and her desires. She could be, it was felt,
very dangerous for business.

She was, however, Philippe de Montclair's daughter. This
fact was hammered home again and again in staff meetings,
particularly by Robert Beneteau himself, who was getting
old and, the others thought, emotional in his old age. The
younger lawyers, Rousseau and de Mornay and the women,
all shook their heads and talked about him behind his back.
A.R.M. was their lifeline, and they were determined to save
it.

And de Mornay believed he had found a solution.

"Eric Beaumont," he said persuasively to Rousseau one
evening over brandy in his apartment on the rue des Filles
du Roi, "is the secondary heir to the de Montclair will. It
goes to Amanda's daughter, and then to Eric Beaumont, and
then to young Pierre de Montclair."

Rousseau lighted a cigarette. "It only goes to Beaumont if
Caroline Copeland dies without leaving issue," he said.

"Indeed." De Mornay watched and waited as the import
of his words seeped in.

Rousseau frowned. "I don't think that I like what you're
saying," he said, slowly.

De Mornay went over to stand near the mantelpiece and looked into his balloon glass. "Isn't it a little late in the game to start developing a conscience, *mon ami*?" he murmured.

"Conscience be damned," Rousseau said, his voice angry. "Beaumont has no issue nor many hopes of any, if I read his attitude towards women correctly. So eventually A.R.M. would go to the Count de Montclair, Pierre." He glanced up. "I don't know how closely you have been following our monitoring of the de Montclair family, but Pierre is of no more executive material than Caroline. He is not particularly intelligent. He drinks excessively and is devoted to his mother to the exclusion of any original ideas on his part whatsoever." He stubbed out his cigarette and took a sip of brandy. "Besides, it would be sheer pleasure for the Countess to destroy A.R.M. She hated it and everything it has ever stood for. And, I tell you, Pierre listens to his mother."

"I still think," de Mornay said stubbornly, "that the company would be better off without Mademoiselle Copeland as director."

"We all agree with that. We simply have to find a way to persuade her away from it."

"And if she won't be persuaded? I tell you, we need to be prepared for action!"

"What are we to become, then? Terrorists? Are we to use violence simply to suit our purposes?"

De Mornay turned to face him squarely. "That's what it's all about, isn't it? The company manufactures machines for war, machines for killing people. From what I hear, Monsieur Beaumont is working on ways of killing people even more efficiently. What is the difference? We all use violence, don't you see? It's just that some of us are more honest about it than others."

"Implying what?"

"Implying that you're all so neat and clean here. Implying that you don't mind who gets killed, as long as you don't do the killing. As long as it's far removed from your neat little lives here in Zurich. Well, I'm telling you that I'm not going to bound by any stupid outdated morality!"

Rousseau stood up. "You're insane. The others will never agree. Beneteau and Giroux—"

"—are old men who belong to a different world. I'm a man of action!"

"You're insane," Rousseau repeated.

De Mornay walked to the door. "We'll see," he said softly, "who is insane."

"Where are you going?" Rousseau looked up sharply.

"Towards the future, *mon ami.* Towards the future."

Caroline twisted uncomfortably in the tweed chair. "I don't think I'm angry with Eric," she repeated. "He's done what he can for me."

Dr. Hargrove didn't say anything for a moment, and then he said, "He's sent you away from your friends and your flying."

"I know. But it was really my choice in the end. I mean, I'm old enough now, I could go back to California. But I don't think that I want to."

"Hmm. When do you turn twenty-one?"

She smiled. "In four days."

"I see. So you're a bona fide adult. What does that feel like?"

The smile disappeared. "Horrible."

He waited, but she didn't say anything else, so he asked, "Why horrible?"

"Because it's not as though I can just go on and do whatever I want. There's the company." She wrinkled her nose. "A.R.M., I mean. I guess that I have to do something with them, and I don't really want to."

"What do you want?"

She frowned. "What do I want? I don't know. I want to be able to fly, because I like it so much, it feels so good. And I suppose that I'd like to get married." She leaned forward. "I'd like to be in love with somebody the way that my mother was in love with my father. Like that. Intense and wonderful. But without a wife, of course. The other wife, I mean. I'd like to be the one to marry him. And I'd like to have children."

"And what about the company?"

"I don't *want* the company! I don't want to make decisions and do business deals and have A.R.M. people following me around for the rest of my life. I don't want it." She sighed. "I suppose that I'm a frightful disappointment to Eric."

"Is living your life the way that you want it a frightful disappointment?"

She flashed him a grateful smile. "It is when you're

Philippe de Montclair's daughter, I suppose. But you're right, it shouldn't be."

Dr. Hargrove shook his head. "We've got to take those 'shoulds' out of your vocabulary, Caroline."

She studied the pattern in the arm of her chair for a moment, picking at the threads on the arm, and when at length she looked up at him again there were tears in her eyes. "It won't work, Doctor," she said softly. "As soon as you take them out, A.R.M. will put them back in."

Caroline took the new passenger airplane, a Pan American flight, up to Boston to see her mother.

Before leaving, her grandmother's stern eyes had added up the cost. "It's all right, Grandmother," said Caroline. "I'll pay for it."

"Don't start getting extravagant, my girl. That's the way to end up in the poorhouse. Now, come and give me a kiss."

Caroline walked over to where the wasted body lay by a window, an afghan covering her legs and the sun streaming in on her. Margaret Lewis, she had realized only recently, was getting very old. The blue eyes that had been so sharp now were faded, but the tongue was as tart as ever. Her doctor had prevailed at last in bringing her back to Newport from New Hampshire. "Stuff and nonsense," the old lady had said, vigorously, but there were better doctors and more care for her in Newport. Mrs. Lewis exacted revenge on the doctor by calling him out to the house daily for small errands and flimsy pretexts.

It had been so long since Caroline had been a passenger in an airplane that she found herself drumming her fingers with impatience to be the pilot, to be in control. Her own airplane was still in California. She had been flying at the Allards' school outside of New York on the weekends, but that was all. Eric had offered to have one of the A.R.M. people fly her airplane back east for her, but she had refused. Four years later it still spoke to her all too strongly of Andrew.

And then she was in the taxi, moving quickly past the mud flats where Sarah Martin had died all those years ago, and on into the city, arriving finally at a quiet tree-lined square where tall walls and iron gates locked out the world.

With some trepidation, she rang the bell.

A maid answered the door, and Caroline, still feeling uncomfortable, followed the woman down a long corridor

into a large open sitting room that was furnished with sofas
and chairs covered with faded chintz. There was an Oriental
carpet on the floor, and china dogs keeping vigil on either
side of the fireplace.

A small collection of lead soldiers grouped in a diorama
was a jarring note in that quiet and peaceful room. Caroline
wondered at it; it seemed out of place, somehow.

The room itself was like stepping back in time. Whatever
had happened in the past twenty years was not reflected in
the dust and comfort of Amanda's sitting room, and Caroline sensed that here at least her mother was still, somehow,
trying to catch and hold on to the things that she had never
quite had.

Amanda herself had stood up and was waiting for Caroline. Her hair was cut shorter than it had been the last time
they had seen each other, and Caroline was more than ever
conscious of the flecks of gray in it, of the fine tracing of
wrinkles around the bright eyes and the laughing mouth.
Her skin was slightly tanned, making the color of her eyes
more startling and lovely than ever. Amanda was no longer
a young woman, but she still had an air of—what? Style? It
had something to do with what she was wearing: a long
divided khaki skirt and a crisp white blouse with an
elaborate gold brooch at the collar to the shirt. Very Africa,
Caroline thought as she looked into her mother's smiling
face.

Across from her, sitting stiffly on a tapestry-covered chair,
was Monsieur Rousseau from the law firm in Zurich.

Caroline went across to her mother first, kissing her cheek
and murmuring something. She wasn't ever quite sure what
to say to this woman. Amanda had sent many letters from
Africa describing in detail her experiences and adventures,
but she hadn't seemed to expect any letters in return.
Caroline, not knowing what to say, hadn't replied. Amanda
was still smiling, and more than ever Caroline felt like a
puppet, being moved and manipulated in a play that was not
of her own choosing. She didn't want to be here, she didn't
want to be doing this, and there was absolutely nothing that
she could do about it. Amanda's liaison with a young French
count had seen to that.

"Monsieur Rousseau," Caroline said politely, extending
her hand.

He stood and shook it. "Mademoiselle Copeland. I am

delighted to see you in good health. I trust that you had a pleasant trip?"

"Very pleasant," she said correctly. "And yours, Monsieur?"

He shrugged delicately, and said, not without a trace of humor, "I fear that even as a representative of A.R.M., I still suffer from airsickness."

Amanda gestured towards the table, also chintz-covered, with heavy brass candlesticks on one end. It was as though she suddenly realized how awkward the moment was and wished to get on with the proceedings. "We could use the table, if you want," she suggested.

He nodded. "Yes. Better to get on with it. Mademoiselle Copeland, if you would sit here, please, and you, Madame Osbourne . . ."

Rousseau sat at the head of the table and removed a great number of papers from the briefcase he carried. "Now, then," he said, shuffling through them. "It is my pleasure, Miss Copeland, to wish you a very happy birthday. I understand that you turned twenty-one yesterday."

"Thank you," Caroline said politely. What a silly thing to say, she thought. Why else would we all be here?

"Well, then. We might as well get on to the business at hand, which is the transferral of all A.R.M. stock in your mother's name from your trust fund to you directly. Do you understand that?"

"Yes," Caroline said.

"Good. Now, it is my obligation at this time to remind you both of the terms of the will of Count Philippe de Montclair. He stipulated that a small portion of the de Montclair estate be channeled directly to A.R.M. You understand, of course, that this has become a mere formality at this time. It is my understanding that the Count feared that the company might fall on hard times and that the estate money would be enough to get it through." He coughed discreetly. "Of course, in modern terms, the money amount is negligible. But we are naturally bound by the will and continue to do as instructed."

Caroline said, "And what does the Countess think of all that?"

He raised his eyebrows. "Madame the Countess has nothing to say about it. Naturally, if there were anything she ould do to prevent it, she probably would prefer that the money stay within the estate."

"Do they need it? Are they managing?" asked Amanda.

"I do assure you, Madame Osbourne, that the de Montclair estate is healthy and taking more than adequate care of the Countess and the young Count. You have no need to worry. I was referring, rather, to the Countess's well-known aversion to A.R.M."

"Go on," Caroline said.

"Yes. Well, in any case, that will continue. What changes now is that the trust fund is dissolved and you, Miss Copeland, are to become directly responsible for forty-nine percent of the existing A.R.M. stock. Monsieur Beaumont retains his twenty-five percent, the law firm retains two percent, and of course the remainder is public stock, owned chiefly by the Banque de la Sécurité in France. We remain available to advise you, Mademoiselle, in any capacity that you may require. In addition, your mother"—he inclined his head towards Amanda—"has indicated to me that at this time she is signing over to you the entirety of the Copeland estate, which includes part-ownership of Copeland Industries, a steel-producing firm in the Midlands of England. All of this money, I may say, is well invested and should permit you to live extremely comfortably on it alone. You may well find, as your mother has, that you have no need to touch any of the A.R.M. dividend interest money." He cleared his throat. "What I am saying, Mademoiselle Copeland, is that today you have become a very wealthy young lady indeed."

Caroline looked across the table at Amanda. "Are you sure about this, Mother?"

Amanda made an impatient gesture. "Of course I am. What else would I do with it? I have enough money. . . . Charles endowed me quite adequately through the divorce settlement, and I have money of my own, also adequately invested." She flashed a mischievous smile at the lawyer. "It's time you managed all this, Caroline. It's gotten tiresome."

Caroline said, "All right. Except that if Mother ever needs money, I want to have funds available to her immediately. Can that be arranged?"

The lawyer inclined his head. "It would be perfectly

regular, Mademoiselle. And then there are a few other
points. You are from now on free to do what you will with
the Copeland fortune and any stock purchases which are
part of the estate, including your shares in Copeland Industries. If you have any questions about any of this, an
attorney has been appointed from our firm to work with you
personally and assist you in making these decisions. Her
name is Françoise Duroc. However, the A.R.M. stock
cannot in any case be sold. The terms of the will tie it
directly to you, and through you to your firstborn."

"And if I have no firstborn?" Caroline asked.

"Then it reverts to Monsieur Beaumont and his family. If
he is no longer living, or if he has no issue, then it reverts to
Pierre de Montclair and his issue. It is, in a sense, not yours
as much as it is your family's. Is that all quite clear?"

"Quite clear," Caroline agreed. "Does this mean that I
have to take an active role now with A.R.M.?"

He shuffled the papers again and adjusted his glasses.
"Only if you wish to do so, Mademoiselle." He cleared his
throat. "What are your desires in this area?"

She shrugged. "I'd rather not have anything to do with it,
to be honest. I'm tired of the whole thing. I'm tired of
A.R.M. people watching my every move, all that. I'd rather
not."

Rousseau breathed a sigh of relief. "It is our considered
opinion, Mademoiselle, that Monsieur Beaumont is running the company exceptionally well, and it is our recommendation that he continue to do so. You will of course be
obligated to vote on various occasions, but you may sign a
proxy vote and do not have to trouble yourself to travel to
California."

Caroline nodded. "That's just as well," she said. "Where
do I sign all this?"

The lawyer indicated the spaces on the pages. "Here,
Mademoiselle Copeland," he said. "Sign here."

Amanda had walked her to the front door. "When shall I see
you again?" Caroline asked.

"Whenever you wish. I'm not leaving for Africa until
June. There's plenty of time to visit. Or not, if you wish. I
would quite understand your wishing to keep a distance
from me, after all has been said and done."

"You're still my mother," Caroline said, but without real conviction.

"Yes. I am still your mother," Amanda repeated, opening the front door. There was a mist outside, weaving in and about the trees and benches in the little square in front of Amanda's house. "I'm not sure that's something that you ought to be very proud of, my dear."

"I don't know," Caroline said, uncomfortably. "We all make choices, don't we? And I might have made choices like yours, Mother, if I had had the freedom to do so. Who knows." She shrugged. "I don't expect that you were like most mothers, but I don't know what most mothers were like. And you seem to be at some sort of peace. Are you sure about returning to Africa? Are you sure that you don't want to just stay here in Boston where it's nice and quiet?"

"Caroline, darling, I've never liked things nice and quiet, and I'm not about to start now. Besides, I like it there. People are . . . freer. They don't care so much. I have met a perfectly lovely man. He's quite an adventurer, and when I go back I just may return to him."

"Mother!" Caroline was shocked.

"Well, darling, you can't expect me to start being a different person altogether, can you? And one does get lonely."

"I suppose so." Caroline stared out at the mist for a moment, and then abruptly turned to face Amanda. "Mother, do you miss my father?"

Amanda looked at her for a long moment, and then nodded. "Every day of my life," she said softly.

Caroline nodded, as though that finalized something. "All right. Let me know if you need anything, Mother. I'll be in Newport."

"Of course you will." Amanda patted her back. "Give my love to your grandmother, Caroline."

"I will." She hesitated, torn between what she thought she should say and her own natural inclinations. But Dr. Hargrove had said not to listen to all the "should's." "Good-bye, Mother."

"Good-bye, Caroline." Amanda offered her smooth, sweet-smelling cheek to be kissed. "Have a safe trip back."

"Yes. Good-bye." And then the heavy green door had closed behind her, and it was not just the moisture of the mist that was stinging Caroline's eyes and running down her cheeks. It was something else entirely.

Every day the world marched closer to war.

Eric had begun to understand, at last, the world that Philippe had known in his last days, the world of muddy trenches and rats, of climbing over bodies as if climbing over a hill, of a constantly moving front line and tracer arcs in the night. Eric had read enough and talked to enough people to begin to pierce the romantic version that he and Amanda had always held of the war. He knew, now, what horror it had been.

Despite his newfound knowledge, he began to make plans for the next horror.

It was going to happen anyway, he reasoned. He was no politician. Europe was going to go to war and no one was going to ask his opinion of the venture. And, if it was going to happen anyway, one might as well be prepared. A rationalization, something deep inside told him.

Things were working out better than even he had anticipated. Amanda was occupied in Africa. He didn't have to expend any more useless energy worrying about her, about how she was going to make his life more difficult, or ruin Caroline's. And Caroline had told Rousseau that she wasn't interested in A.R.M., that she simply wanted to be left alone to live her life the way she wanted to. He missed her, of course, but it was a relief nevertheless to know that she was safe. Eric was sure Johnson Industries didn't know about Caroline; didn't know who she was or where she was. And he was determined to keep it that way.

The young man, Andrew Starkey, had been a problem, but as Edward had taught him, every problem has a solution. Andrew had planned to run off with Caroline, Eric knew, but he also knew enough to send people to talk with young Starkey the night before it was to happen. Caroline, they told him, was not the right girl for him. And if they overemphasized their point a little, well, that wasn't for Eric to question. Starkey had taken their point and had gracefully ducked out of Caroline's life. He had broken her heart, of course, but hearts mend. And the threat to A.R.M. had receded.

Now, as the world inched inexorably closer to another war, Eric readied himself. There would need to be increased production, and he was prepared for that. He had already been supplying the Army Air Corps with a number of bombers—B-9's and B-10's, which he manufactured in a factory north of San Jose. It would take but a few modifications to the factory itself to double his present production schedule. He was experimenting with bombers that carried more engines and thus could carry more weight. He could equip them with four engines, and they could carry 5,000 pounds and fly at 30,000 feet.

The War Department had misgivings, of course. The United States hadn't actually entered any conflict, and many felt that signing contracts for a large number of bombers wasn't a particularly good idea. Eric listened to them patiently, nodding and smoking a cigarette in silence, and then he stubbed it out and went into his office and put through a call to Washington. Minutes later he had the President on the line.

"I can start production now," Eric said. "But the War Department won't countersign the order."

"Why not?"

"We're not at war."

"We're not *going* to war. It's simply a defensive measure. We need to reassure the American public that, no matter what happens overseas, we're prepared to defend ourselves. It's all defensive, Beaumont. Got that?"

"Yes, sir."

"Who's there? Who are you talking to? Jennings?"

"Yes, sir."

"Put the man on the damned telephone."

The War Secretary emerged later with an ashen look on his face. "I've been told to countersign the order," he said stiffly. "But only as a *defensive* measure."

"Quite right," Eric agreed, pushing the paper across the table to him.

"Defensive measure. Right. Everyone who believes that can stand on his head and whistle 'Dixie' backwards." He scribbled furiously. "There, Beaumont. Satisfied?"

"I only have the best interests of the United States at heart," Eric said smoothly.

"Of course you do."

De Mornay requested a six months' leave of absence.

There was nothing irregular in the request, and Rousseau,

filled with pleasure at Caroline's reaction to her new status as part-owner of A.R.M., had neglected to tell anyone of their strange conversation.

Françoise Duroc, the new almost-partner who had been assigned as Caroline's mentor, was equally pleased by the young girl's decision. "She is more a housewife," she said. "Let her be one. We will look to the future."

But de Mornay did not believe that it would be that easy. He had said nothing to the partners, because he knew that they would try and keep him from doing what he knew needed to be done.

At the airport, he was stopped. "Monsieur de Mornay? Traveling to New York?"

"That's correct."

"Very good, Monsieur. Business or pleasure?"

"A little of each, I hope."

"I see. Monsieur de Mornay, why are you carrying a weapon?"

"It's for hunting. Here, look, I have a license. I'm going hunting with some friends."

The official looked at the license. "Very well, Monsieur. Have a pleasant and profitable stay in America."

Pleasant, perhaps not, he thought as he made his way across the tarmac to the Air France airplane that was waiting. But profitable, surely.

Caroline Copeland was not to be trusted. If Andrew Starkey were to appear on the scene again, who knew what might happen. No, the best thing to do with people who were not to be trusted, de Mornay thought, was to eliminate them. His partners didn't have the courage to seize the moment.

But he did. He would save A.R.M., and in the end, they would all thank him.

Chapter Twenty-six

Caroline finally had sent for her airplane.

People in Newport didn't understand her desire to fly, not really. They didn't understand that, for her, it wasn't such an extraordinary thing. She had lived for a great many years in the shadow of one of the most famous women pilots of all time, and had been the responsibility during those years of a genius who made airplanes not so much for a living as to satisfy some deep need. To Caroline, flying was as natural as driving a motorcar would have been to any of the friends that she made in Newport. And yet they persisted in seeing it as something that was more than a little strange.

There was no airport near Newport, so she arranged to purchase some land west of the city and to build a small airfield for herself and a few other pilots who, seeing the construction, stopped by to make inquiries. It was a little too reminiscent of the airfield in California where she had first met Andrew Starkey, but she was determined to forget about him, so she set to work making it into her own.

The pilots who leased space from her there were nice and polite and friendly, and some of them were even good-looking. On occasion they asked her out for a drink, or tried to talk with her, but Caroline adopted a pose that was cool and aloof. Not another pilot, she told herself; she didn't want another Andrew in her life—not now and not ever again.

She went on living in the great mansion with the old lady who seemed to age visibly with each passing minute, and she spent her days out at the airfield, winging and soaring over the port and feeling free and safe—safe from all the people who said that they wanted to be with her, because of who she was. If her connection with A.R.M. was obscure, it was certainly no secret in Newport that Caroline was an heiress, and that was recommendation enough.

She was every young man's dream: a slim blond girl with childlike features and dark eyes, beautiful and fragile, and owning more fortunes than anyone else could ever think of. Envied by all and loved by none, she thought.

"I feel like I'm becoming my mother."

Dr. Hargrove narrowed his eyes. "In what way, exactly?" he asked.

"Oh, you know." Caroline made a helpless gesture. "All the parties. All the unnecessary things. All the places I go because I'm supposed to go there. My mother did all that. It was her whole life. I don't want to be just some society person, I want a *life*."

"What kind of life?"

"A husband. Children. A real family, a family that stays together and loves each other. A family where we put up a Christmas tree every year. And dogs and cats."

"I see. And what is keeping you from that?"

Caroline wrinkled her nose. "Everybody I meet at these parties is so artificial. Men who like the society pages, for God's sake. I wouldn't be able to count on them for anything. They all smile and flirt with me, but it's not because of who I am. It's because I'm pretty and because I'm rich. It all makes me sick." She looked at him appraisingly. "I don't suppose that you'd care to marry me?"

"It's not me that we're talking about. It's you."

"I know, I know. I'm getting fixated on my therapist." She smiled with mischief. "At least after all this time I'm learning the language!"

"I'm gratified. Have you learned anything else?"

"I've learned that I'm angry with my mother, but that I understand that on an intellectual level, not on an emotional one. And now she's in Africa and I feel as though she's dead, and I'll probably never tell her my feelings, because if I ever did it would be an intellectual exercise, not a real exchange of feelings. I've learned that I'm not very good at figuring out just what my feelings are. I probably deadened my feelings after I was raped, and I'm just now trying to come alive to them again." Caroline started picking at the old tweed chair. "I've learned that I don't want to be what everybody expects me to be—either a businesswoman or a society lady. I just want to be ordinary. There's nothing wrong with that, is there?"

"Do you think that there's something wrong with that?"

She considered. "No. No, I don't. But everybody else does, I guess. I'm supposed to be living up to some sort of reputation. . . . I guess that my mother and father left me more than just money as a legacy, didn't they?"

"It sounds as though that's the way you're experiencing it."

"Hmm. I suppose that I am." But what other way was there to experience it? Either she moved back to California and lived in Eric's world, under his shadow, and learned how to work at A.R.M., or else she lived here in the shadow of her mother's memory, Amanda Lewis, the mischievous, flirtatious, outrageous girl who had cast a very long shadow indeed here twenty-odd years ago. What was there between those two alternatives? Caroline was feeling very confused, and very tired.

"It seems to me," Dr. Hargrove said carefully, "that you need to go out and do something for yourself. Or, better yet, for somebody else."

"Such as?"

He shrugged. "Good deeds aren't my department. Check back with your rector."

"I don't go to church very often these days."

"No reason why you can't talk to him. He's a sensible person. I think that you need to widen your world a little, Caroline. You need to see real people—not the people at the parties, but the people in the streets. They're there, if you look for them. See if they don't give you a new perspective on what might be."

But even Dr. Hargrove had no idea what it was that she was going to find.

De Mornay arrived in New York on a morning filled with brilliant sunshine. There was snow on the ground, the first snowfall of the winter. Everyone was saying that it was going to be a white Christmas. The sun and the snow together were blinding.

He adjusted his sunglasses to the glare outside of the terminal building and hailed a taxi. "Grand Central Sta-

tion," he requested, and then sat back on the seat, a satisfied
smile on his face.

The time for action had arrived. And he was responding.

Caroline went to work three mornings a week at a soup
kitchen that doubled at night as a shelter for the people who
no longer had homes.

She had no idea that such a thing existed. Caroline had
been, for all of her life, shielded and protected from the
knowledge of poverty. Even as the country groaned under
the weight of the heaviest of all economic hardships, the
Depression, Caroline flew in a brand-new A.R.M. airplane
and spent her time worrying about clothes, not the lack
thereof.

But the back kitchen at Saint John's provided soup and
bread, every noonday, for the hungry and homeless of the
city, and Caroline was sent to work there by the rector. "You
want to know people?" he said. "I'll show you people."

"But they smell!" Caroline wailed on her first visit.

"Indeed they do. Welcome to the real world, my dear."

She gritted her teeth and put on her oldest and plainest
dress, and she knotted a kerchief over her flaxen hair and
tied an apron around her waist. She looked into the faces of
pain and degradation and sorrow. She saw men reeking of
alcohol and women with tattered coats and tattered smiles.
She saw children with grease and grime on their faces and
watched them eat with the single-minded attention of
animals. "They have no manners!" she whispered, scandalized, to the woman standing next to her, who only laughed.

"Survival is more important than manners, Caroline,"
her companion said. "There are those who don't think that
they're synonymous."

More often than she liked to admit, Caroline dashed for
the toilet in the back of the shelter and leaned over it and
threw up.

And, yet, slowly, these people crept into her life. She
started learning names, first names only, that went with
faces. Some weren't even real names. There was Preacher,
who stood outside the door talking about the end of the
world until one of the workers brought him in and sat him
down. "The third angel he come!" Preacher would shout.
"He come and he pour his bowl onto the sea, and the sea it
turned to blood!"

"Come in, Preacher," Caroline would say, standing in the doorway, shivering in the wind, and clutching her shawl about her shoulders. "Come in and get warm."

He looked at her as though he didn't see her. "This is the hour of victory for God!" he intoned. "For Satan will be overthrown! Satan will be overthrown, and his time is short!"

"Yes, Preacher," Caroline said. "But take time out to eat."

She ransacked the mansion for clothing, and came upon closet after closet filled with Amanda's discarded dresses, frilly light things that would be useless in the December wind. "Didn't Mother have anything practical?" she demanded of Jenson, who shook his head.

"Never in her life," he said.

"Then I'll sell all this," Caroline decided. "Help me wrap it all up. It's in good condition; people will buy it."

"Miss Caroline!" He was scandalized. "You can't do that!"

"I can and I will," she said firmly.

She made the round of society teas, and asked everybody she met for help—money, clothing, food. Soon the invitations became less and less frequent. She herself was giving generously—all of her interest income from the Copeland estate. She owed it, she felt, to the man she had never known who had never, after all, been her father. It was a fitting tribute.

"These are the words of the Witness! I will spit you out of my mouth! I know where you live! In the shadow of the throne of Satan."

"Come get some hot soup, Preacher," Caroline coaxed. "I brought a new coat for you. Come eat some soup and try on your new coat."

The elderly man peered at her. "I shall come and remove your lamp from its place! You are a liar and a fraud!"

"Yes," she said. "Please come in, Preacher. It's freezing out here."

"The lake is freezing," he replied. "And then it will be on fire. Repent now! Seven thousand will be killed on that day!"

"Do you need some help?" A giant of a man with a red beard appeared behind her in the doorway. "Preacher still at it?"

"Yes," Caroline said. "I can't get him to come in."

The man stepped past her and out into the street. "Come on, Preacher. You can tell us all about it inside."

Preacher raised a fist. "Happy is the man who shared in the first resurrection!"

The other man nodded. "Happy is he," he agreed, and he put his arm around the old man's shoulders and steered him inside. Caroline held the door open for them and then closed it as they passed through, grateful herself for the warmth.

"Get some soup," she suggested, and watched as they went over to the counter together.

She took a break later and found herself sitting next to her rescuer. "Thanks for helping me with Preacher," she said. "I wasn't sure what to do."

"That's all right," he said. He had bright blue eyes over the dark red beard and a kind smile. "He just needs to feel like people are talking his language."

She laughed. "You've got me there, then," she said. "I don't even understand his language!"

"Don't have to. In fact, I'd worry if you did." He smiled, and carefully wiped his hand on his sleeve before offering it to her. "Steven Asheford," he said.

Caroline shook his hand. "Caroline Copeland."

"Pleased to meet you, Caroline Copeland. Am I missing something, or are you new around here?"

"I started just before Christmas," she said. "About a month ago. Just a few days a week."

"Sometimes," he observed, "a few days a week is enough. It's easy to get sad around here."

"Yes," she said, amazed to find someone who shared her feelings. "Sad and guilty."

"Why guilty?"

"That I have so much more than they do."

"Nothing wrong with having things," Steven replied, wiping his mouth and pushing his chair away from the table. "It's only wrong when you have things and don't share them. See you around, Caroline Copeland."

She opened her mouth to answer, but he was gone.

De Mornay had taken a room at the Ocean House Hotel downtown and stayed there over the Christmas holidays. He had long since learned patience, and holidays meant nothing to him. He was not married, nor had he ever been. Women

were an unnecessary entanglement. Women, as typified by
Caroline Copeland, were a nuisance. The sooner this one
was out of the way, the better.

But still he bided his time. After all, it was essential that
no one discover him, or the motive for Caroline's death.
Even if he succeeded—as he fully intended to—he had to
be very careful. If Johnson Industries caught a whiff of this,
then Eric Beaumont would be in greater danger than ever.
They would get to Eric and then they would get to the young
Count de Montclair and it would be all over.

No, it was far better to bide his time and make certain
that A.R.M. was not connected to the murder—that in her
death Caroline didn't reveal the terms of Philippe's will. If
A.R.M. were to be connected to her death in any way, then
Johnson certainly would become suspicious of her ties to
A.R.M. Wealthy young women die under strange circumstances, from time to time. He would just have to be very
careful and very, very creative in engineering those circumstances. So he waited, and he watched her. He observed her
daily patterns, he watched the people that she talked to,
what she ate for breakfast, her favorite dance. The more he
knew about her, the easier it would be.

For that, de Mornay was willing to wait.

Caroline came out of a shop on Bellevue Avenue and nearly
walked into Steven Asheford.

There was a woman with him, her arm linked through his,
her laughter dancing all around them in the frosty air.
"Excuse me," Caroline said, starting to go around them, but
Steven put out a hand and touched her arm. "Caroline!" he
exclaimed. "It is you, isn't it? Caroline Copeland?"

"Yes," she said, feeling awkward. "It's nice to see you
again."

"It is," he said, still not moving, smiling down at her.
"Oh, my manners. This is Justine Chambers. Justine, Caroline Copeland."

The girl smiled at her and Caroline pretended to return
the smile. Justine was very pretty, with blue ribbons in her
dark curly hair. She had sparkling blue eyes and a cupid's
mouth. For some irrational reason, Caroline was jealous.

"We were going to have lunch," Steven said, "as soon as
Justine picks up a package here. Won't you join us?"

"Thank you," Caroline said. "But I really think—"

Justine placed a hand on Steven's arm. "Why don't I go on in now and pick it up? I'll be right back." She smiled brightly at Caroline and slipped through the shop door. Steven didn't even watch her going. "Please join us?" he asked again.

"I can't," Caroline demurred. "I may see you at the shelter tomorrow."

"I don't go during the week, except in the evenings," he said. "I have to be at work, generally."

"Oh." Stupid, stupid, she berated herself. There are people in the world who work for a living, you know. "I'm sorry."

"So am I. This is my only day off until Saturday, and I'd promised Justine to take her shopping."

"Yes. Well. It was nice to see you again." Caroline started edging away. He'll never speak to me again, she thought. I'm such a silly fool.

Steven glanced into the store. "I thought that—" He was interrupted by Justine's arrival. "I'm ready, Steven," she said, balancing her package and trying to pull on her gloves. "Are you coming for lunch?" The smile she gave Caroline was bright, but Caroline was staring at Justine's hands as she slipped them into gloves. She wore a diamond ring on her left hand.

"No," Caroline blurted, still staring. "I'm sorry. I have to go. I really have to go. . . ." She backed away, and then turned and ran towards Washington Square, hearing Steven's voice raised behind her. "Caroline!"

She walked and walked until she was quite sure that they weren't following her, and then she hailed a taxi. "Lewis estate," she said breathlessly to the driver. "Ocean Drive."

As they drove away, she was aware of the most absurd lump in her throat. What did it matter to her if Steven Asheford was engaged to be married? She barely knew the man. Justine seemed like a nice person, and . . .

She didn't understand at all why she was crying.

A week later Caroline saw Justine at the bank.

It was too late to turn around and walk away again. She saw her and felt her throat tighten in response. This is absurd, Caroline told herself coldly, and walked up to the teller's window. Justine was standing a few feet away, counting her money. She was wearing a blue coat that exactly matched both the ribbons in her hair and the blazing brilliance of her eyes. Caroline decided that she hated her.

She took her own money and, turning, met Justine's eyes. "Hello! I thought it was you. . . ."

"Hello," Caroline said coldly. "Excuse me, I have to be going. . . ."

"Oh," Justine said, looking genuinely disappointed. "And I was so hoping that we could talk. . . ."

"Whatever about?" She was being rude, Caroline knew, but she didn't know how to talk to this woman.

"It's just . . ." Justine gestured a little helplessly, "I hardly know anyone in Newport, and you seem so self-assured. And Steven tells me that you're terribly dedicated, that you work down at the shelter, which is such a good thing to do, only I'm too afraid to try it myself. . . ." Her voice trailed off and she looked at Caroline, biting her full lower lip, and Caroline knew that in spite of herself she liked this woman. She made Caroline feel strong, stronger than she actually knew herself to be.

"We could have coffee," she suggested.

Justine nodded eagerly. "Oh, please! That would be marvelous! I can pay, I just cashed a check. . . ."

Caroline started feeling guilty again. "Nonsense," she said. "It's my treat. There's a tearoom just around the corner, on Bellevue."

Justine relaxed into her chair and looked only slightly shocked when Caroline offered her a cigarette. "Oh, no, thank you, I couldn't."

"Suit yourself." Caroline lit hers with a match that spluttered and went out quickly. "It's a habit I picked up from my mother."

Justine, in the meantime, was talking. "I've been ever so lonely here. There aren't many places to meet people, you see, and I suppose that I'm not very outgoing myself. . . ."

The coffee arrived and they fell silent as the waitress placed the steaming cups in front of them. "Oh no, no sugar, thank you."

Caroline was amused. "Don't you have any vices?"

A quick smile. "I suppose not. Am I fearfully boring?"

"No." Caroline smiled again. "Refreshing, if anything. I tend to know too many people with too many vices, myself."

"You must lead a very exciting life."

"Hardly." Caroline sipped her coffee and regarded Justine over the rim of her cup. "Where do you come from? You said that you've only recently moved to Newport."

"Oh! Yes. I came to get married." She blushed. "My father knew Mr. Asheford when they were both at school—they went to Harvard, you see—and they always said that they would try and get their children together. And I didn't know anybody interesting at home in Connecticut. New Haven, actually. My father is a professor of ancient history at Yale University."

"I see." So there were brains beneath that insecurity. Caroline wondered if she ought to introduce Justine to Dr. Hargrove. There was obviously more to her than met the eye. "What does Mr. Asheford do?"

"You don't know? Oh, yes, that's right, Steven did say that he hardly knew you. Well, they have a shipbuilding business. Here in Newport. Steven works there, too. I guess that all the Ashefords do. It isn't very large, of course, but they're rather hoping for some military contracts, which might make a difference."

Everyone's talking about war without talking about it, Caroline thought. That must mean that it really is going to happen. She pushed the unwelcome thought out of her mind and concentrated on Justine. "Well, perhaps we could do things together sometimes, you and I. When is the wedding?"

"In March. Will you come? Oh, Caroline, please do say that you will!"

Caroline bit her lip. She was being silly, envying this girl her happiness. She had a sudden vision of Steven, his head tipped back, laughing, the red beard catching the light. She liked him. She could love him, but she wouldn't, because this girl was going to marry him. She forced herself to smile. "Of course I will," she assured Justine. "Of course I will."

Two weeks later Caroline worked late at the shelter and was still there when Steven arrived, stamping the snow off his feet and shivering with the cold, a great hulking mountain of a man. "Hello, Rosie!" he greeted one of the regulars, a small woman who collected bits of string in her pockets. "Hello, Preacher!"

"Happy is the man who heeds the prophecy!" Preacher answered, and Steven clapped him on the shoulder. "That's right." And then he saw Caroline.

She was sorting through a pile of donated clothing and stayed where she was as he walked across the room to her. "Caroline! This is great! I never expected to see you here this late."

She pushed a lock of hair off her forehead. "I guess I got a little carried away."

He sat down next to her and picked a sweater off the top of the pile. It had embroidered flowers on it. "Think it's the real me?" he asked, holding it up against his massive chest, and she laughed and shook her head.

Steven tossed the sweater back onto the pile. "Justine tells me that you've been very nice to her lately. I really appreciate that."

"It's nothing. She's a nice person."

"So are you, Caroline Copeland." He was smiling, and she felt uncomfortable. She could love him, she could truly love him, if only . . . "She invited me to the wedding," she said instead. "Where will it be?"

"At Saint John's. My family has gone there for years."

"I used to go there, too. When I was a little girl." She rocked back and encircled her knees with her arms. "I used to wear a little birthstone ring, and I'd sit in the pew and try and make the stained glass windows reflect off it."

He smiled. "Why didn't I ever see you there?"

Caroline shrugged. "I went to live in California when I was eight," she said.

"Family out there? It's a long way to go."

"Yes," she said, after a moment. "I had family out there."

"You miss it," Steven said, softly.

She looked at him sharply. "You see far too much, you know," she said. "I've got to finish this and be getting home, anyway."

"It's dark and cold," he protested. "Why don't you let me run you home? I've got my car here."

"No," she said quickly, almost frightened. "It wouldn't do." And, besides, she wasn't entirely sure that she wanted him seeing where she lived. Asheford Shipbuilding might be a going concern, but she was certain that it didn't come close to rivaling Ocean Drive. And she wasn't entirely sure that she wanted to be alone with him in a car. He was going to marry Justine. She had to keep reminding herself of that. He was going to marry Justine, and Justine was her friend.

"I'll be all right," she said, now. "I'll just call a taxi." Strange how she had learned to fly but had never bothered to learn to drive a car.

He stood up with her. "Caroline, I—" He hesitated, about to say something, and then, without warning, he leaned forward, cradling her face in his hands, and kissed her lips.

Caroline drew back with a gasp, but Steven was smiling. "Good-bye, Caroline Copeland," he said, and she fled without a word.

She was going to have to see either a great deal more or a great deal less of Steven Asheford.

Eric looked up from the letter he was reading as Anna Martin poured him some more coffee. "Thanks," he said. "Caroline is doing volunteer work at some soup kitchen for the homeless. I'm not sure that I like the idea."

"Why not?" Anna sat down across the kitchen table from him. "It might be good for her."

Eric frowned. "I don't like the kind of people that go to that kind of place."

"Poor people? You don't like poor people?"

He sipped his coffee. "Drunkards."

"Oh, I see. I beg your pardon. And when you didn't have a dime to your name and spent all your time drinking cheap wine with your friend Philippe, that was different."

"Damned right it was." He caught her eye and smiled. "You always seem to know how to get to me, Anna."

"I know you too well." She took a sip of coffee and holding her cup in front of her asked casually, "Any other news?"

"She met some fellow she likes, but doesn't think that anything will come of it. Apparently he's marrying someone else next month."

"I would tend to agree, then, that nothing will come of it. Why can't Caroline fall in love with men who are good for her?"

"God only knows," Eric said somberly. "Beneteau and

Giroux are getting after me about her. Seems that they think she should be getting married soon."

Anna laughed. "Since when is Caroline's love life their business?"

"Since her child inherits A.R.M. They have a point," he conceded.

"Oh, God, Eric, she's young. Give her a little time, won't you?" She shook her head. "Men. I'll never understand a single one of you."

He gulped down the rest of his coffee. "That goes for us, too, in spades. I'm off, dear Anna." He walked around the table to kiss her cheek. "Write back to Caroline for me, will you? I haven't got any time."

"You never have any time." But she said it with affection.

"The world isn't going to wait for me, Anna. I have to stay one step ahead."

War games, she thought as she watched him leave. The men all sit around and dream up expensive toys, and then manufacture a need to use them. Eric was talking to Washington once a week these days, and she wasn't naive enough to think that theirs were general industry discussions. There was going to be a war. They hadn't learned anything from the last one except how to make better toys. Men, Anna Martin thought, would never learn. Not ever.

War games. But they were playing for very high stakes.

On the first day of March, de Mornay strolled down to Newport's waterfront, taking a long circuitous walk that brought him finally to Saint John's Church. There he entered and knelt down as if to pray.

Caroline Copeland was spending an inordinate amount of time here, with people who were at best mentally ill. It seemed that she was almost asking for it.

De Mornay smiled. It was going to be easier than he had thought, after all.

Chapter Twenty-seven

The winter days were long and cold, but Caroline wished for them to last forever. With spring would come the wedding when Steven and Justine would be married to each other, and she would lose all of the illusions she had told herself not to have and yet to which she clung so relentlessly. It was permissible, she thought, to flirt with Steven when he was but engaged; to flirt with him once married was impossible.

She saw him more and more frequently, both at Saint John's and elsewhere, for it seemed in those cold dark blustery days that she did very little that did not in some way bring her into his path. She wanted to go shopping, but a word to Justine would bring Steven out as well, on a lunch break from his work at the shipbuilding firm. She went to consult with the rector about arranging for a donation, but would do it in the evenings when Steven was most likely to be volunteering at the shelter.

"Why do you do this?" she asked Steven one such night, as he cradled in his arms the wasted body of a dying alcoholic. "Why do you do this to yourself?"

Steven looked up at her and there were tears in his eyes. "My mother," he said slowly, "died when I was a child, when Asheford Shipbuilding was just a dream and my father was working sixteen-hour days as a stevedore on the docks. She died in a place like this, because she had decided that it was easier to drink herself to death than to pay a doctor to keep her alive. I owe it to her. I owe more to her than I can ever repay."

Caroline was touched. "You," she said softly, "are a nice person, Steven Asheford."

He was a nice person. He was filled with laughter and love, and she had to keep reminding herself that it was offered to her only in the spirit of friendship. He was going to marry Justine, and she wanted to remain friends with Justine.

Whenever the subject of Justine's marriage came up, Caroline would change the subject—sometimes so abruptly that Caroline was certain that Justine must suspect her true feelings. Yet Justine seemed to be untouched by Caroline's struggle. "Why don't you get Steven to take you," she would suggest, when Caroline mentioned wanting to go to one place or another. "He has a car, there's no sense in spending money on a taxi." And sometimes Caroline wondered whether Justine really loved Steven. From Justine's initial conversation about her wedding, Caroline half-suspected that the marriage had been arranged between the two families as had Philippe's with his wife.

For all of their developing friendship, the women led distinct and distanced lives. Caroline had not yet told Justine—much less Steven—that she lived on a large estate on Ocean Drive, or that she was in any way connected with such vast amounts of money. It wasn't, she told herself, that she was ashamed of it. It just seemed awkward. And it wasn't what really mattered. They told each other the things that mattered: Caroline spoke frequently of her struggles in coming to terms with her anger about her mother, and Justine in turn talked about her insecurity living in the shadow of her father's reputation in the academic world. That was what made sense. All the rest seemed, somehow, superfluous.

"Have you told her that you're in love with her fiancé?"

Caroline looked up sharply. "Who said that I'm in love with him?"

Dr. Hargrove shrugged. "No one has articulated it yet. But you say it all the time, in different ways."

She relaxed. "I suppose that it's true," she admitted. "He's friendly, and caring, and good-looking. But he feels, oh, I don't know—steady, somehow. As though he would never let one down."

"Hmm. Who else have you felt that way about?"

Caroline was used to his questions by now, and responded without thinking. "Mrs. Martin. Cricket. That was my pony, when I was a little girl. And Eric, but less so now, because I got so angry with him for putting the company first."

"But not your parents."

She laughed. "Good heavens, no. There's no one in the world less steady than my mother. And who knows about my father? Dying isn't exactly the best way to make people think that they can count on you."

A glimmer of a smile. Caroline was finally developing a sense of humor, Dr. Hargrove thought. About time. "Fair enough. Can you think of why that attracts you in a person?"

"Because I never had it, not really, not when it mattered. I want to feel . . . safe. I want to feel like there are some things in life that don't change."

"People change. Even safe people."

"Yes, but with safe people, at least you have a sense of what direction they're going to change in, if you know what I mean. I think Steven will change, but only to become more Steven. The basic character is there, already. I think that time will just make it deeper."

"Interesting observation." But he didn't say anything else, and Caroline was looking for answers. "So what do I do?"

"Do about what?"

"My feelings! I am in love with Steven Asheford. I also like Justine quite a lot. It changes everything for me, don't you see! I can't go on just living here in Newport, near them, knowing that. What do I do?"

Dr. Hargrove smiled. "As you grow, Caroline, I think you'll begin to find that feelings are a great deal less important than we think they are."

"Meaning what?" She hadn't meant to sound belligerent.

"Meaning, quite simply, that life isn't lived at a purely 'feeling' level. It can't be. It would be too confusing, and much too exhausting." She still looked uncomprehending, so he tried again. "Close your eyes, Caroline. Imagine the ocean. Can you see it?" She nodded and he went on. "The ocean is your life, Caroline—deep and mysterious and filled with many things, some things that you like, some things that you don't like." He paused. "Now imagine the waves on the surface of the ocean. They're caused by a lot of different things: tides, winds, and the passage of ships across the surface. They're moving all around at the whim of forces that are external to the ocean itself. Your feelings are like that, Caroline. They rush around because of things that are external to you. But that's only happening on a surface level. Under the waves, under the feelings, everything is still dark and deep and peaceful. You're still you. And that part doesn't change unless you make it change, yourself."

Caroline sat for a few moments, thinking about it, and then finally opened her eyes. "So it doesn't matter what I feel, because the feelings are just on the surface."

He shrugged. "They'll come and they'll go. It's not a very stable thing to base your life decisions on, especially for someone who is looking for safety."

She smiled. "I don't suppose that the ocean is a very safe place."

"Nor is life."

Eric picked up the report from the law firm and frowned, first at the folder, and then at Rousseau. "You've gone to a great deal of trouble."

The lawyer smiled and sat down on one of the chairs opposite Eric's mahogany desk. "It's our job."

Eric was still frowning. "I should resent this intrusion on Caroline's personal life."

"Why? You didn't resent it when we told you that the Starkey fellow was unacceptable."

"That was different. She was clearly in love with him, and making plans. Who knows what will come of this . . . infatuation?"

"Marriage all too often comes of infatuations."

Eric sat down and hunted around his desktop for his cigarettes. "And does this Mr. Asheford meet with your approval?"

"Indeed. Excellent breeding. Good genes."

Eric frowned. "You make Caroline sound like a brood mare."

"It's time that you came to the realization that that is, in effect, exactly what she is. Mademoiselle Copeland is never going to be the head of A.R.M. You know that as well as I do."

"She's still young," Eric protested. He had finally found the cigarettes.

"She is the same age as you were when you were creating

Aeroméchanique. She is politically immature. She has no sense of business. She lets herself become victim to her emotions."

"I thought that that was why you people decided to send her to see that psychologist."

"Yes. Fortunately her grandmother agreed and cooperated so that Caroline did not know we were involved. And Dr. Hargrove reports that Mademoiselle Copeland has made enormous progress since entering therapy. He also reports that she is still confused and uncertain, and desiring a domestic life for herself."

"Then something terrible has happened to her since she moved back east! The Caroline I knew loved the challenge of flying, for example. . . ."

Rousseau nodded. "And so she does, Monsieur Beaumont. So she does. She loves flying. Not planes. For her, flying is a pastime, not a career. She's too softhearted. She would do A.R.M. no good and could do it a world of harm."

Eric lit the cigarette. "I don't know. Philippe wanted her to be part of the company. . . ."

"It is our understanding that Monsieur the Count wanted his lineage to be protected and supported. We will always strive to see that Mademoiselle Copeland lacks for nothing. She has a substantial fortune at her fingertips. She has a number of people—yourself included—who sincerely care for her and are present in her life to support her. She has, it would seem, found a young man whom she loves, and who is eminently acceptable to us. Why do you wish to force her to accept a life that she does not desire? Are you not asking her to do what you want, rather than what she wants?"

Eric sat back in his chair and slowly inhaled on the cigarette and then exhaled. What did he want from Caroline? To take over A.R.M.? To appreciate a company *he* had built? "This Hargrove fellow is certain that this is what she wants?"

"He has been seeing her on a weekly basis for the past four years. If anybody can be sure, it is he."

Eric nodded to himself as though finalizing a decision. Caroline should be allowed to choose her own life. He had to accept that she wanted no part of his dreams. He looked up at the lawyer. "So what now?"

Rousseau leaned forward. "What we suggest is that you remain as president of A.R.M. There is much work to be done in the future, and you are, unquestionably, the person to undertake it. Continue, in short, as you have up until now."

"And Caroline?"

"Mademoiselle Copeland shall be encouraged to marry, and to start a family as soon as possible. That is where the future of A.R.M. lies, Monsieur Beaumont. Not in the count's daughter, but in his continued lineage. Not now, but thirty years from now."

"That's a long time to wait."

"There is no hurry. You yourself are still young and able to be a strong leader and innovator in the field. . . . There is no need to rush the future. We will have the opportunity to have a hand in the education and the upbringing of the next leader, an opportunity that we were in essence denied with Mademoiselle Copeland due to her mother's influence. It will work out, you will see."

"I suppose that it shall," Eric said slowly. "I suppose that it shall."

After church on Sunday, Steven took Caroline aside. "I'd like to take you to supper tonight. Will you come?"

She glanced around. "Would it be proper?"

"Why not? I'm just asking you to supper, Caroline, not away for a weekend."

"I should hope not," she said stiffly.

Steven looked perplexed. "I'm sorry," he said. "Perhaps I misunderstood. But I thought that you would want to . . . After last Wednesday . . ."

After last Wednesday, indeed. They had both been at the soup kitchen when the overnight staff—the rector, as it happened—found himself unable to be there, mired in snowdrifts in Providence. Wordlessly, both Steven and Caroline had agreed to stay on until morning.

It had been a long night, punctuated by cigarettes and cups of coffee. In the small pool of light from the desk lamp, Steven had looked old beyond his years. "I feel so for these people," he said, over and over again, and Caroline felt the old inexplicable warmth building inside of her. Around two in the morning an old man had stumbled in, reeking of wine and vomit, and had collapsed on the floor. Steven and Caroline had worked together to carry him to a bed and clean him and wake him enough to force some soup down his throat. They had stayed with him, throughout the night, one sitting on either side of the bed; and in the chill of false dawn when the sky lightened before retreating back into darkness, the old man died. They never knew his name.

"But he had love and caring, Caroline, maybe for the first time."

"And the last," she had cried.

"It was all that mattered," Steven said.

She stood across the bed from Steven as he pulled the sheet up over the old man's face, and the love she felt for him shimmered in the air between them. He felt it, reaching across, and their eyes locked in silent communication. As of one accord they moved away from the bed and closer to each other. Caroline had held her breath as Steven kissed her, and then hugged him tightly to her and felt the hammering of his heart in his chest. This was what she had been looking for. This was love. This was love, and he belonged to Justine.

Now she frowned at him. Was she trusting too much in her own feelings—in the waves that Dr. Hargrove had described to her? Did she let her heart rule her whole being? Were her decisions based on reality, or on an elaborate fantasy that existed nowhere but in her own mind?

Still, Steven knew what had happened. He had shared in it. He had felt for her, she was sure, the same thing that she had felt for him.

And his wedding was a mere two weeks away.

"I don't think it's such a good idea," she said, softly, suddenly aware of the tears that were flooding her eyes. "Perhaps we should stop this while we still can."

"Stop what?" Steven glanced around them, at the steady line of people leaving the church, and drew her to one side, to the churchyard where the gravestones were iced with snow. "What are you talking about, Caroline? I like spending time with you. I have strong feelings for you. I thought that they were returned." His eyes above the full red beard were searching, troubled. "Was I so very wrong?"

"No," she whispered. "No. But we have to stop."

"Why?" The feelings behind the word were explosive. "For God's sake, Caroline, why?"

She turned her tear-filled eyes to him. "Because of Justine, of course! Have you no feelings for her at all?"

There was a moment of silence. "What are you talking about?" Steven finally asked in a voice that was calm and sincere. "What on earth are you talking about?"

"You and Justine." Absurdly, the tears were now rolling down her cheeks. She brushed them angrily away with mittened hands. "I love you, Steven! I love you! But there's nothing that I can do about it and nothing that you can do about it, because in two weeks you'll be married and it will be all over." She drew in a deep shuddering breath. "It's better to stop, now, while we still can be friends."

He was staring at her as though she were insane. "What are you talking about, Caroline? I'm not getting married. . . ." His voice trailed off and his eyes widened in realization. "You think . . . you mean . . . you think that Justine is marrying *me*?"

"Who else?"

"Oh, God, Caroline. Justine's marrying my brother William. . . . Oh, God. I don't believe that this has happened. . . ." He put his hands on her shoulders. "I see how it happened, but I swear to you I never realized . . . I thought that Justine would have talked to you. William's never around. He's married already to his work if you ask me. He has a personal interest in Asheford Shipbuilding. So I spend a lot of time with Justine—she's sweet, she's been lonely—trying to make her feel at home in the family. Caroline, I swear to you—" He broke off and pulled her up against him then and kissed her, a long, hard, searching kiss, and Caroline felt all the cares and worries and misgivings melt away from her as she relaxed into his arms.

Steven held her against him in silence for a moment and then drew back to look at her. "What are you thinking, Caroline?"

She said the first thing that came into her mind. "That there is a God in heaven."

Steven grinned and said, "Then I take it you accept my apology?"

"What apology?" Caroline giggled nervously. "Oh, Steven, it was my fault, I just assumed the worst. And I do love you, you know."

He tightened his arms around her. "I know. I love you, too, Caroline."

She smiled foolishly. "What was it that you were saying about supper?"

De Mornay saw with irritation that Caroline was spending more and more time with a red-bearded giant, a man large and capable, who seemed not only to enjoy Caroline's company but also to positively look out for her.

There was an incident he observed, standing across the street from the church: One of the derelicts that frequented the place advanced upon Caroline, bottle in hand, swinging viciously. The red-bearded fellow was there at once, vigilant, with an arm and a stern word to the culprit, and an immediate hug thereafter for Caroline.

The sight gave de Mornay pause. Once he had seen how Caroline spent her days, his original plan had been to dress himself in the rags and tatters of the street people, and possibly get close enough to her to use a knife. It would have been easy—quick, silent, and efficient. But the presence of the red-bearded man was a strong deterrent. For, whatever reasons de Mornay had for his actions, whatever zeal motivated him, he was quite sure that he wanted to emerge alive and guiltless from the entire episode. With the red-bearded man around, he wasn't so sure how that would work.

But there were other ways of getting to her. . . .

In 1937 Eric was running to meet the future, and he was dragging A.R.M. along with him.

Rousseau and others were urging him to step up production of fighter planes, bombers, and rockets. Two separate divisions of A.R.M. were doing so, with the blessing of President Roosevelt and the funding of the War Department. Eric had cultivated his relationship with the President, and there was not a week that went by without a telephone call or memo from Washington. Eric himself flew to the White House with some frequency, taking part in high-level political meetings. Eric was the President's favorite "industry source," and he was astonished at the ease he had, suddenly, in manipulating policy. In France, one had to be of a certain family in order to be able to influence government in any way. This would never have happened in France—the farrier's son talking to the President. But this was America, and Roosevelt was leaning more and more heavily on this Frenchman who seemed to have the situation so well in hand. Gone were the days when he could claim that he was only fulfilling needs; now he was exercising power to create the need.

The President envisaged a war fought—and won—in the air, but Eric knew that fighter planes would not be enough. Developments were afoot that could revolutionize the concept of an aerial war.

Eric was determined to lead A.R.M. into the future. He offered incentives for scientists to come and locate their laboratories on the A.R.M. compound, and he was successful in gathering under his aegis some of the best and the brightest. The universities where they taught could not match A.R.M.'s salaries, its location, Eric's guarantee of endless supplies of raw materials, and time to work on pet projects. Some went on sabbatical, others commuted from Caltech and the University of California. All were intent on one thing, and one thing only—physics. It would be physics, and not mechanics, that would direct the future.

And that spring of 1937, the spring that William Asheford married Justine Chambers, Eric hired his single most important scientist, a young newly appointed professor of physics at Caltech, named Julius Robert Oppenheimer.

Together they were to change the shape of history.

Caroline attended Justine and William's wedding with a heart as light as air, because Steven, the best man, was watching her throughout the ceremony and she could feel the intensity of his gaze, electric and stimulating, across the width of the church.

Her wedding present to William and Justine was transportation to their honeymoon spot, an isolated town on Cape Cod where they were to spend a week together, far from friends, relatives, and well-wishers. There was an airport nearby, Caroline had ascertained from her maps and charts, and she offered to take them there:

William had proven to be a shadow of his younger brother. He had the same red hair, but brushed short and fine, and a small moustache. He was as large as Steven, though, and even though he was a man of few words Justine seemed happy enough, once she had recovered from her embarrassment at the confusion between the Asheford brothers that she had so unwittingly engendered. "Caroline, you thought that I was marrying Steven? Dear heavens, what an idea! I'm so sorry. . . ."

All three were united, however, in their shock at Caroline's offer. "You fly airplanes?" William had asked incredulously. "That's not exactly a thing for a woman to do. . . ."

Justine had squeaked about how dangerous it must be, and how cunning Caroline was to learn such a thing, and what a generous gift it was, and had led William away to talk with her parents, up from Connecticut for the wedding. Steven and Caroline were finally left alone.

She glanced at him nervously. "Are you going to tell me that I shouldn't be flying, too?"

"Of course not. I think it's a great thing." But he was frowning nevertheless.

Caroline dampened her lips. "So what is the problem?"

Steven shrugged. "Nothing. I just thought—well, nothing, really. It's stupid."

"No," Caroline said, catching his arm. "I'm sure it's not. Oh, Steven, please tell me?"

"It's just—a different image of you than I had before."

She raised her eyebrows. "You didn't think I was competent enough to fly a plane?"

"Oh, God, Caroline, not that. Never that. It's just, one has to have money to own an airplane."

She met his gaze. "That's true."

Steven's face flushed red. "I just never thought of you as having that kind of wealth, that's all."

Oh, my, she found herself thinking. Have you got a surprise in store. You think that's money. . . . "Looks can be deceiving, I suppose," she said softly. "Do you love me any less?"

"I couldn't love you any less. Just more and more, with each passing day . . ." He pulled her against him, and she encircled him with her arms, feeling again the comfort of his broad chest, his strong arms, his measured heartbeat.

"Steven?"

"Mmm?"

"What if—what if I was different than you thought?"

He smoothed her hair. She had allowed it to grow long again, and it tumbled down her back in soft golden waves. "In what sense?"

"Well, what if there was something important that I hadn't told you, or something like that? Would it make a difference to you?"

Steven laughed. "I know the important things. I know that you care about people. I know that you're gentle and sensitive and kind. I don't suppose there's anything you can tell me that would change my opinion of those things. And those things are the important ones. No, my dear, I don't think anything would make a difference."

"That's all right, then," Caroline said contentedly. "The rest will keep."

William and Justine were married on a blustery March day, when the wind picked up dead leaves from the previous fall and swirled them all around, and the air smelled fresh and clean and new. They said their vows solemnly and seriously, and then ran from the church to Steven's waiting car, which sped all four of them out to the small airport that Caroline had donated to the city for Newport's use—and hers, of course.

There was a tower there, because there were towers everywhere now, allowing controllers to watch one's flight and help pilots take off and land. Something else that Sarah had never had, thought Caroline. After a few months of using them, she couldn't dream how she had ever managed to navigate without their vision and guidance.

They belted themselves in as Caroline performed the routine checks all around the outside of the aircraft, and then went through her preflight internal checks, monitoring every instrument on the panel in front of her, adjusting her earphones, checking that the gas and oil pressure were correct. She started the engines and listened in satisfaction as they revved up and growled steadily. A loud noise to some, she thought, glancing at Justine, but music to her.

Taxiing to the end of the runway, she asked the tower for clearance to take off, acknowledged permission, and brought the engines up to a high whine before releasing the airplane down the runway, the tires screaming on the tarmac and the throttles open. She moved the controls back and they were up, off the ground, climbing steadily into the March sky.

Caroline retracted the undercarriage, checked her instruments again, and moved onto the heading for Cape Cod. She watched the hands creep round the face of the altimeter, two thousand feet, three thousand feet. . . . She leveled off at four thousand and looked over at Steven, sitting in the copilot's seat.

He was smiling at her.

The flight was much too short, and every moment of it was pure joy. Caroline couldn't hear what William and Justine, in the passenger seats, were saying to each other, but she saw Justine pointing out various landmarks, and she was laughing in apparent delight. Steven put on his headphones and jiggled them a little. "Can we talk to each other, now?"

"Depress the button by your throat when you want to transmit," Caroline instructed, and he nodded, pressing it in. "Can you hear me now?"

"Splendidly."

"I love you."

She smiled idiotically. "I love you, too."

The wind was blowing at about five knots out of the northwest, and Caroline made course corrections as she needed them, navigating almost entirely by sight as it was such a fine morning. The sun was playing hide-and-seek with the clouds, and Caroline felt the happiness inside her expand. Life didn't get much better than this, she thought. Flying on a fine day with the man you love sitting next to you.

She wondered in passing if this was how it had been for those other lovers, for Sarah and Eric, the day that Sarah had taken him up in one of his little flying machines. Hardly the same, with the exposed cockpit and the faulty engines, but no doubt the feelings were the same. Caroline smiled. She remembered envying Eric and Sarah and their happiness and love for each other. Now she, too, had found it. Here in the skies, love by her side. She was free, content, removed from the cares of the world below. It was the closest she had ever felt to the woman in the pictures on the walls of the house on Western Avenue.

And then they were slipping over the canal and moving over the island itself, flying northeast up to the point at Provincetown where William and Justine were spending their honeymoon. The airport was small there, too, but the sun was reflecting off its tower. Caroline picked up the radio. "Race Point Tower, this is Alpha Kilo November, do you read me?"

A man's voice crackled in her headset. "Alpha Kilo November, I hear you, go ahead."

"Requesting landing instructions, approaching from southwest, do you have me in sight?"

"I see you, Alpha Kilo November. You are cleared to join right base for runway zero-one, surface wind is zero-two-zero."

Caroline nodded. "Race Point Tower, I read you, runway zero-one."

Steven was watching her, an amused expression on his face. She went through her landing checks, lowering the wheels, banking the airplane around so that she landed on the correct runway, into the wind. Justine and William, when she checked, were kissing each other.

She glanced one more time at the instruments, then started her descent. Six hundred feet. Five hundred feet. Her hand went to the flaps and she pushed the lever in, creating maximum drag to slow her down still more. Two hundred feet, and the beginning of the runway was coming up under her. She closed the throttles completely and the little airplane leveled out, the wheels bouncing once, twice, before they stayed down and she was driving down the runway, slowing, slowing . . . braking gently, the way that the A.R.M. people had taught her. Always be gentle with your airplane, they said. Actually, they told each other to treat airplanes like women, but no one had ever dared say that to Caroline.

And then the plane had come to a complete halt and they were crawling out, Justine laughing in delight and William carrying suitcases, and Steven still smiling at Caroline.

After Justine and William disappeared to their picturesque little inn, Steven and Caroline strolled through the town, staying for the evening. They ate seafood at a café on Commercial Street, and Caroline flew them home in the dark, on instruments alone.

It was when they landed that he asked her, "Marry me, Caroline. Please marry me."

And it was much later, still sitting in the cold cockpit together, that she said, "Yes."

Chapter Twenty-eight

I still say," Anna Martin said carefully to Eric, never turning from the sink where she was washing dishes, "that you're meddling in something you shouldn't be. People can't play God, you know."

"I'm not playing God," Eric said, toying with his cake. "If the work is there to be done, then someone has to do it. You know that if it wasn't me it would be somebody else."

"I know," she said tartly, "that if it wasn't you I would sleep better at night."

Eric pushed his chair back from the table and reached for a cigarette package. "What are you trying to say, Anna?"

She wiped her hands on the dishcloth and turned from the sink. Eric had offered her a maid to help with her house-keeping, a chauffeur to drive her places, a mansion on the better side of town, but she had refused them all. "I see you changing," she said slowly. "And the changes in you frighten me."

He lit his cigarette and tossed the match into the ashtray, where it spluttered and went out. "I don't know what you're talking about." But he wouldn't meet her eyes.

Anna sighed and came over to sit at the table across from him. "I was afraid you wouldn't," she said softly. "Eric, you know that you are my son. More than Peter ever could be. More a child to me than Sarah was—I've known you longer, after all, than I knew her." There was a glint in her eyes that might have been tears. "I care about you. I care about what happens to you and how you live your life. And I have to tell you when I see you heading someplace I think isn't safe for you."

Eric exhaled a stream of smoke. "Please get to the point, Anna. I don't understand what you're saying."

"All right. I'll make it perfectly clear." She took a deep breath. "You say that we're moving towards war. Well, I think that war is what you want, and I think that you're doing everything in your power, which appears just now to be considerable, to move us in that direction. And I wonder what happened to your conscience. Your best friend died in the last one, in case you've forgotten."

Eric raised his eyebrows. "What makes you think I'd forgotten?"

"If you remembered how horrible that war was, you wouldn't be—you wouldn't be instigating another one. You would let us all live in peace."

"Some peace, Anna. Half of the United States can't afford to put anything but macaroni and cheese on the table for supper, when there is supper, that is, and this is living in peace? If we went to war the economy would be stimulated. People would have jobs. People could afford to eat again."

"People would die, Eric."

He shrugged. "People are dying now. Besides, you don't understand what you're talking about. This wouldn't be a war like the last one, with the trenches and the mud and the disease. We'd fight from planes, now. And tanks. And ships."

"Your bombers will be aimed at cities and will kill innocent people. That's worse than the trenches, Eric. People should have to see the people that they kill. They should have to know that it hurts. They should have to know what it means. Then maybe we'd all give up this senseless addiction to war."

"It won't happen, Anna," Eric said comfortably. "There have been wars since the beginning of time."

"Why?" Anna cried, and there was some despair in her voice. "Why? What is the purpose of all of this?"

"I wouldn't know," Eric said blandly, tapping ash off the tip of his cigarette. "Why does it matter so much to you, Anna? You'll be quite safe. I'll see to that."

"Why do you think that my own comfort is my first priority? Think, for God's sake, Eric! You're helping to start a war and you don't even know what it's about. You don't even care what it's about! You just want to work on your pretty little toys and watch them blow up in other people's faces! What kind of man wants to do that? What kind of man have you become?"

He stubbed out the cigarette, angrily, and turned to face her. "Don't be so goddamned sanctimonious, Anna! Listen to me: The war is going to happen. If I participate in it, the war is going to happen. If I don't participate in it, the war is going to happen. There is nothing in the world that I can do to stop it. What I can do is influence policy, and there's nothing that any of us can do to change that, either! We're moving into a new era, Anna. Technology is going to decide policy, instead of the other way around. The generals aren't going to call back to us and say, 'We need such-and-such.' We're going to tell Washington, 'This is what we can do,' and Washington will tell the generals what to do based on that." He took a deep breath. "In the house in Boulogne-Billiancourt there was a diorama, Anna. Some little lead soldiers. The man who owned the house put them there. They were fighting one of Napoleon's battles. And that's where that kind of war is going to stay—in dioramas, with little lead soldiers. The real world is moving in a different direction. And A.R.M. is going to help decide that direction. Anna, we can make the world into the kind of place we want it to be! Don't you understand the kind of power that is?"

She was looking at him as though she had never seen him before. He slumped back in his chair. "All right, Anna. I don't expect you to understand. Just don't lecture me, all right?"

Anna Martin stood up, slowly, and neatly tucked her chair under the table. "I want you out of my house, Eric Beaumont," she said. "I want you out of my house, now, and I don't want you coming back. Not tonight. Not tomorrow. Not ever."

Eric sucked in his breath. "What are you saying?"

"I'm saying that you have changed. I'm saying that I have loved you as my own son, and if you were my own son I would be doing this same thing. No one will sit in my kitchen and say the words that you have said." She shook her head. "God help you, Eric, you've changed."

He stayed where he was. "You can't do this to me, Anna! This is the only place I can come . . . you're the only friend I have." He looked at her imploringly. "Sarah was your daughter, Anna. Think of what she would say."

"Sarah," Anna said steadily, "would not know you if she saw you now. You have become many things in these last few years, Eric Beaumont, and none of them are anything that my daughter would recognize. Leave now. Please leave now." She turned back to the sink and began rinsing some dishes that had already been rinsed.

Eric stood up slowly, uncertainly, like an old man. He looked at Anna and started to speak, but thought better of it and shook his head. Slowly he pulled on his coat and hat, waiting with every gesture for Anna to say something, turn back to him, bridge the chasm that had suddenly opened between them.

But she said nothing, and at length, still without speaking, he let himself out into the night.

Standing at the sink, Anna felt the hot tears running down her cheeks, and dashed them away with a soapy hand. "Damn you, Eric Beaumont," she whispered. "You were my only friend, too."

Eric lay in bed that night, staring at the ceiling, unable to sleep.

Was Anna right? Had he sacrificed all of his morals for the good of A.R.M.? But didn't the end justify the means? He had promised Philippe to build up the company, to make it into something that they could be proud of. It was Philippe's legacy, and Eric had done everything—everything—for Philippe.

Philippe. What would he say, if he were here today? There would be flecks of gray in his moustache, and he might have put on a little weight. . . . But he would be the same, of that Eric was sure—serious and farsighted and deeply pondering the issues of the day.

Eric reached over to his nightstand, picked up a cigarette, and lit it. The burning tip glowed brightly in the darkness. What would Philippe have to say about the issues of the day? What would he say to the President of the United States, who called Eric by his first name and urged him to do the same? What direction would Philippe say that A.R.M. ought to take?

"Something terrible is about to happen." Eric jumped at the words, as though they had been spoken into the darkness and silence of his bedroom. That was nonsense, of course. Philippe had spoken them a quarter of a century ago, at one of those silly dinner parties that Amanda had so insisted upon in the days before the war. It was the incident at Sarajevo, Eric remembered, nodding. Philippe had been talking about the assassination at Sarajevo, and how it was heading them all towards war. He had been right, of course.

There were other words, too. "Do you really think that you can spend all your days out here working on airplanes and not think about what they mean to people?" Philippe had chided him in the old Aeroméchanique hangar, but Eric hadn't listened. He had told Philippe that he didn't make policy, he only made airplanes.

And now he was making both.

"Fighting airplanes don't exist in a void, *mon ami*." And suddenly Eric couldn't stand it any more. The panic was rising fast and hot, choking him. Grabbing the bedside lamp, he heaved it across the room, smashing it into the opposite wall. The porcelain shattered and fell in glittering shards of light, but all that Eric could see was his old friend, all he could hear were Philippe's words of reproach. "Shut up, shut up!" he screamed, his hands over his ears. "Stop it!"

There was sweat on his forehead and his neck; the room was unbearably hot. He threw the bedclothes off him, and lit the lamp of his dressing table. The dark held too many specters. As he turned to the closet to reach for his dressing gown, this time it was Sarah who stood before him. Sarah, young and beautiful and innocent, as she had been in the days on the rue de Verdun, as she had been on the day that she died; Sarah, who had pushed aside her own misgivings about his work so that she could go on loving him; Sarah, who urged him to build her an airplane to cross the English channel, but who frowned on his participation in the Tripolitan conflict. Sarah . . .

She was so real, he held out his arms to her, but she shook her head. "My mother is right," she said. "I don't know you. I don't know you. I don't know you."

He reeled away from her then, falling to the floor and clutching at the side of the bed to support him. I don't know you, her voice said. But I'm doing it for us, he pleaded with her silently. For our company. We were all so involved in it . . . We were all so happy . . .

And Sarah shook her head. "You think you're doing

something for us. You're only doing it so that you can continue to live in the past. We don't care anymore."

"You don't understand," Eric cried. "The world has changed."

"Not that much. If it's a choice between your company or your soul, Eric, which will you choose?"

"You're seeing the world in black and white. You and Philippe, that's all that you ever did. Black and white. Right and wrong. It's not that simple anymore. You don't know what it's like now."

Philippe was standing beside Sarah. "We know what you're like now," he said. "You've changed, *mon ami*."

"I don't know you," Sarah repeated, and Eric covered his ears again. "Stop! Stop it! Both of you! Shut up! I can't take it anymore! I can't take it anymore!"

His voice had risen to a frenzied pitch, and the words seemed to echo around the bedroom. When he opened his eyes, the closet door was standing open, just as he had left it, with his dressing gown on the peg.

He was quite alone.

Eric pulled himself slowly to his feet, and sat down heavily on the bed. They were gone. All of them—Philippe and Sarah, Amanda and Edward, Caroline and Anna. Everyone had left him. He was alone.

Eric put his face in his hands. Had he become such a bad person? He didn't actively mean any harm to anyone. He was just interested in the technologies that he was developing, in the theories that his scientists were postulating, in the strides that were being made in the industry. He just wanted his company to prosper. He wasn't an evil person.

The values that Philippe and Sarah—and Anna—spoke of were archaic. They belonged to another place and another time. That world was gone. Eric reached for the glass of water on his bedside table and drank thirstily. None of them understood, none of them could understand the pressures he was under, to create, to make a significant contribution, to outwit and outmaneuver Johnson Industries. It was easy to criticize when one didn't understand.

He gingerly lowered himself back down on the bed. No one understood, least of all Anna. Well, so that was that. He had always been alone; people had always left him, and

perhaps that was the way it would have to be. He couldn't be
all things to all people. . . . He had a mission in life. He
closed his eyes. Yes, that was the ticket, as Edward would
have said—a mission in life. He liked the sound of that. He
was going to take A.R.M. and make it into something
spectacular. Not just the industry standard, more than that.
He was going to make A.R.M. into the most powerful entity
in the world.

Through A.R.M., he would be more than a politician,
more than a general, more than anything else. He would
make the decisions, and he would have other people
implement them. And if no one liked him because of it?
That wouldn't matter. Whatever he did, he always lost the
people he loved. He would be powerful, and that would be
all that mattered.

The lawyers were right. This was what they had been
telling him, all along: to trust in his brain and not in his
heart; to work for the good of A.R.M. They were undoubtedly right about Caroline, too. Let her marry, let her bear
children. One of those children could be molded, educated,
protected. One day, he would hand over the most powerful
conglomerate on earth to one of those children. He would
have satisfied his debt to Philippe, and he would have
fulfilled their dream. Out of the destruction of their youthful
lives their dream would have survived. One could hardly
blame him for that.

Eric closed his eyes. It was all right. It was going to be all
right.

Marc Giroux knocked on the door. "Private meeting, or
may I come in?"

Beneteau turned from the papers he was glancing through.
The young woman who had been leaning over him straightened quickly, her cheeks flushed. They get younger every
day, Giroux thought. But perhaps that, too, is a sign of
aging.

"Ah, Marc! Louisette was just leaving. Weren't you, my
dear?" The girl nodded quickly, still looking embarrassed,
but as she walked by Giroux she gave him a brilliant smile,
filled with promise. He shut the door behind her. "Robert,
we have a problem. I think that we'd better have Rousseau
and Duroc in on this one, too."

Beneteau lifted his eyebrows and the telephone simultaneously. "Claudine, will you please find Monsieur Rousseau and Madame Duroc, and ask them to come to my office at once? Thank you." He hung up the telephone and folded his hands. "Now, what's this all about, Marc?"

Giroux perched on the edge of a chair. "Routine police report from the airport. We receive them from time to time, you know, any time André thinks there's something that might interest us."

"Any time he thinks we'd pay him for information, yes," Beneteau said wryly. "And?"

"And it seems that our colleague, Monsieur de Mornay, has chosen to take his leave of absence in America."

"I assume that—" Beneteau broke off as the door opened and Rousseau came in.

"Françoise is out of the office," he said. "Do you want me anyway?

"Yes, yes, come in," Giroux said, his voice irritated. "As I was saying, we received a security report from Zurich International. De Mornay went to America some months ago."

"Why are we being told this now?" asked Beneteau softly. His body might have degenerated into craving young girls, but his mind was as sharp as ever.

"I believe," Giroux said, "that André was storing up a number of issues and incidents to give us at one time. Higher asking price, and all that."

"What did he say about de Mornay?" Rousseau asked. He was beginning to feel sick.

"That he flew to New York. That he seemed nervous. And that he was carrying a gun."

"Is that legal?" asked Beneteau.

"If it's licensed and unloaded," Rousseau responded, his stomach lurching uncomfortably.

"The central question," said Giroux, "is why Monsieur de Mornay chose to go to America, and why he chose to go there armed. Do we have any answers?"

Rousseau definitely felt sick, now. "At a guess," he said, "to murder Caroline Copeland."

There was a heart-stopping silence in the room, during which they could faintly hear the voice of Claudine, the secretary, on the telephone in the anteroom.

Beneteau got to his feet and walked away from his desk to the small cocktail table where he kept his spirits. He slowly poured himself a glass of brandy. Sipping it, he turned just as slowly to face the other two men. "Now," he said calmly. "Please tell us why you think that is so."

Rousseau's palms were sweaty. "We talked about it. I mean, what we talked about was how Mademoiselle Copeland was not proving herself adequate to manage' A.R.M. And what to do about it." He cleared his throat uncomfortably. "We were drinking at the time. I don't remember the interview all that clearly."

"Tell us what you remember." Beneteau's voice was cold.

"I said something about waiting until she married—you know, the plan that we had settled on. And de Mornay thought—de Mornay thought that it would be safer to eliminate her altogether and pass control of A.R.M. on to Monsieur Beaumont." He looked unhappily from Beneteau to Giroux. "I swear that I thought he wasn't serious. It was just one of those things, you see—one of those things one says when one has been drinking and trying to find solutions. One says all sorts of impossible things. I didn't take it very seriously at all."

"And," Giroux asked acidly, "why did you not bring this conversation up at a staff meeting? Or with Monsieur Beneteau and myself?"

Rousseau made a helpless gesture. "I swear to you, I didn't know. I didn't think anything of it. Not then, not later, not until now."

"But you did know that—"

Beneteau held up his hand. "Enough, Marc. Enough. We can deal with Monsieur Rousseau later. What we need now is a plan." He sat back down at his desk and folded his hands into a steeple. "The real question, messieurs—in fact, I would hazard to say the only question—is what we are to do now."

Rousseau sounded desperate. "Mademoiselle Copeland must not be harmed! At all costs—"

"Mademoiselle Copeland," said Beneteau, dryly, "is scheduled to become Madame Asheford in precisely five days." He glanced at Giroux. "The announcement came only this morning. Apparently the younger Monsieur Asheford does not believe in long engagements."

Rousseau gasped. "Then we must stop her! A wedding—people milling about—it will be the perfect cover!"

Giroux shook his head. "Don't be a fool, man. We can't interrupt the wedding. We want this marriage for her, or had you forgotten?"

Rousseau moaned. "There will be no wedding if the bride is dead."

"We are jumping to conclusions, gentlemen," Beneteau said. "Monsieur de Mornay has waited this long. I believe he will wait until the wedding itself. I agree, that would be an excellent cover. But we have the advantage: He does not yet know that we are aware of his intentions. All we have to do is stop him."

"How?"

The lawyer shrugged. "It should not be that difficult, after all. We alert Monsieur Beaumont, of course, and the local authorities. And we ourselves stay very, very vigilant, messieurs. We will be able to identify Monsieur de Mornay. No one else will."

"Then we are going to the wedding?"

Beneteau looked at him pityingly. "Sometimes, Monsieur Rousseau, I fail to see what motivated us when we asked you to join our organization. Yes, we will indeed be there. It is only correct."

Rousseau shook his head. "De Mornay will know we're coming. He'll hide. He'll disguise himself. He's not a stupid man."

Giroux said, "He won't expect us. We normally wouldn't actually attend the wedding, only send our congratulations. No, I think Robert is right. We may well be able to pull it off."

"With very little time to spare," Beneteau said heavily as he picked up the telephone. "Claudine? Alert the airport, please. We'd like a flight to New York."

"Great," Giroux said briskly. "Where is Madame Duroc? She should be in Newport, as well."

"She's in Paris, I think." Rousseau said worriedly. "Consulting with our local office."

Beneteau frowned. "They're handling the de Montclair family. Françoise is supposed to have emptied her calendar so that she can concentrate on Mademoiselle Copeland. Monsieur Rousseau, before you entirely ruin your reputation with us, I strongly suggest that you find her and get her to the airport by ten o'clock in the morning."

The door closed, and the two partners exchanged glances. "It will be close," Giroux said, worriedly.

"It is going to be very close, indeed," Beneteau responded. "Pray God, Marc, that the girl doesn't suddenly decide to elope. Just pray God."

Eric received the news just as he was preparing to leave for Newport—separately from Anna, of course. She had refused his offer of a private flight and had booked herself on a Trans World Airways flight for the following day. She still hadn't broken the silence that she had imposed between them, and Eric was beginning to grow accustomed to it.

The telegram from Zurich was tense. "Mlle. Copeland in danger stop plot to kill her discovered stop need to consult prior to ceremony stop" Eric had been burning up the new transoceanic lines, trying to reach the law firm, but so far had been unsuccessful. He was leaving for Newport with nothing to go on but a vague and disquieting sense of dread, which was the most chilling feeling of all.

Caroline turned from the mirror in the small bedroom of Justine and William's house. "Does it look all right?"

Justine surveyed the long white gown critically. It fell in soft satin drapes to the floor with no lace or ribbons or any ornamentation. The fabric simply seemed to cascade down her body, hugging the curves and emphasizing her graceful carriage. Elegant, that was the proper word. "It's gorgeous," she pronounced at last. "Oh, Caroline, you're going to be the most exquisite bride!"

Caroline sat down on the edge of the bed. "Two more days," she said softly. "Oh, Justine, it's so hard to wait! I feel as though I've waited a lifetime already. . . ."

"I know what you mean." Justine's eyes were shining. "I thought that it would never happen. But it did, and now look at me! Look at all this!" She gestured around the small room, encompassing the whole house with her thoughts. "It's a lovely little house, and the best thing is, it's ours! It's nothing that belongs to my parents, or his parents, only to us!" Her cheeks were rosy. Marriage suited Justine Asheford.

Caroline smiled and reached out to clasp Justine's hand in hers. "It must be wonderful," she said softly. "I have news, too. Steven and I just bought a house!"

Justine looked uncertain. "You mean—you're not moving in with your grandmother? Surely there's enough space?"

Caroline nodded. "Oh, lord, yes, there's enough space. We could fit half of Asheford Shipbuilding on the first floor alone. But it's not what I want, and it's not what Steven wants." She smiled. "He doesn't love me because of my money, you know. In fact, I would say that it's a liability, if anything."

Justine sat down on the bed next to her. "I don't know," she said slowly. "I should think that money is useful."

Caroline thought of the times she shared with Steven: the evenings at the shelter, helping people, making a real difference in their lives; the afternoons spent bicycling in the countryside outside of Newport; the tender kisses, the whispered words, her fingers entwined with his; walks through the city; the rides on the trolley that she had been denied as a child. That was what life should be, not living in a mansion and having people follow one everywhere and watch one all the time. She smiled. "It's not everything, Justine. It's not everything. And I think we'll be far happier without tying ourselves to the family estate."

"Yes," persisted Justine, "but what will your family say?"

What would her family say? She had written to Amanda but had not received word from her yet. Amanda, doubtless, would not understand Caroline's need for simplicity. Even in Africa, Amanda lived in high style. Old Mrs. Lewis in her sickbed, frail and a little dotty, kept forgetting who Caroline was, and was already talking about funeral arrangements. Eric, flying in from California, cared only for his company and Caroline's happiness. He would protest, but not loudly, as long as he thought she was safe. Mrs. Martin, still in the same house out on Western Avenue in San Jose—she alone would applaud Caroline's decision. Yet her mother and grandmother had always taken life on its own terms, had lived their lives precisely the way that they wanted to. She was doing the same thing. Her family would have nothing to say about it.

Caroline smiled again. "You'll see, Justine," she said. "It's going to be perfect. You and William living here, and Steven and me living up the hill. . . . We'll see each other all the time. We'll use what money we need. I want to keep on flying—that costs a lot of money—and you might decide that you want something we could help with. But all I want, all that I really want, is Steven. Steven and a simple life as Steven's wife. I've seen a lot of other things, and there's nothing, Justine, that compares with that."

"Well," said Caroline's future sister-in-law comfortably, "that's that, then. Why don't you slip off this gown, and I'll wrap it so it will be fresh for Saturday? And then we can go downstairs and make some iced tea. It's going to be another hot day, from the looks of it."

Caroline caught her arm. "Justine—you do understand, don't you?"

"Of course I do. And I'm glad. It would have been hard to stay friends with you and Steven off in that mansion on the other side of town."

Caroline nodded. "I know. I know," she said happily. "Oh, Justine, you'll see. Everything is going to be just perfect!"

Alone in his hotel room, de Mornay cleaned and polished his gun. He had spent the last three days out in the woods, perfecting his marksmanship. It would be too bad if he found himself in the correct situation and then didn't have the technical proficiency to pull it off.

Putting it away, he drew in a few deep breaths to steady himself. Not long now. He took out the photograph of Caroline Copeland that he had taken some weeks before, catching her in a moment of laughter and fun, holding hands with that huge fiancé of hers. Well, fiancés don't spend time with their brides the morning of their weddings. A pity for the brides.

He studied the photograph for a few minutes, as though committing it to memory. Soon his mission would be completed. He would be able to return to Zurich, and life would go on. A.R.M. would be safe from this silly girl.

Soon it would be all over. He couldn't wait.

Chapter Twenty-nine

They met in Eric's suite at the Ocean House Hotel. It was where they all were staying—where anyone who was anyone, as Amanda would have said, was staying—and the most convenient place for plotting strategy.

They were all worried. Beneteau concealed his anxiety with the most ease, Rousseau with the least, but they were all worried. They chain-smoked cigarettes and sat over endless cups of coffee, discussing options, strategies, and possibilities, and then they talked for hours with the local police, who turned out to be eager to be of whatever assistance was necessary.

"She may well be marrying into Asheford Shipbuilding," the captain said with heavy humor, "but she's still a Lewis. All the fancy foreign names and trappings won't change that. We can't have anything happen to a Lewis, not here in Newport." His men would be about, he promised the lawyers, and vigilant.

"Especially at the wedding!" Giroux insisted. "That is when we think that he will do it."

Yes, the captain assured him. Especially at the wedding.

Françoise Duroc had met with Caroline, briefly, but told her nothing of what might be happening. They were all in agreement on that point: Caroline must not be told. She had her life to live, assuming they could save it. She could not live forever in fear.

So the two women had sipped lemonade together, Françoise extending to Caroline the "best wishes of the law firm of Beneteau and Giroux for a very happy marriage." Caroline thanked her calmly and asked after the weather in

Europe. They were right, Françoise thought: This girl could never manage A.R.M.

Still, it was no reason to wish a death sentence on her.

Caroline had greeted Eric with distracted affection, her mind on the ceremony itself. "Thank you for coming," she said, and he reached past his worry to respond to her. "I wouldn't have missed it for the world. Does he make you happy?"

"Deliriously happy," Caroline said.

"Then that's all I need to know." He needed to know much, much more, but not about Caroline's fiancé, and he smiled for her as though nothing terrible were about to happen, and then with a heavy heart he left her to her preparations. If he couldn't save her . . . If they all couldn't save her . . . For the first time, Eric realized how much of a burden Philippe's legacy had become to his daughter.

Friday night they all went to the White Horse Tavern— the Ashefords, Caroline, Eric, and Anna Martin, recently arrived from California and staying at the Lewis estate. There, toasts were made and wine was consumed, and Caroline's eyes shone in the candlelight as her fiancé protectively kept his arm around her. Eric felt the cold claw of fear in his stomach tighten and tighten. They were good people, Caroline's new family—honest, hardworking people. Violence and intrigue were foreign to them. They would never understand how she came to be in the center of such a plot.

Caroline grew sleepy with the wine. She leaned her head against Steven's shoulder. "Are you all right?" His voice in her ear was music.

"Wonderful," she murmured.

"What are you thinking about?"

She smiled. "About my pony. Cricket. I had him when I lived with my grandmother in New Hampshire. I wonder what's become of him."

Steven's arm tightened around her. "Someday we'll have a pony for our children."

She lifted her face to his. "Promise?"

"On my honor." He kissed her.

Eric, watching them from further down the table, winced. She had grown up. She was about to become somebody's

vife. And, whatever else was happening now, that was pain
nough.

"I think I'm going to throw up."

Justine put her arms around Caroline's shoulder. "Everyone feels that way," she said encouragingly.

"Especially," Anna Martin added, brushing a wisp of hair
off of Caroline's forehead, "the morning of their wedding."

Caroline bit her lip and looked at Mrs. Martin's reflection
next to hers in the mirror. "Did you?"

"Of course I did. It's nervousness, dear heart. Nothing
more."

"But I *want* to marry Steven! Why should I be nervous
about it?"

The older woman put her arms around Caroline. "Because every change in life makes us nervous. Weren't you
nervous on your first solo flight?"

"Of course I was. A little, anyway. But that was different."

"Not very different. You were doing something new and
wonderful and exciting. And when it's right, that's what a
wedding should feel like, too."

"Really?" Caroline's face was pale.

"Absolutely." She was quiet for a moment, and then went
on. "The organ prelude is starting. We ought to finish up in
here."

Justine took a deep breath. "All right. Here's the checklist. I have the ring for Steven. Here's your bouquet,
Caroline—" She broke off her sentence, and for very good
reason.

The door leading from the sacristy to the outside had
opened, and, standing silhouetted against the summer sunshine, was de Mornay.

Inside the church, the organ played on.

Steven and William Asheford had already taken up their
appointed places near the altar. Eric was standing at the
back of the church, ready to walk in with Caroline. The plan
was for the women to join him there, after they were
finished getting ready. He had to smile: Sarah had made no
such preparations for their wedding. But then, no wedding
had ever quite been like theirs.

There were flowers heaped around the altar, white lilies, a gift from Margaret Lewis who lay ill in her room in the mansion over on Ocean Drive. Lilies, she had said only that morning to Caroline, because they would fit equally for a wedding or a funeral.

"You're not dying yet, Grandmother," Caroline had said.

The old lady shook her head. "Sooner than you think, my dear," she sighed. "Sooner than you think."

From Africa had come a long, effusive letter and a fantastic leopard rug. Now where would they put that? Caroline wondered with exasperated mirth.

Eric, adjusting the tie on his tuxedo for the hundredth time, looked around the church. Françoise Duroc was sitting on the bride's side, looking much calmer than she had to be feeling. The other attorneys weren't present, and neither was de Mornay. Eric frowned. It had to be now, they had to be right. If not . . . If not, they would have to start the A.R.M. security again, which might very well cost Caroline her husband and her happiness. From what he could judge of Steven Asheford, that would be a very great loss indeed. Despite his misgivings, Eric found himself liking the quiet giant with the red beard.

He took a deep breath to steady himself. There were a great many strange-looking people in the church, as well— the people who ate the bread and soup over which Caroline and Steven had met each other. One, an old man, hadn't stopped muttering to himself since he had come in, something about fiery flames and the end of time. . . . The A.R.M. people and the police had been suspicious of these ragged people, but Rousseau had scanned every face as it entered the church to ascertain that de Mornay was not among them, and he was satisfied.

De Mornay wasn't there. So far, Caroline was safe. So far.

Caroline cried out as the man shut the door behind him and, for the first time, she saw the gun in his hand. But he immediately held it up and shook his head. "Quiet! Quiet, all three of you! Keep quiet, or I'll hurt somebody. Do you understand?" Three mute nods. He bit his lips. He had made a vital error here, somewhere. He had thought that he would find Caroline alone.

"You don't know me, Mademoiselle Copeland, and I do regret not meeting you under more auspicious circumstances, but such is life. No, Madame Martin, if you please, just stand away from that door. Thank you. Now, Miss Copeland, we have something to talk about."

"What?" It was no more than a whisper.

"How do you know who we are?" That was Anna Martin.

De Mornay smiled again. "So many questions, mes-dames, and unfortunately so little time. I do regret. Now, Mademoiselle Copeland, if you would be so kind as to come with me." He gestured towards the door.

Caroline moistened her lips and smoothed her sweaty palms over her wedding dress. "Please tell me," she said, her voice uneven. "Please tell me why you're doing this."

"Why?" His mouth curved into an unpleasant sneer. "Why, Mademoiselle, because of A.R.M., of course."

Justine Asheford had her hands in back of her, propping herself up against the sacristy sink, and now she clutched the only weapon she was able to reach: a copper vase sitting on the sacristy counter. How to move quickly enough to use it? she wondered. How could she save them?

Anna Martin narrowed her eyes. "There is no reason to involve Caroline with A.R.M.," she said calmly. "If you have any issues with A.R.M., it is Eric Beaumont you need to be speaking to. Caroline has nothing to do with the compa·y."

"Except for owning it," de Mornay said. "You see, Madame Martin, I know much more about this than you think."

"I see," Anna said slowly. "You want to hold her hostage. You want to blackmail money out of the company."

"Madame Martin," he said. "I'm getting tired of you. I have my own reasons. I don't need to listen to your guesswork. I have nothing but the best interests of A.R.M. at heart." He sighed. "Please don't make things more difficult for me." He glanced at the clock and towards the door. "Mesdames, it's time for us to leave."

Eric cleared his throat. The organist was playing the prelude over for a third time and was looking worried. The rector had come out and was standing in front of the altar, looking a little expectant and a little crestfallen. Steven Asheford was frowning.

Eric glanced at his watch. She was late. Well, brides were often late, or so he had been told. Wait another minute, he said to himself. Wait another minute, and then see what's going on.

De Mornay grew tired of waiting and grabbed Caroline around the waist, dragging her up close to him and towards the door. "Stay quiet!" he snarled at Anna and Justine. "Stay quiet, or I'll kill her."

Perhaps it was the use of that word that did it; Justine didn't know. But a voice inside her head was saying, He's going to do it anyway, I may as well do what I can. She summoned all her courage, lifted the vase over her head, and threw it in the direction of de Mornay. It missed.

De Mornay reacted quickly and instinctively, using his pistol to hit her, hard, across the temple. Justine went down on the floor as though she had fainted, fast and in a heap. Anna exclaimed and bent over her.

"Is she alive?" whispered Caroline.

"Yes." Anna looked up at de Mornay. "Stop now," she told him, slowly straightening up. "Stop now, before you hurt anybody anymore. You must listen to me." Anna advanced toward him. "Stop now."

De Mornay shot her.

Caroline could hear someone screaming, and it only registered with part of her mind that it was she. Anna Martin had fallen over backward with the force of the bullet. There was hardly even a stain on her dress where it had entered her chest, just below her left breast.

Caroline kept screaming, and de Mornay pulled her towards the door. "Come on, come on!" he urged her, dragging her away from the sacristy and the two bodies on the floor. "Come on!"

She stumbled after him, hardly realizing where she was placing her feet. "Come on!"

Eric had decided to make his move a few moments before they heard the shot.

He had advanced down the aisle of the church, swiftly and silently, feeling rather than seeing Françoise Duroc rise and follow in his wake. Steven Asheford was looking at him. "Let's go see," Eric said aquietly, gesturing towards the sacristy door. "I think that—"

And then the shot rang out, and they could hear Caroline screaming.

Steven sprinted to the door, tearing it open and running inside. Eric and William were just behind him, looking over Steven's shoulder to see the bodies of Anna Martin and Justine Asheford sprawled out on the floor. Steven saw only the open door on the opposite side of the room and ran for it, leaving Eric and William to the blood and death behind him.

De Mornay had dragged Caroline out into the sunlight, and half across the street. He knew only that something had gone terribly, terribly wrong with his plan, for suddenly there were police cars all around him. He had been so careful. . . . He had thought he was being so careful. . . .

The damned girl kept screaming, and he grabbed a fistful of the flaxen blond hair and pulled her head up against his chest so hard that she gasped. "Shut up!" he shouted at her, looking desperately around them for an escape route. It was then that he heard another voice, speaking French.

"De Mornay! De Mornay, stop it! Let the girl go."

It was Rousseau.

No. A voice in his brain was saying the word urgently: *no.* Anything but that, anyone but Rousseau. He could not face disgrace before the partners, when all that he had sought to do was ameliorate the chances of them doing well with the company. It was too ironic, it was simply too ironic. Rousseau couldn't be here, he couldn't have known.

And then it was Rousseau, walking towards him from behind one of the parked police cars, stretching out his hand. "Give me the gun, de Mornay," he said in French. "Give it to me and let the girl go."

De Mornay did the only thing he could think to do, in the circumstances. He moved the gun from Caroline's temple, and raised it to fire at Rousseau.

Rousseau ducked, but it didn't matter, because at that moment Steven Asheford threw himself at de Mornay, knocking the smaller man to the ground and all of the wind out of him. The gun went off, firing harmlessly up into the trees. Caroline fell aside and was supported by Rousseau until Steven came back. Lifting her up in his arms, he cradled her. She clung to him, sobbing in fear and relief, and buried her face against him. He turned and walked slowly a few paces away from the crowd gathering around de Mornay, still holding her in his arms, the train from her gown dragging behind them on the road.

Behind them all, Françoise Duroc met Rousseau's eyes, and both of them nodded in silence.

The shouts and the police horns and the voices might just have well been coming from another world, as far as Eric Beaumont was concerned.

He was sitting on the sacristy floor, with Anna Martin's head in his lap.

William was in the room attending to Justine Asheford, leaving only to summon an ambulance. Already a policeman had stuck his head in the door, and had withdrawn it at once as soon as he saw the situation. He would get help.

But it would be too late for Anna.

When Eric had entered, her eyes had been wide open, staring lifelessly at the ceiling. He had gently closed her eyelids and then lowered himself to the floor so that he could hold her. It seemed indecent, somehow, to just leave her lying there alone. He had left her alone too many other times.

Too many other times . . . And, for the fourth time in his life, Eric Beaumont wept. He sat and held the lifeless body of Sarah's mother, and he cried for her. He cried for her and for all the deaths, all the needless deaths of the people he loved, and he cried for the harsh words they had spoken to each other, words that had separated them. He had never told Anna that he loved her, and he cried for the times he had disappointed her. They had arrived in Newport not speaking to each other, and there had never been, for them, the opportunity to speak the words that would end their separation. Now, they would be apart, he realized in hopeless misery, forever. There would never be a chance to heal these wounds, because she died with them still in her heart.

Closing his eyes, he saw her again as he had at first on that tentative trip up the coast to meet the woman who had had such kind words for him when Sarah was killed. He saw again her hands on her apron and the sweetness in her eyes. He relived his pleading with her to accept Caroline as a surrogate daughter, and he saw once more the struggles she accepted as she raised still another adolescent girl. He tasted her coffee and her cakes, he saw her laughter and her stubbornness, and he listened to her voice reasoning with him in their late-night discussions. And, his heart breaking, he saw her as he had last seen her in California, angry with him and making him leave her house because she could no longer believe in his dream.

Anna Martin. The very company that had been the source of her concern over him had also been the cause of her death. What had happened was a direct result of the power he had sought to give to A.R.M. He had made it so important that a man could become unbalanced in an effort to keep that power base. He had done that, and in the process he had killed Anna.

Eric sat hunched over her body, the tears running uselessly down his cheeks to splash over her face. At last they came to bundle Justine into an ambulance and to pry him away from Anna. Even then, he was only vaguely aware of the movement around him. In a daze he allowed the doctor to give him an injection, and let Robert Beneteau lead him out into the sunshine. It seemed obscene, somehow, that the day was still so fine.

There were people all over the place, standing about in small groups, talking in hushed voices—the aftermath of disaster. Beneteau moved expertly among them, the ambulance driving off in one direction, the police cars in another. "There will be questions for you, later," Beneteau advised him. "But for now, you have some time to rest."

Caroline half-stood, half-leaned on Steven as Eric passed by them. There were two serious-faced men asking her questions, and her sobs had subsided to hiccups as she tried to answer. Steven was looking both angry and protective. There was a long smear of red on her white gown, and it was ripped in one place. She looked at Eric as he walked by, but her face registered nothing—no recognition, no love, no empathy.

Beneteau drove him back to the hotel, and, still with that automatic drug- and grief-induced emptiness all around him like a tattered cloak, Eric slept.

Anna Martin's body was flown back to California, courtesy of A.R.M., and Caroline and Steven followed it for the funeral. She was buried in the family plot, with her husband and her daughter, and Eric spent the remainder of the day hunched over the grave, rocking back and forth on his heels, mourning a loss he would never come to terms with.

Later, he went to Peter Martin and purchased from him the house out on Western Avenue. It made the most sense to Eric. He began living in it, living with the ghosts that haunted it just as they haunted him, and he began drinking again.

He would recover, he knew. He would go back to the A.R.M. compound and make the machines that would turn the wheels of government and industry. But would he ever again love, would he ever again feel whole? It seemed as if that part of life was completely over for him. It had started to trickle away when a vital beautiful girl fell out of an airplane over Boston Harbor, and it continued to flow when friends died from war wounds or their own hands. But it ended, definitively and completely, when a crazed lawyer put a bullet into the chest of the woman he had come to think of as his mother. It was over.

Work would go on, but life was over.

Before she left for Anna's funeral in California, Caroline had gone to see Justine in the hospital.

"This is what I meant," Caroline explained to the pale face smiling at her from the pillow. "This is what I meant. If I had just been an ordinary person, nothing like this would have happened. Mrs. Martin would still be alive and you wouldn't be hurt and Steven and I would be married now. It's all that damned company and that damned money. All that I want is for it to be out of my life."

Justine smiled. "Well, it can be. Just marry Steven and go on. Life has to go on, Caroline."

"Not for Mrs. Martin. And you—you got a concussion."

"I'm all right. I'm sorry about Mrs. Martin. She seemed to be a nice lady. But don't worry about me, Caroline. I'm all right. In fact," she beamed, "I'm better than you think!"

"What does that mean?"

"Well, they gave me a full physical examination yesterday, and you won't believe this, but I'm pregnant!"

"You're—pregnant? Are you sure? Oh, Justine!"

"Yes," Justine said, contentment in every line of her face. "Yes, I'm sure. They told me it's quite certain. I'm pregnant. William is thrilled!"

"I should think he would be," said Caroline, fighting

down—once again—an odd feeling of envy. "So at least there is some good news."

"There could be good news for you, too," Justine said softly, stretching out her hand for Caroline's. "Why don't you and Steven go on and get married now?"

Caroline was shocked. "Now, Justine? It's hardly the time. Besides, I don't think I can go back—there." She couldn't even speak the words. "It would be too horrible. I would remember too much." She paused, and then said vehemently, "People who kill should burn in hell. People who kill in churches should burn twice as long."

Justine shook her head. "It's not a good time to start hating, Caroline. You're going to get married soon. You've got to try and put this all behind you."

"Yes," Caroline said, her voice flat. "Yes, of course."

Caroline Margaret Copeland and Steven Owens Asheford were married, finally, on the seventeenth of September, 1937, on the Lewis estate on Ocean Drive in Newport. They were married alone by the rector of Saint John's, with only William and Justine Asheford as witnesses. They were married with hopes of putting all the danger, all the blood and the grief and the horror, behind them.

Sarah Martin had fallen from the sky twenty-five years earlier to the day.

Steven took Caroline to the house they had bought so many months before, the house that they had not yet lived in, the house that knew nothing of the terror and grief of the months before. It was fresh, and clean, and filled with new beginnings and great expectations.

Night fell, and with it came the wind off the ocean, cleansing and cold. Steven and Caroline stood in the small garden that she already looked forward to cultivating, and he took her slowly into his arms. "It's going to be a great life, you know," he said softly.

"I know," Caroline whispered. "I just feel—I feel as though I've lost the last bit of my innocence, somehow."

"There is," Steven said carefully, "life after innocence." And then he kissed her.

She responded to him with a passion that she didn't realize was inside her. She kissed him in return, passionately, a kiss sharp with need, filled with desire. And then he was running his hands up her back, and she realized how much she ached for him, ached to be taken, to be cared for, to feel a sense of connectedness and permanence with this man.

Her breath had quickened, and her fingers sought the buttons on his shirt. Hurry, hurry, every impulse in her body was urging her, and Steven was laughing into her hair. "Come on, Caroline, let's go inside."

He pulled her in after him, but she was still unbuttoning his shirt, still trying to take it off him. They stopped for a moment in the living room, dark and dappled with shadows, Steven kissing her again with more insistence, his mouth warm on hers, his tongue probing her mouth. She sighed and pulled his shirt off his shoulders. "Silly girl," Steven said, smiling into the darkness.

She laughed. "Doesn't this feel good?"

"It feels great," he said into her ear. "Don't ever stop."

She didn't. She pulled the undershirt off, too, and licked around the base of his neck, following the contours of his collarbone. He moaned softly and pulled her closer to him, his hands in her hair, and she kissed him and moved down further to lick his nipples. "Caroline, Caroline," Steven said above her, but she was breathing faster and faster, wanting him, needing him, and she didn't listen to what he was saying.

She was fumbling with the buckle on his belt when he reached down, lifted her into his arms, and walked to the staircase. "Steven!" Caroline gasped, and he laughed again.

"It is the custom to carry one's bride over the threshold," he said, "and I am a great believer in custom."

She giggled and reached down for his pants again, and he muttered "shameless hussy" under his breath and hurried up the last few stairs and into the bedroom. Laying her on the bed, he began kissing her neck, her arms, down to her hands where he sucked on her fingers, slowly, one at a time. "Steven," she said again, but this time it was a sigh, a sigh of complete contentment.

And then he was pulling her dress off her, and she was fumbling with his pants, and they rolled around for a bit pulling and tugging until their clothes lay all around them in disarray, and they were both entirely naked. Steven moved over on top of Caroline, a darker shadow in the dimness, his eyes searching for hers. "I love you, Caroline Asheford," he whispered.

She reached up and held his face in her hands. "I love you, Steven Asheford," she responded, and he bent down slowly, slowly, to kiss her lips.

He rolled over, off her, and she moved on top of him, lightly, the passion building and growing again inside of her. It felt as though she was being consumed by fire. She reached down between his legs and touched his penis, tentatively at first, and then with more assurance as she felt it responding to her touch.

"Yes," he was saying, "oh, yes, yes." She bent her head and touched it with her tongue. He moaned again, and she licked the length of him, kissing the hair that grew all around, fondling and touching and kissing and licking until his body was shaking.

She moved up and kissed his chest again, and he made a sound like a sob and turned her on her back and buried his face between her breasts. She held him there for a few minutes, feeling their hearts beating in rhythm, their lives finding each other and interlocking in perfect resonance with each other, and she smiled into the darkness. This was love. This was what she had been looking for.

And then Steven touched her between her legs, feeling the warmth and the moisture there, and his fingers stroked her and stroked her until she could stand it no longer, the fire was banked too high, and sparks were flying all over. "Now," she gasped. "Oh, Steven, please, now!" He reached down again and guided himself and entered her body, and she cried out with joy and relief and pleasure. They moved together as though they were one mind, one body, one soul.

When they climaxed, twisting and moving until the pinnacle had been reached, Caroline screamed and clutched at his shoulders, and Steven cried out and moved and moved and then slowly stopped. They lay together in silence for a few moments, their hearts hammering against each other.

Steven kissed her cheek and was surprised to find tears there. "Did I hurt you?" There was concern in his voice.

Caroline shook her head. "No," she whispered. "It's just that I'm so happy. Oh, God, Steven, I'm so happy."

He lay down next to her and tucked the covers around her

and moved her over so that he could hold her, her head resting on his chest. And it was then that he spoke.

"Let's stay happy," he said.

Caroline smiled. "I'm all for that. How do we do it?"

"Oh, I don't know," he said, yawning. "How about doing this at least once a day, for starters?"

"Sounds good to me," Caroline said sleepily. "What else?"

"Let's work very hard," he said, his voice serious in the darkness, "to keep A.R.M. out of our lives."

"Hear, hear," Caroline said, closing her eyes. "Hear, hear."

Epilogue

June, 1938.

"Well, it seems that we got what we wanted." Giroux turned from the window.

"We paid a remarkably high price for it." Beneteau reminded him. His voice was dry.

"But we did it. Isn't that what really matters, in the end?" Giroux sipped at the scalding liquid.

"I can't help but wonder if we could have avoided that entire de Mornay debacle last summer."

Giroux sighed. "One cannot think of everything, Robert. We did what we could. And we were able to keep it out of the newspapers, thank God, and so out of the attention of Johnson Industries."

"So you think that she is safe from them?"

"For now. For now, yes." Giroux allowed himself a wry smile. "I do believe that, were one to ask her, Madame Asheford would name A.R.M. as her enemy more quickly than she would name Johnson Industries."

Beneteau nodded. "That is doubtless correct. Unfortunate, of course. But times change, and she may well, too. What is the word from California?"

"Rousseau reports that Monsieur Beaumont has instructed the President to appeal to Germany and Italy to solve all of their problems without American intervention. It will never work, of course, which he is fully aware of. Hitler and Mussolini are far too engrossed in their own little empires." He sat down and stretched his legs out in front of the crackling fire. "Still, I gather that Monsieur Beaumont feels it wise to go through the motions."

"He is confident that he will be able to supply the wa
when it starts?"

Giroux looked at him quizzically. "Of course."

Beneteau nodded with satisfaction. "That is a goo
thing."

Giroux sipped again at the tea. "I expect that Roosevel
will be appropriating funds for defense from Congress any
day now," he mused. "We are going to have to expand ou
offices, Robert."

The older man grunted. "Perhaps, Marc. We shall see. W
shall see."

Giroux nodded and smiled. He had seen the future ir
Eric's eyes and knew already what it held. Time would tak
care of the rest.

Eric received the announcement and, without thinking
immediately ordered an airplane to fly him to Rhode
Island.

It was stark enough: "Baby girl, born June 25, 1938, to
Steven and Caroline Asheford. Name Elizabeth Erica."

He reached Caroline before she had even left the hospital
She was sitting up in bed and showing off the baby to all and
sundry. He approached slowly and watched with some
amusement and trepidation as Steven Asheford moved
protectively closer to his wife.

Caroline, looking up from the child held in her arms
smiled when she saw him, and that was all the invitation
Eric needed.

"She's beautiful," he said, bending to kiss her cheek
"And so are you."

"Thanks," Caroline said softly. "Did you see her name?"

"Could I miss her name?" Eric smiled. "Thank you
Thank you both."

Steven nodded. "It seemed to make sense," he said.

Caroline reached out a hand, and Eric squeezed her hand in
his. "I'm sorry," she said slowly and with difficulty, "that I
wasn't what you wanted me to be."

Eric swallowed hard. "I'm sorry," he said, "that I wasn't
what you wanted me to be."

Caroline smiled, but there were tears in her eyes. "We
could be friends," she suggested, tentatively.

Eric nodded vigorously. "Yes," he said firmly, astounded at the tremendous relief he felt. "We can be friends."

Later, he went back down the hall to the nursery to look at Caroline's baby. She was so tiny, and so wrinkled, that one could hardly tell anything about her at all. But Eric had a feeling. Nothing much to go on, feelings, but this one was strong. She could do it. One day, she could do it. Elizabeth Erica Asheford, he thought, and whispered the name to himself. She might well be the one.

For the time being, the peace he was feeling was promise enough.